PRAISE FOR *THE SHELL HOUSE DETECTIVES MYSTERY SERIES*

'A cleverly plotted and thoroughly enjoyable book about dark deeds in beautiful places.'

—Elly Griffiths, author of the Ruth Galloway series

'A total delight.'

—Sarah Winman, author of *Still Life*

'Exquisitely written, set in Cornwall, great characters, and a gripping plot. Who could ask for more?'

—Jill Mansell, author of *Promise Me*

'This beautifully written cosy coastal mystery packs a real punch! With wonderfully atmospheric prose and twists and turns aplenty, the plot will have you riding a wave of suspense long after you've turned the final page. If you love Cornwall, you will adore this book.'

—Sarah Pearse, author of *The Sanatorium*

'Suspenseful, twisty and unputdownable . . . Loved it!'

—Claire Douglas, author of *The Couple at No. 9*

'Clever, plotty and compelling.'

—Jane Shemilt, author of *Daughter*

'If you're looking for a new favourite cosy crime series, here it is!'

—Libby Page, author of *The Lido*

'Emylia was born to write detective fiction.'

—Veronica Henry, author of *The Impulse Purchase*

'An expertly plotted and hugely compelling murder mystery . . . Crime fans are in for a treat.'

—Lucy Clarke, author of *One of the Girls*

'An absolute treat from start to finish! A wickedly plotted whodunnit with a cast of suspects fit for any Christie, all written with Emylia's trademark heart and humour.'

—Hannah Richell, author of *The Search Party*

'A big-hearted page-turner with twists you won't see coming and the best pair of amateur sleuths I've read in a long time. I loved it!'

—Lucy Diamond, author of *Anything Could Happen*

'My favourite new crime series.'

—Ginny Bell, author of the Dover Café series

'Sensationally good: utterly gripping, beautifully written and brilliantly clever. I was up reading way past my bedtime and could not unravel Emylia Hall's fantastically plotted mystery for love nor money! Set in gorgeous Cornwall at the peak of a heatwave, with her best cast of characters yet, this book oozes confidence, style and sparkle, with Emylia's trademark warmth and humanity. I absolutely loved it.'

—Rosie Walsh, author of *The Man Who Didn't Call*

'Gorgeous writing and a plot crammed with suspense, this is your perfect new crime series.'

—Kate Riordan, author of *The Heatwave*

'Beautifully written, gripping, and so atmospheric . . . One for fans of Richard Osman!'

—Emily Koch, author of *What July Knew*

'A clever and complex whodunnit, a deeply compelling human drama and a gorgeously imagined love letter to Cornwall. Every brushstroke is the work of a master . . . and I adored it.'

—Emma Stonex, author of *The Lamplighters*

'A treat of a book: immersive, suspenseful, full of twists and turns . . . It's as captivating as a Cornish summer. I loved it.'

—Susan Fletcher, author of *The Night in Question*

'*The Shell House Detectives* is a hug of a book that is transporting and full of love, with a humdinger of a mystery at its big heart.'

—Amanda Reynolds, author of *Close to Me*

'Captures the magic and beauty of Cornwall wrapped within a warm and engaging detective story. I loved it.'

—Rosanna Ley, author of *The Forever Garden*

'These mysteries are never less than gripping, but are told with so much heart, and with such a vivid sense of place, that each one is a breath of fresh air. I recommend them to all my friends, and can't wait for the next instalment!'

—Kate Webb, author of the DI Lockyer Mysteries

'An intriguing mystery that perfectly captures how a seaside community is rocked by murder.'

—*Sun*

‘Mystery with heart! Fans of intriguing crime mysteries will adore this brand-new series, which is just crying out to become Sunday evening television.’

—*The People’s Friend*

‘Engaging and enjoyable.’

—*Daily Express*

THE HIGH TIDE MURDER

ALSO BY EMYLIA HALL

The Shell House Detectives Mystery series

The Shell House Detectives
The Harbour Lights Mystery
The Rockpool Murder
The Death at the Vineyard
The Arts Trail Killer

Women's Fiction

The Book of Summers
A Heart Bent Out of Shape
The Sea Between Us
The Thousand Lights Hotel

THE HIGH TIDE MURDER

Emylia Hall

This is a work of fiction. Names, characters, organizations, places, events, and incidents are either products of the author's imagination or used fictitiously. Any resemblance to actual persons, living or dead, or actual events is purely coincidental.

Published by Thomas & Mercer, Seattle

www.apub.com

EU Product Safety contact:
Amazon Publishing, Amazon Media EU S.à r.l.
38, avenue John F. Kennedy, L-1855 Luxembourg
amazonpublishing-gpsr@amazon.com

ISBN-13: 9781662521805
eISBN: 9781662521812

Cover design by The Brewster Project
Cover illustration by Handsome Frank Limited – Marianna Tomaselli

Printed in the United States of America

To my dear readers. Thank you for being with me on this adventure.

Prologue

He never thought it would end like this. Blinding torchlight shines in his face, obliterating everything. The wind and the sea are shouting their mouths off. There's even an almighty clap of thunder, like the gods themselves have spoken.

Everything but the kitchen sink, is it?

Whoever came up with the idea that your life flashes before your eyes when you die? Because there's no sign of a highlights reel for him. He presumes it would be highlights, anyway, because it would be a rough exit to be confronted with the worst of yourself: the woes, regrets, missteps, quick-fire and unrelenting, until everything stopped once and for all. He's had reason to think on this before, but the shoe was always on the other foot then. First-hand experience, in this instance, is always going to be a one-off; there are no dispatches to be filed, unless you believe in the word of ghosts. And he might be drunk – stumbling, weakened, damnably easy pickings – but he's not *mad*.

In the event, there is no flashing. Not beyond the wretched torchlight, anyway. Not beyond the glitter of the knife's blade. No highlights, no lowlights, no nothing.

Zilch.

Simply a stone-cold certainty that there is no coming back from this one.

He sways on his feet, lurches backwards, arms flailing. And as he goes over the railing, he screams, for all the good it'll do him.

He is reminded briefly – *so very briefly* – of the whistle of a freight train as it blasts past, simultaneously announcing both its arrival and its departure.

Then, gone before you know it.

1

The day before

When Ally first opens her eyes, she is suspended, neither here nor there.

Where am I?

Then she is righted: The Shell House, of course. She should be used to it now, the temporary discombobulation that greets her when she returns from Suffolk. Two, three nights away, and it's as if she's entered another life altogether.

Ally first visited Ray in late springtime. It was a long drive, and the further east she got, the more the clouds gathered. She stopped in a rainy Aldeburgh to see the seashell sculpture, and the wind along the seafront broke her umbrella; the pebbles clattered angrily with the incoming tide. She might have taken the weather as a sign, but the welcome she received at Ray's – a rose-pink cottage with low beams and the lingering scent of woodsmoke – was warm. Alf the cat jumped into her lap. There was a posy of anemones on the bedside table. And when Ally woke the next morning, sunlight streamed through the window of the east-facing guest bedroom.

When she visited again it was summer and there were ox-eye daisies in the vase. This time the sun came in from the west and golden light tinted the white walls of Ray's room. Swifts swooped and dived outside the window.

None of it was as strange as she'd thought it would be.

I think it's great, her daughter Evie said. *I mean, really great. Dad wouldn't have wanted you to be alone forever.* To which Ally replied that she was still, assuredly, alone, but that was what she wanted. What she and Ray both wanted.

So, you're not in a relationship? asked Evie. *He's not your boyfriend?*

I'm too old to have a boyfriend, dear.

Partner, then.

Goodness, no.

Cue an understanding murmur. Perhaps Evie knew better than to push it. But then she added: *Mum, I have to say, if there was going to be anyone after Dad, I thought it'd be Gus.*

In truth, Ally had thought the same. But Ray came in on the tide, a treasure on the strandline after the storm. He'd been her first boyfriend, forty-seven years ago, when they were art students together at Falmouth. Before her husband Bill. Before Porthpella. And long before she and Gus kissed beneath the mistletoe, or she held his hand in the dark of the ICU.

And now here they are.

And Ally is home again, after three trips to Suffolk in six months, which is, to her, an extraordinary number. They're into autumn now. Not the sun-blushed, mellow kind, of plump blackberries, ripening apples, sunshine like summer. No, this is storm season. The clocks have gone back. The dunes shift nightly. Winds whistle down the chimney, and The Shell House feels as if it's swinging on its ropes. She loves all the seasons, but the beachcomber in her perhaps loves autumn most of all.

And there is an extra crackle of possibility in the air this year.

Ally climbs out of bed and takes her dressing gown from the chair; slides her feet into her slippers. Her little dog Fox stretches in his basket, and she bends to rub his ears. First, coffee. Second, check in with Jayden. After four days away from Porthpella, Ally's eager to know if any new cases have come their way. Ever since the Arts Trail Killer – she can't help but think of the moniker that hit all the headlines, the name that set all of Porthpella abuzz – they've had a steady flow of work. In the early part of the summer, Jayden had his hands full with his young family – Benji is just seven months old, Jasmine is two and a half – and his wife, Cat, needed the extra support. It was up to Ally to take the lead with the detective work then. Nothing as grave as murder or missing persons, but enough to keep her busy. Enough to keep reminding her why this seventh decade of her life is full of surprises.

Just as her stovetop coffee pot is starting to hiss, her phone pings with a message.

It's Jayden.

You back in Porthpella, Al? Hope it was a good trip. Just a reminder that Cat and I are at the High Tide today. Catch you tomorrow?

Of course. It was Jayden's birthday two weeks ago, and Cat booked them a night at a luxury hotel. But then, one by one, all four Westons came down with colds. The treat was rescheduled.

Ally replies, wishing him a relaxing stay, and gets a thumbs-up emoji in return.

She likes the thought of Jayden and Cat having some time to themselves. And the High Tide Hotel, just along the coast at Trebaron Cove, is about the fanciest place around here, these days. It didn't use to be. It always had the dazzling views, the enviable location just steps from the sand of that crescent cove, but inside it was a standard seaside hotel, with worn carpets and creaking pine beds. A passable full English.

Passable. That was Bill's verdict, as he rocked back on his chair, scrunched up his napkin and sent her a wink.

Ally and Bill stayed there the night they came to view The Shell House for the first time. A special treat, as they stood at the brink of their new life together. They never went back, all the years they lived here – why would they need to? They had The Shell House by then. And when the hotel received its luxury makeover and opened a restaurant – *what, twenty years ago?* – it was rather out of their league. Or perhaps they'd just preferred the 'passable' old version. Glitz and glamour were never their style.

Her phone pings with another message from Jayden.

But if a juicy case comes in, feel free to interrupt my hot stone massage, Al.

2

'This'll do,' says Jayden, as he peers through the windscreen at the High Tide Hotel.

The wipers squeak back and forth against the steady drizzle. After a bright start, the weather's muscled in and started throwing punches, but the hotel manages to shimmer out of the gloom. The older building is standard Victorian, somewhere between a large-scale family home and a council-owned mansion, but elegant wood-and-glass structures, mostly on the seaward side, change the whole effect. Proper money has been spent, so the owners are in the market for recouping it. And the car park shows it's working.

There's a racing-green Jaguar by the doors. Two Teslas side by side. Range Rovers are the cheap seats as far as this place is concerned. And their seriously tatty Land Rover? Round here, Jayden's fully prepared to be mistaken for a maintenance man.

'Not too posh for us?' says Cat.

'Totally too posh for us,' he grins.

Cat looks especially amazing today: sea-blue eyes, a cream jumper, her summer tan still on her cheeks. Seven months on from Benji's birth and she's found her rhythm. They both have. Things were rocky for a while back there: a difficult birth, then the jolt of going from one child to two. Cat took it hard, and their responsibilities got on top of them both. It was a new experience for Jayden, worrying about Cat – which is maybe why he was slow to get the memo. He still feels guilty about that, and the way it reached crisis point while he was knee-deep in a case with Ally. The relief Jayden feels now, seeing his wife back to herself again, is immense. Which is why, when she told him she was taking him for a night at the High Tide Hotel for his birthday – *a whole night away, just the two of us, Jay* – he said it was perfect. *I know it's not our usual vibe, but I thought . . . you deserve it, Jay. We both do.*

Leeds are back in the Premier League. A couple of match tickets would have done nicely, but hey. Good food, a cocktail or two, immense amounts of relaxation – he'll take it. And if he's with Cat – and, *no offence, kids,* not with Jazz and Benji – he'll take it with bells on. He loves his kids upside down and back to front, but time together with just his wife is needed.

As they head for the entrance, Jayden takes Cat's hand.

'Still fancy the hot tub in this weather?' she asks.

'With you? You bet, babe,' he says, kissing her on the cheek.

'I can't believe it's just us,' she says. 'No responsibilities, no drama . . . just you and me, Jay.'

Her eyes dance, her smile is electric. And as they reach the covered entranceway, he goes in for a proper kiss.

'Catherine Thomas? Are you kidding me?'

Cat's maiden name.

They turn to see a woman with a pink umbrella and, despite the weather, yellow shades. She pushes up her sunglasses and beams widely.

'Sorry to kill the moment, guys, but . . . You don't recognise me, do you?'

Cat turns a puzzled face to Jayden, then looks back at the woman.

'No, no, I do. I just can't place—'

'Liar,' the woman says with a smile. 'It's Summer. From Penhavern?'

'Oh God, Summer. Of course I recognise you. Ellery! Summer Ellery, isn't it?'

Cat calls out the name like it's the answer in a pub quiz, then looks at Jayden as if he should know her too. He doesn't. And this woman isn't someone you'd be likely to forget. She's tall and very attractive, with the kind of long dark hair that the word *swoosh* is made for.

'Jay, Summer and I went to school together, like . . . *years* ago.'

'Nearly twenty years ago,' says Summer. 'I left Penhavern in Year Nine.'

And is it Jayden's imagination, or is there a little spike in her words?

'Oh, I remember . . . You moved away, didn't you?' says Cat.

'No. Just moved schools.' Summer steps beneath the shelter of the overhang, shaking out her umbrella. 'Anyway, it was a lifetime ago, right? Are you guys staying here too?'

'We are, unbelievably.'

'I'm here for work.'

'Nice work,' says Jayden.

'What a chore, right?' Summer glitters back. 'I'm supposed to be writing about how Cornwall is the perfect place for an out-of-season break, but the weather's not really playing ball . . . Still, cosying up by the fire, Irish coffees, massages, overlooking the sea. That's the angle.' She grins. 'I'm a travel blogger. And I'm on Insta as Summer Holidays. See what I did there? Oh, hey, here's my fella. Come say hi, honey.'

A long-haired guy slopes through the hotel doors. He's of the Broady school, stubbled and surfy; an easy grin on his face, worn-out Vans on his feet. Despite appearances, it's like the High Tide is his natural habitat. He slings an arm around Summer's shoulders and Jayden sees how they look at each other: straight-up adoration.

'Hey, good to meet you,' the man says, holding out his hand. 'I'm Blake. Hey, man.'

'Blake's my plus-one,' says Summer, 'though he won't let me put him in any shots. I get the international-man-of-mystery thing, but kind of annoying when you're in the content game. And he's so pretty too.'

Blake laughs, and Summer leans into his side as though they're basically the same person.

'Mate,' says Blake, winking at Jayden, 'duck and run or you'll be all over Summer's Instagram.'

'You can put us on Instagram so long as you big up our place, Top Field Camping,' says Cat. 'Though I'm not sure it's the same crowd as here . . .'

'What are you talking about?' says Summer, slipping her arm through Cat's. 'Today, *we're* the crowd.'

'Yeah, let's surf this high tide,' laughs Blake, and he claps a hand to Jayden's shoulder as if they're old mates too. Then all four of them are sweeping through the doors and into the warm, dry, and somehow very expensive-smelling lobby.

Cat sends Jayden a look, amusement in her eyes. But she's happy. Laughing. Already asking Summer another question.

Just the two of them? Not for long, then. But Jayden will roll with it like he rolls with most things. *All good.*

And he's got the rest of the season to catch a Leeds game.

3

Kathy Schofield isn't usually the one in the driving seat, but this time she insisted. *You just sit back and relax, Drew.* If anyone else was newly retired they'd want to put their feet up, wouldn't they? Especially after three decades in the police. But not this husband of hers. Kathy got an audiobook for the journey, a tough-guy American thriller, and despite the frequent violence she found it a pleasurable listen – mostly because it sent Drew to sleep. They've made the drive in a little over five hours, and that's with a stop on the M5; overpriced cups of tea and an anaemic lemon drizzle.

As they pitch into the last of the lanes – *three minutes until destination* – Drew suddenly reaches across and snaps off Google Maps.

'I can't stand that woman's voice,' he says. 'What a know-all.'

Kathy elects to stay quiet. She doesn't want an argument now, not when they're here for a lovely time. And she really does want it to be a lovely time. Thirty-five years of marriage has to be worth celebrating, doesn't it? But, lacking confidence that Drew would see that as enough, she pitched the trip as a retirement celebration too: a luxury weekend at a surprise destination. She's still amazed he agreed. The fact that she's paying for it with the bits of housekeeping she's squirrelled away all these years will have helped.

The drive began well enough, but around Bodmin, Drew started getting grouchy. And the further west they headed, the more his mood dropped. *Best you could do, Kath?* he said, as they turned off the A30. *Caribbean all booked up, was it?*

Kathy tried laughing in reply, though there was no humour in her husband's voice. She tells herself that there's still Steve. Steve won't disappoint. And just wait till Drew sees the hotel. The view. The wine list.

Silly, really, how much she still wants to please him. Not least because it's an instinct that stands in direct opposition to her darker thoughts.

Now, the sea appears in front of them, although its effect is diminished by the driving rain. She spies a distinctive tree on the corner and recognises it from a picture on the hotel's website. Has she missed the turn-off? The tree is a sturdy thing but it's listing at a ridiculous angle. She notices Drew looking at it too, and waits for another wisecrack about the weather around here.

'Where exactly are you taking me?' he says. His voice is sharp as a knife, and she winces.

If there was a sign for the hotel, it was far too discreet. The lane starts narrowing, grass running down the middle like a strip of snooker baize. It climbs as steeply as a rollercoaster, and she grips the wheel as if she's throttling it.

'Good question,' she says, trying for a laugh again; it comes out like more of a whimper. 'I think I've missed it.'

'You need to turn round.'

I need my Google Maps lady, she thinks. But saying it will only start something. And there's a hostile current to his voice.

What have I done to deserve this now?

Well, that's a question – and one she's failed to find an answer to all her married life. Instead, she focuses on the immediate problem: she's about to either get wedged in an ever-narrowing lane or be catapulted into the sea. A sea that now seems to be looming directly below them like a grey and roiling plunge pool.

'Turn around and take me somewhere worth going, Kathy.'

Suddenly there's an entranceway, a carved granite stone with *Star Cottage* on it.

'In there,' barks Drew.

'That's someone's house . . .'

But she takes it anyway, ferns swishing the metalwork. As she stalls, her hand slipping on the gear stick, Drew spits out a *God Almighty*. Then out of nowhere there's a man crowding her window; tapping at the pane.

'Looking for the High Tide, are you?'

He's elderly, a flat cap pulled low over his face. Beads of rain sit proud on his wax jacket.

'So sorry,' says Kathy. 'I missed it. Satnav's playing up.'

'Back the way you came,' he says, pleasantly enough, his accent a soft Cornish burr, 'then next left. Just follow the lane down—'

'Back the way we came is about right,' snaps Drew, cutting him off. 'Now drive, woman.'

Kathy sees the man's face change and forces a brittle laugh.

'Drew Schofield, you miserable so-and-so.' She tries to smile at the man; reassuring, apologising, as if it matters what this stranger might think of them. 'It's a surprise weekend – and this one doesn't much care for surprises. But he'll soon change his mind when he's sitting with a glass of something fancy. Thank you. And sorry for the disturbance.'

Drew's still muttering, and she catches the words 'wittering woman'. Heat flares in her cheeks.

I wanted this to be lovely. I should have known better.

She pulls out of the driveway, looking in the rear-view mirror despite herself. She sees the expression on the old man's crumpled face. It's pure pity.

Kathy puts her foot down as they jolt back along the lane. She does so dislike people feeling sorry for her. That's the good thing about someone like Steve: he never does.

4

Elliott King can hear the travel blogger in reception, and he knows he should go out and press the flesh, really. It was Louisa's idea to invite Summer Ellery, and it's Louisa who's been circling the woman like a shark – a highly solicitous shark – sizing up its prey. The High Tide hardly needs the promotion, but Louisa's new thing is about drawing a younger crowd. Which Elliott puts down to the loss of Phoebe.

But then he puts everything down to the loss of Phoebe.

They drove north a few weeks ago, a father–daughter road trip. Phoebe indulged him on the music front – Traveling Wilburys, Johnny Cash – and they had all the sugary sweets that Louisa hates. York came too soon. Elliott lugged his daughter's boxes, trying to ignore the fact that the campus halls looked like a prison, and as they hugged goodbye she said, *You'll be okay, Dad*, as if he was the one embarking on something new and faintly frightening. Somewhere on the M1 he put on Fleetwood Mac – 'Landslide', of course – and cried like he hadn't in a long time.

And now it's just the two of them: Elliott and Louisa, man and wife. It's how they started, so why does it feel more like the end?

Elliott pushes open the office door. Summer and her boyfriend are talking to another young couple, so perhaps there's no need for him to rush out and introduce himself, as Louisa would have him do. *Drop the sad-sack act, darling, you're hardly lonely. You've a whole hotel of people to fuss over.* That's been her line these last few weeks. Elliott notices his wife doesn't include herself as an object for his attention, but then he and Louisa have not been essential to one another's well-being for some time.

As the young couples move away, Elliott sees an older pair standing with their suitcases by the door and no sign of Louisa on reception. *An Englishman's home is his castle*, that's what Elliott's father always told him, *and as ours happens to be a hotel too, we'd best welcome all comers.* So, Elliott's off and out, with a practised smile.

'Hello there, welcome.'

By the looks on their faces, he feels like he's walked into something, like an unseen spider's web on an autumn morning. The man's nose is clearly out of joint, and he doesn't care who knows it. His wife looks puzzled and self-conscious – head bent; shoulders dropped – and Elliott's heart goes out to her. He sees her wipe at her cheek, and he hopes it's just rain splatter.

It's not unheard of for people to arrive feeling out of sorts. A lengthy drive; the tangle of lanes at the end; a bit of anxiety, maybe, stepping into a space that feels so determinedly exclusive. Elliott always tries extra-hard to put people at ease if he suspects they think they're punching above their weight with this booking; Lord knows there are times when he feels an imposter here himself. And of course there's whatever baggage they're carrying too – and he doesn't mean their suitcases. When people book themselves a perfect weekend away – lured by the azure pool, the floor-to-ceiling windows with sparkling vistas, the glittering restaurant – they often fail to remember that they'll be bringing their imperfect selves along with them. As hoteliers it's Elliott and Louisa's job to create an atmosphere where relaxation is organic and inevitable: a true break, not just geographically but emotionally too. Back in his parents' day, there used to be a little wooden sign by the entrance. *Leave your troubles here!* Twee as you like, but it made people chuckle, which was mission accomplished.

Are this couple's troubles of the usual kind? He hopes so.

The woman approaches the desk, her face suddenly as bright as an LED light.

'Good afternoon,' says Elliott, warmly. 'Checking in?'

There's something familiar about her, he thinks. Or maybe she just has one of those faces. She's faintly old-fashioned, like the guests his mum and dad used to welcome back in the day – ladies with handbags hanging from their wrists and wafting clouds of perfume. It's the way her hair is set, her conservative clothes. Her husband, on the other hand, is sharper. With his polo shirt and chinos, and his supercilious expression, he's ready for the golf course or the deck of a yacht. Though what he mainly looks ready for, Elliott thinks, is a fight.

The man's foul mood comes off him in fumes. But then his expression changes, as sudden as the flick of a switch, as he calls out 'Steve-o!'

A new arrival shoulders through the sliding doors.

'Surprise, surprise!'

The newcomer waggles his hands, attempting what Elliott presumes is a Liverpudlian accent, a nod to a long-forgotten television show.

'Drew! Kathy! Your eagle has landed.'

And suddenly the lobby is full of manly slaps on shoulders and laughter for the sake of it. The woman – Kathy – stands back, her arms wrapped around herself in a hug. By the look of cautious satisfaction on her face, Elliott would put money on her being the orchestrator of the surprise.

As a kid, he used to make up stories about all the guests, inventing elaborate and fantastical tales of eloping lovers, backstabbers and spies. As an adult, Elliott's come to realise that truth is often far stranger than fiction, and even the most ordinary-looking people are capable of remarkable drama. What of this Kathy? What of this – *what was his name?* – Drew? This Steve-o? And in the wings another player, a small woman in a smartly belted coat, neat as a doll and younger than the rest. She flutters her fingers at Kathy in an approximation of a wave. Kathy rocks on her heels and smiles like it's Christmas morning, and for no particular reason – or perhaps several – Elliott suddenly feels very sad.

5

'Okay, we need to stay here forever.'

Cat holds out the complimentary box of chocolates – *at least I hope they're complimentary* – and Jayden goes for a posh take on a caramel keg.

'Not too shabby, huh?' he says, popping it in his mouth.

They've never stayed in a place like this before. With floor-to-ceiling glass along one wall, the sea and sky are as much inside the room as out. There's a sumptuous sofa, angled for the view, and a sleek bathtub, hemmed in by a garden's worth of potted exotic plants. A coffee table made of polished driftwood is fanned with coastal living and design books, each one looking like it's never been opened. And the bed – the bed is huge. Huge and inviting. And Jayden's still thinking about that aborted kiss.

Cat slides the balcony doors open and goes to the railing. She peers down towards the terrace, her hair blowing sideways. The soundtrack of the weather – the beats of wind and rain, the bassline of the sea – are turned all the way up.

Definitely an afternoon for staying in.

'Jay, there's no one in the hot tub,' she calls out. 'Let's go.'

~

'Not the worst idea,' says Jayden, as he sits back in the hot tub, drink in hand.

The deck is under shelter and the little bit of rain that's blowing through is, once you're acclimatised, quite refreshing – *bright side, Weston* – though he could do without the wind that's taking the top layer of skin off his face. Beside him, Cat has goose pimples on her cheeks. But underwater they're both warm; legs twined.

The sea is rock-gig loud, and the beach is eerily deserted, but the terrace of the High Tide is designed to keep wildness at bay. Primped palm trees in giant urns and subtle spotlights; nothing as basic as a string of fairy lights. The pair of them soaking in warm bubbles, a couple of fluffy High Tide robes waiting for them for the dash from outside to inside.

Cat raises her Prosecco, and they chink.

'Hey, so Summer suggested a pre-dinner drink later. Do you mind?' she says.

'Sure. If you want.'

So long as the drink doesn't turn into a double date for dinner. Jayden's got no problem going with the flow, and he's formed no particular opinion of Summer and Blake, beyond their supreme confidence and obvious mutual adoration. *Okay, maybe I have formed an opinion.* But he likes the idea of having his wife all to himself on this rare night away.

'Weird thing is,' says Cat, 'I remember Summer at school, but I don't *remember* remember her, you know? She was kind of on the fringes.'

'You wouldn't think it now,' says Jayden.

'Right?' says Cat. 'So glam. I looked at her Instagram and it's gorgeous. She's a proper travel influencer, Jay. Getting freebies like this place. Going wherever she wants, whenever she wants. No responsibilities . . .'

'Hey, look at us,' says Jayden. 'Do we even have kids? I'm so relaxed I've forgotten.'

She laughs. 'No wonder her and Blake look so loved-up. They're living their best lives, aren't they? Imagine us doing it. Travelling with the kids, like . . . a family year out.'

The words *travelling with the kids* don't fill Jayden with instant relaxation. But Cat has the same look in her eyes as when she first started talking about the campsite. *All that prime sea view, wasted on Dad's cauliflowers.* Daydreaming meets steely intent. So Jayden agrees that, yeah, of course it would be amazing, but the campsite barely brings in enough income as it is, and the detective work isn't exactly reliable, and so how are they going to fund this year out of theirs?

Also . . . the detective work.

Cat shrugs. 'Maybe we could document it. Summer says we're a very Instagram-friendly family.'

'When did she say that?'

'She asked if we had kids and so I showed her a pic. Okay, a few pics.'

Jayden raises an eyebrow. 'Oh no. *Content.*'

'And I used to be good at writing back in school.'

'I did hear that.'

'Plus, you're always saying Cornwall isn't exactly diverse.'

'I'm always saying that, am I?'

'What I mean is, there's a whole world out there, Jay. Maybe we should see it before the kids get stuck in school. And we get stuck in a rut.'

A few hours of freedom – a few words from this old schoolmate, and a look at Summer's no doubt massively aspirational Instagram – and Cat's ready to cast off into a new life. Not that Jayden doesn't love his wife's exuberance. And of course it'd be cool to show the kids that the world is a lot bigger than their sandy back garden. They could connect with their roots in Trinidad, for one – that's been on his list since Jazzy's birth; show them their great-grandad's house, where their dad and Auntie Ella spent all those happy holidays as kids. A trip, sure. But leave Porthpella for months on end? He feels weirdly rooted in Cornwall – something that the version of Jayden who first moved here three years ago would struggle to believe.

That word, though: *rut.*

'Hold on, we're not in a rut, are we?'

'Not yet,' says Cat easily, 'but we're not exactly Summer and Blake, are we? They were *glowing*, Jay.'

Fair point.

'Room for one more?'

The question is asked, but then the newcomer's already taking off his robe and climbing into the tub. Observation: guests at the High Tide aren't really into boundaries. Jayden vaguely recognises him as being one of a party of four who checked in just after them. The two men were chests out and back-slapping, reminding him of some of the guys he used to work with in the police. King of the Jungle stuff. A weird mix of comrade and competition.

Never his scene.

The man settles back against the edge and drapes his muscled arms out wide. He's no prizefighter but he works out and wants you to know it. He shuts his eyes and tips his head back, as if he's instantly flicked a switch to relaxation mode.

Cat winks at Jayden and suppresses a laugh. They're basically sharing a bath with a stranger. A non-appealing stranger, at that.

'Check the sky, Jay,' she says.

Out over the water, the sky is so dark it's like night's starting out there – and coming for them. The wind's getting up too: the leaves of the palm trees along the terrace are cracking and snapping.

Maybe it's time to get out? *On numerous fronts.*

'Little birdie tells me you're a copper.'

The man's eyes are still shut, and he tosses the line at Jayden easy as a beach ball. Jayden waits a beat. What, the guy isn't even going to look at him as he speaks?

'Jay?' Cat nudges him, maybe thinking he hasn't heard. Beneath the water, her hand squeezes his leg.

'What birdie was that?' he says.

'That pal of yours. The beautiful girl. We got talking in the lift.'

Summer. She asked Jayden what he'd been doing before he came to Cornwall, then Cat chipped in with the Shell House chat. Summer let fly the OMGs at that.

'Used to be,' says Jayden.

'Likewise. Cheers to getting out, mate. Think I'd be staying at a place like this if I was still on a cop's salary?'

So, he *was* police. *Called it.* Maybe that accounts for the watchfulness too: *that pal of yours.*

The bubbles suddenly get a lot more ferocious, the pitch louder. One of them must have accidentally pushed a button.

'What do you do now?' asks Cat, over the roar of the water.

And Jayden knows she's just being polite, but this guy has no such compulsion. He ignores the question and looks past both of them, his attention caught by something seaward. Jayden follows his eye and sees a figure on the beach. It's a man in a big coat, tramping through the tide pools. Out there the wind's roaring up the sand, wanting to topple anything in its path; the man looks as if he's fighting for every step.

The noise of the hot tub suddenly cuts out, its run ended.

In this sudden lull, Jayden watches the watcher. Their companion hasn't taken his eyes off the person on the beach. Is that muscle memory? A cop noting an anomaly? *IC1 male out walking on beach in storm. No surfboard or fishing rod or dog.*

'What's he up to?' the guy mutters to himself. Then, cupping his hands to his mouth, he yells, 'Drew! Oi, Drew!'

Loud enough to give the wind a run for its money. Loud enough for Jayden and Cat to swap another look. The High Tide Hotel. Peaceful sanctuary? *Yeah, that depends on the guests.*

'Had enough?' says Jayden.

'Had enough,' grins Cat.

As she slips from the tub in one deft manoeuvre, the man finally switches his gaze; he fixes it on Cat's bikini-clad body and his mouth twitches with a smile. *This guy.* Cat pulls on her robe, oblivious, and Jayden swiftly follows. They slide their feet into the freebie white slippers in unison. In this get-up they look more like invalids than people living a life of luxury.

'Private security,' the man calls out. 'In answer to your question, that's what I do now.'

Jayden wraps an arm around Cat's shoulders. Away from the shelter of the overhang, rain stings their faces. He pops a quick thumbs up to acknowledge the man in the tub – his mum's voice in his head: *always keep your manners, Jayden* – then turns back to his wife.

'Run for it?' he says.

6

Louisa King's favourite time of day at the High Tide is evening. Dusk swoops in early in autumn – today, it's been like the dead of night since five o'clock – but inside, the hotel comes into its own. It's a soft-shimmering palace. Louisa loves natural light as much as the next person, and their place has acres of it; at least, it does now, thanks to the improvements they made as soon as they took the reins from Elliott's father. The interior lighting, however, is the work of a magician consultant from Chelsea. As darkness falls, the High Tide glows in all the right places. Everybody looks beautiful here, Louisa's design team even turning their attention to the mirrors too. A little trickery: not a white lie, but a reflective one. Of course, it hits hard when guests re-join the real world and see themselves for what they really are, but it's yet another reason to book a stay, isn't it?

With the foul weather outside, the hotel feels even more like a blissful cocoon. The wind moans like a drunkard, kicking at the windows, but as much as Louisa can't abide Cornwall's darker shades, the guests don't seem to mind. Louisa would like their VIP Summer Ellery to see at least a drop of sunshine while she's here, though. Moody hues are all very well, but Instagram likes its sea and sky to be blue, thank you very much.

As Louisa passes through the restaurant, her heels click over the chevron oak floors. The chefs are putting on their subtle, powerful show in the open-plan theatre, and her waiting staff flow like dancers. Louisa's eyes subtly rove the tables, pendant lights illuminating each one. Naturally, she's looking for Summer and her plus-one. Her brow crinkles when she sees another couple sitting at the table she's reserved for their special guest. Okay, the Westons are a visually pleasing couple – young, quite beautiful – but they're not Louisa's VIP. They must have been seated there by mistake. Because, look, over in the far corner, the deepest recess of the place, is Summer Ellery. Barely visible! It's a crime.

'Milly,' says Louisa, catching the passing waitress's arm. 'A word.'

Milly looks worried. She's a pretty girl, but nervy.

'Why is Summer Ellery stuck out on table eleven? I reserved three.'

The young waitress blinks. Her eyeshadow is kingfisher blue.

'She asked to be moved,' says Milly. 'They wanted a corner table.'

'Then why didn't you give them five? Or eight, for that matter?'

'The guy chose eleven. I guess they wanted privacy.'

Louisa clicks her tongue. Summer is a name in the travel industry, she has a ton of followers, but she's not an actual celebrity, for God's sake. *And she's not here for privacy.* The customer, though? Always right. Some customers, anyway.

'And your make-up, Milly, tone it down, will you?' says Louisa, pointing to her eyes. 'It's a little too showgirl for us.'

She turns on her heel and makes a beeline for the hinterland that is table eleven. Louisa enjoys the walk; she always does. The High Tide sometimes feels like the catwalk she never got to tread, apart from at a fundraiser for the university rowing club, tottering in a barely-there sequinned dress that felt so outrageously downmarket it was like she was playing at being someone else. Is it a coincidence that Louisa first met Elliott that night? Her soulful-eyed Cornish boy – sad-eyed, in certain lights – wearing a tired old lumberjack shirt but rippling with innate handsomeness. And yes, okay, the rumour was that his family owned an eye-wateringly beautiful chunk of beachside real estate and a hotel that was criminally underdone. Louisa saw it for herself that same summer – by which time she had Elliott King wrapped around her little finger – and her whole body tingled as she took in its proximity to the sugar-white sand and the sparkling water, thinking how her family's money could transform the tatty old place into something magnificent.

Tonight, Louisa has chosen white jeans and a wide leather belt; a silk blouse that's like a kiss against her skin. As she moves through the space, she sends charming smiles in the direction of all her diners, including the noisy quartet from Oxfordshire. Or the noisy duo, she should say, as the two men – silverbacks in manner, if not stature – dominate their mousy partners. Not High Tide people, really, but Louisa has learnt to check her snobbery over the years. Nothing to do with the bleeding-heart liberal that she married – *although she hasn't failed to notice that Elliott has given up trying to soften her edges; just like he's given up on a lot of things* – and everything to do with their bottom line.

'Summer, good evening,' she says, with her most expansive smile, taking care to include Summer's boyfriend too.

The boyfriend – Blake – looks back at her, dead-eyed, and Louisa almost does a double take. Earlier, she could see the appeal, if you looked beyond the teenage clothes – the faded surf tee and cheap jeans – and focused on the ruggedly good-looking face, the easy smile, the uncommonly green eyes. But this evening he looks like a different person altogether. His light's gone out, and even Louisa's Chelsea magician isn't helping.

Oh, fabulous. Nothing like relationship trouble to sour a stay.

'What about a couple of glasses of champagne?' she says. 'With our compliments, of course.'

Summer's response is drowned out by an almighty shout from behind. Louisa starts – people do not raise their voices at the High Tide, unless they're calling for their children or their dogs – and is horrified by what she sees.

One of the Oxfordshire party is on his feet, his white shirt blooming red, as if he's been shot in the chest.

'Oh my God,' says Milly, 'I'm so, so sorry.'

And in her hand, an incriminating bottle of Château Margaux. A glass rolls on its side like a bowling pin.

Fury roars in Louisa like a jet engine. *The most basic of mistakes.* She knew the girl wasn't up to snuff, but Elliott, *bloody Elliott*, wanted to give her a chance.

'What are you playing at?' the man bawls, showing all of his class. But, to be fair, he's only voicing Louisa's thoughts – albeit with a macho venom. Milly, meanwhile, stands stock-still, apparently overcome.

'Drew,' says one of the mouse-women, attempting a pacifying hand on his arm, 'I packed other shirts.' But she's batted away – like a six at Lord's, poor thing – and for a moment a small alarm bell goes off somewhere deep inside Louisa. Her father, her mother; the things she saw that no one thought she did.

Ugly, ugly.

Louisa turns quickly to Summer. While her concern is all for their VIP's enjoyment, not this mess between inadequate staff and inferior guests, Louisa must nevertheless attend to it. But then, mercifully, Elliott is there. She didn't even see him in the restaurant, but he's over like a shot, ready to smooth things in his careful, considered way. *Good.* Whatever other feelings have faded, she does on occasion still feel gratitude.

'I'm sorry, sir,' says Elliott, 'but no one speaks to our staff like that.'

And no one speaks to our guests like that, Elliott!

Least of all her husband, Mr Personable.

He stands toe-to-toe with the wine-soaked man, then turns to Milly, and says coaxingly, 'Take a break, Mill. Accidents happen. No one's fault.' Then, addressing the guest, 'Isn't that right, sir?'

Louisa has never heard her husband's voice so barbed. It's Phoebe, that's the trouble. Elliott, the textbook overprotective father, is worried about his darling girl being swallowed up by the horrid wide world, so if he can shelter this inept waitress then he'll go all out, won't he? He'll go all out, the ridiculous man.

'Excuse me,' Louisa says to Summer. 'It looks like the storm's found its way inside.'

'I like your husband's style,' says Summer.

Louisa's eyes widen. Then . . . *Of course*. Summer's social media following is Generation Z. Naturally she'd be on the waitress's side. Obviously, she'd *call it out.* Lost for words, Louisa offers Summer a smile that, she hopes, says all the right things. Then she glides over to table nine – wretched table nine – where whatever fight was in her husband seems to have left him like the air from a balloon. She watches him wilt under their guest's demand for a complimentary bottle and payment for a dry-cleaning bill.

'Least we can do, sir,' says Louisa, taking over, smooth as silk. 'In fact, your entire meal this evening is on us. And with our sincere apologies.'

She looks to her husband. *It's just good business, darling*, her eyes try to say.

But the expression in Elliott's eyes says something quite different. *Disappointment.* And what a grand irony. Because here he is with everything – the beautiful wife, the beautiful daughter, the beautiful hotel – and yet he's still not satisfied. Which makes Elliott just as greedy as anyone, doesn't it?

7

This is how it starts, thinks Ally. The sky darkens, the sea follows. Birds pour from the water and settle inland. As the storm blows in off the Atlantic and tears at the land, somewhere in The Shell House a window frame is rattling. Ally gets the fire going and wind whines in the flue; it sounds like a furious animal, trapped and railing.

She likes wild nights. As a child she stayed up for thunderstorms and that awe has never left her; nor the feeling that, in the eye of a storm, anything can happen. Ally can't help but think of this time last year, when gales galloped over the headland, sand and salt water flying, and Gus was here at The Shell House. A bottle of wine. The fire. Not the kind of night for leaving.

You'd be more than welcome. To stay, I mean, she said.

Gus will never know how much it took to say those words.

That's very kind. But . . . I'll be grand, was the reply.

It came out much later that the reason for Gus's reticence was that he thought Ally was still in love with her late husband, Bill. A feeling that was validated, in Gus's mind, by his discovery of a wardrobe full of Bill's clothes. Well, they're still there. And now, against all odds, there is a Ray. A Ray who just messaged Ally to say: I hear you've got it bad in Cornwall. You should have stayed here! The weather being one of at least fifty reasons. Shall I list the others?

Ally replied saying that she likes a good storm. And then hoped that didn't sound unwilling. As much as she is enjoying Ray being back in her life, she still cherishes time on her own. But she has always been like that, even with Bill.

Her phone buzzes.

She expects it to be Ray, but she has to admit, she always hopes for Jayden. Because Jayden might mean a new case, and of all the new experiences life has brought her in the last two and a half years, the investigative work is her most treasured of all. But her partner is at the High Tide Hotel, his mind on relaxation, not crime.

It's Gus.

You okay in this weather, Ally? Batten down the hatches!

A paper aeroplane, tossed over the dunes.

More than okay, she replies with a smile. Gus knows she loves wild weather. But then might he misinterpret it, her 'more than okayness', as connected to her stay in Suffolk? She can't bear the thought of that. So she deletes it and writes: Okay here! Already looking forward to tomorrow's strandline treasures. And your novel, whenever you want to send it (no pressure).

Gus has been writing a novel for as long as Ally has known him, and earlier in the year he finally managed to attract an agent. However, he's since confided that writer's block has descended. Ally has offered to read it, mostly so she can tell him how wonderful it is. She'd like to lift his spirits; Gus isn't one of life's most confident people.

Not like Ray.

This thought is immediately followed by another: the frustration that she should compare them. Or is that natural? When it comes down to it, Ally chose Ray over Gus – but how can she explain that it wasn't a case of the two men standing side by side and her picking? She knows it's more complicated than that.

Ally sees the three dots that show that Gus is typing. Then they stop. Perhaps Gus doesn't quite trust her to lift his spirits after all.

She looks to the fire and is just wondering whether to toss another log on or let it die down when there's a thump at the window.

Bang!

Loud enough to cut through the wind; the boom of the incoming tide.

Ally's on her feet.

Random crashes are the music of big weather, and out here at the final frontier a storm will take hold of anything that's not tethered. Nevertheless, unease twitches in her chest. Ally goes into the kitchen and immediately spots the dark smear on the windowpane.

She knows blood when she sees it.

She takes her torch from the hook and opens the door. The wind immediately gusts in. As Ally rounds the side of the house, she can't help but think about that night back in the spring, their last murder case, when she trod through a dark interior and found an unimaginable horror. When you've seen the worst, perhaps there's less to be afraid of. Does that hold? Either way, she's spinning her torch beam over the veranda, garden, the gate – then on to the window itself.

The blood is a lurid red, streaked on the pane like an artist's palette.

As Ally looks down, she sees a bird lying at her feet. It's a huge herring gull, its eyes frozen in a look of fury. A bright yellow beak cracked wide. It must have been injured already, because flying into the pane of glass wouldn't have caused it to bleed.

Ally crouches beside it. It will have flown towards the light of her window, like a ship steering towards a lighthouse. She lays a finger on its soft feathers, and refuses superstition; bad omens abound, when it comes to birds and houses. As the storm around her shouts its indifference, Ally whispers an apology.

Tomorrow, she'll bury it in the garden.

8

As soon as Summer wakes, she notices the quiet. There's nothing but the sound of gulls; the rhythmic breaking of waves on the beach. The wind that tore at the High Tide last night has died away. Summer's seen enough big weather on her travels – a monsoon in Goa that was like walking through a power shower; a tornado in Texas, that perfect, terrifying twist of energy, when she was staying on a ranch for *Harper's Bazaar* – but there was something unsettling about last night's storm. It was the way it rolled in off the sea, under the cover of night. Then snapped off all the power, showing that even a place like the High Tide Hotel is no match for dark forces.

Or maybe it's just being back in Cornwall.

But Summer doesn't want to give any headspace to that thought, because it's inconvenient and even a bit pathetic. And she thought she'd activated Summer 2.0.

Summer wasn't so unsettled that she missed the chance to get a reel for Instagram, though. In the middle of the power cut she went out on to their bedroom's balcony. She filmed the sky cracked wide by lightning and the thunder like cannon fire. A fat moon suspended like an unexploded bomb. Summer panned one hundred and eighty degrees, capturing the full spectacle, then tapped out a caption: *Out of season break in Cornwall? Moody!* Then she went back in, sliding the doors closed behind her.

Now, she rolls on to her side and looks at the sleeping Blake. His breathing is deep, even. And as much as she can see in the half-light, his face is untroubled.

He claimed a migraine yesterday, but Summer had migraines as a teenager. They were stress-induced, the doctor said. She'd feel sick with the pain, and a constellation of stars followed her everywhere. Even after they passed, she'd feel as if she were bruised, half-blinded. No, Blake had a headache at best. But it was enough for him to want to skip being sociable all afternoon. Enough to make his whole demeanour change.

You look spooked, babe, she said.

I'm not good with pain.

I've literally seen you land on your head on a snowboard and carry on.

They had to abandon their planned drinks with Cat and Jayden – she didn't feel like doing it on her own – and it was an effort to drag Blake to dinner. Their spell in the restaurant was disappointingly short-lived.

So Summer was uncomfortable before the storm, really. Because he was supposed to be the fun-never-stops Blake. The barman she met in Avoriaz, high in the French Alps, who turned somersaults on his snowboard and danced like he was liquid and made her feel like she was the only woman he'd ever fallen for. But suddenly, he didn't seem himself. Or not himself with *her*, anyway.

Which perhaps says more about Summer, doesn't it?

It would be a cruel kind of trick for Blake to lose interest in her here, of all places. As if just by crossing the Tamar she's reverted to the self she thought she'd left behind. Would someone as cool as Blake have looked twice at her at school? Not for a second. Except pityingly, maybe.

So the raging storm? Yes, that was loud, but so too were the thoughts inside her head. Worries that grew fangs. Lurked.

And others joined them.

Like Cat Thomas again. Or Cat Weston, as she is now.

Cool Cat, that's what Summer used to call Cat in her head. Not one of the mean girls at school, just someone who floated around in her own bubble, never thinking about what it was like for anyone else. Summer could tell that Cat couldn't remember her yesterday. Not really. And maybe that was a good thing, because Summer isn't that person anymore, is she?

Sad Summer. That's what the girls used to call her. Whispered in the corridors and, once, scribbled across the cover of her new jotter, where she'd written her name so carefully in her sparkly birthday pens.

Maybe that's why she went so big yesterday, flaunting her new-made self. What was she thinking, interrupting that kiss between Cat and her husband? On one level, it suited Summer that Blake didn't want to be sociable with them last night. Why put herself under such pressure to prove her worth to someone from a million years ago at school? But then she felt that nagging doubt: *what if Blake's seen through me?* Because when Summer thinks about it, it wasn't long after seeing Cat that Blake lost his zest.

She's restless now. A lie-in is out of the question.

Sensing a lightening of the sky, Summer slips out of bed. Perhaps there'll be a sunrise to catch on the phone: the calm after the storm. Today is a new day. She hopes – oh, how she hopes – that Blake will be his usual self and the pair of them will be shiny at breakfast. Good vibes only.

She pulls on her robe and parts the curtains. Silver light, cautious but determined, filters in. As she steps on to the balcony she feels the whoosh of fresh air. It's brisk, salted, and she closes her eyes, letting herself be in the moment. The sea is a wall of sound. A chorus of seabirds lend their piercing vocals.

Summer thinks she hears Blake call out her name and she snaps her eyes back open. She's turning, an optimistic 'Morning, babe!' ready at her lips, when something catches her attention.

There's a flock of gulls on the terrace, scrapping and flapping. But then something causes them to rise up – wheeling, shrieking – and that's when Summer sees it.

Not it: *him*.

A man.

He's spreadeagled, his limbs at unnatural angles. Even in the delicate light of dawn she can see the dark stain by his head.

Then the gulls bomb back in. Three, four, five of them, darting up and down his body. When one starts pecking at his head, that's when Summer screams.

9

The scream yanks Jayden from a deep sleep. His reaction is pure instinct; he's out of bed and on his feet before he's fully processed what he's heard.

There's a beat of silence, and for a moment he thinks it was a dream, but then Cat bursts out of the bathroom. She's wet from the shower, her eyes wide and questioning.

'Did you hear that?'

Jayden moves fast to the balcony, pulling on his jeans as he goes. He yanks the curtains and throws the door wide open. The fireball sun is on its way up, its rays burning over the water. The wind whips at his face, blasting any last traces of sleep away.

'Summer!'

He didn't know that the couple were in the room next door.

Summer is standing on her balcony, perhaps six or seven metres away. She's in her High Tide dressing gown, her hands gripping the railing as if she's frozen. Her scream hangs in the air like a cloud. Blake surges out in his boxer shorts, his face glaring white, crying out, 'What is it, babe? What's up?' But Jayden is already looking past the pair of them. To the gulls. The man. The blood.

Hearing Cat behind him, Jayden spins round.

'Call 999,' he says. 'I'm going down.'

'Ambulance?'

'Ambulance. And police.'

Questions fire in Jayden's brain as he runs down the hotel corridor, but the biggest is 'dead or alive?' Forget the angle of the limbs, forget the carrion-seeking seabirds, think of Lewis Pascoe. In their very first case, Lewis fell from a great height – and he was still breathing when they got to him.

Jayden pelts down the stairs, his feet skidding as he enters the lounge area. The calm evoked by the low acoustic music and scented candles makes it feel like a stage set. There's no one on the reception desk, but the monitor is on and there's a half-drunk cup of tea in a blue mug. Jayden can see through to the empty dining room. Breakfast starts at 7.30 a.m. and it's not that yet. At the far end, a waitress carries a tray. She doesn't see him.

For a split second, Jayden hesitates. Should he call out for the waitress to get the owners? Say there's been an incident?

Don't delay.

He sprints through the doors, into the gardens and across the terrace. Palm fronds are everywhere, shredded from the trees by last night's storm. He'd forgotten he was barefoot, but the cold, wet ground reminds him. His bare chest prickles with goosebumps.

Half-naked. Ever the professional, Weston.

As Jayden approaches the man, the birds are lairy. They're the sort who bother tourists, all sharp beaks and wide wings, and he runs at them yelling, waving his arms. They scatter, shrieking.

Then he pulls up short.

It's the man who had wine spilt on him, erupting with such violence that Jayden couldn't take his eyes off him for the rest of the night. *Babe, stop staring*, Cat said, *you're worse than Jazz.* The man who went walking on the beach in the gathering storm. *Oi, Drew!* That's his name: Drew. And his friend, their charmless hot tub companion, is Steve; a name that flew about the restaurant last night like a bullet. Steve seemed to enjoy the wine spillage. The kind of person who likes making something out of nothing; who'd be quick with the 'what are you looking at, mate?' on a night out.

Drew.

Jayden kneels beside Drew's body. He can already see the rigor mortis but feels for a pulse anyway. The man's skin is ice cold. His fingers are like talons. The blood on the terrace is already the colour of dark rust.

Jayden rocks back on his heels, looking up at the balcony that Drew fell from. It must be seven or eight metres high. A woman, Drew's wife, stands looking down. She's in a nightdress, the skirt fluttering at her legs. She says something Jayden can't catch, then she covers her face with both hands.

'This scene needs to be secured!'

The voice is a command, as though there's a line of constables waiting to spring into action. Jayden gets to his feet, already guessing the source – and sure enough he sees Steve charging towards him. The guy stops two metres short of the body, his energy creating a force field.

He's angry, thinks Jayden. And although shock has many faces, the emotion jars.

Behind Steve is the hotel owner, Elliott King. Elliott sets a hand on Steve's shoulder, then thinks better of it. He looks to Jayden instead.

'You found him?' says Elliott, a quaver in his voice.

'Another guest saw him from her balcony,' says Jayden, gesturing towards where Summer and Blake are standing. *Were* standing. 'Summer Ellery. Her scream woke me. Woke us all, right? My wife's calling the police.'

Steve's phone starts ringing and he answers it like he's on duty. He paces the scene, his elbow thrust at a right angle.

'Tell her to bloody let you in, Mae,' he says. 'I can see her from here.'

'They're on their way,' says Cat, appearing. Her hair's wrapped in a towel and she's clasping her phone to her chest. Jayden sees her look at the body, the horror in her eyes. She passes him a t-shirt, and he gratefully pulls it on.

Jayden looks again at Drew's wife. She's dropped into one of the outdoor chairs. Through the balcony railing, he can see her crossed ankles; pink slippers she must have brought from home. Someone needs to be with her.

'Kathy!' Steve's voice is rough-edged as he shouts up. 'Mae's at your door. Let her in, love.' Then he rubs his face with both hands, as vigorously as if he's trying to get a stain out. 'Alright, listen up. Deceased's name is Drew Schofield. Fifty-five years of age. Not long retired. Lifelong copper. Up there, that's Kathy. Wife. Next of kin.'

'What on earth happened?' begins Elliott. 'You don't think he . . .'

'Drank enough to sink a ship last night,' says Steve, looking down at his friend. 'He was all over the place.'

Jayden watches for emotion on his face, but Steve gives nothing away.

Elliott, on the other hand, is an open book. He pushes his hands through his hair; his forehead is grooved with deep worry lines. Maybe he's already thinking of bad press. But considering he's in charge round here, he's not asserting his authority.

Steve checks his watch. 'Response times in the sticks are going to be laughable.' He nods to Jayden. 'You and I need to man this scene, mate.' Then he points to Elliott. 'No one leaves this hotel. Staff or guests. We'll need statements. No one slips through the net.'

Elliott looks confused, as if he's thinking, *but didn't he just fall?*

'I don't think we should cause unnecessary alarm. . .' he begins.

'Unnecessary?'

Elliott flinches as if the word is a right hook. Steve's not the biggest of men, but he has the bristling energy of a bantamweight boxer.

'That's my mate dead there. My mentor. Who just happened to be a highly respected police detective too. So everything that happens next – the interrogation, the investigation, the whole dog-and-pony show – is *necessary.* Alright? Because I'll tell you one thing, blokes like Drew Schofield don't just topple off balconies because they have one drink too many. They don't just trip and fall. If they go down, it's because they're pushed.' His voice cracks as he turns to Jayden. 'Right, mate?'

His eyes burn like headlamps. His forehead is pricked with sweat, despite the cold air.

'Mate, I asked you a question,' says Steve.

Jayden makes a non-committal gesture. He's aware that he's standing back; observing, more than taking charge. But it's not through lack of confidence. And he's sure as hell not going to jump because Steve tells him to. Suddenly there's the crunch of tyres on gravel. *The police.* Steve heads towards the patrol car like he just called for back-up.

'*Pushed?*' says Elliott quietly. 'That has to be the shock talking, doesn't it?'

'I'm sure there's shock in there,' says Jayden, diplomatically.

But he's also thinking about the other parts of the man's reaction.

He turns, feeling a hand on his arm. *Cat.* She's biting her lip, her brow crumpled. He wants to take care of her – has she ever seen a dead body? He doesn't think she has. But he also wants to be all eyes on everybody, especially Steve and Kathy. One spitting blood, the other frozen.

And where have Summer and Blake gone?

'Jay,' says Cat, 'can I talk to you for a second?'

As they move a few paces away from Elliott, Cat hands him her phone.

'Sorry, but there's something here you need to see,' she says.

10

Constable Tim Mullins has never been to the High Tide Hotel before. Not his cup of tea, really. But here he is, standing looking up at its palatial façade, and he's suddenly glad of the little bit of extra oomph that his uniform gives him. He glances down at his boots, to check they're polished.

There's a regular in The Wreckers Arms who brought a date here once and went round afterwards saying, *That place cost me an arm and a leg and a roll in the hay*. Seemed like that line – and the titters that followed – was the bloke's only consolation. When the hefty dinner bill came, his card didn't work, and his date didn't take kindly to his insolvency. If Mullins had a date? It'd be the chippie all the way – and chuck in a pickled egg while you're at it. Or The Wreckers for gammon steak. Or Hang Ten for brownies, if he figured that was the girl's speed. *Well, I've been there, done that.*

But it's all a bit pie in the sky, this talk, because there are no dates for Mullins on the horizon. The only excitement he's had lately is a dream where Saffron – otherwise known as Hippy-Dippy, owner of the aforementioned Hang Ten – gave him a surf lesson. There was no actual surfing; instead, they just seemed to be bobbing about on boards on flat water, sun pouring out from the sky, her smile as wide as the bay. But the sensation Mullins was left with once he woke was weird: he felt buzzed and calm at the same time. And, like, really happy.

If Mullins were into the woo-woo stuff, he'd take it as a sign. Of what, though? That he should ask Saffron out? *Yeah, right.* But he could ask her for a surf lesson. What would Saffron say when she worked out that all Mullins wanted to do out there was bob about and smile at her, though?

No, some things are best left to dreams. Which maybe makes him a bit woo-woo after all.

Mullins shoves these thoughts to the back of his mind, and lets the dead bloke take centre stage. *The deceased.* He's seen a few now and it never gets any easier; maybe that's why his head's darting about like a snooker ball.

He looks down at the body, makes a quick assessment.

He'd estimate early sixties. Thick white hair, falling in waves; waves that make Mullins think of the flakes of cod flesh in his Friday-night fish and chips. Grey skin; several hours dead, by the look of him. A bulky body: muscle run to fat. If he was going to call it now, he'd say heart attack – the plunge from the balcony being the unfortunate upshot.

The CSIs, already white-suited, white-booted, move in.

'The victim's Drew Schofield,' says the guy at his elbow – Steve Bradshaw – who first greeted him as though he were lord of the manor and Mullins a visiting peasant. But it turns out he's just a guest. 'Lately of Thames Valley CID. Don't know how much you lot down here have to do with the civilised world, but the brass should know him. Helluva cop, was Drew. Taught me everything I know. And then some.'

Civilised world?

'Hung up my boots a while back. Fool's errand, modern policing. No offence, pal. Politics. Paperwork. Less budget than your average kid's pocket money. Not for me.'

Mullins smiles thinly. 'Someone's got to do it. What's your relationship to the victim?'

'Mate. Good mate. We were here together for the weekend. Kathy, Drew's better half, made it happen.'

'And where's Kathy now?'

Steve jerks his head to the balcony. 'Hasn't come down. Crying her eyes out, probably.'

'I'll need to speak to her.'

'Yes, you will. You'll need to speak to everyone, once you've called in the cavalry. There'll be a lot of eyes on this case. One of our own. One of *your* own. Once your DCI comes down, I'll offer my assistance, obviously. All hands to the pump.'

Saturday morning? Mullins imagines DCI Robinson in a pressed pair of chinos and a polo shirt, slinging his golf clubs in the boot. No way he's turning out for this one.

And DS Skinner? Gone to St Austell for the weekend to see his sister and, in Skinner's words, 'her godawful new husband'. Maybe Skinner would love this as an exit strategy: a dead cop at the High Tide.

Right now, procedure dictates that Mullins secure the scene, let the CSIs get their groove on, supervise the removal of the body and take statements. All in a day's work.

He asks the necessary question:

'Sir, do you have reason to believe this wasn't an accident?'

'Reason?' snaps Steve. 'Course I've got reason. He's not going to just fall off a balcony.'

Mullins waits. Steve glowers back.

No reason, then.

'Look, I think Drew knew someone here. A face from the past.'

'What makes you say that?'

'"A blast from the past." That's the line he used.'

Sterling detection skills from Steve Bradshaw there.

'When was this?'

'Yesterday afternoon. Early evening, maybe.'

'What else did he say about this "blast from the past"?'

Steve shakes his head. 'We got on to something else. That's what it's like once we get going, the conversation moves fast. Smash and grab. He didn't bring it back up and I forgot. Until now.'

'Do you think he was talking about a person, rather than the place? Had he been here before?'

'Don't know,' says Steve, skimming a hand over his buzz cut.

And Mullins can tell how much it's costing him to admit it, this hole in his knowledge. Too bad this Steve is more for broadcasting than for receiving.

'But I'd put money on a person.'

Mullins nods. They'll run a check on all the guests at the hotel, see what comes up.

'How did Drew say it? Was it like he was talking about an old mate, an old enemy, or someone . . . unimportant? In your opinion, Steve?'

Steve sticks his chest out. He's a bloke who likes giving his opinion.

'He said it like it was a bit of a laugh. Not important.'

There we go, then.

'But,' says Steve, 'just because something wasn't important to Drew doesn't mean it wouldn't be to someone else. You know?'

He rubs at his jawline, looks at his boots. For the first time, Mullins sees a little chink in this guy's armour. Then Steve's turning away, saying something about 'covering all bases' and 'your DCI' before striding off.

'Mullins.'

A hand on his shoulder.

'Jayden! What are you doing here?'

Though Mullins should know better than to ask by now, when it comes to crime scenes. He glances round for Ally Bright, but instead of Jayden's partner, Mullins sees his wife. Cat's looking freaked out. Maybe it's her first dead body.

'Can I have a quiet word?' says Jayden.

Jayden's trying to be subtle, but Mullins can feel the hotel owner, Elliott King, watching them. Elliott's been joined by a woman in skin-tight leggings and a big, long, drapey cardigan that looks soft as marshmallows. Lovely hair. Mullins closes his mouth, realising it's in fly-catching mode. Well, she's got her eye on them too.

They head for the patrol car together. Mullins sidesteps a terracotta pot that must have gone over in last night's storm; it lies on its side, cracked open like a nut. Cat follows too, glancing back over her shoulder.

'What have you done with your kiddies, then?' Mullins asks, trying for conversation, but Cat's distracted, and Jayden hands him a phone.

'Take a look at this,' he says.

Jayden's serious voice. *Here we go again.* Shell House equals murder. Not a technical equation, but one that seems to hold.

A fall from a balcony? Always worthy of investigation. But accidents happen and natural causes strike hard. Especially when the bloke you're talking about is retirement age, meat on his bones, known to like a drink or three.

Mullins squints at the phone.

'What am I looking at? Instagram? Not into it, Jayden. Bunch of posers.'

'It's a video of last night's storm. Shot from here.'

Mullins frowns as he watches the film. It's nothing he hasn't seen or heard before. The wind howls like a mad thing. The sea crashes. Bit of thunder and lightning. The camera pans the hotel terrace and the line of balconies; it's dark, despite the big old moon, and Mullins can only just make it all out. Conclusion? It won't be winning any Oscars.

'Who's Summer Holidays?'

'That's one of the guests. Summer Ellery, travel blogger. Old school friend of Cat's, as it happens. Mullins, look. Watch it again.' Jayden's finger hovers above the screen. 'There, mate.'

He speaks quietly, but urgently. And Mullins doesn't get the big deal. Then suddenly he does.

'There's someone on the balcony.'

'Two people. Check it.'

Mullins frowns. Touches the screen to zoom in. 'Yeah, okay. Two people.'

'Mullins, this is Summer's video, shot from her balcony. And that's Drew Schofield's balcony.'

'Flip.'

'Exactly.'

Mullins looks behind him. CSIs doing their thing. That pool of dried blood. And the cluster of people watching. *Suspects.* He plays the video again, zooming in on the two figures as much as he can.

'I can't make them out, Jay. Could be anyone. Woman, man, anyone.'

'But it's Drew's balcony, no doubt about it. And look at the body language.'

Body language that Mullins has seen a thousand times. Blokes squaring up to one another. Pub nights, match day, just about any place there's booze.

'Someone was with Drew on that balcony before he fell,' says Jayden.

'And had a bone to pick with him. Or vice versa. Time of the video?'

'It was posted at 12.30 a.m. We'll need to check the original.'

We. Classic.

'What's her game, do you think? This Summer. Posting this.'

'At a guess, she didn't know what she had. She was just capturing the storm.'

'I'll be interviewing her.'

'I don't know where Summer is,' chips in Cat. 'She was here and now she's not.'

'I'll *definitely* be interviewing her,' says Mullins.

'Along with everyone else,' says Jayden. 'Million-dollar question: who was on that balcony with Drew Schofield?'

Mullins huffs a breath. Thinks of Skinner, getting himself out his sister's door, hustling back before the Newquay lot get a sniff. Right now, Mullins is on his own.

'Victim's mate, Steve Bradshaw, reckons Drew Schofield ran into a "blast from the past" here,' he says.

'At the High Tide?'

'No, Jay, on the moon.' He rubs at his nose. 'Could be relevant, though.'

'You think?'

Jayden's turn for sarcasm.

'And just like that,' says Mullins, puffing out his cheeks, 'we've got ourselves a murder investigation.'

11

Jayden watches as Mullins joins the small group standing at the hotel doors. Steve, like a dog off the leash, jumps on Mullins; the guy's got opinions, and he wants them heard. Meanwhile, Elliott stands back as his wife Louisa moves in on the constable too. The hotel owners will have other things on their minds – not least when things can get back to normal.

Answer? Not any time soon, going by that video.

A blast from the past.

The phrase Mullins relayed is lodged in Jayden's head. If Drew Schofield was here on a surprise weekend, was this 'blast from the past' an extra element? Planned or not planned?

'Jay, I need to phone Mum and Dad,' says Cat. 'If they somehow hear about this, they'll freak out. When shall I tell them we'll be back?'

Jayden looks at his watch. Checkout is midday. They'd planned a long breakfast, and a last rinsing of the facilities before they headed back to reality. But now? Jayden reckons he has at least four hours to be around this murder.

His face is obviously doing something, because Cat sends him a knowing look.

'Oh God, you want to stay, don't you? Now more than ever?'

'I really want to see Jazz and Benji,' he says.

That is true.

'I miss them.'

True too.

He leans closer, drops his voice. 'Cat, this place is secure. You can't get into the main building without an electronic key. Alright, factor in open windows, fire escapes, there's always possible entry points, but . . . whoever's in that video, they most likely came from *inside* the hotel.'

'You think one of the guests killed him? My God, Jay, even more reason to get out of here.'

'Mullins will be taking all of our statements. We have to stay for that at least.'

'It can't just be Mullins.'

'It won't be. Our mate Skinner's going to love seeing me here.'

Cat shakes her head. 'They have to let us go after that, though, don't they?'

Jayden looks at the group at the door again. They've been joined by several other guests. He glances to the balconies, where more people stand like sentries. There's still no sign of Summer, though. Or Blake.

A small alarm bell sounds.

It's the second time they've been missing in action. Last night, Summer and Blake pulled out of the early-evening drinks they'd suggested, then they seemed to be in a world of their own at dinner. Cat thought they were blowing kind of hot and cold.

'Technically we're all suspects,' he says. 'Cat, have you seen Summer?'

She shakes her head. 'God, she might not even realise what she caught on camera.'

Everyone else directly involved – except for Summer, except for Blake – is out here. Kathy Schofield, wrapped in a big coat, has come downstairs and is standing by the hotel doors. The petite dark-haired woman, Steve's partner, is beside her. Other guests have also joined them, trickling out in dressing gowns and speedily pulled on clothes, no doubt wondering how something as real as death has broken into this fantasy place.

Jayden does a quick calculation. There are maybe fifteen rooms. With staff too, there are possibly thirty to forty people on site. That's a lot of statements. And Summer will be right at the top of the list.

'We should check in on Summer,' says Jay. 'Shall we try her room?'

Cat narrows her eyes.

'You can't pump her for info, Jay.'

'She might have seen something and not realised the significance.'

'Not your job. Not this time.'

'Excuse me . . . Jayden, isn't it? Can I have a word?'

Louisa King has glided up soundlessly. She'd make a great spy.

'This is a dreadful business,' she says.

On the surface she looks unruffled, but there's a tension at her delicate jawline.

'It is. . .' begins Jayden.

'That young officer over there,' Louisa goes on. 'He's being very gung-ho and launching a murder investigation. Which feels incredibly over the top to me but . . . what do I know about these things? Fortunately, not much at all. You, on the other hand, Jayden . . .'

She smiles tightly. So, she knows who he is, then. *Okay.*

'You seem to have rather a knack when it comes to this sort of thing. You and your partner. Professional partner, I should say,' she adds, smiling at Cat. She touches Jayden's arm, and he looks down at her manicured fingers. The glittering diamond ring, the size of one of Jazzy's Lego bricks. 'All I know is that I can't have this ugly business dragging on and on. Police clomping around the place. Horrible rumours. That's not High Tide. I want this cleared up, and cleared up quickly.'

No mention of the victim, his wife, his friends. Louisa's priorities are purely selfish. But Jayden thinks he knows what's coming. He glances to Cat. By the look on her face, she's called it too.

'I was brought up to throw money at a problem. I expect you have a rate card, but I'll include a substantial bonus for a quick solution. Solve this by the end of the weekend and you'll be able to afford to stay here any time you like.'

She laughs, as though she's joking – but Jayden suspects she isn't.

He feels himself hesitating. *Have we ever had a client we don't actually like?*

'The police have got this,' he says. 'They were quick to the scene.'

'Look, I don't believe in luck,' says Louisa. 'I think we're responsible for our own fortune in life. But I expect my husband would say it's serendipitous that we have a private detective of some local repute, under our roof, the very night someone's killed. We'd be fools not to get you involved, Jayden. And considering my offer, you'd be a fool not to take it.'

He glances to Cat again and she shrugs. It's not as if they couldn't use the money. *Up to you*, she mouths.

'Let me talk to Ally,' he says.

Louisa shakes his hand like it's a done deal. For a slightly built woman, her grip is nails.

12

'A new case?'

Ally cups her hand around the phone. The wind is nothing compared to during the night, but she doesn't want to miss a word. Her boots are sunk deep in the wet sand of the strandline and the words *suspicious death* glint more brightly than anything she can find on the shore. But *murder*? She feels a now-familiar sense of dread – and anticipation.

How can she admit that some of her best days – days spent investigating with Jayden – are a direct result of somebody else's very worst?

Don't you find it depressing, Ray asked her over a fireside glass of wine, *wading about in someone else's tragedy? I'd worry it'd get inside me and not leave. A kind of contagion.*

Ally tried to explain to Ray that what she and Jayden do is positive action after the most negative act has occurred; that perhaps the bereaved can then take the first step on a long road towards finding something like peace. Each case leaves a mark on her, of course it does. But Ally never wants to stop this hurt, because it means that she cares.

'Skinner would hate it,' says Jayden. 'We'd be right on top of his investigation.'

'Is Skinner hating it a reason to take the case or to *not* take the case?'

Their relationship with the detective sergeant has been up and down over the last couple of years. 'Playing detective' used to be his refrain – and that was when he was being polite. Ally feels he respects them now in a way he didn't before, but Jayden's theory is that, as their success has grown case by case, so too has the green-eyed monster; the Shell House Detectives took the headlines with the Arts Trail Killer case, and Skinner doesn't like playing second fiddle.

And Constable Mullins? Oh, dear Mullins bumbles on. Occasionally surprising them along the way.

'You know I like proving people wrong, Al, but this is going to look like a head-to-head race. Especially with Louisa's mad bonus in the mix.'

'And you think we can't compete?'

Ally feels a dart of pride as she says it.

'I know we can. But we'll be up against the usual. Forensics, warrants, resources . . . Maybe the way to pitch this to Mullins and Skinner is as a team effort. Same side, greater good.'

'Do we need their permission? We haven't before, Jayden.'

But the High Tide Hotel is an intimate setting. And if the killer really came from within, it's a small pool for a lot of fish.

'Technically, we could be getting in the way,' he says. 'Treading on toes.'

'But if we tread *carefully* . . .'

On the other end of the phone, she hears him give a low laugh. 'You know what, I'm not really into swanky hotels. I don't tend to love the crowd they draw. But a murder case for a late birthday present? Now you're talking.'

Ally looks down the beach. By Hang Ten she can see two surfers carrying their boards over the sand. The sky above is a grubby white. The sea the colour of soaked denim. She can feel the wind through the knit of her hat.

Today was a normal day, and now it isn't.

She's already walking; whistling for Fox.

'What about the man who died? How much do you know about him?'

Jayden recounts the basics. Drew Schofield. A retired detective from Thames Valley Police, at the High Tide Hotel for a weekend with his wife and friends. *First impression, Al? Not the nicest guy.*

'Thames Valley? That's Oxford, isn't it? I only know because of Gus's beloved Morse.'

'That's right. Drew's mate Steve was police too, but not anymore. He's a bit of a . . . character.'

'Will he be content sitting on the sidelines, do you think?'

'Not for a second. And there's a possibility Thames Valley might want in as well, so this case is already getting busy. How soon can you get to Trebaron Cove?'

Ally quickens her stride. Beside her, the tide teases in and out, nippy as a puppy.

'I'll leave now,' she says. 'One question: is the High Tide dog-friendly?'

'Friendlier to dogs than some humans, at a guess.'

'Is our client something of a snob, Jayden?'

'Yeah, you could say that.'

Ally looks down at her old hiking boots, her faded jeans and wax jacket. She decides not to get changed on principle.

13

'Make like a cobra,' says Saffron. 'That's it, Gus. Lock out those arms, arch that back.'

Gus has felt ridiculous countless times in his life, but this is right up there. For starters, it's the garb. He imagined himself looking a little bit 007 on a water-based mission, but in reality he feels more like a neoprene-clad baby. An aged baby, mind: sixty-eight years old, and learning to surf for the first time.

Ridiculous.

The idea came to him while he was at his writing desk, working on his agent's edits for his detective novel. A few months ago, that fact would have given him untold glee. *My agent! My edits!* The book that brought Gus to Porthpella is finally going somewhere. But his detective novel is yet to make its way out into the world of publishers, let alone the great reading public. So, Gus is waiting at the gate, and the gatekeeper – the impressive but intimidatingly brisk Marissa – isn't quite ready to open it yet. Gus needs to deliver a draft that has more narrative tension. *Turn the screws,* she's told him. *Up the ante.* Marissa believes in this book of Gus's, but only if he can rise to her vision for it.

And that's proving to be the trouble.

He can't even bring himself to share it with Ally, though she's offered to read the manuscript to help encourage him. While on the one hand he can't think of anything he'd like more, what if Ally thinks it's tosh? He simply doesn't have the backbone.

He's been in this pickle for some time, but then a few weeks ago he looked out his window, past his laptop screen, and had a sudden flash of inspiration. *Surfing! I could take up surfing.*

Because from where he was sitting, it looked a hell of a lot easier than writing.

Dictionary definition of procrastination: the action of delaying or postponing something.

It has nothing, absolutely nothing, to do with Ally's burgeoning relationship with Ray Finch. But if she's reignited an old romance, reclaiming a lost youth, then perhaps Gus can stake a claim on a youth that was never his in the first place. Beach bum. Surf rat. Or at least give himself a reason to believe in the impossible.

'Gus, is that your best cobra?' says Saffron. 'You're going to need that chest up for your pop-up.'

'I think "pop-up" is ambitious. What about "gradually drag one's bones up"?'

'Not as catchy. And definitely not as catchy-wavey.'

Gus straightens his arms, then begins the slow process of getting to his feet, via his knees, before standing astride the board, arms flung out like a telegraph pole.

Zero wipeout.

Because they're still on the sand.

Meanwhile, the sea is a churning mass of white water, the taste of last night's storm still in its mouth. Gus shivers at the thought of going in, let alone being forcibly ejected into its depths – probably head first. Ill-natured things, surfboards. He always thought they looked rather glamorous until he was nose down on one.

'That's it! Nice!'

Saffron is nothing if not enthusiastic.

'Come on, let's do it for real. Catch you your first wave.'

Saffron is nothing if not deluded.

She's already given him one duff idea this morning, though bless her for trying. As Gus bemoaned his writing woes, Saffron suggested that he shadow Ally and Jayden on a case. *Get some first-hand experience, Gus, up close and personal with real-life crime. That'll inspire the writing, won't it?*

But Gus suspects he'd only get in the way.

Does Ally really want him hanging around in the background? Gus has a feeling he does enough of that already. As close as they still are, the fact is, when it came down to it, Ally chose Ray.

She chose Ray.

Gus tucks his board under his arm – and even that's not as easy as it appears, what with the board being the size of a barge and that last pop-up (or thereabouts) still blazing in his chronically underused arm muscles. He readjusts it, huffs a breath, then looks to see if anyone is witnessing this debacle. Someone, of course, is walking down the beach. At quite some speed too.

Ally. In that lovely blue knitted hat she has that brings out the colour of her eyes. Fox yapping at her heels.

'Yo, Ally!' shouts Saffron.

Ally waves as she approaches, calls good morning. Her feet scuff the sand as she stops.

'Are you jogging?' he says.

'Are you surfing?' she replies.

Gus lifts a shoulder. He offers a nonchalant grin – though he suspects it's more of a grimace.

'When in Rome.'

She raises her eyebrows. Perhaps she's thinking that he's been in Rome for two and a half years now, and if you're going to succumb to the surfing life maybe late autumn isn't the time to do it. But then she smiles, and it's sunshine.

'Wonderful, Gus. I think that's wonderful.' Then, 'I've got to dash, I'm sorry. We've got a new case.'

'A case?'

Gus's mind boggles. What he'd really like to do is ditch the board, peel off this dratted wetsuit and settle at a table in Hang Ten with Ally. Hear everything about the case. And hear nothing, nothing at all, about Suffolk. Forget, in fact, that Suffolk even exists. Let alone anyone who might live there.

'Gus!' says Saffron. 'It's meant to be.'

Ally looks confused, and so Saffron explains her bright idea, that Gus should tag along on their next case.

'He could do with a muse,' she finishes. 'Couldn't you, Gus?'

And Gus dies a little inside.

'Would it really help?' asks Ally. 'I know you've been struggling.' And her face is so kind that he drops his guard completely.

'I don't know if it'd help, but I know I'd enjoy it very much.'

'I'd have to ask Jayden,' she says. Her cheeks have gone red in the cold. Just like his have, come to think of it. 'But . . . I can't see why not.'

'See,' says Saffron, grinning wide. 'Told you, Gus.'

Bless the girl. She hasn't given up on the pair of them, even if Ally has.

If.

Ally says she'll be in touch and walks on. As he watches her go, Gus feels the return of something akin to zip.

Saffron holds up her hand for a high five. Says, 'Now that's sorted, shall we hit the water?'

14

'The scene's secure,' says Mullins. 'I've taken statements from the deceased's wife, Kathy Schofield, his two friends Steve Bradshaw and Mae Cunningham, Summer Ellery, the VIP guest who found the body, and the hotel owners, Elliott King and his wife, Louisa. Lots more to get round.'

He sips his coffee, his fingers struggling with the dainty cup handle. *Is this for a dolly, or what?* But the coffee's nearly as good as Saffron's. And that shortcake biscuit has no business being that buttery.

Elliott King showed them to a small room on the ground floor of the hotel. *The library*. There are bookshelves, two sofas and a couple of wingback armchairs. It's full of daylight but the room glows with lamplight too – no one's worrying about dropping coins in the meter here. The carpet is so thick that their feet have left prints in it.

Mullins adjusts his position on the sofa, but finds that, no matter how he sits, the squishy furnishings want to swallow him whole. Which would be fine with him if he were at home watching the box, or settling down with a pint in The Wreckers, but briefing his superior officer on what is now, no joke, a murder investigation? Not a good look.

'Louisa.' Detective Sergeant Skinner narrows his eyes. 'The lady in head-to-toe cashmere?'

'Know cashmere when you see it, do you, Sarge?'

'The ex had a cashmere cardie. No *mere cash* about it. Cash-a-lot, more like. Cost me an arm and a leg.'

Mullins obliges with a grunt-laugh.

Either sit on the very edge, or loll back. Those are the options. Back in the spring – last time he was on a case with Ally and Jayden, in fact – Mullins busted his coccyx, and it still gives him bother from time to time. He goes for lolling, like he's got this whole case in hand, easy as you like.

'And sit up straight, Mullins. You can at least try and look like a professional, even if in every other respect . . .'

The detective sergeant's voice drifts. His eyes are on a movement outside the window. Steve Bradshaw, stalking about, glued to his phone.

'Talking of exes,' says Mullins, dragging himself up, 'that guy Steve Bradshaw, the ex-cop, he's going to be a handful. He was set on this being murder before any evidence—'

'*Evidence.*'

Skinner says the word like he doesn't trust it, but the truth is he zoomed down from St Austell to Trebaron the second he got the message. He watched Summer Ellery's video on Instagram, getting his tech-savvy niece to screen-record it before they told Summer to take it off the internet and turn in the file. They don't need that going viral, or the great British public – 'The Great Unwashed', as Skinner likes to call them – launching a witch hunt for the second person in the film.

They'll be the only ones hunting witches, thanks very much.

'I don't care if he was a ruddy chief constable in a former life,' says Skinner. 'He's not anymore. And he's on our patch now.'

'Steve Bradshaw was a DC in Thames Valley, with Drew Schofield. I've got the lads running a check on him.'

'There you go, then. Small fry.'

Mullins juts out his jaw. *Well, compared to chief constable . . .*

'Small fry and big mouth,' Skinner runs on. 'Not worth our time. I'll leave it to the no-doubt-inbound Major Crimes team to mark him off. Special treat for them. Question is, is Steve Bradshaw bluffing? Anything of interest in his statement?'

'Not *suspicious*, if that's what you're getting at. But he's stuck on Drew mentioning a "blast from the past". Bradshaw didn't zone in on it at the time and their talk went in another direction. But now he's thinking it could be relevant.'

Skinner rubs at his jaw. 'The possibility that Schofield encountered someone he knows here, out of the blue? That's worth following up. Make a note to ask Schofield's wife too.'

'I'm getting a check run on all the registered guests as well.'

'Good.'

'But Bradshaw didn't say anything else that sounded suspicious. And Summer Ellery, the woman who found the body, is in deep shock. Could barely get a word out of her.'

'On her own, was she?'

'She's here with her boyfriend.' Mullins checks his notes. 'Blake Bryant. Yet to take his statement because he was down at the pool.'

'So he wasn't there when his girlfriend found the body?'

'No, he was there. Well, asleep. But then, after, he went for a swim.'

Skinner raises an eyebrow. 'And you call that a natural reaction?'

'Well, no one's going to give him a Boyfriend of the Year award. Summer said he had a mate who broke his back falling off a balcony, so it brought up bad memories for him. He wanted to clear his head, apparently.'

'So, Blake Bryant has been in the vicinity of two different blokes falling off two different balconies? Interesting. Push him up your statement list, Mullins. I don't care if he's having a swim or getting his nails done.' Skinner checks his watch. 'We need a statement from every single person in this hotel, from the pot washer to the porter. And no one leaves without our permission.'

Mullins has already gone door to door, delivering that directive. Aside from a few grumbles from posh people acting like the death of a man was an inconvenience to their neat little lives, most seemed quite happy to be marooned at the High Tide. As Mullins dipped his head inside the pool area – all low light and soft blues, no reeking chlorine or verruca-ripe splash pools – he saw three people calmly doing lengths, one of them presumably Blake Bryant. Another lounging about in a robe with a paperback. You'd never think a man had had his head smashed open. *And the rest.*

'What about this Summer Ellery, then. What did you make of her, Mullins?'

'She kept going on about the gulls, like that was the worst bit or something. She was convinced they were pecking at him.' Mullins shakes his head. 'Lazy blighters, seagulls. They're not going to try getting their beak round an eyeball when there's chips to be had.'

Not that anyone was eating chips at the High Tide at seven o'clock in the morning.

'And she didn't have the faintest idea she'd bagged that footage.' Skinner shakes his head. 'If she'd held her shot just a few more seconds she might have shown what actually happened. Instead, she's given us a major headache. But here's what we know. That video was recorded at 12.27 a.m. and it shows two figures on Drew Schofield's balcony, engaged in an animated conversation, if not a confrontation – waving arms, a bit of pushing and shoving. It's lousy quality, owing to the dark and the distance, but we'll get the tech boys and girls on it, and they may be able to enhance it. At

6.55 a.m. the body of Drew Schofield was discovered, having fallen from said balcony. CSI's first impression is that the obvious injuries are as a result of that fall. No signs of other trauma. Question is – was he pushed? So we need to identify who that second person was on the balcony. I'll want to talk to his wife again.'

'Kathy reckons she was knocked out on sleeping pills. Didn't hear a thing from Drew.'

'Convenient?'

'She's got a prescription, Sarge. Insomnia, apparently.'

'So if Kathy Schofield is telling the truth, someone came into their room and she's none the wiser.'

'It's got to be a hotel guest,' says Mullins. 'Or someone who works here. To get inside the hotel, most people are going to go through reception. Out of hours it's not manned, but you'd need a key card to get inside the building. You can't just walk in.'

'Are you telling me kitchen deliveries go in through the front door, Mullins?'

'No, Sarge. Sorry, Sarge. There are three side doors. One in the old building, one direct to the kitchen. But they're still key card access.'

'The owners are getting us the CCTV footage, are they?'

Mullins nods. 'But it got cut off during the power cut.'

'Convenient,' Skinner says again. This time without the question mark. 'But, alright, it was a hell of a storm.'

'The whole hotel was out for a good three hours. But the main doors fall back on a battery.'

Skinner tugs at his moustache. 'I want to talk to Mr King. And that cashmere-clad lady wife of his. I want to talk to everyone. That footage gives us precious little, but it's all we've got. What was Summer Ellery doing out on the balcony in a storm anyway?'

'She's a travel blogger, Sarge. She was looking for atmosphere or something.'

'School pal of Cat Weston's, isn't she? And you're telling me our friend Jayden's here on pleasure, not business?'

Skinner adds mean little air quotes to that word, *business*, but Mullins knows that the detective sergeant would have Jayden in his ranks all day long if he could. He explains that Cat hadn't seen Summer Ellery in years, and they just happened to be here at the same time.

'I want him and Ally Bright staying out of it.'

'They are, Sarge. Jayden came to me with the video straight away.'

'He's learning, then. Where is he now?'

'Packing, probably. He'll want to be off home to see his kiddies once we've given permission to leave the hotel. Who killed Drew Schofield isn't his problem, is it.'

But as soon as the words are out of his mouth, Mullins doubts them.

15

'Who is it?'

Summer's voice, on the other side of the door, has a tremor in it.

'Us,' says Cat. 'Cat and Jayden.'

Part of Jayden wanted to wait until Ally got here before talking to Summer, but he decided the sooner the better. Plus, Cat's their ticket in; it's natural for them to see how she's doing. And does he think it's strange that she's been lying so low? Well, yeah. A little.

When Summer opens up, her face is pale, her eyes hectic. He can't tell if she's glad to see them.

'Sorry,' she says. 'I've just given my statement to the police and . . . it's unreal. Come . . . come in.'

Her voice breaks like glass.

Cat looks to Jayden, concern across her face. *Go easy*, she mouths to him. Then she wraps an arm around Summer's shoulders, guiding her towards the lounge area.

Summer and Blake's room is like theirs but supersized. It's practically an apartment. Light pours through the vast windows, illuminating every detail. Summer heads for one of two sofas, and settles back against about fifty cushions, Cat beside her.

'It must have been so awful, seeing him like that,' Cat says, as tenderly as if she were speaking to Jazz or Benji.

Summer sinks her face into her hands. When she speaks, her voice sounds very far away.

'I can't get it out of my head. The blood. The birds. One landed on my balcony just now, flapping and screeching. Just like before.'

'Summer,' says Jayden gently, 'other than the gulls, was there anything else you noticed? Sometimes details come back to us later, and we don't even realise their significance.'

Summer closes her eyes, pushes her fingers into her temples and massages them.

'I . . . It's all a blank.'

He doesn't disbelieve her; shock affects people differently, and they can process the same event in any number of ways.

'Hot, sweet tea,' says Cat. 'I'll make some. Times of need, my granny swore by it. Where's Blake?'

Jayden tries not to look too interested in the answer. Perhaps Blake's giving his statement.

'He's . . . gone for a swim.'

Summer pulls a hand through her hair. It's still sleep-mussed, he notes. Yesterday she was immaculate and today she's yet to brush her hair.

'A swim?'

He says it levelly, but why's the guy gone for a swim when his girlfriend so obviously needs him? Cat gets to her feet, says, 'I'll put the kettle on.'

Summer studies her ocean-blue-painted nails. They're chipped, and as she worries at them Jayden sees why.

'It's . . . He was stressed. It hit him hard, seeing the body. He was still half-asleep and then . . . that sight. It'd freak out anyone.'

'It definitely would,' says Cat, as the kettle starts to hum.

'It's complex for Blake,' Summer goes on. 'He . . . he had a friend who fell off a balcony. It was in the ski town they were working in. He broke his back and ended up in a wheelchair and he said it brought it all back.' She looks at them both, her expression searching, 'And swimming's good stress relief, right?'

'Did he ask you to go too?' asks Jayden.

'I wouldn't have wanted to anyway,' she says, looking away. 'Then the police came up and . . . I gave my statement. They were going on about a video I took. Of the storm. But how did they even see it? Why were they looking at my social media?'

Jayden sees her eyes fill. Cat comes over with the tea then, sets the mug carefully down in front of her.

'Summer, Cat and I saw the video on Instagram.'

'I didn't know you followed me on socials.' Then, 'Was it you guys who told the police?'

'I think you captured something important,' says Jayden with a nod. Then, carefully, 'Probably without realising.'

'The police said there were people in the video. Two people on the balcony. I had no idea . . . I've given them the file. I've deleted it from Insta too, obviously. But why did you tell the police? And not me?'

Jayden can't tell whether it's accusation or incomprehension in her voice.

'It all happened quickly,' he says. Then, 'And you weren't there.'

'What do you mean?'

'When people realised what'd happened, a lot of the guests came down. But we couldn't see you.'

'What, and you thought that was *suspicious*?'

'Not at all,' he says reassuringly, 'but Mullins was right there so we mentioned the video to him. Summer, you did a good thing.'

She heaves a breath. Looks down at her nails again.

'Have the police taken Blake's statement too?' asks Jayden.

'I don't know. Maybe at the pool.'

Jayden checks his watch. 'You want me to shoot down and see if he's alright?'

'If it's brought up some trauma for him,' says Cat, 'Jayden's good at that stuff.'

Summer picks up the mug of tea, then puts it down again. She looks from one to the other. For the first time, her expression hardens.

'Is this you offering as a friend, or . . . because you're a detective?'

'Both,' says Jayden.

'Jayden's been hired by Louisa and Elliott,' says Cat. 'He's going to get this solved, I promise.'

Summer swallows, a look of trepidation crossing her face. As if the word *promise* could just as easily be a threat.

16

Ally takes the coast road, heading for Trebaron Cove and the High Tide Hotel. It's exciting, being summoned by Jayden, and questions swoop and dive in her mind like swallows at dusk. The one that looms largest: has the killer left the hotel?

As Ally drives, she's alert to every detail of the landscape and every movement within it: a pair of labourers resting in their truck in a lay-by; a man out walking a German shepherd with the well-grooved gait of two old friends; a cyclist, Lycra-clad and skinny as a whippet, flying down the hill. Evidence of last night's storm is everywhere too. She passes trees showing their roots to the sky; broken branches are caught in the hedgerows, like driftwood in shoreline bladderwrack.

To Ally's right, the ocean unfurls all the way to the horizon, its surface mottled with reflections of fast-moving clouds. After the fury of the night, it's now one of those days where the weather doesn't know what it's doing so tries a bit of everything. Rain patters her windscreen, then stops. Sun glints in her eyes, then stops. The wind is the only constant, pulling the heads of the trees this way and that.

As she turns into the steep driveway, the High Tide comes into view, the original building gleaming bright white against the dark woods behind. The modern additions, on the other hand, subtly blend in with the landscape: sand-coloured wooden structures and sky-grey girders. The hotel isn't as Ally remembers it. And perhaps that's a good thing, given what's now unfolded here. A situation that's complex enough without her bringing her own memories into it.

At least, that's what she tells herself. But there is another feeling too, one that nags like a sore tooth: Ally's concern that what remains of Bill, the beloved patchwork of their life together, is fading; holes appearing. In the time following Bill's death, it was as if all Ally's senses were heightened. The smallest moments in their marriage, the smallest memories, were so vivid. The triangles of toast they ate for breakfast on their honeymoon, with Bill's mother's damson jam that he'd insisted on bringing his own jar of. The time they took Evie to a circus and, as the clowns tumbled and gurned, Bill whispered to her, *Sinister lot, clowns*, in such a grave tone that Ally got the giggles – and must have looked like the biggest clown fan in the big top. The way he always went *ahh* with such sweet satisfaction after that first sip of his pint. Why can't she recall the pair of them arriving at the High Tide with their bags? What was the wallpaper in their room? Did they have dinner in the dining room or go out?

Her phone buzzes, pulling her back to the present.

'Al, are you on your way?'

'I'm just parking.'

'Great. I'm on my way down. And watch out for Mullins and Skinner, they don't know we're on the case yet.'

Ally notes the two police cars parked out front. A uniformed officer she doesn't recognise is at the edge of the terrace, talking into his receiver. Behind him, she can see crime scene tape, flickering in the breeze.

Not wanting to draw attention to herself, Ally doesn't linger. She heads through the sliding doors and into the serene interior of the High Tide. Understated luxury immediately takes her in its soft embrace: warm light, seductive scents; Ally detects rosemary, orange, the effect both invigorating and comforting. Her hand goes to her wind-buffeted hair, patting it down. Beside her, Fox's paws tip-tap on the polished floor in a way that suddenly sounds disorderly. For a moment, Ally can almost believe that she has the wrong place; that nothing bad could have happened here because it simply wouldn't be allowed to. Murder is not something one curates.

Only, sometimes it is, isn't it?

She meets the gaze of a man standing by the reception desk. He's tall and slightly stooping, with salt-and-pepper hair and trendy glasses. Ally recognises him as Elliott King, the owner. After Jayden's first call, she did some quick research as she hurried back down the beach. In the portrait shot she saw of Elliott on the hotel website – standing on the terrace with his wife, Louisa, and their daughter, Phoebe – Elliott looked like he had it all: a dynamic hotelier and proud family man. Today he's sagging, as if he's suffering from a slow puncture.

Ally's thinking how to introduce herself when Jayden appears, saving her the trouble. He treads quickly down the stairs just as Louisa King emerges from the other direction and joins her husband. She looks exactly as if she'd stepped from her portrait photo – her hair perfect, her film-star smile intact.

'Ah,' says Louisa, 'my Shell House Detectives.'

'This is my partner, Ally,' says Jayden.

'Pleased to meet you both,' says Ally.

Louisa sets a hand on her husband's shoulder, and Ally sees Elliott stiffen at the touch.

'Elliott thinks I've gone off-piste bringing in reinforcements but, as I pointed out, you were already in-house – it's simply a case of utilisation. And anyway, as any skier knows, *hors-piste* is where all the fun is.'

'I don't think "fun" is the right word in this situation,' says Elliott, voicing Ally's own thoughts.

'You know exactly what I mean, darling.'

'And I think it's a mistake to undermine the police investigation,' he adds. 'No offence, Ally and Jayden. I'm sure you're very good.'

Elliott's voice is measured and reasonable – if a little taut. But Louisa shrugs, as if his opinion is of no consequence, and Elliott sighs and moves papers around on the desk. It might have been Elliott's family who launched the High Tide but it's Louisa who's the captain of the ship now.

And, like it or not, Ally and Jayden have been hired to solve the murder of Drew Schofield.

'The police have already interviewed Milly Trelawney,' says Elliott, 'our waitress who bore the brunt of the victim's wrath during service last night. Please don't go bothering the poor girl again.'

'Wine spillage,' says Jayden to Ally. 'I saw it happen.'

'Yes, they've already established that she doesn't have a revenge-seeking boyfriend at home,' says Louisa, with a roll of her eyes, 'and Milly herself won't say boo to a goose, so what my husband is saying is that you can tick her off your list.'

Jayden gives a perfunctory nod of acknowledgement, but Ally knows that they'll make their own decisions about who they do or don't talk to.

'And while you're here, just be subtle, won't you?' says Louisa. And is it Ally's imagination or do Louisa's eyes linger on her sand-clogged boots, her old coat, her very much non-pedigree little dog?

'You won't know we're here,' says Jayden easily. Then, with a quick jerk of his thumb, 'Come on, Al. This way.'

And they head towards another pair of sliding doors, Jayden flashing a key card. A sign on the wall says *Pool and Leisure Club.*

‘Hiring us wasn’t a joint decision for the Kings, then?’ says Ally, as the doors close behind them.

‘All Louisa.’

‘Is her husband always so passive, do you think?’

‘Well, he stood up for that poor waitress last night, so maybe not. Okay, Al, full briefing to follow, but first I want us to quickly catch someone who’s gone for a dip. Which is a bizarre thing to do when it’s your girlfriend who found the body, right?’

Jayden pauses outside a glass-paned door. Behind it, Ally can see the deep blue tones of water, the shifting, flickering light. Even the faint tang of chlorine manages to be semi-enticing at the High Tide.

‘His name’s Blake Bryant. Here with Summer Ellery, VIP travel blogger and social media queen. It was also her Instagram video that turned this into a murder investigation. She caught an altercation on Schofield’s balcony when she was filming the storm during the power cut. Didn’t realise what she had. Oh, and she went to the same school as Cat, though they weren’t close.’

‘Have the police already spoken to Blake?’ asks Ally.

Through the door she can see someone moving through the water with strong, fast strokes.

‘Not sure,’ says Jayden. ‘But now it’s our turn.’

As they step into the swimming pool area, Blake glides underwater, kicking quickly towards the bottom, and swims another length completely submerged.

Ally looks beyond the water, through the glass walls to the sea beyond. On a patchy-weather day like today, the effect is impressive, immersive, calming. On a beautiful day, Ally imagines it to be impossibly hypnotic.

As Blake performs a perfect swimmer’s turn, Jayden moves to the edge of the pool. His shadow ripples in the water.

‘I don’t want to go in hard,’ says Jayden.

He quietly tells Ally what Summer said about Blake's past experience with balcony falls; the bad memories that seeing Drew Schofield's body brought back up.

'We could be standing here forever, though,' says Ally as Blake keeps on moving through the water, attuned to nothing except his own rhythm.

Jayden looks around, then grabs a lifebuoy hanging from a peg. As Blake shoots towards them, he lobs it into the water directly in his path. Blake barrels into the ring, tossing it into the air in frustration. His feet find the bottom and he stands, dripping, his face red and angry. Then he appears to reset when he sees it's Jayden.

'What was that, mate?'

'Sorry, Blake,' says Jayden. 'We were just trying to get your attention, and you looked like you were getting ready for the Olympics.'

Blake looks from Jayden to Ally and back again. He's twenty-eight, Jayden said, and his features are boyish; his eyes are grey as pebbles.

'What do you want?' He's adjusting his voice to be gentler. 'Is everything . . . cool?'

'Not really. Summer's in a bit of a state,' says Jayden.

'Course she is,' Blake says quietly. 'Anyone would be.'

'You saw the body too, right?'

'Only for a second. I couldn't look.'

'Are you doing okay now?' asks Jayden, in that kind and direct way he has.

It's a subtle invitation for Blake to tell them about the friend that Summer mentioned, but he doesn't take it. Instead, he looks almost resentful that the question should be warranted at all. He narrows his eyes and looks again at Ally.

'Is this . . . your mum?' he says to Jayden.

Jayden laughs easily. 'Ally's my partner. Blake, have the police taken your statement?'

'Not yet. They've got a lot of people to get through. And I've got nothing to tell them.'

'Well, Ally and I are investigating too.'

'What, unofficially?'

'Officially,' says Ally. 'Louisa King hired us.'

Blake pushes his wet hair back with his hands. 'But it was an accident, right? It must have been.'

'A fall like this is always considered suspicious,' says Jayden. 'And Summer's video . . . It shows there was someone else on the balcony with the victim.'

'What video? Summer *filmed* it?'

As confusion crosses Blake's face, Ally expects Jayden to fill in the blanks. But he says nothing.

Blake drags in a breath. 'So they're looking for . . .'

'They're looking for whoever was on that balcony with him,' says Ally.

Blake stares beyond them to the sea. His eyes hold the movement of the water; grey and restless.

'And they're treating it as murder,' says Jayden.

17

'Before we get into everything, let me give you a quick tour, Al,' says Jayden. 'You need to understand how this place flows.'

Ally and Jayden leave the swimming pool behind them, and head back down the corridor towards reception.

After their conversation, Blake wasted no time getting out of the pool and disappearing to the changing rooms. Jayden would have liked to ask more questions, because the guy's moves are clearly off. Is Blake's behaviour consistent with someone who has past trauma connected to balcony falls? Maybe. But it's also consistent with someone who has something to hide.

Jayden didn't ask Summer if Blake was in the bedroom when she filmed the storm video. If he was there, it rules him out. But nor has she volunteered that information. Is that because only the guilty rush to offer an alibi?

The Blake that Jayden met yesterday was bright and breezy, reassuringly normal among the polished High Tide crowd, in his battered Vans and hoodie. Summer said that they met in the French Alps eight months ago. She was on assignment and Blake was odd-jobbing his way through another winter season, a cool couple who'd ditched the nine-to-five and were living for experiences. But the version of Blake at the pool just now?

Very different.

If Blake was triggered by Drew's balcony fall, then he could still be in the grip of those feelings; unable to control his response. Did Jayden go easy on him because he knows what that's like? After his friend and partner Kieran died on duty, that horrific night in Leeds three years ago, Jayden struggled. And Blake looked like he was struggling too. So, Jayden weighed the odds, just as he had with Summer before, and keeping the pair of them on side – as if they're the newfound mates of yesterday, not suspects in a murder enquiry – won out.

For now.

As they head towards reception, Jayden keeps his eyes peeled for Skinner and Mullins. He's constantly aware of how his and Ally's operations interact with the police. They've found a kind of harmony now, but basically they're only as good as their last case. And if they overstep the mark, Jayden knows Skinner won't hesitate to put him back in his box. A box that, when they first moved to Cornwall, was firmly labelled *Frustrated and slightly broken ex-cop trying to play detective*. And Ally's box? Something like *Curtain-twitching widow of local sergeant*, probably.

'Okay, Al,' he says quietly. 'Main entrance. Someone's on reception through the day and the doors are open to all comers. But after hours it's electronic key card only.'

Jayden looks to the reception desk, where Elliott is tapping at a computer screen, head bent. Deliberately ignoring them? He's made it clear he doesn't love that Louisa's hired them. Or maybe Elliott just doesn't love much that Louisa does. Jayden's no marriage expert, but their relationship dynamic is . . . non-aspirational.

'During a power cut, Louisa said the key card sensors fall back on a battery. Same for the main door and all the bedrooms. So, access works as normal.'

'But during the day anyone could walk in?'

'Well, yeah. But CCTV would capture it – up until the power cut, that is, when all the cameras went down. I'm guessing the police will be working their way through it all, but we can ask too.'

'Because in theory anyone could have entered the hotel and hidden themselves? If not via the main entrance, then a side door?'

The phone on reception rings then and Elliott answers it. Jayden steers Ally past the desk and into the more private space beyond, where two sofas are arranged by a crackling fire. There's a pyramid of manicured-looking logs. A neon-pink surfboard that looks like it's never seen water or wax is propped casually against the wall.

'In theory, yeah. But that means someone from outside the hotel would have to have known that Drew Schofield was staying here. It was a surprise weekend for him, a retirement-slash-anniversary gift from his wife, so that kind of limits the pool.'

'*If* it was premeditated,' says Ally.

'Well, if you're sneaking into a hotel then hiding for hours on end, that makes it premeditated, right? Honestly, Al, I think it's more likely that the attacker came from inside the hotel. Remember, Drew had to let them in to his room too. Which makes me think he knew them.'

Jayden glances back towards Elliott at the desk.

'Let's keep moving,' he says. 'Through there is the library. Louisa said that the police were in there earlier. "Cluttering up the place", I think were her exact words. It's quiet now, though, so if they're still taking witness statements they must be going room to room. Mullins and Skinner have got their hands full.'

'So, they'll be glad of the help?' says Ally with a twinkle.

'Let's hope. Okay, through there, that's a separate cocktail bar. Tiny place. For what it's worth, Cat was blown away by the Manhattan.'

'Is the bar staffed?'

'Yeah, just in the evenings. Young barman, nice guy.'

Ally raises an eyebrow. 'But everyone's a suspect?'

'Okay, *seemingly* nice guy. On the subject, staff-wise there were four waiters on shift last night, and three chefs in the kitchen plus a pot washer. Elliott and Louisa share front-of-house duties, and there's a part-time receptionist too. Fifteen bedrooms, but according to Louisa only twelve are currently occupied. There are two couples from Germany and an American solo traveller; the rest are UK-based. With the restaurant open to non-residents, there's the possibility for a lot of movement, but because of the weather last night it was quiet. All the diners were staying at the hotel.'

'It's still a lot of people,' says Ally. 'More than we've ever dealt with.'

'So we focus our attention on Drew's circle and those closest to the crime.' He jerks his thumb towards the stairs. 'That chat's for behind closed doors. Anywhere else you want to see?'

'I'm just amazed how quiet it all is,' says Ally.

And she's got a point. The fact that the police are treating Drew's death as a murder investigation instead of a tragic accident is not being broadcast throughout the hotel. Few people know about Summer's video confirming an altercation. Elliott and Louisa, meanwhile, have taken pains to soften the drama, gliding about as though everything is wonderful. Only, Elliott is not quite up to the part – which, incidentally, makes Jayden like him way more than his wife.

'You could imagine nothing happened here, right?' says Jayden.

Just then Blake rounds the corner, wearing a towelling robe. He catches sight of them, abruptly turns, and goes in the other direction – out of the main doors and into the car park. Barefoot.

'*Almost* imagine,' says Ally.

18

'Murder?' Kathy looks from Skinner to Mullins and back again. 'Drew was *murdered*?'

In the immediate aftermath of Drew's death, Mullins took an initial statement from Kathy and she was statue-still then, and eerily quiet. It was like shock had struck her with its unmagical wand. Nor did she cry; Kathy's eyes were wide as windows, but there wasn't so much as a smear, let alone a drip. Now, an hour later, they're back in her room talking to her again. She's less frozen, but there's still no sign of tears.

'Video evidence confirms that someone else was on the balcony with Drew before he fell.'

Her mouth gapes. 'But I was here.'

'And, according to your initial statement, you'd taken sleeping pills.'

The pathologist has confirmed that, with Kathy's pills, she'd sleep through just about anything. Including, for instance, an assailant entering the room, arguing with her husband, and pushing him to his death.

'Only when I need to.'

'Why did you need to take them last night?' asks Skinner.

'Strange bed,' says Kathy.

Mullins finds himself nodding. *I hate a strange bed, me.*

She *sounds* convincing, but it still could have been her togged up in a big coat, out there on the balcony, couldn't it?

Kathy sits on the edge of a hard chair, her hands folded in her lap. She hangs her head.

'Mrs Schofield, I know this is very upsetting, but I'd like to ask you some more questions about the weekend,' says Skinner.

'But I already said everything to the boy here.'

Mullins feels his ears go red. *Boy?*

'In light of developments, we need to go over a few details. Drew had no idea he was coming to the High Tide Hotel, is that right? And no idea that Steve and his girlfriend Mae would be here too?'

'It was a surprise. To celebrate his retirement. No one knew.'

'You said it was for your anniversary,' says Mullins, quick as a gull jumping on a chip.

Kathy blinks. 'Well, that too. But really it was about this new chapter for Drew. Not all of our old ones.' She gives a little laugh, tight as a screw. 'And that's why I invited Steve. They worked together for years. Steve really looked up to Drew. I thought it'd be . . . a lovely surprise.'

Mullins had someone check out Steve Bradshaw the minute he knew he'd been a copper. They're waiting on more information, but the headline is that Steve was dismissed from Thames Valley five years ago for misconduct and violation of professional standards. Skinner rubbed his hands together at that.

'Were you aware Steve lost his job with the police?' asks Skinner.

'Of course. It was a difficult time. But, quite honestly, he hasn't looked back since.'

'It didn't present a problem for Steve and Drew's friendship?'

'Drew always looked out for Steve. He was that bit younger, he almost saw him as a son. We don't have any children, you see, and Drew . . . Well, he was never very happy about that.'

'Is that how you see Steve too?'

Kathy's mouth twitches. Mullins can't work out if she's fighting a smile, or a grimace.

'More of a cheeky little brother to Drew, I suppose.'

Cheeky. Mullins's own impression of Steve Bradshaw is not quite so generous. But what energy would Mullins be tossing out if Skinner were to pop his clogs? He doubts he'd be his best self either, as Hippy-Dippy might say.

'Kathy, when I spoke to you earlier, you said Drew was in a bad mood on the drive down,' says Mullins.

'He doesn't like surprises. And he said he wasn't keen on Cornwall. He'd rather have been in the Caribbean.'

Wouldn't we all, mate.

'Yet you chose to surprise him anyway?' says Skinner.

'Yes. It was silly of me, wasn't it?' says Kathy faintly.

'Do you think there was anything else bothering him?' asks Mullins. And he says it softly, because Skinner's being on the harsh side here and this lady is the bereaved, isn't she?

'I'm used to them,' she says. 'His moods, I mean.'

'So the mood wasn't connected to the prospect of a weekend with Steve?' says Skinner.

'The opposite. It was seeing Steve that snapped him out of his temper. I knew it was a good idea to invite them.'

'Are you aware of anyone else being here that Drew knew?' Skinner passes his hand across his moustache. 'Someone he might have referred to as a "blast from the past"?'

Kathy shakes her head. 'Just Steve and Mae. Though . . .'

'Though what?'

'Drew used to holiday in Cornwall as a boy – that's how I got the idea of coming – so I suppose he could have seen someone he knew from back then. Why are you asking about this?'

'Steve remembered him saying it.'

Seeing as they were colleagues, it seems to Mullins that, if Drew was talking about any blasts from the past with Steve, they're likely to have been from his professional life, not his personal life. Thirty years in the force? That's a lot of collars. They'll be looking at Drew's arrest records. Recent prison releases. Anyone coming to Cornwall with a grind-ready axe packed in their suitcase.

Kathy slowly shakes her head. 'You really think someone came into our room . . . and . . . pushed him?'

'There's no access to the balcony from the exterior,' says Skinner, 'so he must have let them in. There's no sign of forced entry, so presumably he knew them. And was on good enough terms to be open to the night-time visit.'

Which probably rules out old foes.

Drew was also happy to let them into the room while his wife was sleeping – he must have known she was knocked out on pills. Or didn't care. Or had no choice?

'Night-time visit?' says Kathy. 'That sounds . . . sordid. It wouldn't have been a *woman*, Officer. Drew was a lot of things, but he's never been unfaithful. Not to my knowledge, anyway.'

Kathy suddenly looks down at her hands, as if realising what she's said.

'We're hoping for a clearer picture from the video,' says Mullins. 'We can't currently tell if we're looking at a male or a female.'

'And anyway,' she says, her voice climbing higher, 'he'd had a skinful. He always does, with Steve. That was why I took the pill, if I'm honest. I knew I couldn't stand him coming in late, banging around like a bear with a sore head. Snoring to high heaven. Drew would have let anyone in, in that state. You can't presume he knew them, not for one minute.'

Kathy presses her fingers to her eyes and Mullins thinks the tears might finally be coming for Drew Schofield's wife. He goes to pat his pockets for a tissue, but Skinner gets there first. He hands over a cotton hanky the size of a tablecloth. Kathy balls it in her fist.

'You know, it's a good job he's dead,' she says, 'because he'd have been livid with me that I let it happen, without even blinking an eye. That I was so useless. He'd be absolutely livid.'

Skinner's face shows that Kathy's strange reaction – murder as a let-off from a scolding? – has registered with him too.

Just then, Mullins's phone goes, and with another quick glance at Kathy he gets up to take the call.

He listens, then hangs up. Kathy's still clutching that hanky like there's no tomorrow.

'Sarge?' he says quietly. 'We need to talk about Blake Bryant.'

19

'Your coffee's on the house, Gus. You worked hard out there.'

Saffron digs the idea of anyone learning to surf, but she has a particular soft spot for Gus's endeavour. Because she gets why he's doing it.

When it comes to matters of the heart, Saffron knows how rough it can be. Try having a business right next door to your ex-boyfriend's, for instance. Hang Ten is just steps across the sand from Mahalo, Broady's surf school, but currently they're as separate as planets. They broke up in April, by semi-mutual consent. And as for Milo Nash, the graffiti artist who stole Saffron's heart for a little while? He's still on the scene. She still thinks he's kind of wonderful. But it turns out Milo doesn't really do commitment. Even if, in Ally and Jayden's last case, Saffron did technically save his life, which you would have thought would be a bond forever, right?

She watches Gus as he settles back against the tie-dye cushions. He's out of his wetsuit and back in his standard uniform of fisherman's jumper and jeans, his hands wrapped around his mug of coffee. When Gus first started coming to Hang Ten, the vibes he gave off were a mix of hopeful and rueful. Turns out divorcing in his sixties wasn't his plan – *but then nor was living by the seaside, so it's swings and roundabouts, Saffron*. And falling for Ally Bright – artist turned private detective – wouldn't have been in the plan either. Saffron still can't believe that hasn't worked out. Yet.

But maybe if they're on this new case together? She's hoping Ally doesn't leave him hanging on that one.

'I honestly think if I were to close my eyes I'd be sound asleep,' says Gus.

'Well, you can, can't you? Slow morning here, Gus. Kick back.'

You never know what you're going to get at the beach in late October – and weather and custom are directly connected. Some days the sky is a limitless blue, and before long you're taking off your beanie, rolling up your sleeves. But then the next minute the wind gets up, the clouds hustle in, and rain starts coming down like spears. Caribbean to Arctic in moments. Last winter Saffron closed for the season, and she and Broady went to Hawaii – it was the beginning of their end, one way or another. This winter? She's thinking she'll keep Hang Ten open.

And Mahalo? If Broady stays open too, it'll be an even weirder vibe at the beach: an emptied plain, with a couple of outposts. They had so many plans to connect their two places, but that all fell away when they broke up. Maybe she could suggest a partnership to get them both through the off season?

No, he'd never go for it.

'Do you know, I might just . . . rest my eyes,' says Gus.

Saffron heads back behind the counter. She settles on her stool, picks up her phone and scrolls idly through Instagram. Her feed is all free spirits and wanderlusters; Saffron watches a longboarder dance up and down their board on a Californian mountain road, then a surfer do the same on a wave in Sri Lanka. Earlier she saw a post from Summer Ellery – aka Summer Holidays – a travel blogger she likes. The picture was of the distinctive clutch of beech trees on the high hillside by the Cornish border, the ones that get called the 'nearly home' trees or the 'nearly there' trees. For Saffron and her mum? Nearly home trees, all the way. And that was the caption Summer put too; Saffron didn't know that Summer Holidays was a Cornish girl.

Saffron clicks on her feed to see if there are any more Cornwall posts, but, weirdly, Summer's original post with the beech trees has been deleted. Last entry? Paris. The one before that is somewhere tropical – the kind of white-sand, blue-sea paradise that literally makes Saffron's heart beat faster.

Not that she has to travel far for that. In the right light, Porthpella can do white-sand, blue-sea all day long.

Saffron's phone buzzes with a message from her housemate Jodie, interrupting her scrolling. Her eyes widen as she reads, and she taps out a fast reply. Another message drops in, and they're criss-crossing now.

'Gus,' she says, 'that new case of Ally's. I've got the lowdown.'

He snaps his eyes open. 'Oh! What's that?'

'Jodie's little sister Milly is a waitress at the High Tide Hotel – you know, the luxe place over at Trebaron Cove? Well, she had this really rough shift last night. She spilt wine on one of the guests and got totally balled out by him in front of everyone. Milly called Jodie in tears. Anyway – now he's dead!'

'The man who had wine spilt on him by your friend's sister?'

Saffron nods. 'Wild, huh? He was pushed off a balcony. The police have been up there all morning interviewing everyone. Milly wasn't even on shift, so she got a house visit.'

Gus puffs out his cheeks. 'Dear me. You're not saying your friend's sister was somehow involved . . . ?'

Saffron can't help laughing. 'Milly? She wouldn't hurt a fly.'

'Dear me,' says Gus again. 'That sounds a horrible business.'

'According to Jodie, his name was Drew Schofield. A retired cop.'

'No wonder Ally and Jayden have been called in. All hands on deck, I imagine, when someone in the force dies.' He looks thoughtful. 'Goodness, I hope it hasn't brought up memories of Bill. Poor Ally.'

'This guy doesn't sound anything like Bill Bright, Gus. But you're right about all hands on deck. I bet Ally could use your help.'

'I'd hardly be helping. Hindering, perhaps.'

'Come on, Gus. You've got this.'

'I'm going to google the victim.'

'Attaboy.'

And then Saffron does some googling herself. She taps in *Summer Ellery Cornwall* because, if Summer's out west, maybe Saffron can tempt her for a coffee and a brownie at Hang Ten. Now that would be a nice bit of marketing, ahead of the long, quiet winter.

She pauses a second, feeling a stab of guilt that she's not dwelling longer on the murder. But a rude old cop, killed at the High Tide Hotel? Saffron's not going to lose too much sleep over that one. Maybe for his next trick he picked on someone his own size – and they didn't like it.

'Saffron!' cries Gus excitedly. 'I might actually be able to be of some genuine help to Ally.'

He holds up his phone as though it's displaying a set of winning lottery numbers. 'Look! Drew Schofield was Thames Valley CID.'

'I'm sorry, but I have zero idea what that means.'

'What it means is that it's my stomping ground, Saffron. He hailed from Oxford!'

And while it's a push to imagine Gus stomping anywhere, she gives him a high five. Because he's smiling wider than Saffron's seen in a long time.

20

'So this is our HQ,' says Jayden. 'Our new thinking room. Louisa says we can have it for as long as we need. By which she really means the end of the weekend max.'

Ally smiles to herself at the phrase *thinking room*. That's their name for the room at The Shell House – Bill's old office. It wasn't until their fourth big investigation that they started using it; perhaps it was only by then that Ally began to think of herself as a 'proper' detective. It wasn't a case of stepping into Bill's shoes. Far from it: it was more like walking in a different pair herself.

She's sure most people would consider this current space a significant upgrade. The bedding in subtle marine colours. The succulents in artisan pots and walls full of original art. The dry-brushed furniture giving a rustic, coastal look, and all with polish and obvious quality. But Ally would take their whiteboard and squeaky markers, the creak of Bill's old leather chair, any day.

Cat pulls a dress from the wardrobe and folds it into her suitcase.

'I'd say I'd love to stay on too, but . . .' She shivers. 'That's so not true. Jay, I'm out of here.' Cat goes to him and holds his shoulders. Looks into his eyes. 'Please take care,' she says.

There's a note of pain in her voice, which Ally understands. Their cases have a habit of putting him through it – and, as a couple, Jayden and Cat have endured a lot this year too. Ally glances away from this intimate moment. She goes to the window and takes in the expansive view. Out on the water, a little fishing boat rocks up and down on the waves, trailed by a cloud of gulls.

'Tell Jazz and Benji I'll see them really soon,' she hears Jayden say. 'And tell them I love them.'

Cat says something quietly, and Ally turns to see them folded in an embrace. She turns back again, not wanting to intrude.

'Bye, Ally,' calls Cat. 'Take care of him for me, won't you? And yourself too.'

Ally smiles her assurances. She's been here herself, the wife of an officer, watching her husband suit-and-boot and head out to answer a call. For all the freedoms that Jayden enjoys now that he's out of the police, there are dangers too. They don't have the force of the law and they don't have back-up – but they do have each other. Though Ally knows she has the better end of the bargain in that respect.

'Hey, Jay,' says Cat. 'I'm going to say goodbye to Summer before I go.'

Jayden puffs out his cheeks. 'She's a suspect, Cat.'

'Only like I'm a suspect. Or you.'

'Come on, we don't really know Summer at all. Or her boyfriend . . .'

He shoots Ally a look as he says it, and she wonders if he's going to mention Blake's demeanour at the pool – and in the lobby.

Cat checks her watch. 'Okay, fine. I'm late as it is. But if she writes on her blog that she bumped into an old schoolmate who turned out to be cold as ice, that's on you, Jay.'

'I'll take the hit,' he says, and kisses her again at the door.

Cat waves to Ally too, then disappears, back to their children, back to the farm, back to normality.

'Alright,' says Jayden, turning to her. He takes a breath. 'Let's do this. Shall I start at the beginning?'

'Please,' says Ally.

She settles on a sofa that isn't half as comfortable as it looks. Jayden stands with his feet planted on an elaborately patterned rug.

'Someone went to Drew Schofield's room, in the middle of the night, during the power cut, and had a conversation with him on the balcony – that looks a lot like an altercation. Subsequently, Drew Schofield fell to his death. Which makes it look a lot like murder.'

'Will the pathologist be able to put a time on it?' asks Ally.

'They'll estimate based on rigor mortis, but the workable theory will be that the incident occurred as a result of that night-time visit. And because the hotel is largely locked down, the focus has to be on the guests and the staff. Which, with the former, puts a timer on our investigation. Our best bet for making headway is talking to the suspects while they're all still under this roof.'

'And the police can't keep them here?'

'No. It's not like with Rockpool House.'

Their third major case, when musician Baz Carson was found floating face down in his infinity pool. With the security cameras and locked gates, the killer was, without doubt, one of Baz's private party guests, and Skinner got to say, *Don't leave town*. But the High Tide Hotel has too many people with no connection to Drew Schofield whatsoever.

On the face of it.

'So, talk me through the suspects,' says Ally.

'Okay, let's start with Kathy Schofield, Drew's wife. She organised this weekend as a surprise for her husband. I haven't spoken to her yet, but when I first got to Drew's body I looked up and Kathy was staring out like she was frozen. I expected her to run down but she didn't.'

'Could it have been a more complex reaction than simple shock?'

'Maybe. But she obviously didn't say anything in her police statement that got alarm bells ringing, or she'd have been taken in by now. As to the surprise weekend, it was Steve Bradshaw who mentioned it. Drew's mate from back in the day.'

'The bullish man you told me about? The one who relished the scene with that poor waitress?'

'That's him. Real charmer. Ex-copper. Works in private security now, which could mean anything from a security guard in a supermarket to a VIP bodyguard. He's here with his girlfriend, Mae Cunningham, but beyond seeing her in the restaurant last night, I haven't had any contact with her. She seems to be keeping herself on the fringes, although she was trying to get in to see Kathy straight after Drew's body was found. Steve, though, we've been up close and personal with him. Cat and I had the dubious pleasure of sharing a hot tub with him yesterday.'

Jayden pulls a face and Ally laughs.

'After the incident with the wine, Al, I couldn't take my eyes off their group. Cat told me off for staring but, honestly, my alarm bells were ringing. There was just . . . a bad energy. Drew's reaction was massively over the top. But his wife didn't act like it was anything unusual. Drew struck me as the kind of guy who likes to make people feel small. Which . . . Hold on a sec.' Jayden pulls out his phone and performs a few quick taps. '*There*. Which is supported by the quick bit of desk research I did earlier. The *Oxford Mail* – the local paper for his patch – ran at least two pieces questioning his arrest methods. Suggestions of excessive force. They're from a few years back, and I know you've got to take online comments with a pinch of salt, but they're worth reading. Take a look.'

Ally's eyes widen as she reads them.

Roddy17: *I heard the bloke kicked a bloody door in. No reason whatsoever.*

JudgeAndJury: *The non-estimable DS Schofield has a different idea of what 'use reasonable force when a suspect is resisting arrest' means. The bruises I've seen.*

BoyFromUpTheHill: *police brutality in action. Don't know how he's still here. Oh yeah, that's right, that's who we are now.*

'So that's interesting, right?' says Jayden. 'I want us to dig deeper, because it looks like he wasn't everyone's idea of a good copper – to put it lightly. But if the guy hung on until retirement, then clearly nothing stuck.'

Ally can't help but think of Bill retiring. How he gave everything to the force and was thoroughly unimpeachable no matter what he faced. In the weeks and months after Bill's heart attack, she found herself wondering if the job took too much: whether his heart could simply bear no more.

'If this was Drew's reputation,' she says, 'there could be any number of people who might wish him harm.'

'Exactly,' says Jayden. 'It's a line of enquiry, and one that Skinner will no doubt be following. What I'm wondering is how many other people knew about this surprise weekend? Beyond Kathy, Steve Bradshaw and Mae Cunningham. Because Mullins let slip something interesting earlier, Al. Steve Bradshaw told him that Drew said he'd run into a "blast from the past".'

'Did he elaborate?'

'Mullins, you mean? Or Steve? Either way, the answer's no. But Steve thinks it's relevant. Which could be a deliberate move on his part, to switch focus.'

'Or could be genuine,' says Ally. '*A blast from the past.* It's certainly piqued my interest.'

'Mine too. So, two questions. Is there someone else at the High Tide who knew Drew? Or is Steve bolstering his own lie?'

Ally now knows, after five major investigations, not to be intimidated by the number of unknowns at the start of a case. Somehow, they always get there in the end.

So far.

'The obvious people who knew the Schofields were coming here, outside of Drew's group, would be the hotel owners,' she says. 'Louisa and Elliott King.'

'Doesn't constitute a blast from the past, though. Unless one of them knew him already.'

'Exactly.'

'And they do hold a master key, remember. So whether Drew actually opened up his door to his night-time visitor, or was taken by surprise, becomes a question.'

'So should we look for any links between the Kings and Drew Schofield?' asks Ally, already tapping their names into Google. 'Nothing's coming up straight away.'

'Try Blake Bryant and Drew Schofield. Then Summer Ellery and Drew Schofield.'

'Nothing for Blake,' she says. 'Let me try Summer . . .'

Jayden walks to the window – and immediately exclaims: 'Blake!'

Ally jumps to her feet as Jayden throws open the balcony door. She follows him out to see. And gasps.

Mullins is striding across the car park. There's the glint of handcuffs. And Blake Bryant, no longer in his bathrobe, is under arrest.

21

Jayden pelts downstairs, for the second time that day. He's fast through reception, bouncing on his toes as the sliding doors take a beat too long to open.

Mullins is already driving away.

'Jayden.'

Skinner.

They shake hands.

'You've arrested Blake Bryant?'

'No flies on you,' says Skinner, with a twitch of his moustache.

'That was quick. Did he confess or something?'

'Good old-fashioned detective work,' says Skinner, tapping the side of his nose. His face changes as he sees Ally exit the hotel. 'Ally Bright. I didn't know you were having yourself a luxury break too. What is it, Shell House Away Day?'

Jayden gives a low laugh. There was once a time when the detective sergeant's style got right under his skin, but now? They've been through too much together. They rub along alright.

'Blake's girlfriend, Summer Ellery,' Jayden says. 'Have you—'

'Hark at you,' cuts in Skinner, narrowing his eyes. 'How are you getting all these names?'

'Cat knows Summer from school days.'

'What, you're here with them, are you? No one said that.'

'No, it's random. We just ran into them yesterday.'

'So I should be interviewing you too.'

'I gave my statement to Mullins. So did Cat.'

'But now Bryant's in custody,' says Skinner. 'Puts a different light on things. Nothing struck you about him?'

'Not enough for an arrest. What have you got on him?'

'Ask his girlfriend. She played dumb with us, but she might open up to you. We'll be talking to her again if we need to, but right now she can stay where she is.'

Jayden raises his eyebrows. *Is this Skinner willingly getting them involved?*

The DS smacks his shoulder. 'We've got our man. And something tells me he won't be a hard nut to crack despite . . . certain evidence to the contrary.'

'I doubt Summer was "playing dumb",' says Jayden. 'I think she's in shock. First finding the body, then—'

'So give her a shoulder to cry on, son,' says Skinner gruffly, 'but in my experience, the partner always knows. Maybe not the facts, but there's a gut instinct. Like . . . a tectonic plate shifting. You feel it, don't you, even if the whole house doesn't come crashing down. Not right then, anyway. It always does later, Jay—'

Skinner's moment of poetry is interrupted, his words lost, as Steve Bradshaw barrels out of the main doors.

'So you've made an arrest? And I missed it?'

Steve muscles in front of Ally, gets up close to Skinner. The guy's a loaded spring.

'Who have you got? That close-lipped pair on reception won't say.'

Jayden turns to see Louisa and Elliott standing side by side, framed by the doors. For a weird moment he thinks of the cuckoo clock his grandad in Whitby used to have: the little wooden man and woman who came out on the hour, just as the bird made its cry. They look tidy, smart – and, perhaps for the first time, united in the shared drama of a man dying under their roof. *Or off their balcony.*

Meanwhile, there's no sign of Drew's wife. Or Steve's girlfriend, Mae.

'I'm not at liberty to disclose that, sir,' says Skinner, crisp as an apple.

'What about his widow? You can't even tell her?'

'The investigation is ongoing,' says Skinner. He turns back to Jayden, possibly considering him the lesser of two evils. 'Jayden? Ally? Don't go getting in the way.'

At that, Skinner makes for his car.

Steve rounds on them, eyeballing Jayden.

'You know who they've taken in, don't you, mate? Go on, cough up.'

Jayden weighs it up. Skinner thinks it's case closed, but what if it isn't? And if he and Ally need to talk to Steve, having his trust wouldn't hurt. But Jayden's not going to be the one to tell him.

'I didn't see the arrest,' he says.

'Nor me,' says Ally.

Steve pulls an almost-smile, a flash of white teeth. Then he pointedly looks them up and down; the scorn, the judgement, all conveyed without saying a single word. Jayden stands his ground. *Nothing I've not met before.* Then Steve says something Jayden can't catch and muscles back towards the hotel. Jayden stares after him, watching as Elliott and Louisa neatly step aside to let him pass.

'I take it that's the deceased's friend,' says Ally quietly.

'Yep.'

'And you don't trust him?'

'I don't trust him,' says Jayden. 'But I don't know why yet. Apart from the obvious.'

'He's very unpleasant?'

'Got it in one.' Jayden looks back at the hotel, lowers his voice. 'Al, I don't think this is over.'

'You mean you don't think Blake's involved?'

'I don't know,' he says again. 'But one thing's for sure, it's time to introduce you to Summer.'

22

Mae Cunningham lets herself back into her room with a sigh of relief. It was a head-spin seeing Kathy. The woman is obviously in shock, stunned into paralysis. Like that deer that hit their car one winter; the way it teetered on its legs and stared straight through the windscreen at them, as unseeing as a porcelain doll. Steve had a shovel in the boot, and he said he had no choice but to finish it off. *Better that way, Mae.* Was it, though? There was no obvious wound; perhaps it would have recovered its senses. But Steve is a police officer – or he was then, anyway. It wasn't long after they got together; six years ago now. And if you can't trust a police officer, what hope is there?

Mae still finds herself thinking about that deer from time to time. And there was something in the wide eyes of Kathy Schofield that took Mae right back to that moment on the dark road.

The truth is, Mae has never much cared for Drew. And she's never understood how Kathy puts up with him. Mae wasn't going to tell the police that when they asked about their relationship, though, was she? She doesn't actually think Kathy had a hand in her husband's death; she's just not sure she's all that sad about it.

Steve suddenly steps from the bathroom, wiping his hands on a towel, and Mae jumps like she's been caught doing something she shouldn't.

'Oh!' she says. 'You're here.'

She felt sure Steve would be pacing about downstairs still, bending the ear of whoever would listen; especially now the police have made their arrest. If some other person had gone off their balcony, Steve would have acted the same – he always wants to make things his business – but Godly Drew? If she's allowed to turn armchair psychologist, Mae would say that Steve has an unhealthy regard for his former boss. First-degree daddy issues. The sun shone out of Drew's backside and straight into Steve's eyes – blinding him, in Mae's opinion.

And now that he's dead? Steve's going to be in right trouble, emotionally. Mae feels an anticipatory fatigue wash over her, for the weeks to come.

If I'm even still around.

Mae told herself that this weekend would be make-or-break for them. If you can't have a good time together at a luxury hotel, then what's the point? While she can't blame Steve for Drew's death – that would be a whole other level of relationship trouble – she does see it as a sign.

'Did you find out who was arrested?' she asks.

Steve's first response to Drew's death was one of wall-punching anger, and it's obvious that the fury's still in him. The set of his body is so tense, if she touched his shoulder it'd be like tapping a steel girder.

'It's the beautiful girl's boyfriend. Some German geezer just told me he saw him in cuffs.'

'No!'

The exclamation is silly. But Mae noticed the couple as they arrived and thought how in love they looked. The woman's hand slung in the back pocket of his jeans; the kiss the man dropped on the top of her head, light as a flower. And what Mae felt was envy: it was crystalline.

Steve looks up. That vein of his at his temple, the one that she can't take her eyes off when he's cross, appears to pulse. It looks like a tiny purple wriggling worm.

'What I can't figure out is *why*. "Blast from the past," Drew said. He must have meant that scruffy guy. *Must have*. I've a good mind to go and knock on the girlfriend's door.'

'That'd be a bad idea, Steve.'

He grunts a response.

'What's his name?' she asks. 'The young man's? Or don't you know it?'

And it's like she's taken a stick, poking the hornets' nest.

Buzz, buzz.

Mae braces for his reaction but Steve just stares back at her. He looks, she thinks, quite pathetic. She notices his red-rimmed eyes then and she tries to reset. After all, she did love him once. She used to watch him in his five-a-side football team. She'd cheer him on from the sidelines, admiring his sturdy calves, the way his bum looked in those silky shorts. But Mae has come to learn that there's a difference between the way you see someone and the person they actually are. His poster-boy masculinity ticked some box of hers from way back when, but he changed after he lost the job. And like a dripping tap he got worse and worse. She's an idiot for putting up with it for so long.

Steve has never told Mae exactly what happened with his job, and she's never asked. Mostly because she knows he won't give her a straight answer. It'd be loaded with spin: The World According to Steve. The accepted narrative was that he more or less walked straight into another job. One that had better hours, and better pay as well, or so he said. But Mae saw the chip on his shoulder – and it was a heavy one.

'How are you holding up?' she asks.

He rubs a hand at his jaw. He's one of those men that if he doesn't shave you know about it. The bottom half of his face is already in shadow.

'It's a bloody mess.'

A snarl with bark and bite. But a peevishness too.

Make-or-break, Mae, make-or-break. And surely the writing's on the wall?

'I knew that young bloke was shifty,' he goes on. 'Called it a mile off. I said to Drew, "There's no accounting for taste." Woman like that with someone like him.'

'And what did Drew say?'

'What?'

Mae can imagine Drew walking up to the guy and telling him he was punching well above his weight. The male ego is fragile, but is it *that* fragile? Oh yes. She's seen bar fights over less.

'I mean, what did Drew say when you brought that guy to his attention?' says Mae. 'How did he act?'

'He was distracted. Didn't even hear, I don't think. He was just back from that stupid walk he took, probably trying not to have a coronary. And now he's dead . . . and that messes everything up.'

Steve makes a noise somewhere between a growl and a groan. Is this anger giving way to . . . something else? Actual sorrow? He cried like a baby when his mum died three years back. And then he never mentioned her again. Not one word.

'Stevie?'

She's surprised to find there's actual tenderness in her voice. Well, she's not a monster.

'He made me a promise,' he says into his hands. So quiet, so muffled, she can barely hear him now. Like a storm that's blown itself out. 'Drew did.'

A bad feeling blasts in. He *was* beside her bed all night, wasn't he? She's sure he was. She's pretty sure that Steve isn't the killing kind. But the blow-his-top kind? The stupid-accident kind? The run-away-from-the-consequences kind?

'What sort of a promise?' she says, her voice loaded as a gun.

Steve looks up, his mouth askew. Need leaches from him, and she hates herself for finding it so unattractive; for judging his appeal, of all things, in this moment.

That's her problem. Once, she found him alluring – and now she doesn't.

'I never got it in writing. Texts, emails, I've gone through the lot. There's nothing concrete there.'

She waits. No point asking another question; it's just rain against a window, no means of breaking in. Does Mae even want to know the answer? She's out.

Out.

Her resolve is as hard and clear as the diamond he's never given her.

Good job too, because the extraction would be a hell of a lot messier.

'Drew said, "My word is my bond, Steve-o." And I was stupid enough to believe him.'

Steve passes his hand across his mouth. Hope temporarily lights up his features.

'But there's still Kathy,' he says. 'Isn't there?'

23

Summer is curled on the sofa, tight as a mollusc. She's wearing a long cardigan with a vivid Aztec print, and it's wrapped around her like a blanket.

'I don't understand why they'd arrest him,' she says softly. 'I don't . . . understand.'

And nor does Ally. But there has to be a good reason.

Summer's hair falls in front of her eyes, but she doesn't sweep it away. She looks, Ally thinks, as if she wants to disappear.

'Talk us through what happened,' says Jayden.

'Blake came back up from the pool and he was . . . stressed. Just as stressed as before. Maybe even more. We got into a bit of an argument. I guess I wasn't happy at being left like that, and I felt like there was something going on. I mean, there was something. Like maybe he didn't want to be here. But not . . . *that*.'

She nods to beyond the balcony as she says it.

'You thought there was more to Blake's reaction than remembering his friend who got injured in a balcony fall?' says Jayden.

'Yeah, I guess. Deep down.'

'And how did Blake react when you challenged him, Summer?' asks Jayden.

'He just . . . went quiet.'

'He didn't say anything at all?' says Ally.

'He sat in a chair. Head in his hands. I've never seen him like that. I thought . . . Well, I thought it looked bad for us.'

Summer shakes her head.

'Bad for both of you?' says Ally carefully.

'Our relationship, I mean. I thought the problem must be with me. That he wanted to end it. But then there was a knock and . . . it was the police. They walked in and arrested him. And it was crazy because Blake went with them like a lamb. Didn't even question it. And he didn't look at me. Not one glance.' Her voice drops so it's barely audible. 'I don't understand any of it.'

Ally looks to Jayden. His face is open, kind. He rests a hand on Summer's arm.

'So the name Drew Schofield doesn't mean anything to you? Blake never mentioned him?'

Blast from the past?

Summer shakes her head.

'Is there a possibility that Blake could have known Drew and not told you?' asks Ally.

She shakes her head again, says, 'I don't know. No.'

'What about yesterday? Drew made a scene in the restaurant. Cat and I saw it happen. We all did. How did Blake react to that?'

Summer looks towards the view of the ocean. The patches of blue sky have been blotted with dark clouds. Rain streaks the vast glass.

'Blake wouldn't hurt anyone,' she says eventually. Her lips are tightly pressed together, her cheeks white. 'I swear on my life he wouldn't.'

She didn't answer Jayden's question.

'Summer, how did you both spend yesterday afternoon?' Ally asks.

'Blake got a migraine and . . . he wanted to lie down. I sat downstairs and made a few notes for my piece. Louisa organised for us to have massages, but Blake passed so I went on my own. When I got back, we went down for dinner.' She looks at Jayden apologetically. 'I know we were supposed to have a drink with you and Cat, but he wasn't feeling up to it.'

'But he felt okay to go for dinner?' says Jayden.

With the migraine? Or with the knowledge that Drew Schofield was in the hotel? Because they both saw the way Summer avoided the question about the scene at dinner.

Summer hesitates. 'I persuaded him. After I got back from the spa, Blake was on his phone, scrolling away, so I knew his migraine had lifted.' She looks down. 'If you're okay to stare at a screen, you're okay to have dinner, right?'

Jayden nods, and Ally thinks he's doing a great job of keeping her on side.

'I think I was a bit mean, actually,' she says, her pale cheeks colouring now. 'It's just I had this idea of what it'd be like for us two, staying here together, and . . . it wasn't playing out.'

And now he's been arrested.

'And how was dinner?' asks Jayden gently.

Summer chews at the corner of her lip. She looks from one to the other, as if she's weighing something up.

'Honestly? Dinner was awful. I could tell that Blake didn't want to be there. First, he made us move. They'd put us on the best table, but he wanted to be in a corner instead. He said it was more intimate, but he didn't mean it as he was totally distracted. He was sitting with his back to the room, but he was tuned in to everything and everyone. When there was the stupid mess with that poor waitress, he told me we should just leave and get room service instead. He said it'd be more relaxing, but I think he just didn't want to be there.' Her voice chokes. 'But, honestly, Blake did not do this. You have to believe me. He's a good person. There's just no way . . .'

'Did he leave the room at any point during the night?'

'He . . . No.'

'What about when you were filming the storm? During the power cut?'

Ally sees her hesitate.

'Summer?' says Jayden, clocking it too.

'For two seconds. He went down to reception to see what was going on about the power cut.'

'And did he talk to anyone at reception?' asks Ally.

'He said there was no one there.'

If Summer was busy filming, and Blake was away substantially longer than 'seconds', would she even have noticed? Ally and Jayden swap a look.

'I know what you're thinking,' says Summer, 'but he was hardly out of the room.'

But all Ally can think is that it's rather strange that, in the middle of a power cut, the hotel owners weren't making themselves available to their guests.

'Okay, so you're his alibi,' says Jayden. 'The police will be following up with you. Unless . . .'

'Unless what?' says Summer.

Unless Blake confesses.

'He didn't do it, Jayden.'

Jayden rubs his head, and his razor-short hair crackles.

'Okay,' he says, 'here's where we are. The police have made the arrest. And they've obviously got something substantial, because as far as I know they didn't even take Blake's statement before they arrested him.'

Ally watches a single tear escape Summer's lashes and trickle down her cheek.

'So, I'm thinking it's one of two things. Either a witness saw Blake with Drew and was able to clearly identify him, or Drew told someone something incriminating about Blake, and they've communicated that to the police. His wife, maybe.'

Not Drew's friend Steve, though. He had no clue who'd been arrested.

'None of that makes sense,' Summer says quietly.

'Or . . . third option . . . they've run their own checks, and found Blake has a criminal record. Depending on the charge, in a situation like this, that could be enough to take him in.'

Summer looks from one to the other.

'He doesn't have a criminal record,' she says.

Ally mouths one word to Jayden. *Fatima?* His friend in the force, who he trained with way back. She's helped in the past.

Jayden shakes his head. Says quietly, 'Honeymoon.' Then, 'Summer, where did Blake live before he moved to France?'

'He . . . moved around, I think. "It's always snowing somewhere", that's what he used to say. He's like me. We both live to travel.'

'Where did he grow up?' asks Ally.

'Grow up?' Summer blinks. She looks perplexed, as if she's never considered this part of Blake before. 'What's that got to do with anything?' Then, 'I think it was Oxford.'

24

Gus sits at his desk, tapping at the keys of his laptop with fervour. Lord knows it's been a long time since he's done this. In the last half an hour he's been down a 'Drew Schofield Thames Valley Police' rabbit hole – and he's still in it. There is of course the chance that Gus is covering well-trodden ground, but he can't help feeling that he's bringing some invaluable local knowledge to proceedings. That photograph of Drew Schofield outside the central police station, for instance. Well, goodness me if Gus didn't drive past that building on his way to Sainsbury's just about every week, back in the day. There's an utterly unfounded feeling of glamour about the recognition. *I know that road!*

And he knows the estate that the *Oxford Mail* piece talks about too. Gus used to teach at a school where the catchment stopped just short of Hawthorn Way, and some of the teachers – the ones he'd do anything to avoid at the kettle – used to harp on that it was a good thing too. DS Schofield was accused of excessive force at the Hawthorn – kicking down a door, duffing up a suspect who was 'resisting arrest' – but the mud didn't stick. Plenty of dirt in the comments section, though, and Gus combs through every line; half cringing, half enjoying it. When he lifts his head up and reconnects with the actual world – or at least his little corner of it: pine panelling, salt-smeared window, bad-tempered ocean slapping at the shore – he feels rather grubby himself. It's the effect of being caught up in the minutiae of other people's existences; the bewildering number of other lives out there.

The conclusion, though? Perhaps not a shining beacon of the police force, this Drew Schofield.

For a moment, Gus imagines how he himself would react when push came to shove – and when shove then came to the waving of a knife, say. Would he keep a cool head, when everyone about him was losing theirs? *Shouldn't think so.* But then Gus never signed up for law and order. Though Year Nines, last period on a Friday, required a degree of policing.

Next, he unearths a Facebook post from the force, wishing Drew well in his retirement. It has rather fewer 'likes' and accompanying well-wishes than Gus would have imagined. He thinks of his own retirement from teaching. It was a decent show. He sat up on the stage in a final assembly, smoothing his tie, feeling a tad awkward as he looked out over the sea of children's faces that had changed over the years, but also hadn't really. *The pupils.* He still thinks fondly – all the more so for the distance, the absence of marking, the lack of playground duty – of that semi-abstracted body of individuals. Gus was presented with a silver compass by the head; a thoughtful gift for someone embarking upon a new direction in their life, especially a geographer. Gus had to work hard not to get misty-eyed, especially as things with Mona were already iffy; the structures of his life were buckling and he wasn't sure which way was north, even with his new compass in hand.

Gus enlarges the picture of Drew Schofield, posing with a framed certificate. His thick hair is a dirty white. The bloke has a drinker's nose. A drinker's midriff too: his suit jacket hangs open, as if it's given up trying. His eyes, though? Steely as you like.

I wouldn't go up against him. That's the thought that flashes into Gus's mind – though, to be fair, there's precious few he would go up against.

His hand reaches for his phone. He must contact Ally.

Then he stops himself. *And say what?* He's hardly got the scoop of the year. He could just reiterate his interest in shadowing her and Jayden – for the good of his stop-start novel. Which is either a barmy idea of Saffron's or more or less the status quo, because hasn't Gus been involved in every one of Ally and Jayden's cases, in some small way? Peering from windows to identify vehicles; getting up close and personal with the victims' relatives, like an ersatz liaison officer; photographing gravel. *Oh yes.* He's proved himself useful, one way or another.

And, of course, this victim hails from Oxford. *I know that road!* Et cetera.

Gus jumps as his phone goes, and he feels a starburst of pleasure at the sight of Ally's name. Maybe this is it: his call-up. *Get me Munro! Only Munro will do!*

'Gus,' she says when he picks up, 'this is very much a long shot, but I don't suppose the name Blake Bryant means anything to you, does it? He's twenty-eight, so he'd have left school about a decade ago.'

Blake Bryant. He'd remember the pleasing assonance of a name like that. But he's drawing a blank.

'Why do you ask, Ally?'

'We're trying to establish some background,' she says quietly and, Gus thinks, incredibly professionally. As if she's a real detective.

I mean, she is a real detective. The very loveliest real detective.

'And you thought I might have taught him?'

'I told you it was a long shot.'

'Is it important?' he asks. 'I mean, what do you want to know about him?'

'If there was any trouble, I suppose. If someone who knew him in Oxford would remember anything. Clutching at straws here rather, but . . . we're trying to catch up to where Mullins and Skinner are.'

'You can't just ask them?' Then he corrects himself: 'No, of course you can't.'

Authenticity of police procedure is one of the areas Gus needs to work on in his book. *It doesn't need to be probable*, said his agent, *it just needs to feel possible. Or at least not* impossible.

Gus bends over his laptop, taps in the name *Blake Bryant*. Two chaps come up: one's a weightlifter in Perth, the other a real estate agent in Colorado. And neither looks as if he left school in Oxford around a decade ago.

'You know who I can ask?' he says suddenly. 'Rich and Clive. Nearly sixty years of teaching between them, Ally, and most of them in Oxford. Clive spent his later years as a supply teacher. Talk about thankless, but he's always been good at taking the rough with the smooth, has Clive. And of course that means he got around. Gun for hire, you see. If either of them has come across a Blake Bryant, they'll come back to me quick as a whistle.'

Ally expresses her thanks. And then Gus is jumping straight on WhatsApp. While he and his two friends have enjoyed correspondence by letter ever since he moved to Cornwall, they also occasionally converse on the messaging app. Indeed Clive – always the most technologically minded of the trio – set up a group just for them, when there was once talk of a boys' trip out west; everyone bunking down at All Swell, with a crate or two of Doom Bar and *Pet Sounds* on the turntable. It didn't come to fruition, but never say never.

Blake Bryant, writes Gus. Does the name ring any bells with you chaps? Left school in Oxford around 2013–15.

Almost immediately Rich is typing. Gus watches the three dots in anticipation. Then his response pings in:

I've made it a duty of self-care to erase the name of every kid I ever taught.

Then:

Did you like how I said 'self-care'? It's the Lisa effect.

Lisa being Rich's new girlfriend. Divorcing at fifty-seven did Rich no harm whatsoever. Gus, on the other hand, still feels squashed by his split from Mona. Not every day, but some: when the weather closes in, say, or when Ally goes to Suffolk. It's been three years and counting.

And now Clive is typing. Three dots, alongside the tiny circle showing a picture of him in sunglasses looking like any number of people, and none of them Clive. People go on about teenagers tied to their phones, but retirees – including would-be novelists – would give them a run for their money. It's all that time, see.

What do you want to know, mate?

Is that a hit? Clive can be a little opaque.

Did you know him? types Gus.

Not personally, comes the reply.

Gus snorts. Inscrutable fellow. What he needs, what Ally needs, are facts.

Facts – and fast.

Gus clicks out of WhatsApp, putting an end to this infernal tossing of paper planes, and rings the man instead. That's what his DI Larkin would do. And it's what the Shell House Detectives would do too.

'Oh good,' says Clive, 'I was hoping you'd phone for a natter. But, Gus, why on earth are you asking after that poor kid?'

25

In the interview room, Mullins eyes Blake Bryant. The handcuffs are off, and his hands are folded on the table in front of him. He was dead quiet on the drive from the High Tide; none of the jawing you have sometimes. Mullins was worried they'd get the old 'no comment' when it came to it, but so far Blake has answered their questions straightforwardly. With just the one sticking point: that he had anything to do with Drew Schofield nosediving off that balcony.

'So let me get this right,' says Skinner. 'Drew Schofield arrested you, and as a consequence you were sent to a young offender institution for GBH. Now, I know you pleaded self-defence, Blake, but you must have got yourself a little bit carried away there, because there wasn't any downgrading. I've seen your record. You broke bones.'

'I broke *my* arm. Two ribs.'

'You broke *other* people's bones.'

'It was self-defence. And it was ruled without intent.'

'And yet you've never told anyone about this. You moved out to France, just as soon as you could, and kept it all quiet.'

'I went travelling. I've only been in France five years.'

'Trying to forget that it ever happened?'

'What's so bad about that?' says Blake.

'What's so bad is that, suddenly, Drew Schofield turns up when you're on a luxury break with your girlfriend. A girlfriend who, presumably, knows nothing about this other side of you?'

Mullins sees Blake flinch.

'I don't have another side,' he says.

'Schofield recognised you, didn't he? Just like you recognised him.'

Blake looks down at his hands.

'He could have done it in an innocent way. "Good to see you again! You've turned it all around, son. Staying here? Made something good of yourself." That sort of thing.'

Skinner pauses. And Blake squirms like a worm on a hook.

'But, Blake, the more I find out about Drew Schofield, the more I'm thinking that wouldn't be his style.'

Old-school copper, that was one of the phrases used. Which round here is code for . . . not very good things, basically. They're still waiting on a call from Thames Valley's Professional Standards department for more details.

'What happened, Blake? What did Drew Schofield say to you?'

Two spots of colour have appeared in Blake's cheeks. They're round and red as snooker balls.

'Right now, this doesn't look very good for you, Blake. Added to the fact that you left your bedroom in the same window of time that your girlfriend caught a man on camera confronting the victim.'

'That wasn't me.'

'When did you first realise you were staying in the same hotel as Drew Schofield?'

'I don't know, middle of the afternoon. I can't remember.'

'And what did you do once you realised who he was?'

'I . . . kept my head down. Hoped he didn't recognise me. I faked a migraine just so I didn't have to sit in the bar with my girlfriend and risk him seeing me. Confronting him was the total opposite of what I wanted to do.' Blake rubs at his wrists, as if they hurt from the cuffs. 'But he did see me. And he did recognise me.'

And he's staring into the middle distance; he's right back there.

'I was by the lifts. Summer asked me to grab a bag she'd left downstairs, and I heard this voice call out "Don't I know you?" I tried to brush it off but . . . I'm not actually very good at lying.'

'That right?' says Skinner, eyebrow raised.

'Detective Schofield jumped on it, though. He was like, "Fry's Hill Park." Then he said, "Boom."'

Boom? Mullins is pretty sure he'd internalise that one, even if he thought it.

'He loved how uncomfortable it made me. I should have just walked away, but instead I said . . .' Blake groans like it's uncomfortable to remember. 'I said, "Please don't say anything to my girlfriend. I've put it behind me." Stupid of me.'

'Right,' says Skinner.

'And his whole face lit up. Like I'd just handed him a blank cheque or something. He jumped on it, started giving it the "Oh, she doesn't know, does she? That her boyfriend's got a temper on him." All that. He was rubbing my face in it.'

'And where were you as this conversation was taking place?' says Mullins.

'By the lift.'

'Not in his room?' says Mullins. 'His balcony?'

'No,' says Blake. '*No.*'

'What happened then?'

'I walked away.'

Like you did in Fry's Hill Park, you mean? thinks Mullins.

'Like you did in Fry's Hill Park?' says Skinner.

Mullins's chest puffs out like a turkey's. Maybe he's getting better at this! But the moment of triumph is soon replaced by a different feeling. A weird one. Because the look on Blake's face is so injured, so bloody pained, it's as if they just inflicted some grievous bodily harm of their own.

26

'Gus said his friend didn't know what happened to Blake after he was released from the young offender institution,' says Ally. 'But he didn't return to the school, and he didn't take his A levels there.'

Jayden nods, the picture clicking into view. It explains why Blake's name didn't come up in his searches: juveniles are granted automatic anonymity. Does it also explain why the police were so quick to bring him in? A criminal record would light up their radar, but to make an arrest, surely there's got to be more.

They're back in Jayden's room, the door firmly closed. He's glad they weren't with Summer when the call from Gus came in. It's tough enough not understanding why your boyfriend has been arrested, but suddenly learning they have a criminal record for a serious offence? It's a lot. And unless Summer asks, it's not up to them to tell her.

Jayden and Ally are sitting in the lounge area, a pot of coffee between them. They've turned the lamps on too, because the sky outside has darkened like a whole new storm is brewing.

'He's got a good head for detail, this mate of Gus's,' says Jayden.

'I think it was a shock to everyone in the school community at the time. Apparently, Blake Bryant wasn't typically a troublemaker. What does it mean exactly, "grievous bodily harm without intent"?'

'The "without intent" part means he didn't set out to inflict harm,' says Jayden. 'There's a possibility it could also mean it was self-defence. What was he sentenced to? Two months? That's not nothing, Al. He could have just been given a community order, but he wasn't.'

'Gus said that Clive's friend was his form tutor. He wanted to visit him, apparently, but Blake wouldn't see anyone. This friend, the teacher, he reached out to the family afterwards as well, but they shut him down.'

'Okay,' says Jayden, tapping a drumbeat on his knees. 'We're caught up. A decade ago, Blake Bryant got in a violent fight and ended up in a young offender institution as a result. Because of how quickly Blake was arrested this morning, I'm thinking Drew Schofield must have been involved back then.'

'Could Drew have been the arresting officer?' asks Ally.

'I reckon he could have been, Al. Because there's got to be a tangible link.'

'So if Drew was involved in Blake's arrest ten years ago, perhaps Blake blamed him for his life going wrong.'

'We're busking but . . . yeah. I'd say that's what Skinner's thinking. We know from Gus's pal that Blake wasn't considered a troublemaker. An experience like that is going to leave a scar on anyone, let alone someone who's new to breaking the law. You saw Blake at the pool, Al. He looked . . . scared.'

But was he scared because of what he'd done to Drew on the balcony?

'At least this makes sense of the "blast from the past" line. It means Drew recognised him too.'

'Gus saw the same reports online that you did, Jayden. The accusations of excessive force. That could be a factor, couldn't it? Perhaps Drew arrested him with some aggression, and it impacted Blake.'

For sure.

'Hold on – is Gus moonlighting for us?'

'I think perhaps he is,' says Ally with a half-smile. She mentions his request at the beach, to shadow them in the name of his novel.

'A murder case as a cure for writer's block? That's a new one.'

'Saffron's idea,' says Ally.

Jayden raises an eyebrow. He knows Saffron's modus operandi – and there's always good at the heart of it. And Jayden reckons he can guess the particular good she has in mind.

'Well, he's proved himself useful,' says Jayden. 'He could be a good man to have on hand, with the Oxford connection.'

Ally's face brightens. 'You mean . . .'

'That this isn't over? No way. Here's what I'm thinking, Al. Blake wasn't trying to act normal, was he? His girlfriend found the body, but instead of comforting her he went swimming. He didn't try to hide the fact that what'd happened was messing with his head. And at that point he didn't know Summer had anything on film. So, as far as he knew, there was no reason for the police to believe that it was anything but a self-inflicted accident.'

'But not everyone would try to act normal in a situation like that, would they? He could have caused Drew's death but still have been badly shaken by it. And, Jayden, I do think it's strange that when Blake left the room to go to reception during the power cut there was no one there. Surely in a place like this, staff would be on hand in a situation like that?'

'Middle of the night? Depends how long Blake stuck around. If it was just a minute or two, like Summer says, he could have missed them.'

'Or perhaps he didn't go down to reception at all,' says Ally.

'Even if he was gone for the length of the video, Al, it still wouldn't be enough time to go to Drew Schofield's room, out on to the balcony, confront Drew, and then get back.'

'I do agree with you there.'

'Gut instinct? It rules him out, Al.'

Jayden jumps as there's a sharp rapping at the balcony glass.

Just rain.

Rain with intent. It's coming down in sheets now, the wind getting up too; the palm trees down on the terrace have their heads dipped in defeat.

'Unless Summer is a good liar,' says Ally, her eyes following his to the window, 'and he was gone from the room for longer than she says.'

'A hundred per cent. But I don't think she's lying. I think she's confused. And upset.'

There's another assault of rain and wind on glass.

'Gosh, look at it out there,' murmurs Ally. 'The sea's so dark.'

As dark as fresh-poured tarmac. And it's like it's pressing closer and closer.

'I'm calling it, Al,' says Jayden. 'I don't think Blake did it. Which, as far as I'm concerned, means the killer is still in this hotel.'

27

The killer is still in this hotel.

Jayden's words ring in Ally's ears as she treads down the corridor, Fox close beside her. Despite the warm glow of the spotlights, the colour and vivacity of the paintings on the walls, Ally feels a chill at the back of her neck. Everything at the High Tide has been designed for serenity, but serenity has long since checked out.

They've decided to split up for this next part; Jayden's thinking is that it'll make them a less intimidating prospect. Ally is headed for the room of Drew's widow, Kathy Schofield. Meanwhile, Jayden is going first to Louisa, to tell the hotel owner that the police making an arrest doesn't mean that he and Ally are stopping investigating. Then he'll seek out Steve Bradshaw and his girlfriend, Mae.

Ally arrives at room number five and lifts her hand to knock. Then she pauses. She can hear voices coming from inside. She puts her ear close to the door, discerns one male voice, one female. The words lift and drop, as if caught on the tide; some she can catch, others slip away from her, just out of her grasp.

'. . . what he always said . . .'

'. . . this weekend . . .'

'Drew promised . . .'

Could it be Steve Bradshaw? He's the only other man at the High Tide that's connected to Kathy.

'. . . promise . . .'

'. . . twenty-five . . .'

'. . . heart bleeds . . .'

Interspersed are Kathy's responses – a low murmuring, with occasional rises in pitch – but no obvious words.

'I can't think, Steve! Don't make me think.'

Suddenly her voice is ringing out, clear as a bell.

'. . . leave you to it.'

Ally holds her breath, pulls back. She hears the creak of a board as someone approaches. With her heart in her mouth, she scurries on down the corridor until she and Fox are six, seven paces away. Then she slows to normal walking speed and holds her phone to her ear. She speaks casually, as if deeply involved in her own business.

'Bill, darling, I know. But it would have been so fun.'

The first words to come into my head.

The corridor opens to a recess, with a small table and a lamp. Ally hovers, half turning. Steve must have gone the other way. She lets loose a sigh of relief, and bends down to stroke Fox.

Bill, darling, I know. But it would have been so fun.

What was she thinking? Words hastily plucked and thrown together, but nevertheless she examines them. And 'darling'? She and Bill never called one another darling.

Ray calls me darling.

Ally takes a quick breath and retraces her footsteps. As she walks, she messages Jayden:

Steve was just in Kathy's room. Sounded heated. I'm going in now.

Kathy doesn't answer Ally's knock straight away. Perhaps she thinks it's Steve again. It's clear that Steve wanted something, and it sounded like Kathy wasn't prepared to give it to him. Ally stands back from the door so that, if Kathy peeps through the spyhole, she'll get a clear view of her. Just a harmless sixty-something woman. Jayden once described Ally's invisibility as her superpower. *Round here, people see me coming, Al, they're already forming opinions. But not you.*

'Yes?'

Kathy opens the door guardedly. Ally has the impression that if the woman could shrink away, she would.

Drew was fifty-five and Kathy is perhaps the same, or older. She's medium-height and very thin. Her grey hair is cut in a short style that used to be fashionable. She wears a cream polo neck with a silver cross on a chain.

'I'm sorry to disturb you,' says Ally. 'And I'm so sorry for your loss.'

Perhaps she thinks I'm from the Church, thinks Ally. *Or a fast-acting local support group.*

Ally had a number of such knocks at her door after Bill died. Sometimes she answered and sometimes she didn't. Once or twice, she found oven dishes covered with tin foil, the edges lifting in the onshore wind. A bouquet of flowers, without a note.

Kathy's eyes go to Fox – and they light up.

'Can I pet him?' she asks.

'He'd like nothing more,' says Ally. 'In fact, could we come in for a moment?'

It would feel like an overstep, but Jayden said that all the rooms at the High Tide are sizeable. Even the smallest have seating areas, so there will be none of the strange intimacy of a conversation over the bed.

'I'm Ally. And I'm . . . part of the team investigating your husband's death.'

'It's been come and go all morning,' says Kathy quietly.

But she stands aside to let Ally in. Fox immediately rolls on to his back at Kathy's feet; paws up, eyes appealing.

Good boy.

'Oh, you,' says Kathy, stooping to rub his belly.

Ally looks to the balcony, where the doors are shut fast. The view shows an unrelentingly grey sky. The horizon line is as dark as a pencil lead, but nevertheless the sea is a deep teal. Ally's lived by the ocean for over forty years, but she's still amazed by how the water summons its colour, even if, today, a sky full of fast-moving clouds makes its surface look like a stained carpet. She turns her attention to the room: the coffee table, with the same books and magazines as in Summer and Blake's room; a bed that hasn't been slept in. This isn't the room where Drew opened the door to a visitor then fell to his death. Kathy must have been moved almost instantly, as the CSIs set to work on the original room. Fingerprints. Hairs. Fibres. Anything that might provide a link between Drew Schofield and his assailant.

A large black suitcase is open on the floor and Ally sees perfectly folded men's shirts; the soft velour of a pink dressing gown rolled as if in a shop. Perhaps someone else repacked for Kathy: this was no desperate pulling of clothes from the wardrobe; none of the disorder of shock.

'You don't look like you're with the police,' says Kathy, glancing up.

'Technically, I'm not,' says Ally smoothly. Then, because she thinks it'll help, 'But my husband was. For his whole working life.'

'Oh. So you know.'

Ally gives a small smile. Kathy could mean any number of things.

'So I know,' she agrees.

There's a beat of quiet. Nothing but Kathy's soft murmuring to Fox. He's always been a good judge of character, Ally thinks. And he likes Kathy Schofield. *Or is he just a well-trained detective's dog?*

'I'm a detective myself, these days,' says Ally. 'That's why I'm here.'

'He gave the job everything,' says Kathy, as if she hasn't heard. 'Not much left to go around after.' A laugh, high as a gull's cry. 'Part of me was dreading his retirement, but I expect he'd have had his fingers in other pies before long. That was Drew. Non-stop. Bang at it. That's what he used to say. "I'm bang at it, Kath. Take no prisoners."' She rocks back on her heels; puts a hand to her forehead. 'Your husband like that, was he?'

And because connection feels more important than truth, Ally says yes.

'There's a reason they get the payout. It should come straight to us. The long-suffering wives.'

'The payout?'

'The pension. Drew got a twenty-five per cent lump sum up front. We didn't use it to book this place, though. I scrimped and saved. Kept it a secret.'

'So, it was a surprise weekend?'

Kathy sits on the very edge of the sofa. She wears polyester trousers with pleats down the front and the material rises, showing her pale legs. Fox twists on his belly and Kathy bends to him, her fingers playing with his soft fur. Ally notices Kathy's wedding ring. She also notices her own reaction – or rather lack of it: the sight of the ring brings no additional feelings of poignancy for Kathy's loss.

Now why is that?

'He hated surprises too,' says Kathy, shaking her head. 'He was in a foul mood all the way here. Even worse when he saw that it was Cornwall. We came down the road for the High Tide and I thought he was going to grab the wheel off me and turn us around. But he soon changed his tune when he saw how nice it was. And Steve was the cherry on the cake.'

'Steve and Drew were good friends?'

Kathy's hand rests in Fox's fur.

'They were,' she says.

'And how is Steve doing after his death?'

'Men. They don't show it like us women.'

'What – grief, you mean?'

Kathy makes a murmur of acknowledgement. 'Grief, affection . . . Everything, really.'

'Was Steve with you just now?' asks Ally.

Kathy levels a look at her – one she can't quite read. Should Ally say that she heard snippets of their conversation? Dare she ask what Steve wanted, or is that too invasive? She doesn't want Kathy to shut down. And she can't count on Fox to keep the belly rubs going indefinitely.

'He was. That young man they arrested,' says Kathy, changing direction, 'his name means nothing to me. But then I wouldn't expect it to. Drew never talked about his work, but Steve says Drew saw someone he knew here.'

Ally nods. She must be careful here. Jayden said it wouldn't be in their interests to suggest that Drew's killer is still at large. Not with Kathy.

'Kathy, is it true that you were asleep when it happened?'

'My sleeping pills knocked me out. The hotel could have been on fire and I wouldn't have known. She'll blame me, of course.'

'Who'll blame you?'

'Drew's mother, Margaret. Eighty-two, and she's got every single one of her marbles. More's the pity. I was never good enough for her, Ally.'

Fox suddenly gets to his feet. Kathy sighs and does the same.

'Everyone wants a piece of me,' she says. 'I don't know what to do, really. And now I need to phone Margaret and tell her what's happened. I should have done it already, but I couldn't face it. I shall have to pretend that I've been inconsolable all morning.' She puts a hand to her mouth. Her wrist bone is sharp as a blade. 'Did I just say that out loud?'

'You mean you're not . . .' Ally searches for the right words. '. . . as upset as you could be?'

'Just the shock,' says Kathy stiffly. She licks her lips, and Ally sees how dry they are; lipstick settled in the cracks.

'I'll leave you. Just . . . Can I ask, how did you choose the High Tide?'

'He used to come to Trebaron as a boy, and I remember his mother once saying he loved it. I do listen to her occasionally, see.'

Ally smiles sadly.

'I thought it'd be nice,' says Kathy. 'And it was. For a few minutes, it was.' She hauls in a big breath. 'Right. Phone Margaret. I can't put it off anymore, can I?'

At the door, Ally turns. 'Was yours a happy marriage, Kathy?' she asks.

'Was yours?'

Ally hesitates. She can't lie, not on this.

'I was lucky,' she says.

Kathy's hand goes to her necklace. 'It's a dice roll, then, isn't it?' she says.

28

The reception area looks deserted at first, but then Elliott emerges from a room tucked away behind the desk. His grey hair stands on end, as if he's repeatedly tracked his fingers through it. His expression is fretful. Louisa follows behind and immediately sends Jayden that glittering smile of hers. It goes nowhere near her eyes.

'Ah, Jayden, I was wondering when you'd be checking in,' she says, enjoying the pun. 'In an update sense, that is. Unless . . . with all that kerfuffle with the handcuffs, you're wanting to check out? Though I sincerely hope that's not the case.'

'Not checking out,' says Jayden.

'Jayden, please tell me you're here to say they have the wrong man. We've just been speculating as if we're in a particularly distressing game of Cluedo and . . . Well, I need some good news.'

'I'm not sure "good news" is right . . .'

'Call it what you want, so long as you're not on the same page as those bolshy officers. I know I wanted things cleared up quickly, but I can't help feeling that the arrest of Summer Ellery's beloved might tarnish her experience with us.'

Wow. That's what she's worked up about. A travel blogger having a less than five-star experience.

'While Blake Bryant's helping the police with their enquiries,' he says, choosing his words carefully, 'Ally and I are continuing our investigation.'

Louisa smiles – and this time it does reach her eyes.

'Are you charging by the hour, then?' says Elliott quietly.

'Oh, for goodness' sake,' says Louisa, rounding on her husband. 'Jayden's doing the job I gave him. And I think we'd both prefer any line of enquiry that doesn't include our VIP.'

'The police were swift to act, and I for one am grateful to them,' says Elliott, making no attempt to disguise his disapproval of his wife's lack of perspective.

But Louisa waves her hand as if she's swiping at a fly – or an inconsequential husband. 'Less haste, more speed. That's the phrase I'm looking for. And it's clear Jayden agrees, he's just too diplomatic to say so. Look, what's happened here is dreadful and I was already hoping Summer wouldn't hold it against us in her review, but now that the PC Plods have arrested her boyfriend? It's a disaster. Only you can save us, Jayden,' she finishes with a light laugh.

Jayden glances to Elliott. He's looking at his wife as if she's crazy. Or just grotesquely ambitious when it comes to their hotel's fortunes.

'I just hope that Summer will come back again under better circumstances,' Louisa goes on. 'I've already had some flowers sent up. Offered another massage. It's as good a moment as any to enjoy the facilities and try to relax. Jayden, you and your wife are friendly with her. Please do reassure her that we at the High Tide are here for her. She must be going through . . . hell.'

Louisa struggles with the word, like she's only loosely familiar with the concept but has never known it personally.

'Do you have any idea why the police made the arrest?' asks Elliott, changing direction. 'They looked like they meant business, that's all. It seemed to happen very quickly.'

'You saw it happen?' asks Jayden.

'No, no,' cuts in Louisa. 'But they led him through here in handcuffs. That's a first for the High Tide, I can tell you. Or . . .' She pulls an amused face. 'Perhaps not. Who knows what people get up to in their rooms.'

There's a flicker at Elliott's jaw. 'Louisa,' he mutters.

'I think, for the good of your guests, don't advertise the fact that you know who was arrested,' says Jayden, dodging the original question.

'Oh, they'll all know by now,' says Louisa blithely. She drops her voice. 'That friend of Drew's has been running around with his chest stuck out, badgering anything that moves for information. Now why doesn't someone arrest him? For crimes against . . . good manners. Amongst other things.'

'We're reassuring the guests that it's all over,' says Elliott. 'Back to business as usual. With respect, et cetera.'

'While being enormously relieved that you don't think that it *is* over, Jayden,' says Louisa.

At his bedroom door, Steve shakes Jayden's hand – and dispenses a knuckle-crusher.

'As I think you know, my partner and I are conducting some enquiries,' says Jayden, all politeness. 'We were hoping we could pick your brains. Can I come in for a sec?'

'What are you going on about? They've made an arrest. You were right there, mate.'

'The investigation's ongoing,' Jayden says crisply. Then, adjusting his tone, 'These local boys, not sure they're getting the full picture. We want this solved, right?'

But it doesn't land.

'Yeah, who's paying you?' says Steve, eyes narrowing. 'Not Blake Bryant's girlfriend? Because I'll tell you what, anything from her is going to be dirty money.'

'She's not our client. And Blake has an alibi.'

'Everyone's always got an alibi. And prison's full of innocent men. Keep talking.'

Jayden nods to the room. He can see Mae, Steve's girlfriend, getting to her feet, and he raises his hand.

'Spare me two minutes?' he says.

'Two minutes max,' says Steve. He stands aside, but only just. A cheap power play, but no less than Jayden expects.

Meanwhile Mae smiles economically in response to Jayden's greeting. She's wearing a short dress with tights and boots; her coat is in her hand.

'What happened to you getting some air?' Steve says, turning to her.

'Changed my mind.' Mae perches on the edge of an armchair. 'I want to know what's going on.'

Jayden looks back to Steve. There's a vein pulsing at his temple; his mouth is set hard.

'There you go, Jayden' – his voice all punch. 'You've got your audience. And the clock's ticking.'

'Alright,' Jayden says coolly. 'There's no evidence to suggest that Blake had anything to do with Drew's death. And there's plenty to say he didn't.'

'Yeah, yeah. Poxy private detective outfit? You're on the outside looking in.'

'Does Blake Bryant's name mean anything to you?'

'Donkey,' Steve shoots out. His forehead is a mess of lines. 'Should it?'

So, Steve's not clued in – and hates admitting it. If he still had friends at Thames Valley, he'd know Blake Bryant has a criminal record. Maybe Drew was his last surviving mate from the force. And not everyone has a Fatima up their sleeve. *When she's not on honeymoon, anyway.* Enter – surprisingly – Gus and his pals. Fatima likes to remind Jayden how much he's pushing it from time to time: *You know this is a sackable offence, right, Jay? That what you want for me? The dole queue?* But Jayden also knows that, as an officer, Fatima is unimpeachable. And unimpeachable officers don't get watched 24/7.

'Blake Bryant was with his girlfriend all night long,' says Jayden.

He deliberately doesn't use Summer's name. Jayden doesn't love talking about her with Steve at all, to be honest; she's just a few rooms away – and going out of her mind. He also avoids mentioning the fact that Blake briefly slipped out of the room during the power cut: forget the implausible timings, that'd be a slam dunk as far as Steve is concerned.

'Look, I'm interested in what you think, Steve,' he says, going for flattery. 'Because you called this as murder before anyone else.'

'That's instinct,' says Steve. 'They can't teach you that in training.'

Jayden glances to Mae. Her foot's tip-tapping against the chair leg. Did Jayden just see her roll her eyes? He shifts his attention back to Steve.

'Right? So imagine for a minute that his girlfriend's telling the truth, and Blake *was* with her all night. Who else is there? What's your instinct?'

'This is game-playing. I'm not into that.'

'Humour me.'

Steve screws his face up, like trying to imagine anyone other than Blake being guilty is a real stretch.

'Drew was talking about a blast from the past. Obviously, that was Blake.'

Without knowing any of the details, Steve's nailed it.

'When Drew said that, was he referring to someone he arrested in the past?' asks Jayden, as if it's news to him.

'Didn't say. Didn't need to. Cops like me and Drew, thief-takers, old-school, we make a lot of enemies. A twerp like Blake Bryant doesn't look like he'd be on anyone's Most Wanted list, but sometimes it's the quiet ones. The dark little horses.'

'I hear you. But pretend for a minute that it's not Blake. Is there anyone else who knew Drew was going to be in Cornwall this weekend?'

'Drew didn't even know he was going to be in Cornwall this weekend. It was a surprise thing. Kathy sorted it.'

'Did she pay for you and Mae to come too?'

Steve furrows his brow. 'We pay our way. Always have. *More than*. What's that got to do with anything, anyway?'

Mae makes a noise as if she's about to say something, then stops. Jayden turns to her again, his face a question, and she just shakes her head.

'Look, it's not our patch,' says Steve, heading off on a different tack. 'We're in the arse end of nowhere here. We're city cops, Drew and me. Don't be fooled by the pretty pictures, all that university stuff. Oxford's got every problem going. We made a lot of collars. Anyone looking to get their own back? List of people as long as your arm, probably. But then you know what that's like.' He looks Jayden up and down. 'Unless you were a desk jockey.'

'Response,' says Jayden. 'Leeds city centre.'

Steve whistles; grins wolfishly.

'Saturday nights a bit lively, were they?'

'You know it.'

For a moment the camaraderie is convincing.

'Listen,' says Steve, 'I know what my gut's telling me, I knew it from the minute I saw my mate on the terrace with his head smashed in. But there's got to be something else to make the cops so sure that someone else was involved. See, that's how I know they've got something tasty on Blake Bryant. Hard evidence, Jayden. Whatever you or that girlfriend of his says.'

So Steve doesn't know about Summer's video either.

The guy's right that his certainty was there from the get-go, though. Could it be a case of Steve thinking the best defence is a good offence?

'Maybe they've got something,' says Jayden carefully, 'but it can't be specific to Blake. Partially applicable, maybe, to make the arrest, but not conclusive.'

'Yeah, yeah. Whoever did this – and when I say "who", I mean Blake Bryant, make no mistake – they'll pay. And the rest of us? We'll pick up the pieces. Won't we, Mae? We'll be there for Kathy. She can count on that.'

'She can count on us,' she echoes.

Is that the same obedience that would fake a night-time alibi? Or, like Kathy, is Mae a taker of sleeping pills: a sure-fire exit from the alibi conversation. Jayden can't get a read on her. He'd like a conversation on their own.

Steve jerks his head up, sending him a hard look.

'I suppose the girlfriend's checked out, has she? Run a mile? Tail between her legs? Better hope she has, anyway. She'd have a nerve, staying on here.'

And the way Steve says it makes Jayden think Summer ought to check out. The last thing she needs, on top of everything, is a run-in with Steve.

Jayden gives a vague nod and stands up. 'Thanks for your time.'

'Give up the private eye work, mate. It's a mug's game – and you're clutching at straws.'

29

Ally pulls her coat around her. The heavy rain has slackened, turning into a persistent but inoffensive drizzle. The wind is sound and fury one moment, then in the next a whisper. It feels good to be outside, however restless the weather.

The beach is strewn with debris from last night's storm: vast sea-wrecked branches; half a packing crate; bone-white driftwood flung high up the beach. There will be all manner of treasures along the strandline. On any other day Ally would be head down and in amongst it, but instead she looks back towards the hotel. The oceanfront section is open, though no one's sitting out there, despite the outdoor heaters and sheepskin throws. The biting breeze is not the only reason. Further back, directly below the balconies, Ally can just glimpse the police tape cracking and snapping in the wind. Above, the sequence of balconies and windows appear stern; impassive. A shadow moves behind one of the panes on the second floor, as if someone was standing by the glass then quickly stepped back.

Ally feels a prickle at her spine that's nothing to do with the cold.

She sees Jayden heading down the sand, hands stuffed into his big puffa jacket. *Oh good.* After talking to Kathy, Ally suggested they meet at the beach. In the High Tide Hotel, the walls have ears; what she heard of Steve's conversation is proof of that.

'You go first,' she says.

Jayden relays his conversation with Steve Bradshaw – and his lack of willingness to entertain any possibility beyond Blake Bryant.

'Do you think Steve's hiding something?' asks Ally.

'There's definitely something going on. Maybe he's cut up about Drew's death, but there's anger there too. I don't know if that's because he's a former cop and he's gutted that it's happened on his watch, or . . . something else. I don't love his dynamic with Mae either. They present a united front but there's something uneasy there.'

'Do you think she's suspicious?'

'I don't know,' says Jayden. 'I'd like to speak to Mae again on her own. She was about to head out, but when I turned up she stayed.'

'That's natural, isn't it?'

'I don't know,' says Jayden again, scuffing the toe of his trainer in the sand. 'To be honest I'm not feeling like I've made much headway, beyond reinforcing the fact that my initial impression of Steve was correct. Not a great guy.'

'Well, how about I tell you about Steve's conversation with Kathy?' she says.

Ally takes her notebook from her pocket and opens it to the notes she made earlier. The drizzle spots the page, and she cups her hand to protect it. She shares the fragments that she overheard and watches as Jayden processes.

'Good work, Al. Man, I wish you'd heard the lot, though.'

'I know. But it was obvious it was a heated conversation,' she says. 'It wasn't consoling, like two friends united in grief.'

'Do you reckon they could be in on it together?'

'Go on.'

'Well, it sounds like Steve went to Kathy's room asking for something, right? Did it sound like it was something Steve thought he was owed, do you reckon? That they had a prior agreement?'

Ally looks down again at her notebook.

'Steve said, "Drew promised." But I've no idea *what* he promised.' Ally sighs. 'I should have asked Kathy outright. Did I make a mistake?'

'Not if it didn't feel natural. Better to keep her on side, Al. Is she, by the way? On side?'

'Oh, Fox made sure of that,' she smiles.

'Kathy could have done it,' says Jayden. 'She could have put on a coat, hood up to disguise herself, and pushed him off the balcony. All day long, Al.'

'Apart from anything, she doesn't look strong enough.'

'Steve said Drew had had a skinful. If he was unsteady on his feet, maybe you wouldn't need to be strong. Kathy Schofield had means and opportunity for sure. Motive?'

'Reading between the lines, I don't think their marriage was a happy one. In fact, Kathy struck me as rather a sad person. But there was no nervousness in our conversation, Jayden. I didn't feel as though she was hiding anything. Although . . .'

'Although what?'

'She seemed as if her emotions were dulled. Which makes her harder to read.'

'Unlike Steve,' says Jayden, pacing the sand, 'who's going out of his way to chuck his weight about and doesn't care who knows. I want to find out more about Steve and Drew's working relationship. I get the impression that Steve's disconnected from his old colleagues. Think about it: he's right on the spot when his mate, his ex-boss, gets murdered, but he's got nothing. He doesn't know about Blake's criminal record, or Summer's video. If it was me, I'd have been pulling any favour I could to find out about the guy the police have taken in. But Steve hasn't done that – or *can't* do that. But he did stay mates with Drew, his senior officer. Why?'

'How can we find out more there? Talk to Mae separately?'

'Yeah, we should definitely try and speak to her on her own. I'm not getting much off her. Here's the thing, when Mullins and Skinner realise that they're getting nowhere with Blake – and I'll put money on that, Al – they'll turn to Steve. On paper, he's an obvious suspect. He must have given a good account of himself in his initial statement, but they'll be digging deeper. And there's still forensics to come. Situation like this, death of a former cop, they'll be fast-tracking those results.'

'So they'll talk to Drew's former colleagues, which include Steve's too?'

'Exactly. And based on those articles in the *Oxford Mail*, they'll be talking to Thames Valley's Professional Standards department and finding out what the score is there. Steve's got an aggressive side too – that's obvious a mile off. Maybe it came out on the job and that's why he had to go. Meanwhile Drew, who definitely came under fire for excessive force – or at least that was the word on the street, if not made official – stays on until his retirement. That's not going to seem fair to Steve, is it?'

Ally exclaims suddenly. 'Kathy mentioned a lump sum. A pension payout for Drew's retirement. What if Steve found out about that and didn't think it was right?'

Jayden stops his pacing; rubs his hands together. 'Okay, good thinking. How did that come up?'

'We were talking about being married to police officers,' says Ally. 'I suppose I let her think that . . . we were in a similar boat. But Drew and Bill, they couldn't have been more different, I . . .'

'Nice work, Al,' says Jayden. 'When I quit, my dad brought up the pension, like I was kissing goodbye to something really valuable. Bill would have had the same, right?'

'How do you think I get by?' says Ally with a sad smile. 'Kathy said Drew took a quarter of it as a lump sum.'

'Which is a lot of money. Tens of thousands. A lot of campsite bookings.' Jayden grins. 'A lot of Shell House cases. Hold up, a quarter. Twenty-five per cent. You said Steve said the word "twenty-five"?'

Ally looks back at her notebook; the wind flaps the pages, and she holds it tight. 'You're right,' she says, a tremor of excitement in her voice. 'Steve said twenty-five.'

'That *cannot* be a coincidence. Alright, now we're on to something. Just hours after Drew's murder, Steve's at Kathy's door talking about Drew's retirement payout. What's that about?'

Ally pictures the scene – and everything Kathy said afterwards. *Everyone wants a piece of me.* She tells Jayden, and he bobs his head, grins.

'What if Steve had a deal with Kathy? Steve kills him, they split the money.'

'I can't see Kathy plotting to have her husband killed. But . . .'

Ally pauses, thinks back on all their previous cases. People who smiled at them, chatted amiably, offered them tea. People that Ally would never have believed could kill according to their own determined rationales, defending their choices to the end. People whose surety, and cold-bloodedness, chilled Ally to the bone. And taught her to never say never; not when it comes to human beings and their infinite complexity. The tsunamis of rage, of passion, of revenge.

Kathy Schofield? Perhaps.

'Unless . . . Could Steve have manipulated her into it?' she says.

She watches Jayden turn it over in his mind.

'Maybe. Trouble is, Steve isn't acting like someone who just got what he wanted, is he? He's not turning victory laps, Al. He's angry.'

'There's no triumph in Kathy either, or if there is it's incredibly well disguised. And her conversation with Steve was fractious.'

'Not a carefully laid plan coming into fruition, then?'

'Steve was frustrated and emotional.'

'And he's going on about this twenty-five per cent payout. But, from what you heard, Kathy held out on him, right? She said, "I can't think," and after that Steve left.'

'That's right.'

'Okay,' says Jayden, back to pacing the sand. 'Let's park Steve for a minute. Let's go back to Kathy. She gives the impression to you, a complete stranger, that her marriage wasn't a happy one. And yet she made this romantic gesture of a surprise weekend away, and invited Drew's close friends along as well. Does that add up?'

'Perhaps she hoped Drew's retirement would be a new chapter for them.'

'So why invite Steve and Mae too?'

'Perhaps she didn't want to be solely responsible for Drew having a good time. And she knew he wouldn't like the surprise element . . .'

'So why do it at all?' says Jayden. 'Okay, maybe she was afraid that Drew would say no to the weekend otherwise. Maybe she really wanted to come here herself. She could have just liked the look of the High Tide and figured she deserved a relaxing weekend away.'

'Kathy said she chose the hotel because Drew used to holiday in the area as a child. Drew's mother told her. Who, by the way, Kathy can't stand. Kathy hadn't even told her Drew had died yet.'

Jayden stops. He's looking out at the water, his hand held pensively to his chin. A brace of gulls fly past, screaming to high heaven.

'Drew knows the area?' he says, turning. 'What, the High Tide, or this part of Cornwall?'

'Kathy said that he used to come to Trebaron as a child. Though he can't have enjoyed it very much as she also said Drew was in an ugly mood as soon as he realised that they'd be staying in

Cornwall. Whatever nostalgia Kathy was hoping to summon, I'm not sure it worked.'

'The blast from the past,' says Jayden.

'Hmm?'

'We presumed Drew meant Blake, but what if he was talking about someone from further back? Because the fact that Drew's been here before, that's interesting.'

'Agreed,' says Ally. 'It's interesting.'

She writes down in her notebook: *Drew, childhood holidays, Cornwall.* And: *Where? When?* Then puts it safely in her coat pocket.

'Hey, Al, I just remembered something. Yesterday afternoon, just when the weather was turning, I saw Drew walking down the beach on his own. Now I'm thinking . . . was that a memory lane thing? Could he have been going to meet someone? I think we should ask Kathy about it. See what kind of a mood Drew was in when he came back.'

Ally nods. 'I think Kathy would be open to talking to me again. If I bring Fox, anyway.'

'Great. Pin her down on Drew's Trebaron connection. And, Al, if things are going your way, try to find out more about that conversation with Steve too. Lock in this pension payout theory. That's two very different lines of enquiry, but both are valid at this point. Let's head back in.'

As they make their way up the beach, Ally hurries to keep up with Jayden's quick stride.

'I'm going to check in with Summer,' he says.

'Are you going to tell her what we know about Blake's past?'

He hesitates. 'I'll play it by ear. What's worrying me is that Steve is so vocal about Blake's guilt – whether he's bluffing or not. I don't think the High Tide is a good place for Summer right now. Which Louisa is going to hate me for saying, obviously.'

'Surely Louisa would understand, under the circumstances.'

'The Kings have massively different agendas. Elliott thinks we're just in it for the money and should leave the police to get on with it. And Louisa just wants her star guest to give them a rave review.'

'Well, surely that ship has sailed?'

'Sailed and sunk, Al. Sailed and sunk.'

The light rain turns heavier again, and a gusting wind tries to get its hands on Ally's hat. They quicken their step, heads down. They're almost at the hotel and Ally feels a tightening in her chest: nerves; adrenalin. Ordinarily the hotel would look inviting on a day like this – an especially elegant port in a storm – but Ally can't help feeling as if they're heading towards trouble. A place is only as good as its people.

'Jayden,' she says suddenly, 'if there is anything in Drew's Trebaron connection, and that's the blast from the past, how does that sit with our theory that the killer came from inside the hotel?'

He furrows his brow. 'Well, it'd potentially put the owners and staff front of centre. And there's nothing to say one of the guests isn't local, right? Let's explore it, then strike it from the list.'

'You sound like you don't want it to be relevant.'

'Only because, if Drew's death does connect to the past, and somehow the killer came in from the outside, then all bets are off,' says Jayden. 'Because who are our suspects?'

30

'Blake Bryant swears blind that he's innocent, and until Forensics pull their finger out, we've got nothing to say that he isn't.'

DS Skinner is in his familiar position in front of the whiteboard. Mullins swivels on his chair, gnawing the end of his pen. It tastes faintly of liquorice, but that could be the last traces of the Pontefract cakes he put away earlier. *Grandad Jack's favourite sweet; he was always clogging his chops with them.*

All around Mullins sit 'the suits'. The Major Crimes lot have whistled down from Newquay; Drew Schofield carried the badge, and the words *one of our own* are being bandied about. 'Minimum requirement is maximum effort' is the directive from DCI Robinson, which Mullins thought was how they were supposed to operate anyway.

Mullins definitely put in maximum effort when he got that intel on Blake Bryant's juvenile conviction, anyway. He shifted like a bat out of hell, slapped those cuffs on him and thought it was job done, case closed, handshakes all round. But Blake Bryant won't yield. And the worst bit? Mullins doesn't *not* believe him.

'Bryant will be spending the night in custody, but after that we can't hold him unless we make a damn good case for it,' says Skinner, his voice ripe with frustration. 'Which means either Summer Ellery reneging on her alibi, or a new witness turning up.

A sighting of Bryant in the vicinity of Schofield's room would be nice, because the only thing that video's giving us at the moment is a headache. Mullins, how are the tech team getting on with the enhancement?'

'Nothing conclusive, Sarge. It was a power cut and so the moon's the only light source. Best estimate is a male or female of moderate build, height between five foot seven and five foot eleven . . .'

'Surely they can be more exact than that?' says a voice from behind.

DS Chang, back from maternity leave. Mullins has always quite liked DS Chang. She's the only one of the Newquay lot who doesn't treat him like an idiot.

'You'd think, hey?' he says. 'But it's because of the hood. The coat has this big, bulky hood, which means it's hard to tell the exact height of the person inside it.'

'What about a trace on the coat itself? Presumably all rooms in the hotel have been searched?'

'Yup,' says Mullins.

'Bins in the vicinity?' pipes up someone else.

'Bins too,' says Mullins.

'What we're looking at,' says Skinner, 'is someone either very lucky, or very opportunistic. Thanks to the power cut, nothing's caught on CCTV. Total black hole. If it wasn't for Summer Ellery capturing her footage, the assumption would have been that Schofield went over that balcony by accident – unless the post-mortem and forensics told us otherwise. Phone records are giving us nothing worth looking at either. Let's take it back to the victim. Drew Schofield, formerly Detective Sergeant Schofield of Thames Valley CID, up until his retirement six weeks ago. Not that the press knows that yet. DS Chang, you've been speaking to our friends in Oxford, have you not?'

'I have,' she says, standing up.

DS Chang is a neat-looking woman, her dark bobbed hair smooth as a skullcap. She always looks – and sounds – like she means business. Mullins's hand goes to his midriff; it's definitely not iron-clad. He becomes acutely aware of a long streak of biro on his shirt cuff. Tim Mullins: *shabby chic.* That's the kind of thing Hippy-Dippy would say – and mean it kind of kindly. Laughing at him, but with nice eyes. Terrible combination, that. It leaves a bloke all at sea.

Sea. That dream of his rises up again. Bobbing about on surfboards. Her smile. All that flipping sunshine. He wouldn't mind slipping off for a kip now, so he can get himself back there.

'Depending on who you speak to,' says DS Chang, 'Drew Schofield was either a legend or a dinosaur. Some reckoned he was a copper's copper, old-fashioned police, a good thief-taker.'

'Good bloke,' murmurs someone at the back.

'But others thought his retirement couldn't come soon enough. That someone like Schofield wouldn't have lasted long in these days of increased accountability and regulation. He had "an edge". He stayed a DS because he "liked walking the floor". "Wasn't interested in an ivory tower." Those are verbatim quotes. Although the top brass—'

'Had a different view?' says Skinner. 'Go on, give me the "but". I sense a "but".'

'Indeed. And that "but" comes courtesy of Professional Standards. Over the years there were several allegations of excessive force, even brutality, but nothing that could be proven. For instance, a suspect comes in with bumps and bruises, but the line from Schofield is that he resisted arrest, and it was reasonable force. Joe Bloggs's front door gets kicked in, but Schofield claims he heard someone screaming inside. Turns out that screaming is just a toddler having a tantrum, and meanwhile Joe Bloggs is stuck with a bill for a broken door.'

'So no blemishes on his record?' says Skinner.

'No, but numerous questions. I can't help thinking where there's smoke there's fire.'

'That's not the attitude,' says someone from behind. 'What happened to "one of our own"?'

Mullins sends a hard look in their direction, then turns back to DS Chang.

'Did he get a good send-off? For his retirement, I mean?'

'Mullins,' tuts Skinner. 'What's that got to do with the price of apples?'

Mullins can feel his ears going: bright red, they'll be.

'Actually, it is relevant,' says DS Chang.

And now his cheeks are red too. He might actually love DS Chang a bit.

'Rumour is he was pushed out. For the last eighteen months he was put in charge of a youth crime reduction programme in south-east Oxford.'

Skinner nods. 'Classic move.'

'And for someone like Schofield, the "thief-taker and copper's copper", that's hell. And it worked: he put in for retirement.'

Though from where Mullins is standing, it doesn't sound too bad. He likes kids, even the naughty ones. He was probably one himself.

'The *Oxford Mail* went for him a few times, didn't they?' says Mullins.

'They did. And there's some names in the comments I want to follow up on as well. I'd say if this enquiry was unfolding in Oxfordshire, we'd be on to something with his, erm, chequered past. But at the High Tide Hotel? Not even Drew Schofield himself knew he was going to be here this weekend.'

'That's correct,' says Skinner. 'Magical mystery tour courtesy of his wife, Kathy. Who, for a brand-new widow, doesn't seem terribly cut up. But it's unlikely she pulled on a big coat just to go out on the balcony and shove her husband over. She could have done it in her PJs. DS Chang, I'd like you to follow up with Kathy. Find out why she picked the High Tide for this weekend. And whether she broadcast the destination to the Oxfordshire underworld.'

Cue low-level laughter.

'I'm serious,' says Skinner. 'We've only Kathy's word that she took those sleeping pills. She could know full well who was on that balcony with her husband. She could even have set it up.'

'Before that,' says DS Chang, 'I've got more. Steve Bradshaw.'

'Ah, now,' says Skinner, rubbing his hands together. 'This better be good.'

'Professional Standards confirmed that DC Bradshaw was dismissed five years ago for misconduct. Inappropriate computer misuse and breach of policy – at the least. He ran a plate, then, two days later, the vehicle owner reported major damage to his car. Bradshaw's paw prints were on the file. If not on the vehicle, otherwise the charge would have been a lot worse.'

Mullins frowns. He doesn't get it.

'So, you're saying it looks like Steve Bradshaw turned vigilante?' says someone at the back. 'Against . . . a car?'

'Well, it's something of a coincidence, isn't it?' says DS Chang. 'But he no-commented his way through the internal investigation and was subsequently dismissed.'

And now Mullins does get it.

Okay, so Steve Bradshaw is a right plonker. But is he a murderous plonker?

31

Summer takes a circuitous route to exit the hotel. The last thing she wants is to be pulled into a conversation with Louisa or Elliott. *Thank you, the flowers are beautiful. Thank you, yes, I'm sure your massages are great stress-relievers. Thank you for everything that this disastrous weekend at your hotel is currently delivering.* Actually, that's not the last thing Summer wants; that would be facing Drew Schofield's widow or his friends. Or the invasive questions of a journalist, hanging around looking for the story behind the story. The only people that she wouldn't mind seeing, in fact, are Jayden and Ally.

Summer can't help feeling that Jayden is her lifeline in all this. Because whatever awfulness has been happening at the High Tide this weekend, the one good thing is that Jayden is here too.

Summer presses her key card to the wall and slips out the side door. She hurries down a short path, and suddenly she's on the beach. As soon as her feet hit the sand, she runs like someone is chasing her. The wind catches her hair, yanking it like a bully would. At least the rain has stopped. A few steps from the water, she sheds her dry robe. As she enters the sea, the water cuts like a knife. Her skin rings with pain, and she screams.

It's guttural. Hoarse. A death cry.

No one can hear her out here, and it feels so good to get it off her chest, out of her lungs.

Summer braces herself as another wave breaks, hitting her calves, her thighs. With sudden determination, she surges forward. As she throws herself into the water, the breath is punched from her chest and it's as if her mind disappears entirely. All that remains is body, sensation, survival. She swims four, five fast strokes. Her teeth clatter. She gasps, trying to get her breathing under control. *In and out. In and out.* Her arms and legs move frantically.

She's not one of those elegant cold-water swimmers you see all over Instagram in their bobble hats and cossies, dancing into the ocean. But nevertheless, the water is giving Summer something she couldn't find on land. It's taking her out of herself. Her goose-pimpled, ice-blasted skin is shed – and all that is left is her heart's core.

Oh, Blake.

Summer's crying now, the tears hot on her cheeks. She takes a juddering breath that turns into a sob. It's useless now. She splashes towards the shore, and everything she left behind for those few minutes – *or was it only seconds?* – comes with her.

Why did they arrest him?

Why didn't he say anything to me as he was led away?

Why wasn't I his one phone call once he was in custody?

And when I phoned the police station, begging for more information, why would no one tell me anything?

Blake didn't kill Drew Schofield; Summer knows he didn't, he was right beside her all night long – except for those few brief moments when he popped to reception. But . . . what if he slipped out of the room again later, once she was asleep? That's the malignant thought that creeps into her head, one she hasn't voiced to even Jayden and Ally. What if, in that disturbed night, where she tossed and turned and fretted, she did, in fact, fall into a small hole of sleep. A sudden, deep drop?

No. Because she would *know*, wouldn't she?

But Summer can't get past Blake's mood change. She can't get past her other worry – so inconsequential, compared to life and death – that, yesterday, Blake stopped wanting to be with her. It was like a switch had been flipped and he looked at her and thought, *You? Yeah, not for me.*

Summer kicks through the shallows, the water snarling at her ankles. Already she's thinking of the warmth of her dry robe, the quick walk up the beach, avoiding reception and going in through that side door then straight into a hot shower. Okay, so those four walls will start closing in on her again, these spiked thoughts will pain her once more, but she will, at least, be warm.

Summer jogs with her head down, her breath coming in huffs. Her feet – tanned from all her travels – look shrunken and pale.

She senses someone else's presence before she sees them.

Just a feeling.

She looks up sharply from her sad feet, and there they are. It's a man – and it takes Summer a moment to realise that he's holding her dry robe. The gesture already feels like a violation.

Then, for the second time in short order, the breath is slammed from her. Because she realises it's the dead man's friend.

Summer wraps her arms around herself; the breeze is needles on her wet skin. Despite her swimming costume, she feels completely naked.

The girls at school hid her swimming towel once. She tried so hard not to cry as she rooted through her bag, hunted under all the benches in the changing room, said, pathetically, *Have you seen my towel?* She had to dry herself on her school jumper and was the last to leave the pool, the last to get on the bus, and all the seats were taken except for one right at the back – in the middle of them all.

Come on, it was a different life.

Summer holds the man's eye. When she tries to speak, she realises the bottom half of her face doesn't work properly. Her teeth chatter, banging together as if they're going to break.

'C-c-can I have th-that?'

But he doesn't reply. And he doesn't hand back her coat.

32

When there's no answer at Summer's bedroom door, Jayden heads down to reception. Louisa has her head bent over a glossy magazine and she's frowning.

'Can you believe it? A piece on luxury UK coastal breaks and we're not included.'

'Disaster,' says Jayden.

'You simply can't rest on your laurels in this business,' she rolls on, as if she hasn't heard. 'It's non-stop PR. That's why Summer is so important to us.'

'Talking of . . . have you seen Summer, Louisa?'

'No, I haven't. Now that the story's on the local news I imagine she's keeping a low profile. There were two journalists sniffing around earlier. And a photographer. I told them it was private property, and they had to leave.' She snaps her head up. 'My God, you're not worried about Summer, are you? Now that *would* be bad press.'

She laughs nervously, and Jayden moves on past her. The doors part soundlessly.

Summer is allowed to leave the hotel. She could have been contacted by the police and be on her way to the station. She could have just gone for a walk to clear her head. But Jayden's messaged her, and she hasn't replied – and that feels off.

As Jayden heads outside, he glances up at the balconies. A light rain is falling, and no one is out. He zips his coat up and quickens his stride. It's low tide and the water feels miles away, but he can see a small figure down on the shore. They look so lonely, he thinks. A twig, buffeted by all that sea and sky. Is it Summer? It could be.

Maybe what she needs right now is to be alone with the sea. Part of him doesn't want to interrupt this moment she's given herself. He knows that people like Cat and Saffron see spirituality in the ocean. Not so Jayden, but he does like the way it empties his head out.

As he moves closer, the figure shifts, and he sees it's not one person, but two.

Summer – and who?

Maybe she called a friend to join her.

But instinctively, Jayden lengthens his stride, because he's still thinking about Steve Bradshaw. The way Steve said *tail between her legs* in a way that was half salacious and half vicious.

As Jayden gets closer, he sees it *is* Steve. Steve in a big coat – a green coat with a furry hood, not the one in the video – and he's holding something in his hands. *A blanket?*

And Jayden's running.

Because he can see that Summer's pulling at it; the wind whipping her hair across her face, leaning back like it's a tug-of-war. The wind switches direction and Jayden hears her cry out.

He shouts out, 'Leave her alone!'

Steve wheels round, letting his hands drop. Then he holds them up, as though he's under arrest. His mouth is laughing but, as Jayden reaches them, his eyes are hard as stone.

'What, a bloke can't help a lady with her jacket these days?'

Summer presses the coat to her body. She's shivering, her hair soaked. Her lips are close to blue. Jayden's quick to her side.

'Summer, are you okay?'

She nods. He gets the feeling that if she tried to speak, she wouldn't be able to. She's trying to wrestle the coat on, but she's shaking. Her arms won't go in.

'Want a hand?' he asks softly, not wanting to riff on Steve. Steve, who he'll deal with in a minute.

Summer is crying now. Tears course down her cheeks and something wrenches inside of him. Jayden gently helps her into the coat, then wraps an arm around her shoulders. She leans into him, burying her face in his shoulder.

'Ah, I see,' says Steve. 'I get what this is. There's a reason your lady wife went home early, is there?'

'You need to leave now, Steve.'

'I don't need to do anything, mate.'

'I know you're upset about Drew.'

'You don't know the first thing about me.'

Jayden's well trained in de-escalation. Back in the day he broke up enough verbal battles that were just tipping to physical, enough full-blown fights. But there were also the times where the intervention of a third party – a third party you didn't want to get on the wrong side of or you'd be facing charges – only made a bad situation worse. The badge counted for little then.

And I don't have a badge.

'Come on,' he says to Summer. 'Let's go.'

Because sometimes the best thing to do is walk away.

'Her boyfriend's a killer,' says Steve. 'You're alright with that, are you? Or is that the point? She likes the bad boys. Are you a bad boy, Jayden? That why you were booted out, is it?' He laughs nastily. 'Dishonourably discharged, was it?'

They keep walking.

'I said, is that why you were booted out?'

Steve plants his hand on Jayden's shoulder, and he shakes him off.

'It's alright,' he says quietly to Summer, 'just keep walking.'

'You're not trying to solve this case, mate,' shouts Steve – and he's close, Jayden's skin prickles at how close he is – 'you're just trying to get an easy—'

Jayden spins round. He takes his phone from his pocket.

'Back off, Steve. Or I'm calling the police.'

Steve laughs cruelly. 'We are the police. You and me. So what are they going to do that we can't, mate?' He holds out a finger; taps Jayden hard on his chest. 'You and me. Let's go.'

Jayden's hand, the one that's not holding his phone, curls into a fist.

Steve's face is leering; daring him. Jayden imagines the feeling of landing a punch: the split second of temporary satisfaction. He's only hit someone once in his life. He was eleven years old, and there was a kid at school who wouldn't stop calling his family names. He can still remember the feeling of the boy's nose giving way beneath his fist. The shock of the jetting blood. *I'd have done the same, son*, his dad said to him before bed that night. To which Jayden's mum, in a voice he'd never heard her use before, said, *But you wouldn't have to, John.*

The finger in his chest becomes a palm – a shove.

Summer is beside him, crying again now.

A rush of blood to his head.

Jayden steps back, fingers itching.

'Police.'

The voice is clear and cool and crisp, and as welcome as any he's ever heard. Jayden sucks in a breath as Mullins the archangel comes lumbering over the sand.

33

'Ally, I still haven't told her.'

Kathy ushered her into the room this time as though they were old friends. Fox played his part, bumping Kathy's legs, slipping his nose into her outstretched hand. Now, they sit in the lounge area as, outside, light rain patters the windowpane.

'Drew's mother,' she says. 'Is it very silly that I'm afraid to do it?'

It's warm in the room but Kathy shivers, pulling her cardigan tightly around her.

'I think that's understandable,' says Ally. 'It's a telephone call no one should have to make.'

Tell a mother that their son has died? Even if that son is fifty-five, Drew will doubtless still be a child to her. It's the same with Evie, all the way on the other side of the world in Sydney. When Ally worries for her daughter, she feels a physical ache. She would take any pain from her, if she could. And die for her? Without question. That's what Bill said, that first morning in the hospital, as he held their daughter in his arms. Evie was a prune in a crocheted blanket, mouth pinching and crying blue murder. *I'd die for this child, Ally.* A look of such loving ferocity on his face.

'Ally,' says Kathy, 'you're sort of police, aren't you? Could you stay here with me while I do it?'

'Of course I will. Kathy, I'm not police, though.'

'I know who you are. I looked you up. You're better than them, I'll bet. In some ways. Some . . . important ways.'

Kathy looks as if she's about to say more but then stops. She stares down at the phone in her hand. She has an expression of trepidation on her face, as if her mother-in-law is already on the line.

'Margaret has a sharp tongue. Like mother like son. It doesn't help that I'm so timid . . . I encourage it, you see. The sharpness.'

And Kathy's demeanour is so defeated, so resigned, that Ally wonders if this is Drew speaking.

'You'll feel better once you've made the call,' she says. She looks towards the elegant table, the sleek silver kettle and arrangement of luxury teas and coffees. 'How about I put the kettle on? We'll have a nice cup of tea afterwards.'

'That's kind.'

Ally thinks of the questions she came to ask. If Kathy's rattled after speaking to Drew's mother, the moment may be lost.

'Kathy, before you use the phone, there's something I want to ask you. Drew went for a walk yesterday, didn't he? In the late afternoon. Do you know where he was going?'

'He said he needed to stretch his legs after the drive. That was all.'

'Was he gone for long?'

'Not really. Thirty, forty minutes.'

Which is quite long, for a beach walk in foul weather.

'And he didn't mention seeing anyone he knew?'

Kathy shakes her head.

'It's only that you said that Drew used to come here on holiday, and I wondered if he was retreading old paths. Did he actually stay at Trebaron Cove?'

'He did, yes. So Margaret said.'

Kathy's eyes go to the phone in her hand, and Ally takes the hint. Her question about Steve and the payout will have to wait.

'I'll get the kettle boiling. You call.'

Ally discreetly moves away, while sending Kathy a look of kindly encouragement. She notices how the woman sits so stiffly, chewing at her lip. Kathy holds the phone to her ear while the other pinches at the fabric of her trousers.

Margaret Schofield appears to answer almost straight away.

'Margaret, hello. It's Kathy.'

And then Kathy goes a long time without saying anything. Ally wonders if Drew's mother has already heard the news, but his name hasn't been released in the media yet. Has Margaret heard from some other source?

'I'm sorry your hip's playing up again,' says Kathy, without a trace of contrition. Ally turns away slightly, so she doesn't look as if she's listening. But her ears are pricked, surprised at the change in Kathy's tone.

She hears Kathy deliver the facts of Drew's death: the trip to Cornwall; the balcony; the police. Ally has to admit, she does it quite well. There's a coldness, but it seems that Kathy knows, deep down, just how to handle her mother-in-law – however much she dreads doing it. But then she hears Kathy gasp suddenly, and Ally turns back.

Kathy's free hand is held to her mouth and her eyes are closed. Ally can hear the timbre of a distant but clearly raised voice coming through the receiver. Margaret evidently has a lot to say.

'I'm sorry,' whispers Kathy. 'I'm . . . sorry.'

But Margaret goes on. Words reach Ally's ears, jumping as if from a spitting pan: *stupid*; *typical*; *my son*. And Kathy crumples.

Ally watches as the phone slips from Kathy's fingers and falls to the floor. She hurries over, the woman sending her a beseeching look, whispering *please*.

Ally picks up the phone.

'Hello, Mrs Schofield?' She hesitates. 'It's Ally Bright here. A friend of Kathy's.'

She's met with silence, and for a second Ally thinks the other woman has hung up, or the phone disconnected as it fell. Then she hears a huff of breath.

'Fainted, did she?' snaps Drew's mother.

'Kathy's very upset,' says Ally, 'as I'm sure you are too. I'm so sorry for your loss, Mrs Schofield.'

More silence.

'Thank you,' says the voice eventually. Then, 'Thank you, dear. And call me Margaret, for goodness' sake.'

Ally notices the honeyed tone. This is, undoubtedly, a different Margaret to the one who just spoke to Kathy. It's understandable if manners go out the window in a moment like this, but from the way Kathy curled in on herself, Margaret delivered body blows.

'Drew would love that the police are investigating,' says Margaret conversationally. 'He'll send his old mates a message from beyond the grave if there's anything to know.'

She sounds perversely cheerful.

'But he'll have had a heart attack and gone over,' she says. 'That's what it'll be. He drank like a fish, just like his father. Used to be on forty a day too. Fifty-five years old, that's nothing in today's money, but it's more than he probably should have had.'

Ally keeps her counsel.

'At least he was in a place he loved,' says Margaret. 'I will say that. Just along from Porthpella, she said. Trebaron Cove?'

'That's right.'

'My goodness, we had happy times there. I had no idea he was going back there after all these years. That's my son, though, always held his cards close. Course, we wouldn't have stayed anywhere as fancy as that hotel on the beach. We were caravanners, us lot. Three families together. Every summer we went.'

Ally hears her take a rasping breath.

'They were golden days.'

Ally looks to Kathy. She's holding the kettle in her hand as if she doesn't know what to do with it. Ally suspects that Margaret conversing so amiably with a total stranger is a deliberate move to undermine her daughter-in-law. She feels sorry for Kathy, but this opportunity might not come again. Because Ally the Detective is thinking of Kathy's account of Drew being so sullen in the car as they crossed into Cornwall; his complaints growing worse as he saw where they were staying. Were they really such golden days?

'Memories like that are so precious,' says Ally, moving to the window. 'So . . . Drew loved Cornwall, did he? And Trebaron Cove especially?'

'Of course he did. And we all missed it when we stopped going.'

Far below, Ally notices a movement down on the beach. Two figures. No, three. But at this distance, she can't make them out.

'But it lost its shine after what happened to that poor boy. A great shame. None of us saw it quite the same way again. It hit Drew hard.'

A flicker of possibility. Like glimpsing shoreline treasure through a tangle of bladderwrack. *What poor boy?*

'And it hit the others too. Especially Rebecca, bless her. We started going to Tenby and that was it. Though Rebecca's family said they didn't care for Wales and so there was a splintering. Inevitable, I suppose; the kids were all but grown by then. Such a pity, though. Lovely girl, she was. I always thought she and Drew would marry one day. So very different to Kathy in every way, was Rebecca.'

Margaret's conversation zigzags, but Ally holds on; tracks back.

'The boy you mentioned,' says Ally, 'what happened to him?'

Because it might be nothing, or it might be something.

'He got himself drowned. Stuck in a cave and the tide came in. Not like my son . . . His health failing him . . .' Margaret's voice wobbles for the first time. 'Well, Drew had a good few years more than that lad, didn't he? Forty more, near enough.'

'So was it 1985, the last year you came here on holiday?'

'No, later than that. It'd have been 1988. Drew turned eighteen later that summer.'

'And the boy who died,' says Ally, 'can you remember his name?'

'No, no. I tried hard to forget him, if I'm honest, and I expect Drew did too. But Drew always loved Trebaron Cove, and I'm glad that's stayed with him all these years. At least there's that. Here, are you on the email, Alison?'

'Do I have email? Yes, I do.'

'Tell me it, will you? Let me write it down. I might be ancient but I'm no technophobe. Whatever that useless daughter-in-law of mine says.'

So Ally gives Margaret her address, half wondering what she's getting into.

'I'll send you a picture of Drew at Trebaron Cove. You'll see him in his heyday then. I've got it framed here. In fact, I'm looking at it now, the whole gang of them. That dear Rebecca with all her red hair. And my boy. My handsome boy.' Her voice splinters. 'Tell Kathy she needs to pull herself together. She'd do well to remember that I'm the mother who's lost a son here. And there's nothing more terrible in the world than that.'

Then she's gone.

Ally looks towards the water as she lets the conversation settle in her mind: Margaret's initial response to Kathy, then her pragmatism, forced or otherwise; her flurry of reminiscences.

'Thank you for taking over,' says Kathy quietly. 'What on earth was she going on about?'

But, as the figures on the beach come clearly into view, Ally hardly hears. She opens the balcony door, the wind buffeting her as she steps out.

Mullins has a man in handcuffs. He stops every moment and waits, as though the man is a stubborn donkey, digging his hooves in. Jayden and Summer follow behind.

Beside Ally, Kathy leans on the railing.

'Oh, Steve,' says Kathy quietly. 'What have you gone and done now?'

34

'I overreacted,' says Summer. 'I should have handled it.'

'You didn't overreact. And no one should have to handle a situation like that.'

Louisa has responded to the scene on the beach by offering an in-room massage, off-menu room service – *Anything you want, Summer! Childhood favourite? Our chef will oblige!* Even a 'sound bath' from a boho-luxe therapist based along the coast. But Summer said that all she really wanted was to be left alone. To which she added, *Not by you, Jayden, I don't mean you.*

Now, as if Summer is Jazzy, Jayden is running a bath for her. The door to the bathroom is open and there's the comforting sound of the tub filling. Summer sits in a dressing gown, a towel around her sea-wet hair.

'If I'm honest, I don't feel very safe here,' she says.

'I get that.'

If Mae decides it's her turn to talk to Summer, how can Jayden stop her? And what about Kathy? At least Jayden doesn't have to worry about Summer having another run-in with Steve Bradshaw, because Steve has been arrested by Mullins and taken down to the station. Steve didn't take kindly to Mullins's intervention on the beach, so he turned the same dumb aggression on him, and before he knew it, 'resisting arrest' was added to the ex-cop's achievements for the day. Then *actual* arrest. Because when Steve laughed in the constable's face, shouting *on what charge?*, a flurry of spittle landed across Mullins's cheeks. Deliberate? *Meh.* But Mullins was in no mood to take it. *Assaulting a police officer too now, eh?* he said with a tut. And for the second time in just a few short minutes, Jayden was a little bit in love with Mullins.

'Is there anywhere else you'd rather be, Summer?' he asks her.

Summer offers him a thin smile. 'Try . . . anywhere.'

'Have you still got family locally, or friends?'

It seems a pointless question, because if she did, wouldn't she have gone there already? Summer just shakes her head.

'My parents aren't around anymore.' Then, after a pause, 'And . . . I lost touch with school people.'

'Maybe you could come to ours,' says Jayden. 'You could meet the kids. Cat would like that.'

Summer rubs her finger along the hem of her dressing gown, worrying at it.

'Cat and I were never really friends,' she says quietly.

Jayden offers her an easy grin. 'Well, neither were you and me, but look at us now.'

But Summer doesn't respond. She seems to have slipped into her own world.

'I didn't have a great time at school, Jayden.'

He waits, sensing more coming.

'I didn't look like I do now. I was . . . big for my age. Puberty hit early. I was kind of clumsy.' She darts a quick look at him. 'And girls can be really mean.'

Jayden feels his brow furrowing. 'Not Cat, though?'

A stupid question to ask, really. And shamefully leading.

'No, not Cat. She was always just . . . oblivious. Doing her thing. One of those happy people who thinks everyone else is happy too.'

Jayden nods, wanting to show he understands without being disloyal.

'She was probably going through her own stuff too,' he says. 'Everyone always is. But we forget that when we're young. Or we just haven't figured it out yet.'

Summer looks up; tucks her hair behind her ear.

'And all bullies are cowards? Sad and troubled and we should feel sorry for them?' Her voice has an edge to it. 'Yeah, I didn't have that level of empathy when I was thirteen. And most of the girls I knew didn't even have the basic kind.' She sighs. 'Sorry,' she says, her voice softening. 'I changed schools, and it was a bit better at the new place. Or maybe my expectations were just set super-low by then. I worked hard for my GCSEs and A levels, spent most of the time in the library, and soon as I could, I got out of there. Went travelling.'

'Is that how the travel blogging started?'

'I loved it. No one knew me. I could be who I wanted. Go where I wanted. And I had money . . .' She worries at the hem of her dressing gown again. 'Dad had died by then, and my mum left a few years back, so . . . I sold the house. And, well, I've been on the move ever since. When I met Blake, it was the first time I felt like I wanted to settle down. But now . . . I'm just doubting everything.'

'But not his innocence?'

Because, beyond Blake's word, it's only Summer saying Blake didn't leave the room all night long. Before Mullins took Steve Bradshaw off in the patrol car, he and Jayden had a chat – Jayden had sent Summer in ahead to start warming up – and the constable confirmed that it was Drew Schofield who'd arrested Blake back in the day. And even though it was what Jayden had basically guessed, the intel still hit hard.

No wonder they clapped the cuffs on Blake.

Summer hesitates, then says, 'No, not his innocence. My head's trying to trip me up, spinning all these "what if?" lines, but my heart knows. He didn't do it, Jayden.'

'Summer, we know why the police brought Blake in,' he says.

Her mouth drops. 'Tell me.'

'You're sure? You don't want to hear it from Blake?'

'I want to hear it from you.'

So, Jayden tells her what he knows as gently as he can. And he makes sure to flag that there are a whole lot of things they *don't* know.

'You're saying he went to prison,' says Summer, 'for GBH?'

'He was a juvenile,' says Jayden. 'It was "without intent". We don't know the circumstances . . .'

'And it was Drew Schofield who sent him there?'

Summer's eyes are wide and swimming. Jayden has the impression that he can see right through her: all the way into her doubt, her confusion. But then something else . . . something he can't get a read on.

It can't be relief, can it?

'He looked defeated,' she says, 'but it makes sense now. Blake must have seen him and . . . freaked out. I just . . . I just wish he could have talked to me. Before all this. Or way back, when we started going out. But we didn't talk about our teenage years, we just didn't, and . . . Jayden, does it look bad for him?'

'They might hold him for twenty-four hours,' says Jayden. 'They've enough circumstantial evidence for that.' *More than enough.* 'But Blake won't have anything to worry about if he's telling the truth.'

'That's not always how it goes, though, is it?'

Jayden hesitates.

'And this is the death of a retired police officer. They'll be going all out . . . and Blake's got violence in his past. And an obvious reason to have a grudge against Drew Schofield.'

'Whoever went to Drew's room,' says Jayden, 'the timing on your video confirms it was during the power cut. So that's opportunism. Or maybe luck. But if it was a snap decision to confront Drew, then I'd be really surprised if there's no evidence at the scene. Crimes of passion are messy, chaotic. Forensics will prove who was on that balcony with Drew. Any motive that Blake might have on paper pales in the face of hard evidence, Summer.'

'Promise?'

Jayden hesitates again. Then says, 'Promise.'

'God,' says Summer. 'I thought . . . I thought Blake wanted to break up with me. I thought that's why he was suddenly acting strangely.'

So that's the relief.

'As if,' smiles Jayden.

Then her tears start falling.

'You're kind,' she says, wiping her sleeve across her eyes. 'You wanted to hit him, didn't you? The man on the beach. Steve Bradshaw.'

Jayden rubs at the back of his head. 'Nearly,' he says.

'See, people can control themselves, can't they? It is possible.' She shakes her hair loose of the towel. 'You're a good man, Jayden.'

The sound of the bath suddenly changes tenor, and Jayden jumps up. He gets to the taps just as the water is about to slop over the edges.

'Yeah, so, your bath's ready,' he calls out with a laugh, and when he turns, she's right there behind him.

'Thank you. For telling me about Blake. For being honest. It's hard to hear but . . . I'm grateful.'

Jayden's aware of her proximity. The clouds of steam in the bathroom. The way she's looking at him from beneath her lashes. The room suddenly feels very small.

'I always knew Cat would end up with someone great.'

'Hey, it's what Ally and I are here for. Right, I'm going to leave you to it . . .'

'Jayden.'

Her hand is on his shoulder. Her dressing gown gapes as she leans towards him.

'Sorry,' he says, 'I've got to go.'

And Jayden darts past her. As he crosses the bedroom, he whacks his knee on the corner of the coffee table and his thought from the beach comes back to him: *Sometimes the best thing to do is walk away.* Or run smack into a blunt object.

35

Ally is looking at a young Drew Schofield. She enlarges the image on her phone, zooming in on his face. He could be anywhere between fifteen and twenty, one of those boys who already looks like a man. His jaw is set determinedly and his eyes gaze directly into the camera. *Glowering* – that's the word.

There are five teenagers in the photograph, and they're clustered together looking thick as thieves. Drew is in the middle and beside him must be the girl Margaret spoke so fondly of. *Rebecca.* Rebecca has long auburn hair and a freckled face. The other boys are laughing, their faces caught in motion, but Drew is perfectly still – with all of his sharp edges. And Rebecca? She's mid-twist, one hand lifted; her fingers blurred. Ally zooms in on this section of the picture and sees Drew's hand planted firmly around her waist.

She's pulling away from him.

Margaret loves this photograph, thinking it so evocative of the golden days that she keeps it close to hand – on a mantelpiece, perhaps, or a bedside table. Her son and his friends having the time of their lives at Trebaron Cove. But Ally thinks there's something unsettling about Drew and Rebecca's pose.

Her eyes pull to the window. The tide is making its steady way in. A couple stroll with their heads down against the wind, their dog flying ahead of them. After what happened with Steve Bradshaw, Jayden saw Summer safely inside. And Mullins took Steve off in the patrol car. So, it's official: Steve Bradshaw is bad news. But now he's in the hands of Devon and Cornwall Police, and whether he's bad news enough to kill his friend will be answered by them.

Where does that leave their investigation? Perhaps with this photograph. Because Ally can't stop thinking about the fact that Margaret's take on her son's relationship to Trebaron Cove is so different to what Kathy observed of Drew's behaviour here. Isn't that just the kind of anomaly that Jayden talks about? The piece of the picture that doesn't fit.

As they made their way down to the beach earlier, Kathy preternaturally untroubled about Steve's arrest, Ally brought up the Cornwall connection again.

Kathy, did Drew ever tell you how much he loved coming here as a boy?

Kathy stopped, her hand on the banister.

No. I took a punt. Margaret told me once, and I stored it away. I just thought it'd be lovely for us to go somewhere meaningful. I mean, I know he's not sentimental, but I was surprised when it turned out he couldn't care less about the place.

But Drew wasn't devoid of feeling. Because Kathy clearly said that his mood got worse as he saw where they were staying. Perhaps Drew was every bit as wistful about Rebecca as his mother. Perhaps Trebaron Cove held an unpleasant memory: the path not taken.

Perhaps, perhaps. Not for the first time, Ally wishes the dead could speak. For all the wizardry of forensics, Drew's feelings can't be known. All they have are other people's perceptions.

The door opens and it's Jayden. Jayden looking unusually flustered. As he drops into a chair his hand goes to his knee, and he rubs it.

'Are you alright?'

'Whacked it. Right on the bone.' He puffs his cheeks out. 'All good, Al. So, what's happening?'

She sends him a questioning look. There's a strange energy to her friend. Perhaps the confrontation on the beach is still sitting uneasily for him.

'You seem . . . agitated.'

He rubs the back of his neck. 'Summer's emotions are all over the shop. I don't think it's a great idea her staying at the hotel tonight.'

Her boyfriend arrested; her relationship destabilised; harassed on the beach by a possible murder suspect. If her emotions are awry, it's no wonder.

'The info you texted me from Mullins, that it was Drew who arrested Blake . . . I know we suspected as much but is it making you doubt Blake, Jayden? Or, rather, is it making you doubt Summer too?'

'No, it's not that. By the way, I told Summer about Blake's juvenile conviction. I didn't plan to, but it would have felt like withholding if I didn't.'

'How did she take it?'

'Actually . . . she took it well. I *think*. It's hard to explain, but I think it squared off a few things for her, like why he was acting weirdly the day before. She really did think that the problem was with her and their relationship. So yeah . . . All good. But I am concerned for her being here.'

'Does she have anywhere else she can go?'

He shakes his head. 'No. We could find her another hotel, I guess.'

'What about Cat? If they know one another, could you put her up for the night?'

'No, that wouldn't work,' he says quickly. 'Our place is so small. And it's not exactly relaxing with a toddler and a baby in the mix. That'd do anyone's head in.'

Ally narrows her eyes. Jayden's usual style is to offer solutions, not problems. He's glass-half-full.

'What about The Shell House?' he asks tentatively, his eyes not quite meeting hers.

And it's not without precedent. After the Rockpool House case last summer, their client stayed with Ally in the dunes. But the memory is complex; tainted. Could Ally host Summer at The Shell House? Well, yes. There's fresh linen in the spare room. She could pick a sprig of gorse flowers and set them in a vase beside the bed. The young woman's company the next morning, over coffee, with the rising sun, might be rather nice.

'She'd be welcome,' says Ally.

'You sure? I just think she'd be safer away from here. Kathy and Mae are still in the mix. Louisa means well – actually, I'm not sure she does – but she's massively intense. I think distance would be good. Just for tonight, Al. Blake'll be released tomorrow morning – hopefully – then they can go on their way. Try to put this behind them. Are you sure it's okay?'

'Of course.'

'Legend. I'll message her. Unless, Al, you want to go and . . . ?' He shakes his head. 'No, all good. I'll message her.'

He sighs and sits back; one hand still on his knee.

'Jayden, can we talk about Steve Bradshaw? What are your thoughts now?'

'The polite version? I think he's a deeply unpleasant individual and it's a good thing he's out of the force.' He sits forward again, reanimated. 'But even with our speculation around the retirement payout, I don't think he killed Drew Schofield.'

'Because if he did, he'd be incredibly foolish to draw attention to himself like he did at the beach?'

'Got it in one. There's always the chance he is that dumb but . . . I'm not feeling it. Anyway, it's for the police now, and for once I don't mind that it's out of our hands. I told Mullins about our twenty-five per cent theory, by the way. Because whether Steve killed Drew or not, I think he wanted to get his hands on Drew's money.'

'Was Mullins interested?'

'You know our mate Mullins. Hard to tell.'

Ally smiles. But she also knows that Mullins will take the theory to Skinner nevertheless.

'Okay, so . . . I've got a new lead,' she says. '*Maybe.*'

And she holds up her phone with the old holiday photograph.

'Who am I looking at?' says Jayden.

'You're looking at Drew Schofield and his friends. Here at Trebaron Cove.'

Five minutes later and Ally has told Jayden all she knows, from the girl Margaret Schofield thought Drew should have married, to the sea cave tragedy.

'Was the boy who drowned one of their friends?'

Ally shrugs. 'Margaret didn't dwell on him, other than his death being the blight on their holiday. I don't know if he was a tourist or a local.'

'Tide catching someone unawares in a sea cave? I'd guess tourist. The story doesn't ring a bell with you? Porthpella's only round the corner.'

'Margaret says it was in 1988, so we'd been here a few years by then. I've been racking my brain, but I can't remember it.'

'I wonder if Elliott remembers. He's younger than Drew, but not by too many years. And Elliott grew up here, didn't he? I read that on the hotel website somewhere – that the King family started this hotel years back.'

'So you agree we should look into it?'

'It's a link between Drew and the area. It's definitely worth looking at.' He nods, as if thinking to himself. 'Plus, the death of the boy is a traumatic event, which means big emotions, right? Big emotions can equal crimes of passion. Whoever killed Drew, I think there has to have been an element of chance involved. He's an out-of-towner, and no one knew he was coming here. *Drew* didn't even know he was coming here. I don't see how his death could have been planned and plotted, unless one of his inner circle is the killer.'

Jayden hesitates; rubs at the back of his head.

'And if one of his Oxford gang wanted him dead – or anyone, in fact – would they pick a balcony fall as a method for murder?'

'I think I probably would,' says Ally. 'Because if it wasn't for Summer's video, there's a good chance it would have looked like an accident.'

'Not if it was planned, though, Al. There are too many variables with it, right? Too many things can go wrong. Like trying to shove Drew but not having the strength to actually get him over. Or Drew surviving the fall. It's way too risky, in my opinion, unless you can be one hundred per cent sure he's going to go over – and then be dead from the fall.'

'So if the murder wasn't planned, then it happened in the heat of the moment?'

'Exactly,' says Jayden. 'Let's say someone went to Drew's room last night, wanting to talk to him, perhaps scare him. And it escalated. Drew went off the balcony and died.'

'Is that still murder, then?' asks Ally.

'If the confrontation can be proven, yes. And the video evidence is part of that. So, what we're looking for now is someone with an emotional connection to Drew. Someone for whom a crime of passion isn't out of the question, right? It could have been Blake – but I don't think it was. It could have been Steve – but, despite everything, I don't think it was. It could have been Mae, but I can't see a motive. And it could have been Kathy.'

'I don't think it was Kathy.'

'So where does that leave us? Maybe who we're looking for is someone connected to Drew's past. He's got a few enemies, by the sounds of it, but they're all up in Oxford. So then we're looking here, aren't we? The High Tide. Trebaron Cove. Around Porthpella. And you're saying the last summer that Drew was here, way, way back, a boy died?' Jayden takes a breath. 'Yeah, it's definitely worth exploring. Okay, let's divide and conquer. One of us goes to talk to Elliott, while the other gets into some desk research. Preference?'

'You've had a busy last hour, Jayden,' says Ally. 'How about you stay here with a coffee and do the desk research? I'll go and talk to Elliott and Louisa.'

And Ally's surprised by the look of gratitude that crosses Jayden's face. The scene on the beach must have taken it out of him.

'In fact, it's gone lunchtime, why don't you order some room service? I know the prices are steep but surely our funds will stretch to that?' she says with a smile. 'Desk research always best fuelled by . . .' She picks up the menu from the coffee table, scans her eyes down the list. 'Steak burger and thrice-cooked chips? Sticky toffee pudding?'

'I could do a sticky toffee pudding. Get my blood sugar back up.'

'So, it's medicinal. Quite right.'

'Thanks, Al. I need to check in with Cat too.'

Jayden is always a loving husband, but Ally's noticed that since the tough start to Benji's infancy he's even more attentive. She remembers their embrace as Cat left, her words: *Take care*. Taking care is relative when there's a case at stake – and the murderous to pursue.

'And . . . good luck with Elliott, okay, Al? Louisa's more forthcoming, but it's Elliott who's been here man and boy.'

A sudden thought lands.

'Jayden, Elliott King is the only person who knew in advance that Drew was coming to stay at the High Tide and was also, in all likelihood, here the same summer that the boy died.'

Jayden raises his eyebrows. 'Nice, Al. And I definitely detect a resistance in Elliott. The guy doesn't want us here. But . . . if you owned this place, wouldn't you do your dirty work elsewhere?'

'But how many chances would there feasibly be? You saw Drew walking down on the beach, but other than that, what sort of opportunity could present itself?'

'Yeah, you're right. And I'm contradicting myself anyway, because I don't think this murder was planned. So, there's no strategy at play, is there? So . . . Okay. Elliott King. He goes to Drew's room during the blackout, a conversation escalates, he panics . . .' Jayden shrugs. He doesn't look convinced by the idea. 'What's Elliott's motive?'

'Something about that summer. If the boy who died in the cave was a tourist, he could have been a guest at the High Tide. Perhaps he and Elliott were even friends.'

'You said 1988, right? Elliott would have been a little kid, Al.'

'You're right. I asked Kathy about Drew's walk, by the way. He was gone for thirty to forty minutes. He said he wanted to stretch his legs after the long drive. Tell me again the direction he was walking in?'

'He was heading down the beach on the right side.'

'Did you see him come back up?'

'Steve Bradshaw distracted me,' says Jayden with a roll of his eyes. 'And I wasn't paying attention to Drew at that point. He wasn't dead.'

'Well, quite.' She smiles wryly.

'Go into the chat with Elliott eyes wide open, Al. You're right about that double connection: past and present.'

'Are you sure you don't want to talk to him with me?' she says.

Jayden hesitates, then says, 'No. No, let's keep it light. If he does have anything to hide, we don't want him thinking we're on to him.'

Ally nods. She can do light. She suddenly remembers Gus's request, and the fact that she hasn't got back to him. But when she asks Jayden, he looks sceptical.

'Shadowing us at the hotel? He did great, but the Oxford connection feels less relevant now. And if we're honestly starting to suspect the husband of our client . . . ? No, best will in the world, tell Gus to stay at his desk and get on with his book, Al.'

She stands up. As much as Ally hates to let Gus down, his request does feel like another form of procrastination. She calls for Fox, but her dog shows no sign of moving. He's busy snoozing with his head on his paws.

'My assistant,' says Jayden, nodding to him. 'He's got work to do here too. Unless you want him with you?' He winks. 'Instead of a Gus?'

'I'm fine on my own,' she says with a pointed smile.

36

Mullins is waiting for the station kettle to boil. He drums his fingers on the countertop as his mum's voice comes into his head: *Watched pots, Tim, watched pots.* Not that he's in a hurry. They've got all the time in the world now that this case is near enough closed. Alright, maybe that's exaggerating, but let's just say it doesn't look good for Steve Bradshaw.

Which means it does look better for Blake Bryant. But they're still hanging on to him – you know, to be sure.

'Enough in there for me too?'

DS Chang has her own mug, one of those trendy-looking travel-cup things. She waves a tea bag that isn't builder's or even Earl Grey (which Skinner occasionally dips a toe in the water of, when nobody's looking).

'Peace tea,' she says. 'Want one?'

'Peace tea?'

It sounds dodgy to Mullins. Like wacky baccy in cup form; something for the darker side of Hippy-Dippy. Not that she has a dark side, that girl, but given that she's hanging out with that little street-rat graffiti artist, who knows? Mullins wasted a good hour a few nights ago reading an interview with Milo Nash in some grungy online magazine. Why exactly? Who knows. Maybe he was looking for a chink in the kid's armour. Or maybe Mullins just has nothing better to do.

Was his surf lesson dream that same night? Or another?

'Camomile, ginger and lemon. I swear by it,' she says, smiling. 'I reckon you could do with a cup after nicking Steve Bradshaw.'

'Yeah, he did not go quietly.'

She's married, DS Chang, two kiddies, and she's obviously not in the least bit interested in Tim Mullins. But it's a sign of his current love life – as dry and empty as the Sahara – that his cheeks burn up a bit as she talks to him.

'The sarge is in with him now,' he adds.

'Nice timing with forensics coming back on those prints of his. All over the crime scene, including the balcony. You didn't want in on this one?'

Mullins shrugs. Says airily, 'I think Luke's stepped up.'

One of the DCs from Newquay, who's been following Skinner around like a lap dog.

'The financial motivation was a good thought, Tim,' says DS Chang. 'It's a workable theory that Bradshaw was blackmailing Schofield to get a chunk of his retirement payout. As his partner, he'd have seen how Schofield operated on the street and heard those rumours of excessive force too. Maybe he held his tongue, knowing that when the time was right, and Drew had come into money . . . he'd strike.'

The kettle clicks off and Mullins fills DS Chang's cup first. When he goes to his, there's barely enough, so he tops up from the hot tap.

'Tim, ugh, don't do that!'

'Drinking temperature,' he says. 'How I like it.'

'You're a gent.'

Cheeks. Red.

'It was Jayden's idea, as it happens,' he says.

'What's that?'

'Steve wanting in on Drew's twenty-five per cent lump sum. Jayden and Ally put it together.'

'Ah, your Shell House friends.'

'Course, they don't know about the fingerprints. And they don't know about Bradshaw's dismissal, unless they've sweet-talked that out of him. So, they basically lobbed a dart with their eyes closed and somehow it hit the bull's eye. Classic Shell House.'

'But we still owe them a pint, no?'

'We owe them a lot of pints.'

And Mullins chews the inside of his mouth for a second, trying to figure out if this is DS Chang asking him out for a drink, and if it is, is she inviting Ally and Jayden along just to make it look legit? He frowns and takes a glug of tea. *Gross.*

'Once this is over . . .' he begins, but his pitch for the pub is cut short by Skinner barrelling into the room. Face? Stormy as yesterday's big boy.

'Bradshaw's having none of it,' says Skinner. 'Absolute classic manoeuvre, admitting to the one thing that makes him look guilty as all hell, to show us that he is, in fact, innocent.'

'Blackmail?' says DS Chang.

'Blackmail, is it?' says Mullins.

Their voices chime like a barbershop duo. Mullins gives a goofy grin and puts his hand up for a high five. Chang leaves him hanging.

'That dismissal from Thames Valley?' says Skinner. 'Steve Bradshaw was doing Schofield's dirty work. He'll admit that now the bloke's dead, apparently. Allegedly, Drew was off duty and got into a road rage tussle with some idiot. He asked Steve to run the plate for him, looking for some sort of retribution, and Steve was stupid enough to do it. And even stupider to be caught. He was sacked for it, lost his whole career, and was suspected of much worse than a breach of data. And he never breathed a word. Until now.'

DS Chang takes a sip of her tea, and says, cool as you like – *peaceful* as you like – 'Are you saying Drew Schofield went round to a private address and inflicted damage on the vehicle, in retaliation?'

'It would seem so. Exemplary officer, our DS Drew Schofield. No wonder Bradshaw thought he was sitting on a gold mine.'

'Hold on,' says Mullins, 'Steve's admitted this?'

'Admitted it with bells on,' says Skinner. 'Once he saw the fix he was in, he was very forthcoming. Said Drew promised he'd "take care of him" as soon as he could afford to. That he "wouldn't forget what a friend he'd been". Those were his words. So when Kathy invites Steve and Mae to the High Tide for the weekend, Steve thinks his ship's come in and that there'll be a nice cheque waiting for him.'

'But there wasn't?' says DS Chang.

'No, there wasn't.' Skinner drops into a chair, pushes his hands through his thinning hair. 'According to Steve, Drew starts playing games. Reckons he'd made no such promises. That this weekend away was the only thanks he ever intended. Which was tripe, because it was Kathy's idea – and she knew nothing about what Drew had done, or said, or promised.'

This all sounds great to Mullins. This all sounds like it's on the way to a confession. Only Skinner's already gone in with the spoiler: *Bradshaw's having none of it.*

'So Steve's nose is well out of joint, but he's still thinking he can get what he's owed,' says Skinner.

'And that's where the blackmail comes in?' says DS Chang.

'Nope. Despite appearances to the contrary, I think Steve Bradshaw is too under the thumb for blackmail. He still thought he could talk Drew round. But then Drew goes and dies. And Steve's hopes of any kind of payout, any kind of recompense for the fall he took for him, die too.'

Mullins thinks about drawing attention to Skinner's turn of phrase – *the fall he took* – but they've moved on before he can find a way into it. *Bums.*

'And that's why he was so angry,' says DS Chang. 'Not because his friend died, but because he lost his pay day. Damn, it adds up. But what about the prints?'

Skinner shakes his head. 'Bradshaw says of course his prints would be all over the room. He and Drew had beers in there while the ladies were at the pool. And the room service bill confirms it for the same time, as does the hotel CCTV. Luke got on that one nice and fast.'

Did he now? Good little Luke.

'But there were fingerprints on the balcony too?' says Mullins.

'Nothing to say they didn't take a little fresh air, is there? That's Steve's line. No, we've got nothing, chaps. Not until Forensics can dig up something, anyway. Something genuinely conclusive. Because Steve and Drew were mates, weren't they? On the face of it, anyway. Who needs enemies, et cetera. Hugs and handshakes, DNA-a-go-go. No, what we need is that ruddy great coat the assailant was wearing, but that could be at the bottom of the sea by now. Or burnt to ashes.' Skinner shakes his head. 'Bent coppers. The pair of them. I'd love to say Bradshaw did Schofield in, but we're not there yet. We're not anywhere near that.'

'Sarge,' says DS Chang, 'what about Steve's girlfriend, Mae? She's alibied him at the moment, hasn't she?'

'That's the next move. Talk to her again and let's see if she changes her tune. Meanwhile, Mullins, I want you combing the hotel CCTV footage. Last twenty-four hours. There's the black hole of the power cut, but I want you looking for a flash of that jacket. Anyone wearing anything like it, at any point in the run-up to, and after, Schofield's death.'

Mullins's heart drops like a bowling ball.

'That'll take a fair while, Sarge.'

'It will, won't it?' Skinner looks at his watch. 'I'm holding Bradshaw for twenty-four hours. Clock's ticking.'

'And Blake Bryant, Sarge?'

'Bryant's going nowhere. There was bad blood between him and Schofield, just like there was bad blood between Bradshaw and Schofield. I like either one of them for it.'

Mullins crumples his brow. 'But Blake Bryant's prints weren't found in Drew's room, were they, Sarge? Not like Steve Bradshaw's?'

'Ever heard of gloves, Mullins?' Skinner holds up his hands and waggles his fingers. And to Mullins's misery, DS Chang stifles a laugh.

Normal service resumes, then.

'I'd best get started on that CCTV,' Mullins says, slinging his undrunk cuppa down the sink.

37

'Now you're asking me,' says Elliott. 'I'd have been knee-high to a grasshopper.'

'It was 1988,' says Ally. 'The summer holidays. Did you want to . . . have this chat elsewhere?'

The reception area is the heart of the High Tide. It's a thoroughfare, but it's serene; discreet. A couple are stretched out on the sofa reading with their black Labrador at their feet, looking for all the world as if they're at home. A woman in a dressing gown and pool shoes glides through; her phone is glued to her ear and her voice is brisk, at odds with her appearance. 'Tell Gabby I need it by five latest.'

No sign of Kathy or Mae or Summer.

No sign, either, of the tumultuous aftermath of murder.

'No, here's fine,' says Elliott. 'There's not much to say.' But, nevertheless, he drops his voice. 'I do remember. Of course I do. I was ten years old. Something like that . . . Well, you don't forget it, do you? Much as my parents tried not to make a fuss about it. They didn't want to spook me. And, without sounding callous, it wasn't good for business. A boy dying in a holiday resort.'

'Was he a guest of the High Tide?'

'A guest here?'

'He was a local boy,' says Louisa, sweeping in, a bouquet of exotic-looking flowers in her arms. 'You're talking about the teenager who died, years back? Aren't these beautiful. They're for the lounge.'

'Let me help you with those,' says Elliott, jumping to attention.

Louisa raises an eyebrow. 'Since when have you had an interest in flower-arranging, darling?' She turns, laughing, to Ally. 'Probably since the news that his father's cancelled his return flight to Mallorca and is now on his way back here. *Again.* We only got rid of him two days ago. He went on to friends in Bath, but then he heard about what's happened here and still thinks he runs the place. No, don't get me wrong, we love Malcolm. He just can't help . . . sticking his oar in.'

Elliott shrugs apologetically. 'Dad handed over the reins nearly twenty years ago, but I don't think he ever really detached. Not emotionally.'

'He's bored to tears on that island in the sun,' says Louisa. 'That's the trouble.'

Ally can't help feeling the conversation is going in the wrong direction.

'So he was local,' says Ally, steering it back. 'The boy who died. You don't know his name, do you?'

'He was called Peter, wasn't he?' says Louisa, on the move again. 'Torren and Lizzy Jago's son. Elliott, have you seen sight or sound of our VIP? I feel terrible for her after whatever happened on the beach. Your partner Jayden was there, Ally, smoothing things over as ever.'

'Summer's in her room,' she says. But Ally doesn't add that they intend to offer her a different place to stay.

'I don't like how all this is dragging on,' says Louisa. 'I do hope you and Jayden are making progress. Don't go getting caught up in stories of the past with my husband. He's nostalgic enough as it is.'

But then something else catches her eye, and Louisa is off and away; heels clicking across the reception, arms full of flowers, and a cloud of perfume in her wake.

'My wife likes to make things beautiful,' says Elliott, in a tone that is, it seems to Ally, apologetic. 'How is Summer? We don't want to pry, but she is our guest and . . . speaking as a father, not to mention a decent human being, I didn't like the atmosphere between her and Steve Bradshaw when they came back in.'

'She's still very upset about Blake's arrest,' says Ally.

'And *have* you made any progress? I know I wasn't enthusiastic when Louisa hired you. I didn't like thinking of the police investigation being clouded, too many cooks and all that, but . . . there's been two arrests and very little information coming back our way. I'd have thought they'd have a duty to keep us apprised. The guests keep asking me and I sound like I'm fobbing them off. And there was a weaselly journalist in here too earlier, though Louisa's doing a stellar job of scaring anyone like that off.'

'Just say that the investigation is ongoing,' says Ally. 'And it's still early days.'

For all that has happened since, less than eight hours have passed since the discovery of Drew's body. While the High Tide might wear its tragedy lightly – the cushions are plumped, fresh flowers are placed in vases, guests are relaxing with paperbacks and pool time – Elliott seems genuinely affected. He has deep lines in his brow, and his hand goes repeatedly to his hair, in a gesture that could be well grooved or newly nervous.

But does he seem suspicious?

Does Elliott's double connection to Drew – being here in the summer of 1988; knowing the Schofields were booked to stay this weekend – count for anything?

'Elliott,' says Ally. 'Before this weekend, had you ever met Drew Schofield?'

'Sadly not.'

'Sadly?'

Elliott looks momentarily confused. 'Well, the man's died. We do take pride in our relationships with our guests. Now, if that's all . . .'

'Peter Jago,' says Ally abruptly. 'Did you know him?'

'I was only ten,' he says again. 'He was a good deal older than me.'

'Louisa mentioned his parents, Lizzy and Torren. Do they still live in the area?'

Elliott's hand goes to his hair. 'Well, yes. Yes, they're very much Trebaron Cove people. The family's been here for generations. Not like mine, we're nothing but incomers, us Kings.' He gives a laugh. 'But Dad did a decent job of passing, when he was sinking ale with the locals.'

'I'd love to speak to them,' says Ally. 'If you think they'd be willing.'

Elliott frowns. 'You can't think that has anything to do with what happened here?'

The investigation is ongoing.

'Or are you working on a different case now? A different case altogether?'

'Is there a case there?' she says. 'With Peter Jago?'

'God, no. Just a terrible tragedy. Torren and Lizzy . . . Well, they're elderly. And they've tried very hard to put it all behind them. They live quietly. Hermits, more or less. I dread to think what they think of all of our guests, blasting down the lanes in their four-by-fours. We draw a different crowd these days. When my parents were at the helm, well, it was rather less exclusive . . . Louisa's changed a lot. We both have. Together, I mean. We're very proud of what we've done.' He pushes a hand through his hair. 'Sorry, rambling. But what I'm saying is, I don't think it's fair to go and dredge everything up again with Torren and Lizzy. You never get over a thing like that, do you? But they've tried to. And they've done bloody well. That deserves to be respected.'

Ally nods. 'You're right,' she says. 'I'm sorry.'

She turns to go.

'You didn't answer my question,' he calls out, 'on why you're bringing it up? The sea cave accident.'

'I don't really know myself,' says Ally truthfully. 'Not yet.'

Outside, the temperature has dropped, and the wind has picked back up. Ally wonders if the storm is gathering its strength again. She looks towards the water. It's an incoming tide, but it's a way off yet. Nevertheless, Ally walks quickly. She keeps to the right-hand side of the cove, following the line of rocks, tracing what Jayden saw of Drew's route. It immediately strikes her that this isn't a natural path to take.

Ally looks back the way she came. Most people coming from the hotel would enter the cove in the middle, and the angle of the beach is such that the left-hand side unfolds more invitingly: there are rockpools aplenty; rough-cut steps and a path leading up the cliff; a pleasing view down the coast. Meanwhile, the right side looks closed off – an abrupt finish. It's only at low tide that it links to the next-door cove. The cove with the sea caves.

Did Drew know that?

As Ally walks, her boots sink. The tide has ruffled the surface of the beach, drawing delicate ripples across the sand. Drew's tracks from over twelve hours ago are long gone. She checks her watch. In just ten minutes, she's reached the limit of the beach. And Drew was gone for thirty or forty? It's possible he stopped in the bar on the way back, or settled in the lounge to warm up after a cold walk, but . . . what if he didn't? Could he have met someone?

Ally stays close to the rocks. They're vast black boulders, their surfaces mottled with weed and barnacles – a tall and forbidding outcrop – and she follows them round until the next cove opens up. It's far smaller, the cliffs looming close. Ally sees the sea caves straight away. Two black gashes in the cliff face, partly obscured by rocks.

She walks towards them, glancing over her shoulder at the tide. It's a way off yet. She puts her head down and walks on towards the cliff as the wind pummels her back.

Ally stops at the first, the larger of the two. It's a diamond-shaped opening in the rocks; a tunnel of black beyond. A wooden sign marks the entrance: *Danger! Do Not Enter.* It's unofficial, roughly hewn, and Ally looks to see how it's fixed to the rock. At high tide, it'd be deep underwater.

A memory flashes back. Her and Evie, standing by this very entrance. Tiny Evie in a swimming costume, her shoulder blades like wings, her legs fawn-like. Pointing her fishing net into the darkness.

Come away, dear, it's dangerous.

Which means Ally must have known about Peter Jago, because otherwise she would have gone in a few steps, just to see. Her daughter's hand tight in hers, two adventurers, trying out their voices on the echo. But instead?

Come away, dear.

Ally shivers suddenly – then leaps out of her skin as her phone bleats shrilly. She expects it to be Jayden but it's not.

'Gus, hello! I was meaning to call you.'

She moves slightly, the rocks protecting her from the worst of the wind. Gus's voice is a comfort, and she turns her back on the disquieting mouth of the cave.

'So what do you think, Ally?' he says. 'Could I come on up to the hotel? Lend a bit more of a hand? Or at least observe at close range . . .'

Reluctantly – Ally does hate disappointing him – she says that Jayden thinks if Gus really wants to crack this novel of his, then his time's best spent at his desk.

'Oh. Well, quite. It's not going to write itself and all that.'

'The thing is,' she says, 'Jayden and I aren't police. Well, you know that. And if the point was to learn about official practices, then I fear we'd only be leading you up the garden path.'

'Of course you would. Hopeless amateurs,' he says, with a thin-bodied laugh.

'And it's all rather sensitive here at the hotel. There was a nasty incident earlier with the victim's friend assaulting the suspect's girlfriend, and . . .'

'Gosh,' says Gus, 'it sounds like it's all action. Last thing I want to do is get in the way. Jayden's quite right. I need to strap myself into that chair and just . . . get on with it. Of course I do.'

'You know I'd love to read your book, Gus,' she says, 'if you thought it'd help.'

'I know. And you're very kind.'

'I don't think I'd be much use for feedback, but . . . encouragement, well, I can certainly promise that.'

'Very kind. You always are, Ally.' She hears him hesitate. 'What about Oxford? Anything more required there? If I'm at my desk, then I might as well . . .'

'Actually,' says Ally, 'we've a new line of enquiry. It's rather more local. I don't know if there's anything in it, but . . .'

'So, Oxford's old news, is it? Fair enough.' He laughs. 'Used to that. Onwards, eh.'

'Gus,' she says, 'would it help to be blunt?'

‘It might, yes. Well, it wouldn’t hinder. Although . . . No, go on, bluntness. Please.’

‘You’re a very good writer. Perhaps the thing to do is just . . . go and write.’

They hang up after that, Ally hoping that Gus isn’t too downhearted.

When she turns, she sees the tide has drawn closer. It’ll stop for nothing. She strides back the way she came, turning over the question in her mind: *Did Drew Schofield walk this way too?*

38

'Peter Jago,' says Jayden. 'His parents are called Torren and Lizzy and still live in the area.'

'You stole my thunder. The sticky toffee pudding worked its magic, then?'

'Al, consider me refuelled. I found an online newspaper archive. Look, I screenshotted these pieces from 1988. The initial report and then a follow-up. The coroner ruled Peter's death an accident, but his parents were unhappy with that. They couldn't believe that their son would read the tides wrong.'

Ally goes and sits beside him.

There's a photograph of Peter. A sandy-haired teenager in a school shirt and tie. He has a sturdy smile and kind eyes – eyes that Jayden has trouble looking into. Because like all photos of the dead, it's as if the image is heightened by tragedy: all the colours turned up. And there's something about this boy – living by the sea, basically playing in his back garden – that makes Jayden think of Jazzy and Benji. His heart clenches. *Note to self: tell the kids never to go near a sea cave.*

'How sad,' she says quietly. 'But anyone can misread the tides, even the most informed of people. One slip, one moment of inattention. The sea is unforgiving. I've just been down there,

Jayden. I wanted to trace Drew's steps. You said Drew was following the right-hand side of the beach, didn't you?'

'He was. But like I said, I wasn't tracking him.'

'Drew's walk was at almost this exact time yesterday, which means the sea would have been on its way in, but further out. High tide was fifty minutes earlier yesterday.'

Ally moves to the window and points.

'See those rocks at the far end? At low tide you can walk around them into the next cove. It's only a small cove on the other side and the cliffs are very steep. That's where the caves are.'

Jayden comes to stand beside her.

'You think Drew was headed in that direction?' He gives a low whistle. 'It's a long shot, Al.'

'If you saw Drew walking down the right-hand side of the beach, and walking with purpose, I think it's a possibility. Not a given, but a possibility.'

'You didn't go into the caves, no?'

Ally shakes her head. 'But a memory came back to me. I was here with Evie, and it can't have been long after Peter Jago died, because Evie wanted to explore, and I said no.' Ally pauses. 'I distinctly remember telling her it was dangerous. I don't think I would have said that unless the incident was in my mind. I can understand the thrill of a cave. It's instinct, isn't it, to want to go in?'

'Erm, not from where I'm sitting,' says Jayden. 'How come they didn't seal them up or something?'

It's wild to Jayden how the countryside works. People talk about cities being dangerous, but this place? Sheer cliffs you can step right off, no barrier in sight. A sea that'll literally kill you in seconds if you're not careful. And now caves. Caves that even a boy who grew up here – who knew, according to his parents, every inch of the place – could get trapped and drown in. Maybe he and Cat got it wrong, deciding to raise the kids here. Maybe the inner city is where it's at.

'There was a warning sign there,' says Ally. 'Not an official one, though.'

Jayden shakes his head. 'It's a sad story, but the link to Drew feels tenuous. He was an occasional summer visitor. And he hadn't been here for decades.'

'Margaret said they spent every summer here. Those childhood holidays, those teenage years, they're indelible, Jayden. Aren't they?'

And Ally has a point. But, as meaningful as memories can be, what's to say they matter in the present?

'What did Elliott say?'

'Ah, now, Elliott was interesting.'

Ally tells him how the hotel owner remembered Peter's death. That he was ten years old at the time, and his parents had wanted to shield him from it. 'Bad for business, was Elliott's insinuation.'

Jayden tuts. 'Cut from the same cloth as Louisa.'

'I suspect he was being glib. Incidentally, until two days ago, Elliott's father was staying here. He went on to friends in Bath and was supposed to be flying home to Mallorca today, but instead he's cancelled it and is headed back to the High Tide. I don't think Elliott and Louisa are terribly happy about it.'

'He left two days ago, did he? When Drew was still alive and well in Oxfordshire.'

'That's what they said. Elliott confirmed that Peter's parents still live locally, and that they're very private people. Reading between the lines, he seemed rather embarrassed about what the High Tide's become under his stewardship, and how an older generation like the Jagos might feel about it.'

'But Elliott's made it what it is,' says Jayden.

Rich people wringing their hands? No thanks.

'But we both know it's Louisa who pulls the strings. Perhaps the High Tide has evolved in her vision. Anyway, Elliott made it clear that the Jagos wouldn't welcome a conversation about Peter.'

Jayden takes a sip of his coffee. 'I'm trying to think what we'd get from that anyway. Elliott's got a point. Two complete strangers turn up and start asking about their son's death nearly forty years ago. It'd be confusing. And upsetting.'

'But what if the name Drew Schofield means something to them? Or they recognise his picture? Drew and Peter were a similar age, Jayden.'

'Do tourists and locals mix around here?'

'Okay, good point. But remember it was the late eighties. I'm not sure Cornwall was as overrun then as it is now. Certainly, there weren't so many second homes or luxury destinations.'

'Okay, so there's a chance that Drew and his friends might have come across Peter that summer. But it's a long shot.'

'The police have both Blake and Steve in custody. All we have left are long shots,' says Ally.

Jayden cradles his coffee cup, trying to order his thoughts. There's something there. *Is there?* He rubs at his forehead. Other things keep pushing in. Like the fact that Summer hasn't replied to his message yet about the Shell House idea. Is she annoyed at him for the way he ran? Maybe he misread the situation. *I didn't misread the situation.* Does Summer think she's being dispatched from the hotel because Jayden finds her presence awkward?

It's not that at all.

Like, ninety-five per cent not that.

'I'd like to talk to them,' says Ally. 'Torren and Lizzy Jago. I'd tread very carefully.'

'I know you would, Al.'

'It's getting on for three o'clock. The light will be fading soon, and I don't want to knock on their door after dark. Has Summer come back to you yet about staying at The Shell House?'

'Not yet.'

'Let's fit this in now, then. That said, I didn't ask Elliott for their address – he was already wary about me bothering them. But someone round here will know. Trebaron is no more than a hamlet.'

Jayden taps at his phone, says, 'I can help you there, Al. There's this picture in the follow-up article of Torren outside his house. See, he's leaning on this wooden gate. Big tree beside it. White cottage up behind it.' He crosses to Google Street View and buzzes down the lane, past the turning for the High Tide. 'Look, that's the same gate, right?'

'Excellent detective work,' says Ally. 'It's a ten-minute walk from here, if that. Shall we?'

39

There's a fine rain still falling as they approach the Jagos' house. They see the wide-open gate, the beech tree, the just-visible gable of the white stone cottage beyond. The ever-narrowing lane runs on, appearing to plummet towards the sea. Ally pulls the collar of her coat up; pats her damp knitted hat. The water is almost cerulean, with eerie drifts blurring the horizon: far out at sea, a hard rain must be falling.

'Star Cottage,' says Jayden.

The name is etched into a slab of granite. Beside it, a wooden sign says *Private Road, No Turning*. It's the same style as the sign by the cave, the one that said *Danger! Do Not Enter.*

They tread down a driveway overgrown with ferns and lavish heads of pampas grass; a flame-stemmed shrub that Ally can't remember the name of. The cottage crouches at the end of the track, its slate roof blackened with rain. There's a faint glow from an upstairs window. A compact silver Honda is parked to one side.

Fox stops. Nose to the air, he yaps, and from somewhere a muffled bark responds.

'You want to lead, Al?' says Jayden.

Ally nods.

They step up to the porch. The wood is saturated and splintering, bearing the last traces of pale blue paint. Two pairs of wellingtons, one black, one green, are tucked beneath a bench seat, along with a wooden trug holding a trowel and a pair of well-worn gardening gloves.

Ally knocks and they wait.

The bark sounds again, but this time Fox stays quiet.

Ally's conscious of their presence; strangers on the doorstep. Elliott said how the couple live quietly, privately. She wishes she could have forewarned them of their visit. Perhaps a note through the letterbox would have been gentler.

'Could be out?' says Jayden, just as a dim light clicks on downstairs, illuminating the pane in the door.

'Help you?'

Lizzy Jago is a small woman. She wears an apron that's dusted with flour, sheepskin slippers on her feet. She is perhaps eighty, her skin papery, but behind her glasses her eyes are bright – and round as buttons.

'We're sorry to disturb you,' says Ally, carefully. 'We're private detectives.'

Ally looks for a flicker of unease but sees nothing. Ally introduces herself and Jayden, and Lizzy nods. Her hand rests on the doorframe, as if at any moment she'll coolly send them away like they're door-to-door salespeople.

'You've probably seen a fair amount of coming and going in the lanes today,' says Ally. 'There was a death at the High Tide Hotel, you see.'

'We keep ourselves to ourselves here,' says Lizzy. 'But we couldn't miss that. We heard it on the local news. Terrible business.'

'Well, we're looking into it,' says Ally. 'It appears that the man who died, Drew Schofield, had a connection with the area.'

It sounds so tenuous. How to frame it? *And we wondered if your son's death has any bearing on who might have pushed Drew Schofield from the balcony thirty-seven years later.*

‘He used to come on holiday here as a teenager,’ says Jayden.

‘A lot of people do,’ says Lizzy. ‘It’s a popular area. Even more so, with the High Tide being what it is now.’

Ally thinks of Elliott’s warning, that Mr and Mrs Jago didn’t take kindly to the evolution of the hotel.

‘Who is it, Lizzy?’

A man, presumably Torren Jago, crowds into the narrow hallway. His knitted jumper is full of holes, but a chequered collar peeps smartly from the top.

‘They’re private detectives, Torren.’

He takes out a handkerchief and dabs at his nose. ‘What’s that? Detectives? What?’

‘His hearing isn’t what it was,’ says Lizzy, apologetically. Then, in a lower voice, ‘Nor his memory, but we don’t like to talk about that.’ She turns to her husband, laying a hand on his arm. ‘The man who fell off the balcony at the hotel, Torren. They’re looking into his death.’ Her gentle voice sounds strange raised; each syllable enunciated.

Torren looks confused. ‘These two are police, are they?’

‘We’re not police,’ says Ally. ‘We’ve actually been hired by the owners of the High Tide. You might have heard on the radio that the police have made two arrests.’

Lizzy nods.

‘But we’re pursuing a different line of enquiry.’

‘But why are you here, dear?’ says Lizzy. ‘We can’t help you. We don’t know the man who died.’

Ally glances to Jayden. He will be better at this, won’t he? Jayden gives a just-perceptible nod – and takes the baton.

‘We heard about the tragic death of your son.’

Lizzy tips her chin. ‘It was a long time ago.’

Ally recognises her tone only too well: Lizzy doesn’t want to talk about it.

'Would you be willing to tell us about Peter,' says Jayden, 'and what happened?'

Torren – not the biggest man – draws himself up to his full height.

'What's Peter got to do with it?'

And it's a good question.

'Perhaps nothing,' he says gently. 'Probably nothing. But . . . we're trying to build a picture of Drew Schofield, and why someone around here might wish him harm.'

Lizzy looks confused, and Ally can't blame her.

'But it'll have been an accident,' says Torren, his brow furrowing. 'Fellow like that falls from a balcony?'

'The police are treating his death as suspicious.'

'Torren, we know that from the news,' says Lizzy, irritation just creeping into her voice.

'Then you've got to be looking to the hotel, haven't you? All sorts of people running around there these days. There was a pop star last summer. Or was it this summer? Drug addict pop star, here in Trebaron! All manner of people who think they're God's gift, who think they can get anywhere with anything, trample over anyone . . .'

'Shh, Torren,' says Lizzy, with an indulgent smile. 'He can't help getting on his soapbox. He harks back to the good old days, you see. We all do. Trebaron used to be a bit of a secret.'

'But the High Tide Hotel was always here, wasn't it?' says Ally. 'I stayed myself, years and years ago.'

'Oh, but it was a different place then, wasn't it? Malcolm and Frieda wanted to welcome a family crowd. And they didn't charge the earth. Frieda said to me once that she didn't think it was fair to put a price on a view like that.'

It's certainly changed now, thinks Ally.

'Are you friendly with Elliott and Louisa King?' she asks.

Torren grunts. Lizzy shakes her head.

'I'm afraid, after Peter died, we withdrew rather. All we had was one another and . . . so we didn't look for more. Once that's your way, well . . .' She waves her hand. 'They're perfectly pleasant, I dare say, but . . . we're not friends as such. And, of course, they're much younger than us.'

'What about Elliott's father? He's been visiting the last week,' says Jayden.

'Malcolm? He did stick his head in to say a brief hello. He's living a different life now. Married a Spanish woman and lives abroad. A long way from Trebaron.' Lizzy's hands smooth her apron. 'Good luck to him.'

'It's cold with that door open. I'm going back to the fire.' Torren catches at her arm. 'Lizzy, don't let them keep you.'

Lizzy watches him shuffle back into the gloom of the house.

'I'm sorry about my husband,' she says, turning back with a sigh. 'He can be a little abrupt. I'd invite you in, only . . . I really don't think we can help.'

'So Drew Schofield wasn't a friend of Peter's?' says Jayden.

Lizzy blinks. Ally sees it from her perspective: she must think they're mad, trying to find a link.

'It's not a name I've ever heard,' says Lizzy.

'Could we show you a picture?' asks Jayden. 'Al?'

Ally pulls out her phone. A gust of wind blows around her ankles, and she sees Lizzy shiver. It doesn't feel fair to keep her on the doorstep anymore.

'Here,' she says. 'This was Drew in 1988. It was taken at Trebaron Cove.'

Lizzy's lips are tight together. *1988: the year Peter died.* Ally feels sadness pushing at her chest. It feels cruel, bringing it all back up.

Lizzy pushes her glasses into her hair.

'Which one is he?' she asks, peering at the picture.

Ally points.

'I'm sorry,' says Lizzy, 'I don't recognise him. But the summers here were full of holidaymakers. Torren thinks they weren't, a case of rose-tinted spectacles, but they were. A different kind, perhaps, less money flying about, but still.'

'Okay,' says Jayden, glancing to Ally. 'Thanks for your time, and we're sorry to intrude, Mrs Jago. And we're sorry for your loss.'

Lizzy pulls her cardigan tight around her; holds her head high. She seems, to Ally, quietly valiant.

'You get to my age, and you realise that life is nothing but loss. For everybody. We're not exceptional. What happened to Peter was terribly sad, but it was between him and the sea. It took time, but we've come to accept that now. The man who died at the hotel, I send my condolences to his people. And I wish you both well in your investigation.'

As they turn and tread back down the track, Jayden is quiet beside her. Dusk is rolling in. Out over the water, the clouds are as dark as ink blots, a blaze of yellow behind. A scene of otherworldly beauty. Ally hauls in a deep breath.

Life is nothing but loss.

And Ally has nothing but respect for the quiet dignity of Lizzy Jago.

40

Malcolm King arrives at the High Tide just as the last of the light is slipping from the sky. He didn't expect to be back so soon, but he had no choice, did he? Elliott will be putting on a brave face, but he'll be rocked by this death. He was always a sensitive boy, and there seemed to be something particularly fragile about him this last week. A certain . . . thinness. Malcolm's son reminds him on occasion of one of those paper dolls that Elliott and Frieda used to love making together when he was small: a square of folded paper, a few quick cuts, then a string of little people connected by hand and foot. When Malcolm broached the topic – *you okay, are you, son?* – Elliott put it down to a combination of his ongoing back pain, and missing Phoebe. She flew the nest over a month ago, the whole world ahead of her – or at least the corner that the University of York occupies – but Elliott is apparently still in mope mode. A parent who prefers the company of their child to their spouse? That's not something Malcolm can identify with. He was always such a fool for Frieda. When she died, Malcolm felt sure he could never be happy again. But it's a strange old thing, the human heart; it's capable of the most remarkable regeneration.

Louisa, meanwhile, was her usual vibrant self – and, knowing his daughter-in-law, Malcolm suspects that vigour will not have been dimmed by recent events at the High Tide. She'll no doubt be eying the opportunity, the pitch: *Murder mystery party at the High*

Tide Hotel, anyone? He wouldn't put it past her. While Malcolm is fond of Louisa on a number of levels – she did, after all, give them the phenomenal Phoebe – he finds her relentless commercial ambition, and ruthless pursuit of superiority, somewhat distasteful.

No, that's not quite fair. Perhaps 'not to his own personal taste' is more accurate. Frieda always teased Malcolm that he'd give away half of every summer's room allocations to charity cases, if he could. The fact is, they ran a sustainable business for more than three decades – he hasn't retired a millionaire, but who needs to anyway? Within the relative terms of what his life is now, Malcolm has everything he could ever want.

When he handed over the running of the High Tide to Elliott and Louisa, people thought it was because he was ready to put his feet up. But the truth is, after Frieda died, the place was too full of ghosts. Malcolm saw his wife everywhere – snipping roses in the garden, brushing sand from the terrace with a long-handled broom, folding cotton napkins in the dining room – and the fact that she was in fact nowhere was too much to compute. Better a sun-scorched hill town on a Spanish island that meant nothing to him. And, precisely when Malcolm was intentionally taking leave of the known world, he met Gabriella – thus sealing a different sort of fate.

Malcolm turns off the engine of his hire car and sits for a moment, gathering himself. It was a decent drive from Bath, and he can't pretend he doesn't tire more easily these days. The car park is reasonably busy: the usual mix of high-end vehicles that he knows to expect now. At least he can't see any press photographers lurking in the shadows; if they turned up at all, no doubt Louisa will have charmed them – then sent them packing.

From this angle, the hotel looks completely different to how it was in Malcolm's day. The extended structure – all wood and steel and glass – seems to define the place. The original white stone building tucked behind it, like a barnacle on a rock, hanging on, despite showing no evidence of life. It was from one of those fancy box-like balconies that the man toppled and fell.

Malcolm's High Tide didn't have balconies – nor most of the other facilities the hotel boasts these days. He obviously can't blame the current situation on the redesign, but, quietly, he's always preferred his and Frieda's version. Malcolm's afraid to say that, deep down, he thinks his boy probably does too. But Elliott made his own bed, in taking up with Louisa – so he must lie on it. And the injection of cash that she provided – a sizeable inheritance after her father, a hedge fund manager in the City, passed away early in her and Elliott's relationship – certainly took the High Tide into a new era.

Malcolm has learnt to do as all good parents should: let their children live their own lives. Which, inevitably, means letting them make their own mistakes. But he couldn't let this death of a guest lie. Fly back to Mallorca, knowing that an ill wind was blowing at the High Tide? *No.* It would have felt like the worst kind of luck, or at least unforgiveable inattention, to shun his once-beloved home in its hour of need.

Frieda said it once: *What if someone dies here, Malc? Stands to reason that they might, doesn't it?* On account of all the comings and goings, all that life passing through, so why not death? But in all their years of running the High Tide, no one did; not under their roof, anyway. Not even Frieda, who died in the hospice in Truro.

Until now.

Malcolm is climbing slowly out of his car, just as two people come strolling through the entrance. He greets them with gusto; old habits die hard, and when he was the host, he was a good one. They regard him with more interest than usual; they both have friendly, open faces, but are unaccountably sharp-eyed. Malcolm immediately knows who they are. Elliott mentioned them briefly, then Malcolm did his own homework.

'Malcolm King,' he says, holding out his hand. 'My son and daughter-in-law run the place.'

He sees the brief look that passes between them.

'Ally Bright and Jayden Weston, yes? Your reputation precedes you, as they say.'

And he's opening it right up, but why not? Malcolm knows that the moment he steps inside he'll be ushered away by Elliott and Louisa. His son tends to think he interferes – which Gabriella, with her degree in psychology, has reasoned comes from Elliott's own lack of self-confidence: Elliott is only offended by advice because he already doubts his own decisions. Louisa, meanwhile? She considers him a relic from a bygone era. *I remember when this place was all fields*, et cetera. And no doubt afraid he'll ham up his working-class roots in front of their high-end guests, demanding to know why you need anything else on a breakfast menu other than a full English. That sort of thing.

'The police have this one sewn up, don't they? Two people in custody, I heard.'

'The investigation is ongoing,' says Ally, with what feels to Malcolm like a studied demureness. 'You were staying here last week, were you not?'

'I was. I always enjoy autumn here.'

'And a good opportunity to catch up with your old neighbours,' says Jayden, which seems like it should be a question but isn't.

Maybe Malcolm's face does something, as Ally says, 'We just came from Torren and Lizzy Jago's.'

Malcolm can feel his brow creasing. 'What did you want with them?'

'We're just building a picture of the place,' says Jayden.

'You're not opening up what happened with Peter again, are you?'

'Not at all,' says Ally. 'We were respectful.'

Malcolm pantomimes looking at his watch. 'You came from there, you say? I'm amazed they let you go. Two out-of-towners asking about Peter? And detectives, at that.'

He looks from one to the other. The quip hasn't landed. *Too callous?* And unfair, because Malcolm has always liked the Jagos.

'Lizzy and Torren have lived under the shadow of their son's tragic death for decades,' he goes on. 'Sometimes it felt like the only thing that kept them going was their anger. I should think you got the whole sad story, beginning to end, didn't you?'

The woman, Ally, tips her head. 'They didn't talk much about Peter,' she says.

Malcolm's eyebrows lift.

'Their anger,' says Jayden, 'was it directed somewhere specific?'

'Dad!'

Elliott comes striding across the car park, arms outstretched in welcome. *Sort-of welcome.* The expression on his face is a little more complex than that. Which, of course, Malcolm anticipated: Elliott didn't want him coming back here, sticking his oar in. But it's simply a case of Malcolm's protective paternal instinct. The High Tide Hotel will never stop being his baby, just because he's passed it to someone else to hold.

'Dad, come on inside. It's freezing out here.'

Malcolm sends a supercilious smile in Ally and Jayden's direction. 'My son thinks I'm terribly frail these days.'

'More that in Pollensa you've forgotten what a proper south-westerly feels like.'

Elliott claps an arm around his shoulders and – *why not give the boy this small win* – Malcolm lets himself be steered towards the door. It's only when he's halfway there that he remembers his suitcase in the car. When Malcolm turns back to get it, he sees the detectives are standing there watching them, so he says something light and silly, lifting his hand in greeting-cum-farewell. But deep in his chest there's a prickle of unease that's as sharp as indigestion.

41

Jayden's phone finally buzzes with a message from Cat.

Sorry I missed your call babe. Epic nappy change. Don't ask. How's it going up there? Any idea when you'll be back?

Then a photo drops in: a selfie, their three faces pushed together. Cat's laughing, Jazzy is blurred and mid-screech, and Benji is perfectly still, his eyes moon-big and gazing directly at the camera. Jayden's gang. He can feel himself smiling as another message arrives.

How's Summer holding up?

His smile sags. Turning to Ally, he passes her his key and says, 'I'm just going to give Cat a quick buzz. You go on up to the room.'

'Coffee and a debrief, when you're ready?'

'Coffee and a debrief.' And he pops a thumbs up. 'I have thoughts.'

'I wonder if they're the same as mine.'

Jayden's phone buzzes again, and this time? It's Summer. He reads her message – stupidly, with some trepidation.

Thanks for the idea. If it's okay with Ally, I'd rather be out of the hotel. Tell her yes please, if she's really sure. Sorry about earlier.

His finger hovers, ready to reply, when Cat rings. He jumps. It feels weird, their contact criss-crossing. Even though he has no reason for it to feel weird.

'Cat.'

'Hey, sorry to disturb. I didn't know if you and Ally were in the middle of something, but then we all really wanted to hear your voice.'

'I really wanted to hear your voice too.'

'Are you making progress?'

'Kind of. Well, not really, but . . .'

'Jazz has something important to tell you.'

'Yeah? Put her on.'

'Wuv oooh, Dadatz.'

'Wuv oooh too, babe. That's funny because I was just thinking that exact same thing. Wuv Jazz, wuv Benji, wuv Mummy.'

He can hear his daughter peel away laughing, already on to the next thing.

'Told you it was important,' says Cat, retrieving the phone from wherever Jazz dropped it. 'How's Summer doing? Any word on Blake?'

Jayden gave her the basics on Blake earlier, and Cat – just like when he was in the force – didn't press it.

'They'll keep him until tomorrow morning, but they've arrested Steve, Drew's mate, now too.'

'Hot tub creep?'

'Hot tub creep.'

'God. Do you think he did it?'

'I don't think he did. It's complicated but . . . no.'

'And is Summer freaking out?'

'She's definitely . . . under strain. I suggested to Ally that she spend the night at The Shell House instead of here. She already had a run-in with Steve before he was arrested. The men's wives are still around; I just think—'

'Jay, she should come here. Shouldn't she? I mean, we can offer. It's strange not to. I know Summer and I weren't mates as such, but . . .'

Jayden rubs the back of his head.

'Yeah, no, but it might be easier for her to just . . . detach. And with Jazz and Benji, it's not exactly a peaceful retreat, is it?'

'Maybe she'd love the distraction. Too much time with your own thoughts can do your head in, right? I mean, she must be questioning her whole relationship, let alone anything to do with this guy's death. I feel so sorry for her.'

Part of Jayden can just picture Summer at theirs, at the kitchen table with Cat, a bottle of wine between them. Cat loves her girlfriends. And she loves a deep conversation. Maybe she would give Summer everything she needs right now. But . . . he just can't do it. It's uncomfortable. And he's not about to tell Cat that Summer maybe tried to kiss him, not when they're still entwined on this case. For all that Cat trusts him, he doesn't think she'd welcome Summer into their home with open arms with that knowledge.

No, The Shell House is the right call.

'But okay,' says Cat, 'I can see The Shell House and Ally's company being a real refuge.'

'I love you.'

'Huh?'

'Just saying. I love you, wife of mine.'

'At least get it right, Jay. It's "wuv ooh".'

Then they're saying goodbye, and two minutes later Jayden's back in the room, stepping from one world to another. Ally looks up as he comes in.

'I've an anomaly to report,' she says, her face bright.

'Likewise.'

'What Malcolm King said about the Jagos?'

Jayden drops into a chair. 'The Jagos didn't want to talk about their son with us, did they?'

'Not with anyone, that's what Elliott said to me. That they'd put it behind them, and it wasn't fair to bring it all back up. Yet Malcolm said the opposite.'

'And they weren't angry either,' says Jayden. 'Alright, so why would Malcolm King paint the Jagos like that – two people looking to blame someone for Peter's death and willing to tell anyone about it – if it's just not true?'

'Perhaps Malcolm wants to point the finger in their direction.'

'He's doing it very subtly if so, Al.'

'Anyone harbouring anger for a past tragedy could be emotional enough to commit a serious crime, couldn't they? Arguably?'

'Definitely. But the Jagos are old and frail, Al. And Drew was one of hundreds if not thousands of tourists that were here the summer that Peter died. Without anything to link them, it's tenuous to the max.'

'But the link is the time and the place. It's something.'

'It is something,' he agrees.

'I do think it's interesting that Malcolm was here this week,' says Ally, changing tack. 'He left before the death and now he's come back again.'

Jayden stretches his legs out; taps a beat on the arm of the chair. 'I follow. You're wondering if he actually went anywhere, aren't you? But what could link Malcolm King, ex-owner of the High Tide, and Drew Schofield?'

Jayden pulls out his phone, does a quick Google search. Nothing comes up.

'We could find out whether Malcolm has any links to Oxford,' says Ally. 'What happened to his wife? Neither Elliott nor Malcolm have mentioned her, have they?'

Jayden does another search: *Malcolm King High Tide wife.*

He scans through a few entries, then clicks on one.

'"Frieda King, co-owner of the High Tide Hotel at Trebaron Cove, passed away peacefully after a short illness",' he reads. '"Donations in her memory to Truro Hospice."'

'Date?'

'Twenty years ago. So, around the time that Elliott and Louisa took over the hotel.'

Jayden starts up his tapping again. *Paradiddle-paradiddle.*

'What if it's the other way round,' he says, 'and it's Elliott who's playing games. What if he wanted to give the impression that the Jagos shouldn't be disturbed. He didn't want us bringing up Peter's death with them, because there *is* a connection. And think about the way he steamed over when he saw his dad talking to us just now. You could tell by Elliott's face he didn't like it.'

'But Elliott was right,' says Ally. 'Lizzy and Torren didn't want to be disturbed. And they didn't want to talk about Peter with us.'

'So we're back to Malcolm.'

Jayden looks at his watch.

'Al, by the way, Summer messaged. She'd like to take you up on the Shell House offer. Are you happy to run her over?'

'Of course. And what will you do?'

'I'm going to be eyes and ears here. I'll park myself downstairs in the bar and see who's around. Get talking to the staff. I'd like to chat to Malcolm again. And check in with Kathy too. There might still be something she knows that she hasn't realised is significant.'

Ally looks slightly disappointed. Perhaps she'd like to be in the thick of things too.

'Same goes for Summer, Al. She might relax more away from this place and remember something important. She was actually *there*, just before Drew fell. See what you can glean.'

'Anything else I can do?'

'Well, if you're in the mood for some desk research, I think it's worth drilling into any connections between Malcolm King, Frieda King and Drew Schofield. You never know.'

Ally nods.

'And in the morning, how do you feel about a return trip to see the Jagos? Because even though we can't see a link, it *is* an anomaly. Malcolm says they're angry, Elliott says they've made their peace, and they say . . . not much at all.'

'Lizzy said they'd made their peace too,' says Ally. '"It was between him and the sea",' that's how she put it. I feel uncomfortable pushing it, Jayden.'

But Jayden has witnessed Ally learn that sometimes you have to make people uncomfortable in this job: people you like, people you pity, people you fear. Her gentle way means that she gets to the truth quietly – but no less persistently.

'I think it's a case of just chatting with them more generally,' he says. 'I like the fact that they're close to the hotel but not part of it. They could have seen something and, again, not realised its significance. We didn't explore that earlier; we were just focused on seeing if the name Drew Schofield meant anything to them.'

'Alright,' says Ally, 'let's go in the morning. And you're right, they'll have a bird's-eye view from the top floor of their cottage. Though I expect they were tucked up during the storm.'

'You never know. If a vehicle drove to the hotel late at night, I reckon they'd have heard it.'

'Through the storm?'

'Maybe.'

'When the wind got up in the dunes, Bill would always go outside to check the roof wasn't about to blow off.'

'There you go. The Jagos' cottage is surrounded by trees. If I was Torren or Lizzy, I wouldn't be sleeping easy. Okay . . . so we've a plan?'

'We've a plan. And Jayden, how much do you want me to tell Summer about the investigation? If she asks, I mean.'

Jayden hesitates. 'I think we keep our cards close to our chests,' he says. 'But at least you can reassure her that we've a few lines of enquiry.'

The timing of Malcolm King's visit – and return. The significance of Peter Jago's death. Elliott's reluctance for them to talk to Malcolm, to talk to the Jagos, to talk to anyone, basically. Calling them 'lines of enquiry' might be a stretch, but it's all they've got. Million-dollar question: how does any of it connect to dodgy cop Drew Schofield?

42

Blake sits on the edge of the hard, narrow bed; his hands rest on his knees. Everything's coming back up and there's nothing he can do to stop it. It's these four walls, the tang of disinfectant, the smell of concrete and linoleum and then that other scent, the one that sits in the atmosphere like a toxic cloud: anger, pain, violence, regret. *All that.*

The solicitor said they'll keep him the full twenty-four hours but then he'll be out of here. Like it's a win. *You'll be on your way, Blake.* But that means a night – a long, long night – and every single ghost he's ever been afraid of, lurking in the dark.

Those two months he spent in the detention centre, he thought he could shed them like a snake slips its skin. But they're deep in his marrow. Imprinted in his DNA.

Blake closes his eyes and tries to disappear. To go to the place where he remade himself, where feather-soft powder falls and coats everything, making even the ugly look beautiful. Blue skies as wide as you like, the sun like a lollipop, the moon so big and close you could lob a snowball at it. Surrounded by high mountain peaks, Blake hurt himself on his own terms: he learnt to snowboard. Every bruise was a badge of honour; it meant he'd tried and tried again. With his goggles and his helmet he was near invisible, and this gave him courage too. He scraped by with grunt jobs – he was a good, hard worker – and over two, three, four seasons, he befriended the owner of a bar. It suited him, having the countertop between him and the crowd; easy chat and all smiles and 'what are you having?' He was a good rider by then, known for acrobatic feats – *you backflipped off what?!* – and, more than that, he was happy. It gave him a kind of shimmer, a glow that he emitted without even realising it.

That was what Summer saw, maybe.

Is there any feeling in the world worse than shame?

Blake pushes his back against the wall and draws up his legs; folds his arms around them and presses his forehead against his knees. When he sucks in a breath, it shakes his whole body.

He dreads to think what Summer will make of him now. She thought he was someone else, that's the problem. And how badly he wanted to be that person too; not just for her but for himself.

All it took was one fateful encounter with DS Drew Schofield to blow the whole sham to pieces.

Blake flinches as the door opens. But it's the young officer – the one with the not unfriendly face – and his shoulders relax just slightly.

'Hungry?' he says. 'It's lasagne or chilli. And neither are as bad as they could be.'

43

'Are you sure you won't eat anything?' says Ally.

Summer shakes her head and cradles her teacup in her hands. 'I'm sorry. I'm just not hungry.'

'If I heat up some soup, perhaps the smell will tempt you.' It's the gently spiced carrot soup that Jayden has been known to fill a flask with. 'Jayden's favourite,' Ally adds with a smile.

But it doesn't have the intended effect. Summer worries at her lip, and her hair falls across her face like a curtain. In the quiet of The Shell House, Ally feels the young woman's pain anew.

'It's so good of you to have me here,' she says for perhaps the tenth time. 'It's above and beyond.' Then, suddenly, 'If the police can only hold Blake for twenty-four hours, does that mean he'll be released tomorrow morning?'

'That's right,' says Ally.

She doesn't mention that the police could apply to extend it.

'It's going to be difficult,' says Summer. 'A difficult conversation.'

'I know,' says Ally, coming to sit beside her on the sofa.

'Jayden says it was Drew Schofield who arrested him, all those years ago.' Summer heaves a sigh. 'This was supposed to be a relaxing break. I mean, it's work for me but . . . travel writing isn't exactly going down a mine, is it? It's not nursing or . . . anything important. It's not what *you* do. And now this man dies and . . . everything's wrecked. Blake and I feel wrecked.'

'With a murder investigation, other things always come out. It's part of it, Summer. And that can feel upsetting, and unsettling, but . . . I suppose we have to remember it's a small price to pay. Comparatively.'

'You mean because neither of us are dead, and Blake didn't kill anyone? So finding out this massive secret from his past is . . . no big deal?' Summer gives a low laugh. 'You're right. Perspective.'

'It's not *not* a big deal,' says Ally, 'but it's up to you how you decide to feel about it.'

'Until I know the full story, I don't know how to feel.'

'You've the opportunity to be really honest with one another. Perhaps that's a good thing.'

'That's scary, though, isn't it?' says Summer quietly. 'And until the killer is caught, I won't stop thinking about it either. It'll just be hanging over us . . . Blake and I . . . and some part of me will be thinking, "If he lied about this, what if he lied about that?"' Her wide eyes swim with tears. 'I'm sorry. I can't believe I said that.'

'I can understand it,' says Ally.

'Really? You're not just saying that?'

And Ally reassures her, because no one can predict how they'll feel when life gets complicated.

'Let me get a fire going,' she says, getting to her feet.

'Lovely,' says Summer. But her voice is hollow as a cup.

Ally takes the box of matches from the mantelpiece, then remembers – she used the last one to light the fire last night. Has she ever, in her life, run out of matches? She goes to the kitchen drawer and roots through the contents: a torch, a ball of string, ancient birthday candles, a key, but . . . no matches. Suddenly having firelight feels like the most important thing; a small, meaningful act to chase the dark away. She checks her watch. *Drat.* The store will be long closed.

'Ally,' says Summer, 'how did you know he was the one?'

Summer is looking over at the picture of Bill, the one in his barbecue apron, grinning that sturdy grin. He looks so alive it's as if he could step from the frame. It's impossible that he can't.

'Ah, now,' says Ally. 'I'm not sure I did. Not at first.'

Summer tucks her hair behind her ears; blinks.

'Really?'

'All I knew was that he was the right person in that moment, I suppose. I was a student at art school. I'd been rather bruised by another love affair, and then . . . there was Bill. Wonderful Bill. In his police officer's uniform, so reliable and so kind and so . . . comfortable. I was comfortable with him right from the beginning. I had no idea that we'd spend the rest of our lives together.' She pauses. 'The rest of . . . Bill's life.'

Suddenly this feels like half a story. Should she confess that Ray Finch – the love affair – is back in her life? That two days ago she was by the fireside in Ray's Suffolk cottage? But if she does, it pulls focus. She and Bill should have spent the rest of their lives together. *Together*. Whatever Ally is now enjoying with Ray, it's . . . different. Incomparably different.

'What about when Bill asked you to marry him, though?'

'Oh, I said yes without even thinking.' Ally smiles at the memory; it warms her like sunlight.

'How did he propose?' Summer is smiling too; the first Ally has seen in a while.

'We were out getting fish and chips. It was a blustery night, and we were scurrying along, heads down. He stopped on a corner by a lamp post, so we were pooled in all this light, and he said, "Marry me, Al."'

Out of nowhere, Ally feels a rush of emotion, fast as an incoming tide.

'So, I said . . . "Yes, please." For goodness' sake, as if he'd just asked me if I wanted a cup of tea. *Yes, please.*'

Summer holds her hand to her mouth. 'I love that.'

'It was the best moment of my life. It was before our daughter was born, of course, before our wedding day . . .' Ally pauses. 'Actually no, our wedding day was rather too full of other people. I always liked it best when it was just Bill and me. And then Evie too. The three of us together.'

Oh, we were a wonderful three.

'I've never felt as happy as when I'm with Blake. But now . . .'

Ally waits, holding the empty matchbox in her hand. Grateful, actually, that the attention has shifted.

'If he'd proposed at the High Tide, I'd have been like you. *Yes, please*. But now I have no idea . . .'

'Sometimes the worst things can bring people closer together.'

'And sometimes they split them apart.'

There's a beat of quiet. Outside, the wind is getting up again. Ally thinks of the fallen bird and the blood on her pane – everything that's happened since. An ominous feeling builds in her chest. The night ahead suddenly feels long.

They need firelight.

'Summer, this is ridiculous, but I've run out of matches to light the fire. You don't have a lighter, I suppose?'

Summer shakes her head. 'Maybe a neighbour? If you even have them out here?'

'Gus!' Ally exclaims. 'Our saviour.'

When Ally phones, Gus answers with such warmth in his voice that she feels sorry to only be asking him for matches. She apologises for interrupting his flow – if indeed the work has been flowing – and he responds with enthusiasm. *Your words were just what I needed, Ally. Get on and do it! So I did. A decent day at the coalface, all in all.* Gus insists on delivering the matches and, as Ally hangs up, she sends him a quick message explaining that she has a guest. *Someone involved with our case; her boyfriend is a suspect, but we don't think he did it.* He responds with a thumbs-up emoji, which is as new as his surfing. It's a matter of minutes before he appears, brushing raindrops from his shoulders, his cheeks pink beneath his knitted hat. He takes the matches from his pocket and holds them out to her. He's tied a red ribbon around them.

'Oh, Gus.'

'Pleasure to serve.'

'I'd ask you in . . .'

'No, no. I won't intrude. Will she be . . .' He rocks on his toes, peers past Ally, as if to catch a glimpse. '. . . here all evening?'

'She's staying the night.'

Gus's eyes widen. His hand unconsciously goes to his head – and she knows why. *Tallulah*. The last time that someone involved with a case stayed at The Shell House is a painful recollection, especially for Gus, but perhaps there is another sensation too. The blue sky that comes after dark clouds: brave, bright, unbelievably blue. Ally and Gus grew close, and it was partly on account of everything with Tallulah.

'And you're alright with that, are you, Ally? Because . . .'

His eyes brim with concern.

'I am, Gus,' she says. 'It's very different, this time.' But he looks uncertain still, so she finds herself saying, 'Why don't you come in? I'm just heating some soup. You can meet her.'

And as he takes off his hat, the look he sends her is so full of gratitude that for a moment she feels uncertain. Gus seems to be happy with so little. And given where Ally is with Ray now, that has to be a relief. Relief, perhaps coupled with – *and this is hard to admit, because I have no right to it* – just the smallest tint of disappointment.

44

'I was enjoying chatting with your father-in-law earlier,' says Jayden. 'Is he around this evening?'

Jayden imagined Malcolm holding court in a corner of the bar – the former host, enjoying a reprisal of his role – but he's yet to spot him.

'He said the same,' says Louisa, tossing her golden hair over her shoulder, 'but he's exhausted from the drive. He doesn't seem to realise he's eighty and should probably slow down now.'

Louisa is perched on a stool behind the reception desk. The lamplight is soft; two scented candles dispense their pricey aroma. Jayden gets the impression that Louisa likes this front-of-house spot. The computer gives an illusion of admin – perhaps someone other than Louisa might have employed a receptionist – but she sees everything here. It's both eyrie and shop floor. And if anyone looks remotely like a journalist – news, not travel – they wouldn't have a hope of getting past her.

'Elliott's with him, is he?'

'He is, yes. And please don't go bothering them, Jayden. They're having some rare father–son bonding time with a bottle of whisky.'

'Why do you think I'd want to bother them?'

'Because you're asking more questions than a pre-schooler. Now, Jayden, did I see Summer Ellery leaving with your partner earlier?'

Now who's asking questions?

Jayden explains that Summer wasn't leaving in a checkout sense, she just felt like she needed some space.

'But space is all we offer,' says Louisa, with a show of incredulity. 'Tranquillity, relaxation, luxury, and bags and bags of space. Jayden, I rather thought that my hiring you was in direct alignment with Summer . . . continuing to enjoy her stay.'

'I thought it was about solving a murder, Louisa.'

Louisa looks affronted, so he softens up; she's a paying client – and he's got every intention of banking her cheque. 'It's complicated for her, right? But it's no reflection on the High Tide.'

'And what about you? You're enjoying your stay, are you?'

Her look, and her inflection, makes the subtext clear: *the likes of you are lucky to be here on a freebie.* Private detectives aren't exactly 'influencer' status.

'To a point.'

'My husband was concerned about you upsetting our guests, but I reassured him that wouldn't be the case.'

'I thought he was concerned about us getting in the way of the police?'

'Oh, Elliott's concerned about everything, or haven't you noticed that?' Louisa sends him a conspiratorial look that Jayden suspects she thinks is charming. 'If it's not his aching back or his emotionally distant father or the fact that he'd rather I'd left home instead of our darling daughter, then . . . it's this gruesome business.'

'You won't know we're here,' says Jayden.

And he slides off towards the bar, before she can say any more.

Float like a butterfly, sting like a bee.

The High Tide bar is intimate, little more than a low-lit living room area with an attentive host and a drinks cabinet. There are fifteen bedrooms in the hotel and, in the case of four rooms, occupancy has already been halved. Cat is back home with the kids,

Steve and Blake are in custody, and Drew Schofield is dead. There are just four people in the bar tonight. A middle-aged couple sit with a champagne bucket between them, but any kind of celebratory atmosphere is missing in action: both study their phones with a look of unified boredom. By the fireside, though, there's a different kind of couple. Kathy Schofield and Mae Cunningham.

Just who I wanted.

The phrase *thick as thieves* jumps to mind as he takes in the two women. Heads bent together, postures mirroring. When Jayden saw them at dinner yesterday, it was the two men who dominated; Mae and Kathy were in attendance, rather than vibing off each other like genuine friends. But perhaps it's to be expected that recent events have brought them closer.

He wonders how long he can get away with observing them and decides not very. Piped jazz fills the space. Coltrane? His dad would know. His dad would despair of him *not* knowing. Either way, a manic saxophonist is currently overriding all of Kathy and Mae's conversation. Jayden needs to get in on it.

'Evening, sir.'

The barman is in his late twenties. With his neat black shirt and super-styled hair, he looks like a Premier League footballer on a night out.

'We briefly met earlier,' says Jayden. 'Ethan, right?'

'And you're Jayden Weston. Lou briefed us. And we all gave statements to the police.'

'Quick word?' Jayden glances towards Mae and Kathy. 'Just out here?'

And together they step into the corridor.

'Drew Schofield was in here last night, right?'

'He was. Putting them away with that friend of his who got arrested.'

'How was the mood?'

'Little bit "lads, lads, lads". But the old-boy version.'

'Good-humoured?'

The barman pulls a 'not sure' face. 'Yeah, I'd say. At least, when his mate got arrested, I didn't think "Oh yeah, that makes sense".'

'They put in a late one?'

'The mate left first. Drew had another couple of drinks. Double whiskies. Sat there on his phone, mostly. I thought . . . there's a bloke who's avoiding his wife.' The barman glances down towards reception. 'Look, I've got to get back . . .'

'Sure. One last question. I noticed Elliott and Louisa were both in the restaurant last night. Showing people to tables, chatting. Is that usual?'

'Yeah, course. They're not ivory-tower types.'

'Did either of them spend much time with Drew Schofield's group?'

'Before or after Milly tipped wine all over Drew Schofield? Elliott bit the guy's head off – and fair play, because he had no right kicking off like that – but Louisa was on it after. Free dinner, drinks, the works.'

'And what about Elliott?'

The barman shrugs. 'Lying low, I expect. Lou's got a sharp tongue when she wants. If I was Elliott, I wouldn't appreciate her wading in and contradicting me. She should be standing up for her staff, man, even if the customer is always right, yada yada. Anyway . . . this kind of gossip about the bosses will get me fired. Drink?'

'A beer when you've a minute. A Slipway. One last thing . . . The two women in there. You know who they are, right?'

'Course. Drowning their sorrows. And fair play to them.'

Jayden follows him back in and strolls straight on over to Kathy and Mae.

'Mind if I join?' he says casually.

The two women look up sharply and Jayden feels like he's interrupting something.

Course you're interrupting something, Weston. One's husband was killed, the other's partner is under arrest.

He offers some comforting words; mentions Ally talking to Kathy, how he's been wanting to chat to Mae.

Mae gestures to the armchair beside them. 'Have you heard something?' she asks.

It's a heavily cushioned chair and Jayden's immediately tipped backwards. The heat of the fire radiates out. He glances to their drinks: a large glass of white wine and a cocktail with a cherry bobbing in it.

Cosy.

'The police have been here again,' says Kathy. 'But the questions they're asking, it shows they've got nothing.'

Jayden lifts an eyebrow. He and Ally must have missed them, when they were at the Jagos'.

'What did the police want to know?'

'They wanted to know if I was lying about Steve being in bed beside me,' says Mae. 'But I'll tell you what I told them. He came in at 11.20. I know the time because he woke me up, and I checked my phone. Then he was tossing and turning all night long.'

If the police are revisiting Mae's alibi, it could mean that the evidence they have against Steve is only circumstantial. Does that mean they've had nothing back from Forensics yet? Or they have, and it's inconclusive?

'It's alright,' says Kathy to Jayden. 'I know Steve didn't do it.'

How do you know?

Ally said that Kathy seemed emotionally shuttered, not outwardly upset by her husband's death. But he's still surprised by her composure. Kathy's cool as you like.

Jayden turns his focus to Mae. Actually, Mae looks kind of cool as well. He's been around enough people whose spouses are in custody – not least Summer Ellery. Sometimes there's a storm of emotion: raging disbelief. Other times a grim inevitability: *here we go again.*

'Look,' says Mae, as if reading his thoughts, 'I know Steve was stupid with that poor woman on the beach. And I know why they're holding on to him, pushing other angles. But I also know that there's nothing in it. He'll be released, his pride will have taken a kicking, but that's it. On he'll go. Same old Steve.'

So, Mae's in the mood for talking? *Great.* It's not lost on Jayden that she seems freer now that her partner is in custody.

'Tell me why you think they're holding on to him,' he says.

'You'll know already if you're any good,' Mae tosses back.

Kathy, meanwhile, sits still as a figurine; her fist closed around the stem of her wine glass.

'Steve thought Drew owed him money,' says Jayden. 'A payout.'

Mae wrinkles her nose. 'Okay, you're good. We've pieced it together, haven't we, Kathy? What Drew said, what Steve said.'

'Tried to,' says Kathy. 'Best we can.'

'I'd only been with Steve a few months when he lost his job,' says Mae. 'He made out it was a Jerry Maguire type thing, like they booted him out just as he was walking away anyway. But Steve always said that Drew thought he was hard done by, and that Drew would see him alright down the line.'

Mae sips at her cocktail. Kathy's wine glass is emptying rapidly.

'He jumped at this weekend. Course he did, it was being paid for by someone else.'

'Steve said you were paying your way,' says Jayden.

'Well, he lied,' says Mae easily. 'And he was only here because he thought there was a bigger prize waiting at the end of it.'

It strikes Jayden that Mae is speaking with almost complete detachment, as if her partner's fortunes, and her own, are totally separate.

'Before you ask,' she says, 'I'm leaving him. It's been on the cards for a while, and I just haven't . . . Well, you know how it is. I was single for years. I thought I was lucky meeting him. Shows what I knew.'

'Steve has a temper on him,' says Jayden carefully. 'That can't be easy to live with.'

'They all have a temper on them,' says Kathy.

And they're the clearest, loudest words she's spoken.

Jayden sits up. *Motive?* Was Drew a bullying husband, and Kathy finally had enough? Was that scene on the balcony a domestic that escalated? Whatever Ally said, there's a bitterness in Kathy. And he suspects it was Drew that put it there.

'This weekend was always going to be make-or-break for me and Steve,' says Mae, cutting back in. 'I knew that, even if he didn't. And seeing how Steve was, after this so-called mate of his died, that was the nail in the coffin. Even before the business with the girl on the beach. Look, we all know Drew wasn't a saint and he probably led Steve up the garden path with the promise of a pension pot payout. That's what you think, isn't it, Kathy?'

'I think probably,' says Kathy, averting her eyes from Jayden's. 'I mean, I don't know, but . . . I think probably.'

'But still. It's the wake-up call I needed. All of it,' says Mae. She holds up her glass. 'So . . . cheers.'

Kathy nods and lifts her near-empty glass mechanically. They chink.

'We're checking out of here tomorrow,' says Mae. 'Aren't we, Kathy? You've found a little place over in St Ives.'

'We are,' says Kathy. A look of doubt crosses her face. 'The police said that was alright. It is, isn't it?'

'Of course.'

Jayden doesn't blame the two women for wanting some distance from the High Tide. But if this is his last chance to easily talk to them, he's going to take it.

And he wants to bring it back to Kathy. And Drew's temper.

'Look, here's a fact,' says Jayden casually. 'Someone was on that balcony with Drew. And I don't think it was either of the men that the police have in custody.'

A bombshell – but they barely flinch.

'Kathy,' says Jayden, 'are you sure you can't remember anything? A name, a voice . . . You were right there.'

'Not a thing,' she says. 'I already told Ally. I'm sorry, but that's just how it is.'

'You're being spared,' says Mae, 'because once you know something, they won't leave you alone. It's a blessing, Kathy.'

'I keep thinking Drew's going to tell me off for it,' says Kathy, with a high laugh. 'Not knowing anything, I mean. Being useless. But he can't, can he? Not now.'

'He's dead,' says Mae, taking the cherry from her cocktail and pinching it between her fingers before popping it into her mouth. 'They both are, in a manner of speaking.'

Now or never.

'Kathy,' says Jayden, 'excuse the bluntness, but you don't seem very upset that your husband's dead.'

Kathy stares at him. Her glass pauses halfway to her mouth. Beneath her breath, Mae swears.

'Upset?' she says quietly. 'That's because I'm not.'

'Kathy,' says Mae, a warning note in her voice. 'You don't have to—'

'No,' she says, 'I want to. It's a relief to finally say it.'

Kathy takes a deep breath, and her slight frame trembles with it.

'Jayden, do you know how many dangerous situations my husband faced as a detective? Quite a few, over the years. And I used to pray, actually pray, that something would happen to him. Can you believe that? Of all the twisted reactions for a police officer's wife. I'm ashamed to my core. Not of my callousness, but my cowardice. I couldn't understand it, you see. Good people die every day, don't they? Good, loving people, who've never done a scrap of wrong. Yet there was Drew. When he put himself in the way of danger it wasn't because he wanted to uphold the law, or protect citizens, or . . . any of the reasons that decent human beings have for joining the police. Drew wanted the bragging rights, Jayden. He wanted the power. He wanted to shove people around, and the more down on their luck they were, the better. Oh, he really put the boot in then.'

Jayden can feel his throat burning, but he holds Kathy's eye. It's the suddenness of her speech; her painful honesty. It's the fact that it's making him think of Kieran, of Bill Bright. And how proud his mum and dad were of him when he joined up. How proud, and how wary.

I left. And people like Drew Schofield stayed.

Kathy holds her head higher.

'And Steve knew how close Drew sailed to the wind, didn't he, Mae? He knew.'

'I think Steve was fully in the boat with him,' says Mae. 'Until he was tossed overboard.'

'Drew used to say, "They need more like me," and I used to think, "Please, no. The fewer like you the better." I mean, where would we be?'

Kathy drains her glass; Jayden follows with a sip of beer.

'And he loved the threat. He actually loved it. A high-speed chase? A violent clash? Face-to-face with a stone-cold killer? He came home like he was drunk on it, or high. The man thought he was invincible! Bloody invincible. And he was, wasn't he? He certainly had me beaten.' Kathy's voice cracks. 'Not that that's hard.'

Beside her, Mae's face is full of emotion. Jayden suspects it's the first time she's heard Kathy speak so freely.

'Kathy . . .' she starts to say.

But Kathy won't be stopped.

'All of that, but then here we are, in this loveliest of places, hundreds of miles from home, and someone walks straight into our great big posh bedroom and kills him. Just like that, Jayden. And it was the last thing I saw coming.'

Kathy's eyes, finally, shimmer with tears.

'But am I upset? You're right. I'm not. I'm really not. Because that would make me a hypocrite, on top of the rest.'

45

'I think it's brilliant that you're learning to surf,' says Summer.

Gus doesn't know what he imagined when Ally talked of 'a suspect's girlfriend', but it certainly wasn't this charming young woman.

Ally caught him in the kitchen a moment ago as he was rooting around for a corkscrew and told him that Summer seems to have cheered up since he arrived. *Me, a harbinger of sunshine!* Gus isn't sure anyone's levelled that one at him before. Meanwhile the fire – his fire – is now blazing in the grate. They couldn't be cosier.

'Well, I'm not sure it can even be called surfing, really,' he twinkles back.

He can feel Ally looking at him. Does she think him a fool or a hero? Somewhere between the two, probably. A common-or-garden Gus.

'Of course, I wish I'd taken it up when I was younger, but I doubt I'd have felt the thrill of it so much then. It's rather wonderful, feeling reckless in one's later life. The thing about—'

He stops himself. One lesson in, and he's a surf bore. Funnily enough, he's never been a novel bore, and he's spent far more hours chained to his computer than he has to a surfboard. *Note to self: ask Saffron if there's an option where one can be affixed to the board.* While Gus likes to talk up the beachside writer's life in his letters to

Rich and Clive, he can't quite pull off the same aplomb in person. Especially now that he's realised that writing a novel is a lot easier than *rewriting* a novel. When his agent – *his agent!* – said that she loved it, what she actually meant was that she loved an as yet non-existent future version of it. But Gus didn't fib to Ally earlier; he *did* put in a good shift this afternoon. Funny how, if Ally tells him to do something, he more or less does it. Alright, perhaps it was Jayden who first told him to get back to his desk – he must phone him and thank him for that well-placed boot to his rear end – but it was Ally who relayed the message, wasn't it? It was Ally.

'Gus is writing a novel as well,' says Ally. 'He's even got an agent for it.'

And gosh, is that *pride* in her voice?

'Mostly not writing a novel. Ally has offered to read it, but . . . it's not there yet.'

'Absolutely no pressure.' Ally smiles. 'But selfishly, I'd love to.'

Part of Gus dares to dream – *deludedly? Maybe* – that Ally is curious for a glimpse inside his mind too. Because despite it all being made up, it's still him, isn't it? His way of seeing. And even though there's a Ray – *a bloody Ray* – where there's life there's hope, as they say.

'Now that's really cool,' says Summer. 'Writing and surfing? I'd like to do something like that when I'm old. Sorry, I don't mean old. *Older*. Something . . . unexpected. Like you too, Ally. With the detective work.'

'Oh, I would never have done that if it wasn't for Jayden.'

'The fact remains,' chips in Gus. 'It's pretty fabulous, Ally.'

Gus has never used the phrase *pretty fabulous* in his life.

'You owe it to yourself, don't you?' says Summer. 'That's how I'd see it. That I'd survived. All the things that can knock us off our feet, and yet we're still standing.'

Gus looks to Ally, and she gives him a small smile. They both know how it feels to be knocked off their feet in their later years.

Saving grace? Perhaps we're simply better prepared for it by now.

'If we get to sixty, or seventy, my God, we deserve to do whatever the hell we want, right?' says Summer. 'I almost wish I could hit fast-forward.'

Summer isn't smiling anymore. There is, in fact, something suddenly very fragile about her, and Gus has to remind himself of Ally's briefing: her boyfriend has been arrested on suspicion of murder. And here he is gassing away about surfing. And silly old novels.

'It'll all be alright,' he says, resisting the urge to pat her hand. 'You'll see.'

'It will, Summer,' says Ally.

'There isn't a case Ally and Jayden haven't solved yet,' says Gus. 'There's no one better.'

Summer gets to her feet. She's wearing trousers that look like baggy pyjamas and some sort of sheepskin boots. She's an advert for winter casuals, but her face shows no such comfort.

'I know it's early,' she says, 'and this has been so nice, but . . . I'm exhausted. Do you mind if I . . .'

'Of course not,' says Ally. 'Why don't I bring you a hot chocolate for bed?'

She's in Evie mode, thinks Gus. Ally's lovely in Evie mode. She's lovely in all modes.

Summer bites her lip. 'God, that would be . . .'

And then she starts to cry. *A hot chocolate tipping point.*

'Oh no,' Gus hears himself say. As if someone's spilt something. *Idiot.*

But Ally is straight to the young woman's side. She puts an arm around her shoulders.

'I hate this,' Summer says, so quietly it's a whisper.

'I know,' says Ally. 'I know.'

As Ally gently guides Summer towards her room, Gus hears the sound of buzzing. He casts around and sees it's Ally's phone. It's turned to silent, but it's pulsing with an incoming call.

Ray.

Before Gus knows what he's doing, he answers it.

'Hello, Ally's phone.'

As if he didn't see the name flashing. As if he doesn't know Ray from Adam. As if it's perfectly natural for him to be at Ally's of an evening, wandering her rooms and answering her calls.

Dear God, I'm petty.

'Oh, hi,' says the voice on the other end. It's rich, deep, and frankly – *delightfully* – rather taken aback. 'Is that . . . Gus?'

46

Jayden lets himself back into his room. He can tell he's had a few beers. He was prepared to take off after Kathy's speech, but they both seemed to want his company, ordering another drink, then another. It seemed rude to slide away, after the floodgates he'd opened.

His learnings?

Mae is now washing her hands of Steve, and Kathy is facing a future that, once she's adjusted, will probably be brighter than her marriage ever was. Jayden doubts that Mae is harbouring any Steve-like expectations of cash from the Schofields, now that Drew is dead. The sisterhood vibe is convincing. Two women who got stuck with unworthy men but are now, one way or another, free.

Could Kathy have pushed Drew off the balcony?

Could it have been Mae in the big coat?

No, Jayden believes them when they say they had nothing to do with Drew's death.

He slides open the balcony door and steps out. A wall of sound and sensation hits him: the crash of the black ocean, the gusting wind. He holds on to the railing, rain splattering his face.

What Kathy said about Drew . . .

Jayden thinks of Drew Schofield's retirement picture that he saw online. In dress uniform: that bull-like posture; the plastered-on grin. *They need more like me*, Drew said to his wife, and Jayden shares the dread that Kathy said she felt. If what she told him was true, then how did Schofield avoid disciplinaries? How was he not hauled over the coals by Professional Standards?

Because no matter how hard you try, there are always people who get away with it.

'You've still got to solve this one, Weston,' he says out loud.

Even if Detective Sergeant Schofield was the worst kind of officer: bullying, aggressive, manipulative. A man who fitted within the blueprint of a force that, in its worst corners, is institutionally racist, misogynistic, homophobic – and corrupt.

I've still got to solve this.

Because for all the bad guys, Jayden knows there are so many, many good. It doesn't matter that he's no longer wearing the uniform; it's still in him. When he took the oath, in Jayden's mind, it was forever.

Now focus, Weston.

He turns and looks around, taking it back to basics and assessing the environment. The new development means that every room in the hotel has a sea view. The next balcony along is Summer's. Maybe in the peace of The Shell House some new information will find its way into the light; Summer was the only one to see the other person on Drew's balcony, even if she says she didn't register them at the time.

Back behind the extension, the upper floor of the original building is mostly given over to the Kings' private home. That's where Elliott and his father have been sequestered all evening. There's nothing strange about them wanting privacy rather than mingling with the guests, but even so. Louisa blatantly steered Jayden away from them earlier, with her flippant talk of pre-schooler questions and father–son bonding. The trouble with the

Louisas of this world is that, with all the fakery, they're hard to read. Are the Kings in on this thing?

Jayden plants his hands on the railing; it's cold and wet beneath his palms. Even with the warm glow from his room, even with the spotlights on the terrace below, it's eerie out here. It's the sound of the sea. A living thing – something wild, barely contained – and it always seems to gain more power coming out of the black.

Last night's power cut plunged the whole place into darkness, and it would have been disorientating out here on the balcony. Why would Drew and his visitor leave the room and go outside into the wildest storm of the year? Drew doesn't sound like someone who'd care about waking his wife. Was he so drunk that his assailant could have easily forced him on to the balcony? No, Drew was a tough-guy ex-cop. If he didn't want to be out here, he wouldn't have been. Unless there was a weapon involved – and there was no sign of that on the video.

The admittedly dark, shaky, lit-only-by-the-moon video.

Jayden turns round and leans his back against the railing. He imagines someone pushing him.

It wouldn't take much.

If Drew's senses were impaired, would it be possible for him to fall purely by accident? Jayden decides no. You'd need to be trying something stupid, like sitting on the railing, or leaning right over. What about a heart attack? Drew doubling over and toppling? It's possible. Mullins and Skinner will be itching to get their hands on the findings from Drew's autopsy. They might even have them, if all the stops are being pulled out. But Jayden would put money on there being no sign of natural causes.

Because the video shows an assailant.

He straightens up. With a last look over his shoulder towards the unending dark sea, he goes back inside and sinks on to the bed.

His head thrums, his thoughts uneven.

It feels weird to be here, in this luxury room, all alone. He checks his watch: it's only 9.30. After Kathy's miserable account of her marriage, Jayden would have liked to have heard Cat's voice. *Man, I've got it good.* But his wife already messaged saying that Benji took ages to go down and so she's giving up and putting herself to bed too. She sounded chirpy about it, though, with her laughing-face emoji.

He pulls out his phone. If Ally's with Summer, he doesn't want to disturb them by calling. Instead, he taps out a long message, filling Ally in on his night. Then he brings up the picture that she sent him earlier. Drew Schofield at Trebaron Cove as a teenager. The same one they showed Lizzy Jago. Jayden would like to show Elliott and Malcolm this picture too, just in case it provokes a memory, but he's not going to force his way in.

He can't force his way in. Not without a badge.

Jayden feels, not for the first time, the limitations. But then he tells himself what he always tells Ally: the fact that they're not police helps them just as much as it hinders. Take tomorrow: they're going to knock on the Jagos' door again, and hope that their friendly faces will get them a ticket in.

But still . . .

He taps out a message to Mullins.

Two suspects in custody. Any progress, mate?

His phone beeps with a response almost immediately.

Wouldn't you like to know, Jay.

He smiles to himself. When will Mullins not be Mullins? He's one of the good guys, though – despite occasional appearances to the contrary.

Jayden's phone beeps again.

What about you?

If Mullins is asking the question, Jayden reads that as no progress. He messages back:

Five minutes to chat?

His phone rings in seconds, which means Mullins must have nothing better to do. Jayden settles back on the big soft bed, and together – almost as if they're colleagues; almost as if they're friends – they kick about the latest.

Jayden builds up to telling Mullins about Kathy Schofield's heartbreaking account.

Mullins goes very quiet, then says, 'I grew up never questioning that the cops were the good guys.'

'Lucky for you.'

'Not sure Bradshaw's much better than Schofield, to be honest.'

'Mae Cunningham's sticking with her alibi, though, right?' says Jayden.

'And Blake Bryant's innocent as they come – according to him. Well, apart from the . . .'

'Juvenile conviction? Yeah, we know.'

'The girlfriend told you that one, did she?' says Mullins.

'Other sources.'

Jayden grins at the thought of Gus and his network of ex-teachers.

'Alright, Jay. Holding out.'

'I've got one thing for you, though . . .'

And Jayden tells him that, nearly forty years ago, Drew Schofield used to come on holiday to Trebaron Cove.

'A teenage holiday?' Mullins snorts. 'You and Ally always find the weirdest tree to bark up. Why do you do that? Why can't it be a normal tree?'

'Weird or normal, if it's right it's right.'

'And most of the time it's wrong, Jay.'

'That's a false statement, that is, Mullins.'

'Yeah, yeah.'

'Look, an obvious motive is that Blake had a problem with Drew because he was threatening to blow his cover as a regular guy with no criminal record. Right? And another obvious motive is that Steve wanted the money he thought he was owed, and Drew wasn't prepared to give it to him. Right again?'

'And they're *obviously* both in custody.'

'And you're getting nowhere fast. They've got alibis, and the only thing you've got is circumstantial evidence at best. But the *non-obvious* motive is that Drew being back in Trebaron Cove upset someone. Or that Drew upset someone while he was back here. He used to come every summer as a kid until a boy died, and then he stopped. There's actually nothing weird about this theory, Mullins.'

'And you're calling our evidence circumstantial? What's this about a boy dying?'

'A local boy, Peter Jago, drowned in a sea cave.'

'And how's that connected to Drew Schofield?'

Jayden hesitates.

'Friends, were they?' says Mullins.

'No.'

'Did they even know each other?'

'Apparently not, but . . .' Mullins stifles a laugh, so Jayden shoots back, 'Have you seriously got no forensic evidence?'

'Seriously no.' Then, 'Like I'd tell you anyway, Jay.'

Jayden frowns. If the forensics haven't yielded anything, that changes things. And that's a fact he needs more time to think about.

He can hear Mullins take a big sip of something, then swallow noisily.

'Drinking on the job, Mullins?'

'I'm off shift, thanks very much. And it's Horlicks.'

'Horlicks? What even is Horlicks?'

'Something my mum likes to . . . Ah, forget it. More to the point, where are you phoning from? Why can't I hear your kids screaming in the background?'

Mullins actually babysat for Jayden and Cat back in the summer. It wasn't a disaster. In fact, Jazz, a bit too liberal with her affection in Jayden's humble opinion, decided the next day that *I wuv Tim*. She clearly scared him off, though, because the guy hasn't offered again.

'I'm still at the High Tide.'

Mullins cracks up laughing. 'Yeah, pull the other one.'

'I am. Cat left, but I'm staying here. I was comped the room.'

'Nice work if you can get it,' says Mullins. 'Well, if that's true, what the hell are you doing wasting your time talking to me? You should be getting busy . . .'

'Interviewing suspects? Been there, done that.'

'Hit the bar. Watch the big telly. Take a night-time spa, or whatever. Sure, Jay, you're at the High Tide. And you're phoning me.'

'Good point,' says Jayden, and hangs up with a grin.

But the next thing he does is open up Google and tap in *Malcolm King Frieda King Drew Schofield.* Just in case there's a bedtime story waiting out there for him.

47

As soon as Ally opens her eyes, she knows that something is different.

I have a house guest.

It's dark outside, the sun isn't even thinking of coming up yet, but she's ready for the day. Ally moves quietly, wary of making any noise that might disturb Summer. The boards creak as she climbs out of bed. The bedroom door shucks as she pushes it to. Fox's feet patter down the hall behind her. *Shh, Fox.* Ally closes the door to the kitchen with a little gust of relief and sets to making coffee.

There are two wine glasses out on the sideboard – hers and Gus's. He left not long after Summer went to bed because it didn't feel right for them to be making merry while she was so troubled, but he did stay to finish his glass. They talked about this and that; the kind of evening that, Ally realises, they haven't had in a while. Just as Gus was at the door, he said, *Oh, Ray phoned you. I forgot to say.* It was too late to phone back by then, so Ally didn't.

She picks up her phone now, thinking she'll send a message, and sees Jayden's name.

> Al, one of the staff told me Torren Jago walks his dog at 8.30 every morning. I think we should go see Lizzy while he's

out. Get her on her own first, then catch him on his return. Meet here at eight?

Ally goes for a Gus-style thumbs-up emoji. First time for everything.

She'll put her coffee in the keep-cup Saffron gave her last Christmas, take Fox down to the beach for an early run – *alright, a potter to the garden gate and back* – and then whizz over to Trebaron Cove. She's just writing a note for Summer – *make yourself at home* is the gist – when the young woman appears in the doorway. She's in her pyjamas, her hair mussed from sleep. Ally thinks straight away of Evie and her heart swells.

'Good morning,' she calls out, as hale as she can.

'It's a miracle,' says Summer. 'I actually slept. I had my window open a bit, and even though it was wild out there, the sea was like a lullaby. I loved it, Ally.'

And that's when Ally knows that Summer will be alright. If she was undone by anxiety, then she wouldn't open her window to the elements; she'd hear the thrash of an incoming tide by night and think only of threat, of invisible but so-powerful forces sweeping in.

That first night after Bill died is the only time in Ally's life that she's been afraid of the sound of the sea. She was afraid of everything then.

'How about a coffee?'

'Coffee would be amazing.'

Without going into detail, Ally explains that she's meeting up with Jayden. Even if Summer was an insider, Ally would feel uncomfortable talking about the Jagos' tragedy, as if it's a jigsaw piece for anyone to pick up and put down at random. As if this great pain the couple carries makes them fair game when anything untoward happens at Trebaron Cove.

Untoward. Not how Ally ever thought she'd describe a death. But she was feeling a disconnect with Drew even before Jayden's message last night. Ally pitied Drew's widow, but there was an energy about Kathy that Ally didn't think was grief. Last night Jayden filled her in on his conversation with Kathy and Mae – and that energy makes sense to her now. Kathy neither loved nor respected her husband. She was possibly even afraid of him.

And as for Drew himself? Bill's words come back to her: *There are rotten apples everywhere, Al, but it breaks my heart that some of them carry the badge.* While there are articles online questioning Drew's behaviour as a detective sergeant, Kathy's account, disturbingly, went much further.

'Ally, do you mind if I hang out here for a bit? I've messaged Blake to tell him where I am, though I know he won't see it until he gets his phone back. I'll go over to the High Tide to meet him then.'

'Of course. And help yourself to anything at all. And, Summer, if you feel like a walk, there's Hang Ten just down the beach. Saffron makes the best coffee around.'

'Sounds cool. I'll do that.' Summer looks down. 'You know, Ally, yesterday . . . I started worrying that maybe I was stupid having this blind faith in Blake. It was making me go a bit mad. Just ask Jayden . . .' She hesitates. 'But . . . I think that's what love is, isn't it? Faith. Just another word for it. Hearing you talk about Bill, and then seeing you and Gus—'

'Gus?'

'Isn't he . . . ? I mean . . . God, sorry, did I get that wrong? I thought you and him . . . Where did I get that?'

'Jayden?'

'Not Jayden.' Her cheeks colour a little. 'Anyway, sorry. But you and Gus are good friends, right? So . . . that is a kind of love, maybe.'

Ally nods. 'I think so.'

'I guess what I'm saying is, this next bit with Blake, I'm keeping the faith.'

Half an hour later, Ally is parking up at the High Tide. Jayden meets her outside and they go on foot to Star Cottage. The wind is at their backs, and they move quickly. Rain spits from a pewter sky.

'I think Summer's turned a corner,' she says. 'The night's sleep did her good.'

'Shell House magic, Al.'

'She admitted she'd been worried that she was wrong about Blake, after all.'

'Mullins basically said the police have got nothing. On either of them. They were pinning hopes on Mae reneging on Steve's alibi or the attacker's coat showing up.'

'And that hasn't happened?'

'Nope. So they can't have anything concrete from Forensics. Mullins as good as said it. Steve and Blake aside, that changes things.'

'Changes things how?'

Jayden stops; turns to her.

'All along we've said that the most likely scenario is that an argument escalated, right? That the other person was known to Drew, and he let them into the room. Once they're out on the balcony, Drew ends up going over.'

'Yes,' says Ally. 'A crime of passion.'

'But a crime of passion is messy. If the attack wasn't planned, then you'd expect there to be traces all over the place. Forensics should be having a field day. But I don't think they've got anything tangible . . . So you know what that says? This killer meant business.'

'You mean the murder was pre-planned? They got exceptionally lucky that it was a power cut, then, didn't they?'

'Well, yeah. Or maybe the power cut was the sign that they needed to strike there and then. A case of opportunism. Al, I spent a bit of time on the balcony last night. I wanted to see how easy it would be to go off it.'

'I'm glad you're still here to tell the tale.'

'You know what, it's really hard to go over completely by accident. So unless Drew jumped – and there's no evidence whatsoever to suggest he was suicidal – he has to have been pushed. And he has to have been pushed by someone who was really careful not to leave DNA. We're talking hat, gloves, no flying spit.'

'No flying spit?'

'A very controlled situation, is what I'm saying. Every contact leaves a trace, remember?'

Locard's Exchange Principle. Jayden's quoted it before.

Ally looks ahead up the lane. She can just see the Jagos' gate.

'But if the police have something like a hair, or saliva, they can only trace it if that person is already in the system. That's right, isn't it?'

'That's it. But if they had anything to go on, they'd be swabbing every single person who gave a statement and trying to find a match. And far as I know they haven't, so . . . yeah. My new theory is that maybe someone saw a chance and took it. The *intent* to kill was there, so in that sense it was premeditated, but the *method* wasn't. The balcony opportunity presented itself and they ended up executing it meticulously. That takes a certain kind of person, Al.'

'Someone who's familiar with crime scenes would know what they had to do to evade capture, wouldn't they?' says Ally. 'Which makes Steve a strong suspect again.'

'But Steve's an idiot,' says Jayden. 'I don't know what he did to lose his job, but I don't think he's capable of being careful enough for this. What I've been turning over is that this modus operandi makes it more likely that it's about Drew's professional past. The police will have a list of everyone Drew ever put away and are likely cross-referencing that against recent prison releases and Cornwall connections. That's the kind of hard yards we can't do, Al. I went down a few rabbit holes online, looking at reporting from criminal courts and articles where Drew was quoted, and nothing jumped out. But the police have got the systems and the resources. Plus, if they tap up Thames Valley, they've got first-hand accounts too. If there's something there, they'll find it.'

As they draw closer to Star Cottage, Ally drops her voice.

'So the chance of this being connected to an old tragedy looks less likely?'

Jayden pulls an uncertain face. 'Not necessarily. All it means is a more professional hit could account for the lack of forensic evidence. But there's no reason that someone else couldn't pull that off, with enough care and commitment.'

'And even with what Kathy said last night, you really don't think she's involved?'

'No, I don't. But I do still think the Jagos could have heard or seen something the night it happened. I mean, look, Al, bird's-eye view. And we're not even on the upper floor of the cottage.'

They turn in the lane and look down towards the hotel, where it seems to squat in a cleft in the cliffs. The terrace stretches to the rain-darkened beach; the hillside behind is densely wooded and somehow forbidding. Ally tries to picture the same view swathed in darkness, the storm blowing; clouds scudding past a fat silver moon.

'The Jagos could have heard a vehicle,' says Ally. 'But it would have been impossible to see anyone unless they came right past the cottage.'

'The dog could have barked if someone went past on foot. Though, yeah, okay, a barking dog isn't going to crack this case for us.' Jayden glances at his watch. 'Speaking of . . . I don't know how long Torren will be out for. Shall we go in?'

'Is that Torren?' asks Ally. She points down to the beach, where a lone dog walker is crossing the sand. Even at this distance she can tell he's moving slowly. The dog pelts across the sand, but the owner has no such legs.

'Either way,' says Jayden, gesturing to the gate, 'Al, you happy leading again?'

48

The Jagos' cottage is like a time trap; not one specific era, just everything is old. Lizzy Jago herself, in a knitted jumper, her white hair coiled in a neat bun, cautiously welcoming them in. Old furniture: dark, wooden, too big for the small space. Old pictures: moody seascapes in slick-looking oils, and then Peter. Peter is everywhere. He looks down at them from the wall, the mantelpiece, the bookcase in the corner. Peter in a school tie, Peter holding up a glistening silver fish, Peter in his swimming shorts with a bucket and spade, laughing at the camera.

Every year of his life, then an abrupt stop.

'It's good of you to talk to us,' Ally is saying.

Lizzy's hands tremble as she sets down a tea tray. Jayden tries to work out her age – Peter was sixteen, thirty-seven years ago, so she's maybe around late seventies or eighty. Similar to Malcolm King, in age if nothing else. Malcolm is like his surname suggests – straight-backed and authoritative, as much of a force as he probably ever was. When Lizzy moves through the room, she's quiet as a shadow, just the chinking of cups to show there's anyone there at all.

'He's a good-looking lad,' says Jayden, nodding towards the pictures of Peter. Because it feels weird to make no acknowledgement; the boy is the fourth in the room.

'He was beautiful inside and out,' says Lizzy.

'I bet he melted a few hearts,' says Ally.

'No, the sea was all he had eyes for. He was going to be a marine biologist. Travel the world.'

Lizzy passes Jayden a cup of tea. It spills and laps in the saucer.

'The shakes,' she says. 'Don't ever get old, dear.'

'Where's your husband this morning?' asks Jayden, as if he doesn't know.

'Walking Reggie. Though he was under the weather, and I told him not to go. Stubborn as an ox, that man.'

Jayden glances to Ally. It might not be a long walk, then.

'Malcolm King's come back to the High Tide,' says Jayden.

Lizzy nods. 'I suppose he would, a thing like this.'

'Malcolm wasn't here the night Drew Schofield died,' says Ally, 'but he came back when he heard.'

Jayden watches Lizzy's face, but there's still no flicker of recognition at the name.

'Terrible thing,' she says quietly.

'What's Malcolm's relationship like with his son Elliott?' asks Jayden.

Lizzy takes a sip of tea. She looks thoughtful suddenly. 'I think things are different these days, but our generation, the fathers could be . . . standoffish. They don't show their emotions, not like us mothers. I should say that was Malcolm.'

'Was Torren like that too?' asks Jayden.

Invasive? Maybe. But Lizzy started it.

She drops a sugar cube in her tea, and it lands with a *plunk.*

'When Peter died, Torren didn't shed a tear for days – weeks. I thought, "Who is this man?" But they came in the end. And it helped, I think. Got the sadness out of him. He was better after that. We both did our best to carry on with our lives. You can't live in the past, can you? Not forever.'

Jayden looks to the wall again. He focuses on a picture of Peter at Jazzy's age – a studio shot by the look of it; the little boy wears a smart shirt, and his arms are full of a teddy bear. His eyes sparkle intelligence and good humour and Jayden finds it hard to meet his gaze. If anything ever happened to Jazz, to Benji, Jayden thinks the past is the only place he'd want to live. He suddenly finds he can't speak. But Lizzy doesn't need his emotion. Lizzy doesn't need to know that Jayden's thinking of his kids – his safe, living kids – and that her tragedy is bringing his own fortune into such sharp relief.

He needs an exit.

'Do you mind if I use the bathroom?' he says.

'Up the stairs and on the right.'

And he takes the stairs quickly, collecting himself as he goes.

Jayden pushes open the first door on the right, but it's a bedroom, not a bathroom. He's about to turn when he realises: this is Peter's room. He steps inside, knowing he's trespassing.

Just a quick look.

If it was an indistinct time trap downstairs, here it's a capsule: a teenage boy's room from the 1980s, and everything preserved. A Dire Straits print is the only concession to pop culture; there are no football banners, no film posters. A large and ancient-looking globe sits on a little wooden desk, and on the shelf above there's an intricate ship in a bottle. Jayden peers closely, looking at its papery sails and delicate hull. Peter's bookshelves are full. Geography, mostly. The animal kingdom. Oceans of the world. He spies a spine he recognises, *The Observer Book of Sea and Seashore*, and smiles to himself. When he left the police, Jayden's workmates made him a care package to take with him into his new life. It was full of tat, mostly – crazy-patterned board shorts, a pasty-shaped cushion – but there was also a vintage copy of *The Observer Book of Sea and Seashore*. He knew it was Mina who'd chosen it, one of the admin team, and the only bookworm he knew at the station. She'd written *Your new beat* inside the front cover, and for all the banter elsewhere – the jokes about this new surfing, pasty-eating Jayden moving to the back of beyond – he found the gift touching.

As he takes down Peter's copy, idly wondering if it has the same cover, something falls out and flutters to the floor. There's a noise from downstairs: *Okay, time to go*. He bends to pick up whatever slipped from the book.

It's a Polaroid photograph.

And the face staring back at Jayden is one he's seen before.

49

Saffron watches Broady head back up the beach, his board under his arm. Even from here she can see his post-surfing happy face. She used to love splashing out of the ocean beside him, the joy beaming off the pair of them as they dumped their boards on the sand and shared a salty kiss.

The old days.

She turns from the window, checking her phone. Milo is in Berlin, meeting the organisers of a street art festival. It's cool here, I might stay for a bit, his last message said. Wanna come? The thing is, Saffron *could* come. It's not like customers are banging down the door through the off season. And maybe she could use a winter travel reset after the miserable trip to Hawaii last year, where she not only fractured her wrist but her relationship with Broady started showing cracks too. But she's looked it up, and Berlin is 112 miles from the Baltic Sea. If surfing in Cornwall is cold in winter, surfing in the Baltic Sea is going to be . . . well, it's in the name. And that van of Milo's? Also Baltic.

Plus, when Milo says 'a bit', Saffron now understands that that is an indeterminate length of time: a week, a month, three months, who knows?

Or maybe Saffron's just not as freewheeling as she thinks she is.

Or maybe you're not that into Milo.

She looks up as the door clangs, pleased to have the distraction of a customer. Then she does a double take.

Is that . . . Summer Ellery, aka Summer Holidays?

It's the long brown hair and thick fringe. Whether Summer's lounging on a beach in the Bahamas, strolling down a Parisian street or trekking in a Rwandan forest, her hair is somehow always the same.

'Hey,' Saffron says. 'Welcome.'

'Morning,' says Summer, with a shy smile. 'Could I just get a flat white, please?'

Is it her?

This girl's physical presence is quiet, almost apologetic. When Summer's travelling, she delights in everything – and that joy is all over her Instagram. If she posts a selfie, she radiates warmth; her wide smile makes her look like she's always about to laugh. And her pictures are amazing: she sees the beauty, notices the detail, not just the obvious stuff but the everyday. Saffron has always thought that if she and Summer ever met, they'd be kindred spirits. Now Saffron wonders if she'd be too full-on for her.

'Can't tempt you to a brownie? Best in the West, apparently.'

Yeah, she'd definitely be too much.

'I heard that was your coffee,' says Summer with a bigger smile this time. 'Go on, then.'

No, it is her.

Because Saffron clocked the 'nearly home' trees on her Instagram, even if Summer has since deleted them. Summer is in Cornwall. Summer is in Hang Ten. And this might never happen again.

'I've got to say it . . . I love your blog. And your Instagram.'

The girl looks confused for a second.

'You are Summer Holidays, right?'

'Yeah. Yes! Sorry. I didn't . . . Yes. It feels weird to be recognised.'

'Don't you get it all the time?'

'Not at all,' she says, laughing now.

Saffron passes Summer her coffee, and her face lights up at the perfect heart swirled in the micro-foam.

'Are you writing about Porthpella?'

Summer hesitates. 'Yeah . . . Not really.'

Saffron picks out the biggest brownie – the glint of sea-salt crystals, the ripples of caramel like tidelines on the beach – and puts it on a sky-blue stoneware plate.

Very Instagrammable.

'Here,' she says. 'On the house.'

'No, no.' Summer's taking out her wallet. 'You don't have to do that.'

'It's a pleasure. It's great meeting you. And I'm just stoked you've come to Hang Ten.'

Summer looks awkward suddenly. 'Look, I'm not planning on writing while I'm here. I don't want to take a freebie then not give you anything in return.'

'I don't want anything in return,' says Saffron easily. 'I'm just saying thanks for sharing your travels.'

Summer takes a beat – then thanks her.

'Porthpella's got enough people writing about it right now anyway,' says Saffron, holding up her phone with the *Suspicious death at luxury coastal hotel* headline on it. 'Have you heard? My friend's sister is a waitress there.'

'I was there.'

'At the High Tide?'

Summer checks her own phone, as if she's expecting a message, then slides it back into her pocket. She looks at Saffron like she's weighing something up.

'I was the first to see the body. My boyfriend has been arrested.'

Saffron can feel her jaw drop. *Be cool.* She quickly adjusts.

'How are you holding up?'

But the question is lost as the door clangs and a uniformed Mullins strides in; chest puffed out, elbows at right angles. Most of the time he looks just like good old Mullins, but right now, given the company – *and that revelation* – he looks a hundred per cent police. Looming, official, a little bit big for his boots. Saffron notices that Summer has already faded into the background. She's taken a seat at a corner table, her head dipped.

'Alright, Saff. Coffee, please. Make it a big one.'

'Sure,' she says.

Her brain darts about for a subject that has nothing to do with crimes, arrests, the High Tide. Diversionary tactics are the name of the game.

'Hey, guess what, Mullins? I'm teaching Gus to surf.'

Mullins's eyes go very wide. 'You're not, are you?'

And it's a look of genuine astonishment. Saffron didn't expect such a throwaway line to land with such impact. *Nice.*

'Come and watch our next lesson. In fact . . . we should get you in the water too, Mullins.'

'Huh?' He blinks. 'Say that again?'

'I reckon you could be pretty good.'

She's lying through her teeth now, but it's for a good cause. Operation Save Summer. And the effect on Mullins is . . . deep. His cheeks are red as beets.

'What, me and you? Surf lesson?'

'Why not? Like I said, you could be good. And it'd definitely be fun.'

'It would be fun,' he says, with a music to his voice she hasn't heard before. 'Weird thing is, I was thinking the same recently.'

She hesitates. 'Were you? What . . . surf lessons?'

'Well, bobbing about, to begin with. Then . . . ripping it, obviously.'

And he looks so stupidly happy, she feels a pang of guilt. Why does Saffron often feel like this when it comes to Mullins? They've come a long way, though, from their school days, when she thought he was a pure idiot. Now she thinks he's, like, fifty per cent idiot.

'Let's do it. Let's get you on a board.'

His receiver crackles, and he sets a hand on it.

'Gotta go.'

But Mullins doesn't look like he wants to go anywhere.

'You left your wallet at home, right?' she says, handing him his coffee. 'I'll add it to the surf lesson price.'

'What, you're charging me? I thought you were talent-spotting. *Mentoring*.' He grins goofily. 'I'm joking. An hour's one-on-one? I'll pay for that anytime, Saff.'

'Yeah, yeah.'

'I mean it. Don't lump me in with Gus's session.' His eyes suddenly narrow. 'Hold on, all these lessons, this isn't just about making Broady jealous, is it?'

'With you?' A laugh escapes. She can't help it.

He juts his jaw. 'Building up a rival business. First Gus, then me. That's what I meant.'

But those round cheeks of his are flared pink, and Saffron feels another stab of guilt. She knows he likes her. But only in the way he likes any girl who gives him the time of day. Which – actually – is probably kind of a small pool. He's an acquired taste, is Mullins.

'Not at all,' she says. 'I promise.'

And that much is true.

'Gotta go,' he says again, his smile fully returned.

It's a nice smile, actually. When the rest of him isn't messing it up.

Mullins's hand is on the door when he says, 'By the way, you've heard about the High Tide? Ally and Jayden are dragging their heels on this one. They've got nothing. Meanwhile we've got not one suspect in custody, but two: a couple of right chumps. Laters, Saff.'

And he's gone.

Saffron looks to Summer sitting in the corner. Did she hear the line about the chumps? She's pulled on her beanie, her long hair a protective curtain. But Summer needn't have worried about Mullins clocking her: he was crazy easy to distract this morning. Who knew the surf chat would land?

'Are you okay?' Saffron asks.

Summer nods, then says, 'Do you know Ally and Jayden?'

50

Reggie bounds into the room, Torren following some time afterwards. He takes off his bodywarmer, shaking raindrops from it as he goes. His movements are slow, stiff.

'And get that jumper off too,' says Lizzy, quickly at his side. 'It'll be soaked through. You'll catch your death.'

'Wasn't supposed to rain,' says Torren. His face screws up. 'Who's this, then?'

Ally introduces herself and Jayden again, saying that they met briefly yesterday, but the elderly man shows no sign of recognition. Didn't Lizzy mention that Torren has memory problems?

Lizzy touches his arm, says gently, 'They're investigating the man who died at the hotel, dear. Remember? I told them we didn't hear anything the night of the storm. Not beyond the wind howling, anyway.'

'There was a power cut,' says Torren. Then, 'Wasn't there?'

'There was, love.'

Lizzy takes her husband's flat cap off and passes her hand over his bald head. Then she helps him out of his damp jumper. They're tender, intimate gestures, and Ally has the impression of a mother and a child.

She's aware, too, of Jayden beside her. Ever since he came back from the bathroom he's been possessed of a peculiar energy. He nods at her – but Ally doesn't know what her partner's telling her.

'Torren,' begins Ally, 'can I ask you about Malcolm?'

Without the bulky jumper, Torren is a slight figure. He stands looking rather lost, one hand pressed to his chest, and doesn't appear to hear the question. It's clear the walk's taken it out of him.

'Look, we won't disturb you both any longer,' says Jayden, chipping in. 'We should be heading off.'

Ally tries to hide her surprise. Isn't it worth trying to ask Torren the same questions they had for Lizzy? Or does Jayden think Torren is all too unreliable, if he can't even remember meeting them?

'I'm sorry we couldn't help,' says Lizzy. 'I know it's an obvious question but . . . all this fuss, couldn't the man have just fallen off the balcony by himself? Accidents happen, don't they . . .'

Ally's eyes unconsciously go to one of the many pictures of Peter on the wall. *Accidents happen.* She quickly looks away.

'They do,' says Jayden. 'But everything points to someone else being involved. Thank you for the tea. You take care.'

Outside, the rain has slackened, and just above the horizon the sky shows a thin ribbon of blue. Ally scurries to keep up with Jayden's stride.

'Jayden, you've got something, haven't you?'

'Let's get clear of the cottage,' he says, but as they move down the lane his hand is already reaching for his phone. His face is all lit up.

They stand on the verge, looking down over a cascade of dark brown ferns, vivid punctuations of yellow gorse flowers. The High Tide has its face turned to the sea.

Jayden holds up his phone to Ally and says, 'Who's that?'

Ally peers closely at the picture of a teenage girl with long red hair. She's wearing a bikini top, and has her arms folded across her chest. She looks relaxed and happy and full of the joy of youth. Ally knows she's seen her somewhere before, but it takes a moment for the penny to drop.

'Is that . . . ?'

Jayden brings up another picture, the one that Ally sent him yesterday. Drew Schofield and his teenage friends on holiday at Trebaron Cove. Four boys, one girl.

'Rebecca,' breathes Ally. 'Where did you get that other picture?'

'Peter Jago's bedroom.'

Ally goes cold from head to toe; instant goosebumps, her body understanding before her mind.

'Oh, Jayden,' she says.

His face is as close to triumphant as she's ever seen it. He explains how he came across it by chance, how it fell from a book he shouldn't even have been looking at.

'And, Al, look, she wrote a message on the back.'

He pulls up another photo, this time of the back of the picture and its handwritten message.

For Pete, so you can remember me. Love Becky xxx August 1988

'My God,' says Ally. She looks back up the lane as if the Jagos are going to come peeling out, hands thrown in the air over the ransacking of their son's bedroom. 'But you were hardly gone. How did you find it?'

'Honestly? Fate. It came to me, Al.'

'Drew's mother told me that Drew and Rebecca were close. I don't know if they were ever girlfriend and boyfriend, but Margaret certainly wanted them to be.'

'And then suddenly there's local boy Peter, right? Whatever this picture proves, Drew Schofield's group crossed paths with Peter Jago the summer he died.'

'But Lizzy said they'd never heard of him.'

'Peter was a teenager, Al. How much did your parents know about your life then?'

'I'm not sure there was much to report,' says Ally with a smile.

'And this Polaroid was hidden inside a book. It wasn't propped on his desk or pinned on his wall. He wanted to keep it private.' Jayden touches his phone screen, zooms in on Rebecca's face. 'Al, we need to talk to this girl. This woman. She'd be in her fifties now, I reckon.'

'I'll phone Margaret Schofield,' says Ally. After this find of Jayden's, she wants more than ever to do her bit. 'She put her number in her email. However difficult she is with Kathy, she was very forthcoming with me. I'll see if she can give me a surname.'

Jayden checks his watch. 'Do it, Al.'

Ally makes the call, her heart climbing in her chest. When Margaret answers, Ally apologises for the intrusion but Margaret, unlike Torren, remembers Ally right away. And sounds pleased to hear from her.

'Margaret, I was thinking about Drew's friend Rebecca,' says Ally. 'She'd want to know about his death, wouldn't she?'

'Oh, I've no idea where she ended up, dear. Kind of you to think of it, though. Very kind.'

'I'm sure she could be traced easily enough. What's her surname, Margaret?'

'Morrow. Rebecca Morrow.'

'Did she marry, do you know?'

'She did, she did. Crying shame that it wasn't to my Drew. Crouch was his name. And I only know because Ted and Lyn fancied themselves posh and put a notice in the local paper. *Rebecca Crouch.* Not a smart kind of a name, if you ask me. Makes me think of a goblin, crouching to get you. Or a grouch.' She laughs sharply.

'Rebecca Crouch,' repeats Ally.

And Jayden is immediately putting the name into his phone.

'She moved away from Oxfordshire years ago, though. Goodness knows where . . .' Margaret coughs. 'Are you still with my good-for-nothing daughter-in-law?'

'No. No, I'm not.'

'I shall want a hand in the funeral, I'll tell you that for nothing,' barks Margaret. 'I know what Drew would have wanted. Better than Kathy does, any day. And another thing . . .'

Ally lets her run on, weathering the verbal assault. It's easy when it's not personal.

And we have a name.

Jayden holds up his phone. He's found a Facebook profile for a red-headed woman called Rebecca Crouch. She's wearing sunglasses – it's impossible to tell if it's the same person for sure – but the smile? The smile is close. And by the look on Jayden's face, he thinks so too.

At the next pause, Ally manages to interject and wrap things up with Margaret. Even though Drew's mother is hard to warm to, Ally ends the call with a slight feeling of discomfort that she's underserved someone in need.

'Okay, done,' says Jayden.

'Done?'

'I've sent Rebecca a direct message. Asked if her maiden name is Morrow, and whether she knew Drew Schofield back in the day.'

Ally looks back towards Star Cottage again, then down to the High Tide. They could have been in such limbo, but, somehow, they're putting things together. They've unearthed a tangible, and very personal, connection between Drew and Peter Jago – and that connection is Rebecca Crouch, née Morrow.

'Wow, okay,' says Jayden, looking at his phone. 'Rebecca's online. And she's already read it. That was fast.'

Ally pictures Rebecca Crouch, perhaps with her morning coffee at the kitchen table, this message like a stone tossed at a window: a sharp and sudden crack.

'She's replied,' says Jayden. 'Jeez, Al, this verge we're standing on. It's productive. Maybe we should ditch the thinking room and have this as our base. Okay . . . It's her. She's confirmed it. Let me read it. She says, "I knew him as Andrew. I just saw the news of his death in Cornwall. How sad. Why are you getting in touch?"' Jayden gives a low whistle. 'Alright, I'll say we're investigating Drew's death and ask if she can spare some time to chat.'

'Where does she live, Jayden? Does it say on her profile?'

'Ashburton. Where's that?'

'Devon.'

'Devon? Doable.' He taps on his phone. 'Alright, it's a one-hour, forty-five-minute drive. If Rebecca's up for it, I want this chat face-to-face. What do you reckon, Al? She's our best lead. Lizzy says she doesn't know anything, and I don't know about you, but I believe her. And as for Torren, I'm not convinced he knows what day it is. Malcolm's keeping a low profile. Elliott's very guarded. Kathy doesn't seem to have any real clue about those childhood holidays of Drew's, and Mae . . . Mae's busy planning life after Steve. Not that Steve knows it yet.'

'And Summer is waiting for Blake to be released,' says Ally. 'Which should be any minute now, shouldn't it?'

'Yeah, it should. How have you left things with her, Al?'

'I've given her a key to The Shell House. I thought they'd appreciate being away from prying eyes at the High Tide, so I've said she's welcome to tell Blake to come back there first.'

It was a small gesture really, but Summer's eyes filled with tears as she thanked Ally.

'That was nice of you.'

'You needn't sound so surprised,' she laughs.

But maybe Jayden's remembering how the old Ally guarded her privacy. How few people were invited inside The Shell House.

'Okay, so . . . road trip to Ashburton? "Charming South Devon market town", it says here.'

'If Rebecca will see us,' says Ally.

'She'll see us.' Jayden holds up his phone and Ally reads the woman's fast reply. 'No hesitation, is there? I didn't mention Peter Jago, though. Thought that would be better in person. The Drew connection is enough.'

Ally checks her watch. 'It's half past nine. If we leave now, we should be there by half past eleven.'

'So we won't be back until mid-afternoon. Alright.'

Jayden's busy at his phone again and Ally presumes he's messaging Cat. Meanwhile Ally looks to the water. A ribbon of blue sky appears to broaden before her eyes – hope out of gloom.

Ally silently thanks the runaway tongue of Margaret Schofield. Without Margaret, they'd never be asking questions about that summer all those years ago. The summer when Drew Schofield and his friends had the time of their lives. And Peter Jago's life ended.

51

In her house in Ashburton, Rebecca sits and waits. From her chair by the window, she can see next door's horse moving about his field. Out of nowhere the gelding breaks into a gallop, his tail and mane flying. Then he falls to a canter, a trot, a walk, then resumes grazing. Whatever spooked him, whatever sudden energy bolted through him, it's gone.

Rebecca watches with envy. If only it was that easy. If only she could leap to her feet and shake out this feeling of unease.

As soon as she saw the piece on the regional news, Rebecca – her hands trembling; her whole body trembling – googled Drew Schofield. She only knew him as Andrew, and she never cared about keeping up with what he was doing or who he was doing it with. Rebecca has lost touch with most of the people from her childhood. After her parents moved, it was easy to slip away. Easy to pretend that last holiday at Trebaron Cove never happened.

And then Jayden Weston got in touch.

She feels a push at her chest. Her emotion is a physical thing, as obvious as pain. She breathes steadily. *Come on, Rebecca.* She doesn't know what these private detectives will have to say, or whether they'll even know his name.

Peter.

Suddenly, she wants to say it out loud. She wants to remember.

Her husband is on a golf course and won't be home for hours. When they talked about first loves, the ones that got away, she never told him about the Cornish boy who drowned. She never told anyone, really. Unless you counted her pillow at night, so often damp by morning – and her palms, she whispered so many secrets into her palms. Rebecca used to think that her mum would notice that something was wrong, but she never did. And it felt like too big a thing to say, so Rebecca didn't.

She checks her watch again. The second hand appears to stutter; slow. Outside, the horse pulls at the grass as if everything is fine.

Maybe she'll tell the detectives everything.

Maybe she'll tell them nothing.

When the doorbell eventually rings, Rebecca jumps from her skin. She'd fallen into a deep daydream; senselessly scrolling through news articles, eyes blurring. So Andrew Schofield became a detective, did he?

And Peter?

Peter never got to become anything.

52

'Thanks for seeing us,' says Jayden, taking a biscuit from the plate that Rebecca Crouch offers. He doesn't love shortbread, but early in the job he learnt that accepting a little hospitality softens the barriers. 'And thanks for this,' he says, holding up his coffee.

It was a fast drive to Ashburton and the sun joined them for most of it. The moorland landscape slipped past the window, a distant crush of brown and murky green. He and Ally talked all the way, sorting the facts from the supposition. Rebecca knew Peter Jago. Rebecca knew Drew Schofield. Peter is dead. Drew is dead. Is Rebecca a suspect? Was Drew somehow involved in Peter's death? Rebecca gave a Polaroid photograph of herself to Peter the summer he died – and she signed it with a loving message. Could Rebecca have found out that Drew was back at Trebaron Cove and left her home in Ashburton to exact revenge?

They went back and forth, but there were too many unknowns to shape a convincing theory.

What we do know, Jayden said, *is that Rebecca replied to my message straight away. She could have just left it. That makes me think she has nothing to hide.*

Or the opposite, said Ally. *She was in fact anticipating someone getting in touch, and wanted to make you think that.*

Fair play, Al.

Also, Rebecca didn't ask how her name came up, did she? That would have been my first question if I were her. How anyone was connecting me to Drew, and why on earth it might be significant.

Now, in Rebecca's sun-filled conservatory, Jayden and Ally sit side by side on a floral sofa. There's a neat garden, bordered by uniform wooden fences; a field beyond with a grey horse. Rebecca hovers, not settling. Her own cup of coffee hasn't been touched.

'Look, I don't know how this works. I've never been interviewed by the police. Or detectives of any kind.' She smooths her skirt with the palm of her hand. 'And it's a long time since I've thought about Andrew Schofield.'

But when we got in touch, you didn't ask why.

'What was he like when you knew him?' asks Jayden.

'When I knew him? He was just a boy.'

'He was seventeen, wasn't he? Nearly eighteen.'

'Well, yes.'

'You were friends?'

'Our parents were friends,' says Rebecca stiffly. 'And I was two years younger.'

'I spoke to Margaret Schofield,' says Ally. 'Do you remember her?'

'Margaret's still going, is she? She was always tough as boots.'

'She has a soft spot for you,' says Ally with a smile. 'She told me she used to hope that you and Drew would marry.'

Rebecca stands very still, and her hand, still smoothing her skirt, stops suddenly. Her lips quiver.

'Now why on earth would she say a thing like that.'

The sudden passion in her voice shocks them both. Jayden looks to Ally, and she raises her eyebrows.

'Margaret showed us this photograph,' he says, holding up his phone. 'This was the group you used to go on holiday with, right?'

Rebecca nods, her eyes narrowing. 'I remember that being taken. Drew kept trying to put his arm around me and I hated it. He smelt of sweat. It was a really hot summer, that last year.'

That last year.

'You didn't go back to Trebaron Cove after that?'

Rebecca shakes her head. 'I was doing French, so we started going to Normandy instead.'

'Rebecca, can you tell us about that last holiday? There was a boy who drowned,' says Ally, 'Peter Jago.'

'So you already know, then.'

Rebecca lowers herself into a chair. There's a stiffness to her movements; perhaps she's recovering from an operation or has arthritis, but there's a pain on her face that wasn't there before.

'Did Peter Jago and Drew – Andrew – know one another?' asks Jayden.

Rebecca's hand makes a fist, and she presses it to her mouth. Her knuckles are white.

'Teenagers are like heat-seeking missiles,' she says. 'They always find their target.'

Jayden glances to Ally; they wait.

'There were a few of us at the campsite. Our lot, from Oxfordshire, but then other faces we recognised year after year. We all just sort of circled each other. Like an end-of-year disco but . . . all of the time. Everyone watching each other, making up stories, falling in and out of love just like that. I was bored of it. And when the boys didn't get what they wanted from the girls, they took it out on each other. There were always silly scuffles breaking out. But Andrew, it was different with him. It was more. He was angry that summer.'

'Why?' asks Jayden. 'I mean, I remember being seventeen. Hormones have a lot to answer for, but . . .'

Rebecca curls her lip. '*Hormones*. We all have hormones. Andrew wasn't special. But he had a father who was . . . a disciplinarian. Not a nice man. I never understood what my parents saw in him. And Andrew was, like all bullies, a frightened coward.'

Drew the bully. Just as Kathy said. Two dots of colour rise in Rebecca's cheeks; she might not have seen Drew for years, but she makes her assessment emphatically – and with a hot anger.

'He wanted to take it all out on someone, and he chose Peter,' she says.

'So they did know one another?'

Rebecca says something he can't catch. 'What did you say?' asks Ally gently.

'Only because of me. For those two weeks, Andrew made Peter's life hell. He was physically quite imposing, Andrew. Not that tall, but he was broad, muscular. He was always winding people up, wanting to start a fight.'

'Did he start a fight with Peter?' asks Jayden.

'Peter was nothing like Andrew. He was like none of the boys I knew.' And her eyes burn with intensity as she says it. 'Peter and I met at the beach, and we started spending time together. He knew all the names of the creatures in the rockpools. While Andrew and the other boys were having sand fights or throwing a rugby ball at each other, Peter was in the rocks, keeping field notes.' She smiles sadly to herself. 'That's what he called them, "field notes".'

'Was Andrew jealous?' asks Jayden.

'He hated it,' says Rebecca. 'He hated that I liked Peter and not him. So he hated Peter. He spent about a week taunting him. He'd hover around us when we were together, making nasty comments. And then he made it physical. Pushing and shoving. Andrew didn't expect Peter to stand up to him, because Peter was so gentle, you see. Slightly built too. His waist was slimmer than mine. I used to tease him, say that he was like an eel.' She shakes her head. 'But

Peter was tougher than he looked. He pushed back and Andrew wasn't expecting it. Andrew went straight over like a skittle.'

Rebecca describes how Drew fell on his rear end on the sand, and the other boys laughed at him. Rebecca laughed too. And if there was one thing Drew hated, it was being laughed at.

'He went crazy. He ran at Peter and started punching him. I tried to pull him off, but he was far too strong. Peter had a bloody nose, a black eye. It was awful.'

'Did any of the adults know?' asks Ally.

'I wanted to help Peter home afterwards, but he wouldn't let me. He got cross with me, said I should stay with my "friends". That wasn't like him. I think he was embarrassed. Embarrassed to be hurt in front of me. He went off, and I suppose he must have told his dad because that evening Mr Jago came up to the campsite and sought out our group. He had a bit of a set-to with Andrew's dad. After he left, I remember Andrew and his dad going off for a walk together, and when they came back, Andrew – Drew – had bright red cheeks. He looked like he'd been crying. He went inside his caravan and didn't come back out until the next morning. We never did know what happened, if his dad just gave him a dressing-down or something worse. Not that I cared. I hated him for what he did to Peter. And I hated that I was tainted by association, that Peter didn't want anything to do with me either. The next day my parents made us go on a day trip to Penzance and I remember thinking that I was glad to have a bit of space. But when we got back that evening . . . there was an ambulance and a police car by the beach road. All these people gathered down on the sand. That's when I heard. A boy's body had been found. He got trapped in one of the sea caves and the tide came in and he drowned. It was Peter.'

Jayden and Ally let the story settle around them.

So, Drew and Peter fought. Then Drew faced the consequences with his dad. And the next day, Peter died.

'Who found Peter's body?' asks Ally.

'A man and his dog,' says Rebecca. 'When the tide went back out.'

'A local or a tourist?' asks Jayden.

'A tourist. I think he was staying in a holiday cottage nearby.'

'What happened then?' asks Ally. 'Did you ever speak to Peter's parents?'

'No.' Rebecca hangs her head. 'And to this day I wish that I had. I was in shock. And I was heartbroken. I loved him, or as much as any sixteen-year-old can be in love. Two days before, I'd given him a photograph. I thought we'd stay in touch, that I'd be back the next year. But . . . I was scared too. Scared of his parents' grief. They were . . . wild with it. Peter's dad came back to the campsite again, was hammering on the Schofields' caravan, shouting, as if it was Andrew who was to blame. But, of course, it wasn't. It was just a tragic accident.'

Jayden tells Rebecca that they read the newspaper report in an archive; the police investigated and found no evidence of wrongdoing.

'Peter drowned,' says Rebecca with a nod. 'He was caught out by the tide, and he drowned.'

'What do you think he was doing in the cave, Rebecca?' asks Ally. 'A boy like Peter, he'd have known the potential risks, wouldn't he?'

'I thought about it a lot at the time, because it made no sense to me either. But Peter was a bit of a dreamer, and he was obsessed with sea life. If he was following something, I don't know, a rare crab or something like that, I could imagine him losing track of time. Being so focused that he turned his back on the sea. The police theory was that he got trapped or hurt himself trying to escape – they said his ankle was fractured – and the sea rushed into the cave and overpowered him.'

'How did Andrew react?'

'Everyone was in shock, but Andrew . . . I hardly saw him. He and his parents left the next morning, then we all left later the same day. It was the last day of the holiday anyway, but the atmosphere had changed for everyone. My dad said we should get ahead of the weekend traffic and leave early, and that was what the Schofields did, so the rest of us followed suit.'

Jayden nods. 'Did you ever wonder if Andrew was involved?'

But even as he says it, Jayden's wondering *how.* In what possible scenario could Drew Schofield be blamed for Peter's death in the cave?

'Involved?' Rebecca screws up her face. 'Of course Andrew was involved. He made Peter's last day on earth a misery. But the way he died? No.'

'But Peter's dad thought so?'

'I think,' says Rebecca carefully, 'that Mr Jago was just lashing out. He knew Andrew beat up Peter the day before, so he blamed him just like I blamed him. There was no rhyme or reason to it.'

But was there rhyme and reason to Drew's death, all these years later?

'Rebecca,' says Jayden, 'does the name Malcolm King mean anything to you? Or Elliott King?'

'I'm sorry, no. Who are they?'

'Father and son. They ran the High Tide Hotel. Elliott still does.'

'And that's where Andrew died, wasn't it?' says Rebecca. 'I see. No, I'm sorry. We all went in there for a cream tea once, but a lady served us. Do Peter's parents still live at the cove?'

'They do,' says Ally.

Rebecca smiles sadly. 'I wish Peter had introduced me to them. If he had, I'd have spoken to them, that day he died. I'd have said how wonderful he was. And that I was so, so sorry. I'd have liked to have told them that.'

She takes a handkerchief from her cardigan pocket and dabs at her eyes.

'Andrew Schofield was a bully,' she says, 'and everything I've read about him since I found out he was killed suggests he never grew out of it. In fact, he got worse – and was rewarded for it. A detective sergeant retiring in full glory. So, the police haven't solved this yet?'

'Not yet.'

'Well, that's no surprise to me.' Rebecca looks from Jayden to Ally and back again. 'A man like that, they must have a list of suspects as long as their arm, don't you think?'

53

'Torren lied,' says Jayden. 'And I think Lizzy lied to us too.'

They're on the A30 heading west. The road is clear and they're moving fast. Fast towards the end of the land, Porthpella, Trebaron Cove, the High Tide, and, potentially, the truth about what happened to Drew Schofield.

'We can't be sure of that, Jayden,' says Ally.

'If someone beats up your son, you make sure you get their name, right? Peter's dad went up to the campsite, Al. He found Drew's dad and confronted him about it. He went *twice*. Before Peter died, and afterwards too.'

'But Drew went by Andrew back then. Perhaps they didn't make the connection with Drew Schofield in the present day.'

'Oh, come on. If Torren was making noise after Peter died, trying to get the police to believe that there was more to it, then he'd have made it his business to know his surname too. There's no way he wouldn't.'

Ally thinks of the elderly couple, how there were pictures of Peter everywhere, but the effect was somehow less a celebration of someone's life and more a gallery of sadness. She didn't articulate it to Jayden at the time, but she found it oppressive inside Star Cottage. For all Lizzy's gentle ways and quiet fortitude – *we've made our peace* – the atmosphere seemed to say otherwise. It was as if the dust motes were whispering a different story.

Ally cannot pretend to understand grief; all she knows is her own journey. She and Bill had forty-two years together and theirs was a life well lived. Bill died before his time, she feels his loss still every day, she wishes – oh, how she wishes – that they could have just one more moment together, but . . . she bears no anger. How can she, when she has so much to be thankful for? But Peter drowning aged just sixteen, at the beach he called home and loved so much? Now that is a different grief. And perhaps, nearly forty years on, it still rages unabated for his parents. Who is Ally to say otherwise?

'Lizzy did say Torren has memory issues,' says Ally.

'Does he, though? Either way, *she* doesn't. And, Al, it doesn't matter if Drew didn't have anything to do with Peter's death – if the Jagos thought he did, then that could be enough.'

'But do you really think that they'd still hold it against him, all these years on?'

'Drew was nearly eighteen. He wasn't a child. I can understand their feelings towards him at the time, but now?' Jayden puffs out his cheeks. 'I don't know. I think if they're lying to us about knowing who Drew Schofield is, there's got to be a reason for it. Remember what Malcolm said, that he was surprised the Jagos didn't tell us the whole Peter story as soon as we met? What if it's all a pretence, Al? And they haven't made their peace with anything, but we're the last people they're going to show that to. What if Drew turning up here after all this time pushed their buttons?'

'Do you believe that Rebecca hasn't had any contact with them?' asks Ally.

'Yeah, I do. And even though she bears a grudge against Drew, I don't think it makes her a suspect.'

'She was quick to do her research,' says Ally. 'She went online and read all those same articles that we did.'

Rebecca squaring her old view of Andrew, the unequivocal bully, with the adult Drew.

'What if Lizzy and Torren did the same?' says Ally. 'They might have felt that Drew escaped justice as a teenager and went on to live a life where he supposedly upheld the law and protected others. That on its own might feel like bitter irony, but to think that he'd possibly abused that position of power? That would be difficult to accept. But I'm just not sure if it's motive for murder . . .'

'I hear you. And if the police are drawing a blank on forensics, then someone got the job done without leaving any trace. I can't picture the Jagos pulling that off.'

They fall to silence, just the thrum of the road beneath the wheels. After a while, Ally says: 'Malcolm and Elliott King. Where are they in all of this?'

'Well, thirty-seven years ago they'd have been bang in the middle of it. The scenes that Rebecca described would have unfolded more or less in front of the High Tide. But it's a push to imagine the Kings holding a grudge against Drew for anything that happened.'

'Unless Drew was picking on Elliott too,' says Ally.

She says it without thinking, but now she focuses on the thought; holds it carefully to the light.

'Elliott was younger,' she says, 'but there's every chance that he and Drew crossed paths at Trebaron Cove.'

'Okay,' says Jayden, 'let's follow this through. Drew had an obvious reason to take against Peter: Rebecca liked him, and he was jealous. But Rebecca made it sound like Drew was always looking for a fight. So, the little boy who lives in the big hotel? Maybe he was fair game.'

'Perhaps Elliott and Peter were better friends than Elliott's made out. There's an age gap, but Peter sounds like he was a kind boy. And someone who knows their way around rockpools? That'd be seductive to a younger child, I think.'

'Okay, so let's say Elliott's bullied by Drew too, and then he sees his friend Peter – an older boy he admires – get beaten up by him. Then Peter dies the next day. I know we're freestyling a bit here, Al, but . . . it kind of works, doesn't it?'

'What if Kathy booked into the hotel and Elliott recognised the surname Schofield? If Elliott did some digging, he'd have realised it was the same person.'

'And he'd have had weeks to plan it,' says Jayden. 'How to make it look like a drunken fall from a balcony. He even had a master key, so he could just let himself into the room. But what he didn't reckon on was Summer filming the storm from her balcony, categorically proving that someone else was involved.'

'But there's still the problem of method, isn't there? There are so many things that could have gone wrong with that plan. We keep saying it's not sure-fire enough for a premeditated murder, don't we?'

Ally looks out of the window. They're almost home; a strip of sea just visible on the horizon. It seems both close enough to touch and miles distant.

'There's holes,' says Jayden, 'but it's a hell of a lot more than the police have got.'

'Should we tell the police about the connection with Peter Jago?'

'I'd love us to pull together the threads on this one first, Al.'

'What, talk to Elliott and Malcolm?'

'We just need to think about the angle . . . I reckon they'll be tough nuts to crack. They're professional hosts, right? They've got the patter.'

They drive the last couple of miles in quiet. Jayden taps a beat on his jeans, his face lost in thought. Ally sifts through the details in her mind, as if it's shoreline treasure, seeking the shimmer of possibility amongst the tangle of debris.

As they crest the hill on the approach to the High Tide, Ally says, 'I'd like another chance to talk to Lizzy and Torren. Especially Lizzy. Perhaps they do know a good deal more than they're saying, and maybe they have pulled the wool over our eyes, but I think we've a better chance of—'

'Al,' says Jayden, cutting in, his voice urgent, 'Blue lights up ahead.'

54

Ally parks on the verge by Star Cottage. As they climb from the car, the wind whisks through the hedges, rustling the canopies. Everything feels shaken up. They rush through the gates but there's no sign of action. The ambulance is deserted; the cottage door stands open.

Beside Jayden, Ally hesitates, her voice quavering. 'Should we go in, or . . .'

Concern creases her features, and he squeezes her shoulder.

There's a movement at the window, then suddenly people are pouring out. Two paramedics carry a stretcher, and Jayden sees the frail figure of Torren Jago, a mask covering his face. Lizzy is close behind, her hands clasped together as if in prayer. She stumbles as she comes down the step and Jayden surges forward to help, but there's someone already there.

Elliott.

The hotel owner gives Lizzy his arm to lean on, and together they follow the stretcher. As Elliott sees Ally and Jayden, he freezes. Then it's as if he resets. He nods. Straightens up. Says to Lizzy, in a calm and commanding voice, 'There, there. It's alright.'

As Ally goes to them, Lizzy reaches for her arm. Then it's like a baton is being passed, Elliott gently letting go, moving towards

Jayden. He holds out his hand for a shake, and Jayden obliges, even though he thinks it's weird given the time, the place.

'Heart attack,' says Elliott, 'but he's breathing. Lizzy called me right away.'

Jayden takes in every detail of him. His hazel eyes. The stubble at his jawline. The collar of his rugby shirt poking from his wax jacket. He looks incredibly ordinary. Somebody's dad, somebody's son. Wealthy, but not throwing it in anyone's face.

Is Elliott a killer?

Jayden locks on to the bead of sweat that's visible on his forehead.

'He walks that dog of his every morning,' Elliott goes on. 'Lizzy said it's too much for him, but he won't stop . . . I've offered, but it's a point of pride, I think . . .' He stops suddenly, presses a hand to his forehead, wiping the sweat away. 'Sorry, I'm getting twinges. Back's playing up.' He closes his eyes for a second, then opens them again. 'Dear God, it was a shock. Seeing the old boy like that. But Lizzy was calm. So calm. She's . . . remarkable.'

'It was good they phoned you. That they can rely on you.'

'Of course they can rely on me,' says Elliott sharply.

Jayden becomes aware of Elliott's shifting attention. He's watching as Ally and Lizzy, still arm in arm, talk to the ambulance driver.

'I'm taking Lizzy to the hospital,' Ally calls out to Jayden.

'But I can do that,' says Elliott, stepping forward. 'Lizzy, you must let me.'

Jayden can hear a phone ringing and realises it's coming from Elliott's coat. He looks momentarily confused, torn between the phone and Lizzy.

'Lizzy, wait,' says Elliott. He pulls out the phone. Mutters, 'Louisa.'

'Ally has her car here,' says Lizzy, her voice cracked as a broken pane. 'And . . . you said you'd been drinking.'

'Damn, I forgot.' Elliott looks to Jayden. 'It's why I came on foot. I was drinking at lunch. My father, he puts it away. I must be over the limit.'

'Don't worry,' says Jayden, 'Ally's got it.'

The ambulance is on the move, and they're forced to step back to give it space. As the vehicle passes through the gates, Ally and Lizzy are already on their way to the car. Elliott strides after them as they head into the lane. One hand is pressed to his lower back; a glitch in his gait. Even if Elliott wasn't over the limit, it's hard to argue with a car that's right there. And it's hard to argue with the gentle support of Ally.

Is Ally's detective brain firing, though, as she secures this one-on-one time with Lizzy Jago? Jayden knows better than to underestimate her. And it doesn't dilute the compassion in the gesture.

'Jayden, I'll be in touch,' she says.

As the two women climb into the car, and the ambulance grows small in the distance, Jayden is left standing in the lane with Elliott. He turns the full beam of his attention towards him.

What do you know, Elliott King?

'He can't die,' says Elliott quietly. 'He mustn't.'

And he sounds just like a child. A ten-year-old boy. A ten-year-old boy, perhaps, thinking of his friend Peter Jago.

As Jayden is framing a response, Elliott sets off walking. And he's fast, despite the fault in his step. 'Louisa needs me,' he mutters. 'You'll have to excuse me.'

'I'll follow on,' says Jayden.

At which point Elliott all but breaks into a run.

55

Gus gets to Hang Ten just before closing. He's covered the ground between All Swell and Saffron's coffee shop in a kind of dream state. After spending hour after hour deep in the world of his novel, it feels strange being thrust back into reality. For the second day in a row, he's made strides. And for the second day in a row, he's conscious of his inspiration.

All it took was for Ally to tell him to get on with it. Albeit via Jayden.

As biddable as a spaniel, it seems.

Down the beach, the tide is on its way in, and Gus can feel the power of the waves as they break on the shore. It's chaotic out there, the water as unruly as those last-period Year Nines he was thinking of yesterday. *Perhaps I'll stick to writing, not surfing*, he thinks. Recommit to his true calling: *The pen is mightier than the board.* On that thought, he pushes open the door to the café.

'Saffron,' he calls out with gusto, 'I've conquered the novel!'

'You've finished it?' She turns from the coffee machine, cloth in hand, 'Gus, that's amazing.'

A little of the air goes out of him. 'Well, not finished. More . . . restarted. But I've had a cracking couple of days, and it feels great to be back in the saddle. Enjoying the ride. Even jumping the odd fence.'

He's not sure he can stretch the equestrian metaphor any further.

'Nice one, Gus. You look . . . glowy.'

'Glowy?'

Saffron nods. 'Hundred per cent. Coffee? You caught me just in time.'

'Please. And a slice of something to go with it.'

'So, shadowing Ally and Jayden, it's helped, then?'

Gus explains that there hasn't been any shadowing as such, just a little investigative research.

'If I'm honest, they told me to just get on with it. Stop dilly-dallying. Shilly-shallying. Beating about the bally bush. You know.'

'Ally said that?'

'Well, Jayden initially. Not those words, of course. That's the wordmonger in me, Saffron. The ink-slinger.' He can feel himself grinning stupidly, amusing himself. It's as if he's guzzled three pints of Doom Bar on an empty stomach. 'In fact, I should probably call Ally and let her know how helpful she's been.'

'Call Jayden, you mean,' says Saffron, her smile lifting. 'If he's the one who said it.'

Gus looks away first; he knows when his bluff's being called.

'The pair of them,' he says stoically. Because unrequited love is a hopeless sort of look.

The door clangs then, and Broady surges into Hang Ten. The man always looks to be in such iridescently rude health that Gus can't help but sag a bit in his presence. He's in fire-yellow board shorts and flip-flops, despite it being deep autumn.

'Oh, hi,' says Saffron.

Gus notices the drop in her voice; how she tucks a strand of pink hair behind her ear. It must be a strange old feeling, running a business next door to your ex. He could never have weathered living cheek by jowl with Mona once they'd split.

‘What’s this about you doing surf lessons, Saffron?’ says Broady. He looks to Gus, waves his hand dismissively. ‘I don’t mean you, Gus. That’s just messing about. I mean Tim Mullins.’

Saffron laughs. ‘That’s not serious.’

But Broady looks very serious.

‘How did you even—’

‘Word travels,’ says Broady. ‘So, what I want to know is how you’d feel if I got myself a coffee machine? Started flogging flat whites? Porthpella’s not big enough for two surf schools, Saffron. And I was here first.’

‘Milo was right, you’re a capitalist. Your business comes—’

‘It’s not business, it’s . . . personal.’

The weight he puts on that word makes Saffron’s cheeks fill with colour. Gus retreats to a side table; he wishes he had his coffee to fiddle with.

‘And it’s about kicking a man when he’s down,’ says Broady quietly.

‘Broady, I didn’t . . . The thing with Mullins, it’s not real. Can you seriously imagine Mullins surfing? It was a diversionary tactic. I had someone in who didn’t want to attract the attention of the police, and I just said it . . .’

‘One of Milo’s mates?’

‘Not one of Milo’s mates. Not at all. Anyway . . . Milo’s in Berlin. He has been for ages.’

‘What and you’re not?’

‘I’m keeping Hang Ten open through the winter. I want to give it a shot.’ Saffron comes out from behind the counter. She looks as if she doesn’t know what to do with her hands, and in the end she stuffs them in the pocket of her apron. ‘Broady, I’d never take business from you. I want Mahalo to succeed as much as anyone. More than anyone.’

Broady heaves a sigh. Gus knows he should look away, but he can't quite do it. He's never seen a cloud blot out this man's sun before. It's strangely fortifying, seeing someone like Surf God, as Mullins likes to call him, beset by the slings and arrows of romantic misfortune. For a crazed moment Gus imagines leaping to his feet and crying, *For goodness' sake, Milo Nash is in Berlin and Ray Finch is in Suffolk and we're all* here.

'Alright,' says Broady, running a hand through his long hair. 'Guess I'll hit pause on that Gaggia order, then . . .'

'Hey, look, our businesses are neighbours, right? And we're . . . friends? Let's do something. This winter. Together. I've been thinking about it but . . . haven't had the courage to ask.'

'*You* haven't had the courage?' Broady gives a gruff laugh. Then, 'What do you mean, do something together?'

'A collaboration. Like . . .' A sudden smile. 'Winter Waves and Wicked Warm-ups! I just came up with that.'

'Winter Waves and Wicked Warm-ups?'

'I'm thinking . . . like a surf-and-lunch club. You run a lesson, then everyone back here for something hot and tasty. I've been trying a new dahl recipe. Loads of ginger and turmeric – it's so good.'

'What, better than my coconut and cauliflower?'

Broady's voice drips with nostalgia, and Gus still can't look away. Was he a bit of a chef, in his days with Saffron?

'I wouldn't say better,' says Saffron with an easy grin. 'Just . . . different.'

And it's a line that seems to strike a chord with Broady, because the atmosphere changes again. He ducks his head, says something about talking some more, then dips out of the café.

Saffron watches the door, as if she hopes he's going to come back.

'He's got to know I'd never do anything to hurt him,' she says quietly.

And Gus can't help but think beyond Broady, to Tim Mullins and those surf lessons. If Gus knows Tim, he'll think they're real. But it's probably not helpful to point that out right now.

Saffron appears to shake herself and pastes on a grin.

'Hey, guess what, Gus, I had an Instagram-famous travel blogger in here earlier. I wonder if she'd be up for Winter Waves and Wicked Warm-ups?'

'I'm sure she would,' he says distractedly.

But really Gus is still thinking about how easy it is to hurt someone. *Whoever designed human beings to be so damnably emotional? And what a fault it is that, despite our best intentions, we can still make the most dreadful muddle of things.* Gus's presumption about Ally's feelings as a widow; Ray jumping into the ring with his infernal brio just as Gus was on the ropes.

He must call Ally and tell her what a good writing day he's had – and how it's all thanks to her.

An utterance without agenda.

Perhaps some agenda.

Then, yes, okay, he'll call Jayden and thank him too.

56

'You've been here,' says Lizzy.

It's the first time Lizzy has spoken since they got in the car, and Ally has respected her need for quiet. She's understood it too.

'I have,' she says gently.

Should Ally add something reassuring? Torren is breathing; his heart is beating. And for all that Ally has her foot down, the ambulance is far ahead of them; he'll be in safe hands soon. But Lizzy doesn't need false promises.

Ally has been here.

Most people around Porthpella knew Sergeant Bill Bright. Or, at least, they knew *of* him. When Bill died, the tributes poured in. The local press praised his contribution; the funeral was standing room only. It was three and a half years ago. It was yesterday.

Ally can hear Lizzy breathing beside her, over the thrum of the wheels on the road. She glances towards her, sees Lizzy looking straight ahead, her head held high. Her small hands are on top of one another in her lap.

Lizzy is no stranger to the unimaginable.

'Torren's being looked after,' says Ally. 'He's in the best place.'

The woman doesn't reply, but then Ally doesn't expect her to.

It makes sense that extreme emotions might lead to extreme thoughts, but what about extreme action? If the circumstances were different, Ally would be asking Lizzy about Elliott, and whether he and Peter were good friends. Lizzy must be close to Elliott, for her to have phoned him when Torren collapsed; she called 999, and then she called the High Tide. Elliott came straight away.

'We're nearly there,' says Ally.

Then they're pulling into the hospital car park, mercifully finding a space. Ally clicks off the engine and turns to Lizzy. The woman makes no move to get out. In her lap, her fingers are knotted like a cat's cradle.

'I'm scared, Ally.'

Ally covers Lizzy's hands with her own. The elderly lady's skin is papery, sun-spotted. She clasps Ally's fingers tightly.

'Peter went in an ambulance, but he was long dead,' she says in a small voice. 'There was no helping him.'

And in this moment, Ally suspects that thirty-seven years is nothing; nothing at all.

'Life can be very cruel,' she says gently. 'I'm sorry you've had so much pain. But Torren . . .'

'You never get over losing a child. Never.' Lizzy looks up, fixes Ally with her misted blue eyes. 'He told me once he had nothing left to live for. And then . . .'

The sentence goes unfinished.

'And then?'

Lizzy gives a brief shake of her head as she takes her hands away from Ally's. Her engagement ring stands proud beneath her swollen knuckle; she rubs the pad of her thumb on the stone.

'And now this. What if . . . ?'

She closes her eyes, and a tear slips from her pale lashes.

'Lizzy,' says Ally, as carefully as she can, 'is there something you want to tell me?'

57

Mullins and Skinner watch Steve Bradshaw make his way across the car park to a waiting taxi. The detective sergeant is muttering under his breath, his language as colourful as a pirate's. Suffice to say the one-time detective constable of Thames Valley did not endear himself to them during his brief stay under their roof. But despite Steve Bradshaw having every reason to wish Drew ill – Schofield cost him his career for one, and he failed to deliver on a promise for two – they can't prove he had anything to do with Drew's death.

The search teams have failed to turn up the coat.

The tech team have failed to enhance the video image.

The forensics have failed to produce any incriminating DNA.

The hotel's CCTV has yielded diddly squat.

Mae has not reneged on her alibi.

No new witnesses have come forward.

And Blake Bryant? He was released a couple of hours ago, trailing off to the bus stop looking like a lost boy.

All this notwithstanding – including his boss's foul temper – nothing can dent Mullins's mood. Did he seriously walk into Hang Ten earlier and get offered a surf lesson by Saffron? *Dreams do come true.* If he didn't feel so fantastic, he'd be weirded out.

'What have those two got, then?' Skinner says now, turning to Mullins.

Mullins wrinkles his forehead; he'd temporarily floated off elsewhere. 'Who two?'

'Shell House shamateurs.'

'Last I heard . . .' says Mullins, then stops. What was the last he heard? Jayden last night, fishing for leads. 'They're getting nowhere fast, Sarge.'

Skinner grunts. And Mullins can't tell if it's a grunt of relief, that they haven't been outdone, or a grunt of disappointment. On a good day, Skinner also believes in the greater good. But today isn't a good day for the detective sergeant.

For me, though? I'm walking on air. Walking on water.

They currently have zero suspects in the Drew Schofield case. And the fact that Thames Valley haven't sent any extra bodies to trample over their patch is representative of Drew's standing over there. *Not many fans, once you get past the platitudes*, was how Skinner put it.

'The lack of hard evidence points to this being a professional hit,' says Skinner, 'or at least coolly calculated. I don't like it, but we have to keep focusing efforts on Schofield's past arrests. Look for any connective tissue.'

'We've said all along that he had a lot of enemies,' says Mullins. He puffs out his chest a bit. 'This line of work, it comes with the territory, doesn't it?'

'I'm not sure any master criminals are currently plotting your demise, Mullins.'

'Yeah, well, Schofield was a lot of things, but no one can deny he was a thief-taker. I don't get the chance to make many collars, down here. Different lay of the land, isn't it?'

'You saying you want to put in for a transfer, are you?'

For the first time all day, Mullins detects a note of enthusiasm in Skinner's voice. And it stings him like a bee.

'Because the point I was actually making,' Skinner goes on, 'is that you're an honest, fair-minded cop, Mullins. I've never had a single complaint against you.'

Mullins shifts on his feet. 'Nice one.'

'Nice one, *Sarge*.'

'Sarge. Thank you. Sarge.'

Skinner turns to go, then spins back; pulls at his moustache.

'Out of interest, when was the last time you actually heard from Ally and/or Jayden? Because it wouldn't hurt to check in again with them.'

'Jayden wanted a bit of pillow talk last night. He was banging on about Drew holidaying down here as a teen.'

'Drew and the rest of the world,' huffs Skinner. 'And what of it?'

'Not a lot. You want me to find out if they've got any new leads?' he says.

'You might as well. In between going over every single arrest Drew Schofield ever made, checking prison releases, seeing if any of them have a link to Cornwall.'

'But I've done that, Sarge. It's brought up nothing.'

'And it's all we've got, so you'll keep doing it until the next idiot decides it's their day to break the law and our efforts are required elsewhere. Listen, Mullins, I wanted us to tie a nice bow on this one. Drew Schofield's death was not an accident. I know that, you know that, DCI Robinson knows that. The Major Crimes team – despite the fact that they're in the process of shipping out – also know that. But have you noticed that no one's clamouring for justice? Schofield's wife barely seems bothered he's gone. His former colleagues haven't lifted a finger to help catch his killer. So much for "one of our own", hmm?'

'And the person paying Ally and Jayden is Louisa King,' says Mullins, 'just because she wants her precious hotel to get back to normal . . .'

'Quite,' says Skinner. 'But, Mullins, you and I like a job well done. So, call Ally and Jayden, will you? See if they're pursuing any Shell House nonsense, or if they've downed tools on this one.'

Mullins fights a smile.

'What?' says Skinner.

'Just . . . I think we already know the answer, don't we?'

It'll be Shell House nonsense all the way.

58

Blake wonders whether to knock, but in the end he just uses his key card. It was returned to him when he left the police station, along with his belt and his wallet and his phone. Not that the phone has been any use: it's completely dead. Blake hasn't been able to message Summer, and he hasn't been able to see if she's messaged him. He has no idea what she's feeling, so as he pushes open the door, he's trying to arrange his features into something impassive. Only, he can feel the clench to his jaw, and the fact that there's a sore spot on his lip where he keeps chewing it; he's frowning so hard it's making his head sore. Blake cannot pretend that any of this is okay – even if he secured one minor win in getting into the hotel and through reception without being seen by anyone.

Just like Drew Schofield's killer?

But the bedroom is empty.

Summer isn't here.

Did she get tired of waiting? Blake knows he's made a meal of getting back here. First, he caught a bus in the wrong direction, then had to wait over an hour for another. The driver told him it stopped two miles from the High Tide, but the lanes were a maze, and without his phone he found himself lost; he must have walked five miles. He was too self-conscious of where he'd come from to flag down a lift, and hardly any cars passed anyway. In the end, a good three hours late, he made it. The only silver lining? Blake's had plenty of time to work out his speech for Summer.

But . . . where is she?

The next thing Blake notices is that the bed is perfectly made. Housekeeping must have been in; no surprises there. But the book Summer was reading has gone from her side of the bed. Her laptop, notebook and pencil case, which she'd left out on the desk, are also gone. He goes into the bathroom. There's only one toothbrush left in the pot. His washbag, a freebie with some aftershave years ago, is all on its own.

Oh, Summer.

With a sinking feeling, Blake goes to the wardrobe and finds exactly what he now expects: all her clothes have gone. Her wheely suitcase too.

Summer has left the High Tide.

Blake drops on to the bed and sinks his head into his hands. The tears that he's been holding on to for the last twenty-four hours push painfully inside of him. As they rise, they burn his throat, sting his eyes.

No!

He pulls his dead phone out of his pocket. Maybe she's messaged him. *Please can she have messaged me.* He scans the wall sockets in the hope that Summer left her charger plugged in, but no. And obviously Blake forgot to bring his own. They'll have one at reception but there's no way he can face going down to ask.

Stupid. Reckless. Coward.

The words rain down on him like blows. Blake is his own worst enemy: his dad said that to him once and it's true. He'd like not to be, he'd like to be his own best friend, but so it goes.

When Drew Schofield arrested him a decade ago, Blake was protecting a mate of his. James Connell, he was called. James had fallen prey to this gang from school: endless bullying, rising violence. Then came the tipping point in the park, when they were walking together, minding their own business. James was slammed to the ground and set upon – so Blake waded in. Maybe he shouldn't have done but, at the time, it didn't feel like a choice. That's what he told the court. *I had no choice.* He meant that it was a protective instinct, but it was read as latent aggression. A lack of self-control. The judge made an example of him.

He'll have to tell Summer the full story now. That it was self-defence but, at a point, he could have stopped and he didn't. That was what Blake realised, so crushingly, in the detention centre. That the bullies had won. Because, in that fight in the park, he'd been as bad as them – and, when he got out, that was the narrative that flew in the community too. James didn't want anything to do with him; maybe that was down to his parents, but it still hurt. Blake was an outcast. And that's why he's never told Summer about any of it.

Shame on top of shame.

He rubs his eyes; hears a voice.

You were brave, Blake.

Words he's held on to all these years. They came from a kid inside, someone infinitely more troubled than him. The two of them got talking in the library, which was a miracle in itself because he didn't talk to anyone in there unless he had to, but somehow the whole story came out. The younger boy said, *Sounds like you were really brave*. The only person to ever say it. Not Blake's parents, not his lawyer, but a boy whose name he can't even remember.

Is it brave now to walk down into reception and ask for a phone charger? Given the circumstances, yes, it is. Blake wipes his sleeve across his face. Then he decides he needs to up his game and goes into the bathroom, splashes water all over his face.

'Be brave,' he says to his miserable reflection. He tries to find his mountain self. The one Summer fell in love with.

You can do a 540 stalefish. Back-flip off a rock drop. Fly through powder and spin off rails.

'You can sure as hell go downstairs and ask for a phone charger,' he says out loud.

Then he leaves the room before he changes his mind. With luck, he'll be in and out – a quick exchange, ideally with a member of staff who doesn't know who he is – then he can escape back here. Crawl under his rock.

Blake treads down the corridor, rounds the corner and down the next. As he takes the stairs to reception, he hears the sound of a car alarm. Then, as he gets closer, a smashing, shattering sound, followed by another. Raised voices. He feels the hairs stand up on the back of his neck.

Here's trouble.

And, despite his instincts to avoid the stuff, so hardwired now, he goes directly towards it.

There's no one at the desk, but Blake can see the hotel owner, Louisa, standing in the doorway. Her hands are held to her face. Beside her is the small dark-haired woman who was part of the Oxford party of four.

'I don't know how to stop him,' says the dark-haired woman over the shriek of the alarm. Her voice is loud, but weirdly unbothered.

Out in the car park, Detective Sergeant Drew Schofield's mate is attacking a Range Rover with a big lump of rock. It takes Blake a second to realise it's one of the polished-stone sculptures from just inside reception. He can feel his face contorting in surprise, like a cartoon character. Eyes on stalks. Jaw on floor.

Smash.

But then his heart quickens in his chest, because violence of any kind takes him all the way back to the moment in the park. To just about every day in the detention centre, where the constant threat of it buzzed like white noise.

This man – Schofield's mate – is lost in his own fury. His face is as red as spilt blood. He smashes the rock on the car bonnet then aims a kick at the hubcap. Another smash, accompanied by a shout.

'Whose car is that?' Blake says to no one in particular, forgetting he's supposed to be lying low.

'Our car.'

And it's Drew's wife, suddenly appearing behind him. His widow.

Smash.

The Range Rover's bonnet sags like a tent in a storm. The alarm wails on.

'Kathy,' says Mae, turning to her, 'I'm so sorry.'

'I never liked it anyway,' says Kathy.

Mae gives an odd shrill laugh. 'I told Steve I'm leaving him, see, and Steve being Steve, he has to blame someone else.'

'Drew's as good a person to blame as anyone,' says Kathy.

Smash. The windscreen shatters, a spider's web of broken glass.

'He's self-destructing, isn't he?' Mae looks at her watch. 'Kathy, our taxi will be here in a minute. Good bloody riddance.'

The two women stand looking on, as if indifferent spectators with no investment in the outcome of this game. Meanwhile Louisa seems to be frozen in disbelief. But Blake's watching every move this man makes, *feeling* every move, because what's to say he won't turn that lump of rock on these women when he's finished with the car? What's to say he won't lock eyes with Blake and see a new target?

'Someone needs to call the police,' he says. 'This guy's out of control.'

'This is not normal High Tide behaviour,' says Louisa – as if that's the important thing here. Then her face changes. 'Oh, it's you. Is Summer back too?'

59

'I'm sad to hear about Torren Jago, but he's made of stern stuff,' says Malcolm.

Jayden sits on a plush sofa in the Kings' living room, alongside the one-time owner of the High Tide. Their private home is even more opulently styled than the hotel. Jayden's feet are currently lost in a carpet that's as soft as fresh snowfall. Five hundred cushions – or maybe just three – are at his back.

After Torren left in the ambulance, Jayden followed Elliott down the hill to the High Tide. He watched the owner head towards the main entrance – no doubt to find Louisa – then Jayden slipped away around the back, towards the Kings' private quarters. If this is Jayden's only chance to talk to Malcolm without Elliott interrupting, he's going to take it. And he has a feeling the old man will be more forthcoming than his son.

Does Malcolm hold the key to the whole thing? Maybe.

Jayden adjusts himself against the cushions and studies Malcolm's tanned and handsome face. He's clean-shaven and shiny-haired; a smooth operator. Living the good life out in Mallorca, a long way from the High Tide.

'Malcolm, yesterday you said that Torren and Lizzy still carried a lot of resentment for what happened to Peter. Was that ever aimed at someone specific?'

Jayden's trying to be casual, but underneath he's charged. Malcolm narrows his blue eyes as if he's suspicious of so direct a question. Jayden can imagine him being steely when he wants to be.

'Why are you back on that?'

Why? Because this has to be about Peter.

But maybe it's about Elliott too. He was almost frantic, wanting to take Lizzy to the hospital. Was he afraid of what Lizzy, alone with Ally, might say?

Without waiting for an answer, Malcolm says, 'Torren could never win against his adversary. By which I mean the sea.'

Dodging the question.

'I read a news article from the time, where Torren said he thought there was more to Peter's death than met the eye,' says Jayden. 'Was that view shared by anyone else around here? What about you? And Elliott?'

'Elliott? Elliott was a child. He was young when that tragedy happened, no more than nine or ten. He didn't have an opinion on it.'

'Were he and Peter friends?'

'Friends?' Malcolm blinks. 'In a manner of speaking, I suppose. Peter was sixteen. Perhaps on some level Elliott looked up to him. The truth is, I was always so busy with the hotel that I'm not sure I knew a huge amount about Elliott's day-to-day life at that age. He was a bit of a loner, and Peter was too, I suppose. Both only children, you see. Perhaps that did connect them. But . . . Well, you shall have to ask Elliott.'

'At the time, though,' says Jayden, 'you must have talked to your son about what happened to Peter.'

To talk about death – what it was, what it meant – because maybe it was Elliott's first experience of it. To warn his son of the dangers lurking in this paradise: tides, caves, rockfalls, cliff falls, the lot. Surely that conversation was the least a father could do?

'My wife did,' says Malcolm stiffly. 'Elliott's mother. She was better at that kind of thing than I was.'

'Drew Schofield knew Peter Jago,' says Jayden.

He says it out of nowhere, a verbal sucker-punch. But Malcolm just looks puzzled.

'How's that possible?'

'They were around the same age. Drew used to come here on holiday.'

'To the High Tide?'

'No, a campsite up the road. Drew was here the same summer that Peter died.'

'Was he really? How extraordinary.'

'You don't remember? They had some run-ins at the beach. Drew beat Peter up. Torren got involved, going up to the campsite to confront Drew's dad . . .'

Malcolm shakes his head. 'If they weren't my guests then there's little chance I'd have known. I didn't get involved in the soapy stuff. The campsite always drew a fairly raucous crowd. Families from upcountry. Groups of teenagers. But it was harmless fun, mostly.'

'The fight happened the day before Peter died.'

Malcolm's pouring another coffee from the pot on the table. His hand pauses.

'What are you saying?'

'I'm saying . . . it's a coincidence. Isn't it? The timing. The people involved.'

'There was an inquest,' he says, putting the pot down. 'Death by drowning. Terribly sad but that was an end to it. The only people who couldn't accept it were the Jagos.'

'And what about Elliott?'

'Elliott was ten! What kind of an opinion would you expect him to have? Not one worth factoring in to your enquiry, if that's what this is.'

'When a man dies, everything's worth factoring in.'

Malcolm sits back in his chair. He's as still as a painting.

'You can't really think my son had anything to do with it?'

Jayden's about to respond when the door flies open. Louisa bursts in, then stops abruptly when she clocks him. She rolls her eyes in frustration, then focuses on her father-in-law.

'Malcolm, have you any idea where Elliott is? It's absolute chaos. Steve Bradshaw's running riot. The police are apparently on their way. Added to that I've got an airport taxi that hasn't turned up for the German couple in room four. And I simply can't deal with it all on my own . . .'

Malcolm's already on his feet. 'Let me help.'

'But where's Elliott? He's not answering his bloody phone.'

'Louisa, Torren Jago had a heart attack,' says Jayden. 'He's been rushed to hospital. Elliott was with them, but he came back here to see you. What do you mean, Steve Bradshaw's running riot?'

'He's smashed up the Schofields' car,' she says. 'I told you this had to be solved quickly. It's descending into . . .'

Jayden goes to the window before she can finish. The Kings' living room is at the side of the house, with a view of the eastern corner of the beach. How have they not heard the drama?

'. . . and meanwhile Steve Bradshaw's girlfriend seems thoroughly unconcerned. She's merrily gone off in a cab to St Ives with Drew Schofield's widow. Washing their hands of the whole debacle.' Louisa comes and stands beside him. 'Jayden, not to be rude but what are you doing in our home?'

'That maniac hasn't touched any other cars, has he?' says Malcolm. 'I haven't taken out excess insurance on my hire car, and—'

'And where's Elliott?' Louisa says again, ignoring him, the question flying like an arrow.

'He'll have gone to the hospital,' shrugs Malcolm.

'He hasn't gone to the hospital,' says Jayden. 'He came back here. I followed him.'

'You *followed* him?' Louisa flicks a loose strand of hair. 'What is this?'

But Jayden's already making for the door.

'Louisa, where's Steve Bradshaw now?'

'Oh, the little devil's shut himself in his room. As soon as he saw his girlfriend disappear in her cab, he wilted like a tulip.'

Jayden pauses by the window. There's a clear view of the beach, and a movement catches his eye. A lone figure, walking fast towards the sea. At this distance, in the gathering dusk, he can't be sure – but it could be Elliott. And if it is? Jayden doesn't want Louisa and Malcolm to know; they're only going to be obstructive.

And I think Elliott killed Drew Schofield.

Jayden glances to Louisa and Malcolm. Louisa's lost in her drama; Malcolm sits glassy-eyed. Neither one has noticed the figure on the beach.

'Thanks for your time, Malcolm,' he says.

And, before they can respond, Jayden scoots. He takes the stairs two at a time, phone in his hand making a call. As he gets outside, the constable answers.

'I'm already on my way, Jay,' says Mullins. 'Bradshaw's wielding a ruddy great rock, is he? Nice one.'

'He's back in his room, apparently. Mae and Kathy have left.'

'What, you haven't wrestled him to the ground?'

Mullins makes a tutting noise, but it's lost as Jayden rounds the corner of the building and steps right into a gusting wind. He makes straight for the beach, head down. The top layer of soft sand is on the move, blowing around his ankles as if he's in a desert sandstorm.

'Mullins, I've got to go. I can hardly hear you out here. But I'm tailing Elliott King.'

‘What’s that? I can’t hear you, Jayden. I know it’s the bloody wind.’

‘Not the wind, I said Elliott King.’

In the twilight, the man on the beach is only just visible. Jayden squints, trying to see more clearly. If that’s Elliott, he’s at the very edge of the cove and isn’t stopping. Meanwhile the waves are as tall as houses, toppling on to the shore, smithereens of water flying way up the beach.

‘Mullins, get yourself to the High Tide.’

Then Jayden’s ringing off, sliding his phone into his pocket and breaking into a run. Because Elliott has disappeared, and as far as Jayden can see, the only way out is the sea.

60

You've been here.

That was what Lizzy said. And as they sit beside one another on the hard plastic chairs, Ally's stomach clenches, memories swashing into her mind, churning like white water. Bill was pronounced dead in this hospital. Gus lay here in intensive care. Two very different moments, two very different emotions, two very different men.

Please.

That was the binding word then. A six-letter prayer. All kinds of people, all over the world, are probably saying it at this very moment, she thinks. And one is Lizzy Jago.

Please.

Lizzy sits beside Ally, her voice a whisper. There isn't much holding her together, except the hope contained in this one word.

Torren suffered a second heart attack just as they were arriving at the Accident and Emergency ward. He was rushed in on the stretcher, a flood of staff in attendance. Lizzy all but dropped to her knees. She must have thought that the worst was already behind them; that in these safe hands, things would get better, not worse.

They wait together now, side by side. And there is nothing to say, nothing to do.

Ally hears her phone buzzing on silent and discreetly checks who's calling. Only Gus. She leaves it unanswered.

She hasn't repeated the question she asked Lizzy in the car park. *Is there something you want to tell me?* It's lost to the tide of emotion. But stronger than ever, Ally has a feeling that Lizzy knows more.

The woman says something that Ally can't catch; she leans closer.

'Lizzy, what did you say?'

'A punishment.'

Ally waits for more.

'Where does it end?' whispers Lizzy. 'An eye for an eye.'

Ally shifts just perceptibly. It's as if a rare bird has landed in the garden and she can't afford to startle it. She can't break Lizzy's train of thought.

'He tried to talk to him. But he didn't want to know. He acted like Peter was nothing. He was . . . vile. If only he'd . . . said sorry. If only he'd just said that.'

Who is he*?*

The past and the present swirl together: Drew as a teenager beating up Peter; Torren storming to the campsite; Peter dying the next day; Drew dying nearly forty years later. Accidents and non-accidents.

Lizzy unknots her hands and makes two fists. They're as small as walnuts.

'He did what he had to do,' she says, 'and now he's paying the price.'

61

Dusk is falling fast, but Jayden can pick out every single one of Elliott's footprints in the sand. The prints are deep and wide apart, as if he is running.

Why?

As Jayden rounds the rocks and goes into the next cove, a gang of gulls swoop over his head, wailing in that so-human way that he still can't get used to. Here the prints turn sharply, and head back towards the cliffs. Jayden follows, then stops. Suddenly, he knows exactly where Elliott is.

The entrance to the cave is a black gash in the side of the cliff. The wooden sign – the warning notice that he suspects Torren made – is barely visible in the half-light. Jayden takes out his phone and sees he has a message from Ally.

With Lizzy at the hospital. I think she knows something.

No time to reply. Instead, he turns on his phone's torch and treads into the cave.

Just a few steps from the entrance, it's black as night. And cold too. Jayden shivers involuntarily. There's a stench of briny seawater and something foul: rotting seaweed, maybe? The toe of his trainer scuffs something and he looks down to see a dead seabird, a huge gull, half mauled, by animal or time and tide.

'Elliott?' he calls out.

No reply.

Jayden runs the torchlight over the rocky walls, the low roof. How far back does this cave go?

Far enough for Peter Jago to get stuck and drown.

'Elliott!' he shouts again.

Jayden's conscious of the sound of the sea at his back. The waves are big this evening, and close enough to hear the crash and fizz. But still far enough away not to be a worry.

Yet.

He goes deeper into the cave, his torch flashing in the dark. The footprints continue and they're scuffed now, close together.

Then he sees him. A shape in the gloom; totally still.

'Elliott?'

Back in Leeds, Jayden faced it all. He walked into the line of fire; mostly metaphorically, occasionally literally. Because the day-to-day of a response officer is trouble. Chaos is never far away. One man in a sea cave? This shouldn't be a scare. But Jayden shivers again. The truth is, he doesn't love small spaces; he never has. He's conscious of his rising heartbeat, his speeding breath. The sound of the sea fills his ears. He might be a city boy, but he roughly knows how tides work, and this one's on its way in. Jayden wishes Ally were here. Ally would know exactly when high tide is; Ally would know whether the sea fills these caves habitually, or only in a winter storm.

Peter died in the middle of summer.

He steps closer.

'Elliott, it's me. Jayden.'

As Elliott turns, Jayden trains the torch beam on the wall; he doesn't want to blind the guy.

He doesn't want to drive him deeper into this damn cave.

'Why are you here?' Elliott takes the question straight out of Jayden's mouth. 'What do you want?' His voice rises in pitch, and he sounds nothing like the man on the High Tide reception desk.

What do I want?

Where does he start? Jayden has two goals: one, get Elliott out of here; two, get him talking. Because he knows, with absolute certainty now, that Elliott has things to say.

Just look at the guy.

'I want to make sure you're okay, Elliott. The tide's on its way in. We need to go.'

'Don't try to tell me about this cave,' says Elliott, his voice thick with emotion.

Jayden adjusts the torch beam, assessing the environment. Elliott's standing on the other side of a rock. Is there a ledge? Another passage? He treads closer.

'Elliott, you were friends with Peter, weren't you?'

His careful question falls between sets and there's a brief moment of total quiet.

'Yes.'

Then the next wave hits the beach, and the sound cascades through the cave. A forewarning of what's to come, if they don't move.

'Torren . . . Is he alive?' says Elliott.

'I haven't heard otherwise.'

'It's my fault.'

'Torren's heart attack?' *Or Drew Schofield's death?*

Jayden steps closer, careful with his torchlight. Elliott is leaning against a rock; one hand planted on the small of his back. He looks hard at Jayden and fifty different thoughts fly across his shadowy features.

'What happened to Peter . . .' he begins.

Jayden holds his eye but turns an ear to the sea. The tide is incoming, no doubt.

But what about the incoming story?

'I was the one who got him to the cave,' says Elliott, his voice pure pain. 'I was the reason Peter died.' He drags in a breath. '*God.* I've never said that out loud.'

Jayden stays completely still. The sea is still a way off, right? It can wait.

'What happened that day, Elliott? Your dad said you were too young to remember, but—'

'Dad wouldn't know,' he cuts in. 'He never knew.'

'What didn't he know?'

'That I told Peter he had to go to the cave. That Rebecca was stuck. That she was panicking.'

Rebecca?

'There was a girl called Rebecca that summer. Peter loved her, and Drew . . . Drew was jealous. Incredibly jealous. He'd already beaten Peter up, but then his father punished him for that, so suddenly Drew had two things to be furious about, two things to blame Peter for.'

Elliott's talking quickly now; his voice strained as it bears the weight of the past. Elliott can't know that Jayden has met Rebecca; that he's sat in her conservatory and drunk her coffee. But the one inconsistency?

Rebecca getting stuck in the cave.

'I was playing on the beach and Drew came running. He said, "Where's Peter? Find Peter!" He told me that Rebecca had been exploring and got herself trapped in one of the tunnels at the back. Drew said Peter knew this place better than anyone and he was the only one who could help. He looked really scared, so I ran. I ran to find Peter.'

Jayden keeps the torch beam steady. No false moves. His heart is banging, but his head tries not to race ahead.

Keep talking, Elliott. Keep talking.

'I found Peter in his garden and told him. God, I remember the feeling. Of being important, trusted. I felt like the King's messenger. Peter didn't hesitate. He sprinted ahead, and I started to follow but then he told me not to come, that it was dangerous. I felt . . . well, I felt overlooked, I suppose. It was like Drew trusted me and Peter didn't. I know that logic doesn't hold, but . . . Then my mother spotted me, and I was called in for tea. It wasn't late, but people were leaving the beach. They always did at high tide, sandcastles collapsing and people grabbing their deckchairs, and . . .' His voice runs out. 'But then, later that evening, when I was getting ready for bed, I heard a fuss downstairs. There was an ambulance, and police, and all these people. A dog walker had found a body just inside the entrance to the cave. I remember thinking . . . Peter couldn't save her. He couldn't save Rebecca. But when I got down there . . . there she was. Rebecca. The girl with the red hair. And there was Drew and the boys from the campsite and the parents too. There was everyone. Rubberneckers. Me in my pyjamas. And there was Peter too. But . . . it was Peter who was dead.'

Jayden feels the arrival of the thought before it's even fully formed. It hums inside of him. The hairs on the back of his neck stand up.

I know what Elliott is going to say next.

'It was like I was in a dream. I remember looking at Peter's body, and then at Rebecca, and thinking, "But you're not wet. Why aren't you wet?" I pushed through the crowd and got to Drew. I tugged his arm and . . . I can still remember how he looked at me. Like I was something he'd just trodden in. I tried to get the words out, but he said, "What are you talking about? Don't you know it's wrong to tell lies, little boy?" It was like the ground went from beneath my feet. The crowd dispersed. Peter was taken away in the ambulance, even though there was no point, was there? No point. He was dead. And the Jagos, Lizzy and Torren, they were . . . distraught. And all I could think was . . . I did this. This is my fault.'

Elliott stares at Jayden. His face is wide open, as if he's ready to take whatever punch of a response Jayden might throw.

'Drew lied to you, Elliott,' says Jayden. 'You couldn't have known that.'

Elliott winces, leans against the rock as if in pain.

'What I can't remember, what I couldn't remember at the time, is if I said to Peter that it was Drew who told me Rebecca was trapped. Or if I just said that Rebecca was trapped. Because if I mentioned Drew, like I should have, Peter would have smelt a rat. Wouldn't he? I'm sure he would have. So, what if I just said, "Rebecca's trapped"?'

'You were just passing on a message, Elliott. You thought you were doing the right thing.'

'I was gullible. An easy target. Drew knew how pathetic I was.'

'You were ten, Elliott. Just a little boy.' Jayden pauses. 'And you've never told anyone this? You never spoke to Rebecca back then?'

Because Rebecca loved Peter. If she'd known about the lie, she'd have told someone. But Jayden doesn't say it, because Elliott doesn't need to feel any worse.

'I never told anyone. I was ashamed. Scared. I did go up to the campsite two days later, I decided I wanted to try and talk to Rebecca, but . . . they were all gone. That group had shipped out, back to wherever they came from. And I thought . . . I can pretend this didn't happen now. There's no one left who knows. And doing that felt like the safest, least frightening thing.' He looks up at Jayden. 'So I'm a coward, you see. Always was. Then and now.'

Jayden turns, training the torch on the entrance of the cave. The water's coming now; reaching out then pulling back, its wet fingers clawing at the sand. It's dangerous to stay any longer. No matter what Elliott has to say next.

'Elliott,' he says warningly, 'we've got to get out of this cave now.'

'I come here sometimes. I come here and think of Peter. No one knows that.'

'Elliott . . .'

The water flows in, then drops back.

'I made a sort of memorial in one of the tunnels right at the back, just a tower of stones high up on a rock. No one knows it's there. When the tide's really high it gets destroyed by the sea, so I come back and rebuild it. But sometimes it survives. Sometimes it survives for weeks on end. I'll show you . . .'

Jayden puts a hand on his shoulder. 'Come on, we can't mess around now . . .'

'Mess around?' Elliott spins on his heel, and his face is lit with sudden anger. A warning flare goes off in Jayden. When Elliott was ten, he was an innocent victim, manipulated by a much older boy. But Jayden doubts he's so innocent now. He looks down, feeling the swill of water at his feet, just millimetres for now. But then there's a harder push and it covers his trainers. The tick-tick of alarm turns to fear.

'Sorry, wrong word. But the tide's coming in. We need to go, Elliott.'

'Peter died because of me. And now his poor father . . . after a life of nothing but misery . . . That's got to be on me too.'

Jayden can hear his phone buzzing in his pocket. Much as he doesn't want to sever this fragile connection with Elliott, it could be important. Plus, he wouldn't mind telling someone where he is right now.

It's Gus.

'Gus,' he says, 'can you hear me?'

Silence, then a fragmented voice.

'. . . not interrupting . . .'

Course the reception would be dodgy.

'Gus?'

'. . . day's work . . .'

Jayden shines his torch back towards Elliott. He's turned away and is heading deeper into the cave. *No.* He splashes after him. 'Gus, I can't hear you, you're breaking up . . .'

'. . . so thank y . . .'

'Elliott, we need to go the other way,' Jayden calls out.

Gus's voice carries on; distant and broken – but persistent.

'. . . just write and . . .'

'Gus, I'm in a cave at Trebaron Cove, can you—'

Jayden reaches Elliott and gently puts his hand on his shoulder, but Elliott twists away, not wanting the touch. The action pulls Elliott off balance, and he shouts out, reaching for Jayden this time. He yanks heavily at Jayden's arm, the arm that's holding the phone – and on the other end Gus, chattering still, broken-voiced, completely oblivious. As Jayden staggers, surprised by the sudden move, another wave slaps higher, harder, reaching his calves. Elliott clutches again at Jayden, staggering on his feet, pulling again at Jayden's arm – and Jayden feels the phone slip from his fingers.

Whatever sound it makes as it hits the water is lost as Elliott goes over. A splash and a crash. The light goes out.

Fear, sharp as a blade, cuts in. Jayden swears.

'Elliott?'

'My back.'

A pained voice in the dark.

Jayden squats in the water, casting around for the phone. He's wet to his elbows. And if he's waiting for his eyes to adjust, it's not going to happen. It's totally black in this cave. The phone is gone. The light is gone. Gus is gone.

Jayden's hands find Elliott's shoulder in the dark. 'You okay?'

'Back's gone,' he says, through gritted teeth. 'Done it before. Muscle spasm. I can't . . .'

But the last of Elliott's words are lost as a wave – invisible in the darkness – slaps him hard in the face.

62

Ally steps outside and gulps in the cold evening air. It's tobacco-tinged, for there are two smokers outside the hospital doors: a man hunched in a wheelchair; a woman turning slow circles, her phone pressed to her ear. The light falls in puddles as the car park stretches ahead into the darkness; signs are everywhere, directing people's pain left and right. Ally closes her eyes to it all.

Torren Jago is dead; the second heart attack too much for his frail body.

And Lizzy Jago has told her everything.

Ally can feel the sting of hot tears on her cheeks. She takes out her phone, because the one person she wants to speak to, the one person she needs to speak to, is Jayden. But then she pockets it again; she hasn't got the words for him yet.

She starts to walk away from the building, unsure of her direction. She just needs movement. Movement helps her think.

And I need to think.

It's only early evening but it feels like the dead of night. Away from the blare of the building, the floodlit car park, the darkness is swamping. Ally would walk and walk if she could. Think and think and walk and walk. But, even after all that, she knows the conclusion she'd come to is the same as the one she felt on instinct, the moment Lizzy told her desperate story in all its detail.

Drew Schofield came to the Jagos' cottage by chance. His wife missed the turning to the High Tide and used their driveway. Torren talked to them through the window. *Just follow the lane down.* Torren didn't recognise him, of course he didn't, but when he heard the wife say her husband's name in full, *Drew Schofield* – a self-conscious tone, trying for affection, but anyone could see this man was a piece of work – he thought . . . *Schofield. It isn't, is it?* But there was something about the look on the man's face – the angry jut to his jaw, the hard eyes – that added up. When Torren went back inside, he was shaking – *like a leaf,* Lizzy said – and he told his wife his suspicions. They got straight on their old computer, the one that sat upstairs, square as a fish tank, hardly ever used, and looked him up. *Drew Schofield.* They saw he was a police officer, a detective. They saw that he was retired. They saw the complaints against him in the local newspaper. They read the comments: more stories, more aggrieved people lending their voices. They spent one hour, two, finding out everything they could about the man. And their conclusion? Perhaps not a life to be proud of, all in all.

Then they phoned Elliott.

We wanted to know if Schofield was staying there, said Lizzy. *Torren wanted to talk to him, you see.*

And Elliott confirmed the booking. Then asked Torren what he wanted with him.

There was something in his voice, Lizzy said. *I don't know if he sensed something was off. Because what would we want with a man like that? Elliott had no idea.*

From the top of Star Cottage, Torren watched the hotel like a sentry. From Peter's bedroom you can see the terrace, the path to the beach. He wanted to go and find Drew Schofield wherever he was – in the bar, in his bedroom, anywhere – but Torren had a feeling that Elliott, and certainly Louisa, would try to stop him.

So, when Torren saw Drew go out walking down the beach on his own, he fair ran. He went as quickly as his old legs could carry him.

Torren talked to Schofield, Ally. Right by the cave, of all places.

As Lizzy recounted this part of the story, her cheeks glowed like embers. She was burning with emotion, with anger. Because, at the beach, by the cave, Drew brushed Torren off as if he were a fly. He denied even knowing who Peter was. Said, *Stop bothering me, old man. What are you, senile?*

If Torren tried to speak to Drew from a place of equanimity, when he returned to the cottage he was full of rage. It was, Lizzy said, as if the clock had wound full back to their darkest hour. The day that Peter died.

If only Schofield had said, I'm sorry for your loss, said Lizzy. *But to deny that Peter even existed? That Torren had any right to be standing there, talking about his son? It lit a match under Torren, that. And he knew Schofield was involved, because why else would he go to the cave? Why would he stand there looking at it, like it meant something to him too?*

So Torren made his mind up. Lizzy tried to stop him, but she knew she couldn't. He took a gamble, lying in wait, then propping open a side door with a tiny stone. Later, when he returned, the storm seemed to be on Torren's side too, what with gales taking out the power lines, plunging the hotel into darkness and killing the CCTV.

He went to the hotel to kill him, Ally.

Gloves, hat, a big coat. Careful not to touch much. Torren was a neat and careful man. And Drew? Drew made it all so easy.

He was drunken, clumsy, stumbling. He let Torren into the room. He saw the glint of a knife in Torren's hand and backed all the way on to the balcony; lost for words. Probably thinking it was some joke, that he'd let him have his try, this elderly man, then overpower him at the last. But Torren was made of steel. Sadness had toughened every edge of him and resolution did the rest. When Torren brandished the knife, Drew threw up his arms, flailing. He lost his balance and went over.

Torren left as quickly, as cleanly, as he could. Back out into the raging storm. But not before checking – just checking – whether Drew was alive.

He wasn't.

I don't think Torren cared what happened to him that night, Ally. But I did. And I still do. I can't let this be Torren's memory.

And Lizzy looked at Ally with her pale blue eyes, her irises as small as pinpricks. Her hand sought out Ally's like she was a child. Then that one word again: *Please.*

That prayer.

It's one that Ally has the power to answer.

Now, Ally stops. She's circled all the way back to the hospital, and as she looks up at its grim bulk, sadness catches her like a riptide. She doesn't fight it. Inside is Lizzy Jago, distraught. Inside is Torren Jago, dead.

Ally sucks in a breath and the cold air makes her chest ache. She tips her head back, looking for the stars, but there are none to be seen in the sky tonight.

Not a single one.

63

'I can't move,' says Elliott.

Jayden feels a rush of anger at himself. Why did he let this happen? Why didn't he insist that Elliott tell his story from the safety of the beach, or the hotel? Or a police interview room.

Stupid, stupid.

And now Elliott can't move.

Jayden turns. The entrance is visible: a slither of grey, against the pitch black. The water is only at their calves. Jayden could splash out now and be fine. But in the time that it would take to get help, the sea would keep on coming. It would fill the cave. Which means, if Jayden leaves, whatever happens to Elliott afterwards is on him.

Not an option.

Jayden's phone – impossible to find, and probably water-damaged beyond repair even if he could – is not an option either. And Elliott's phone? Also not an option. The man has already confirmed, desperate with apology, that he didn't bring it with him.

Another wave washes into the cave, and this time it has more kick to it. It soaks Jayden's legs. Elliott coughs and splutters.

Nobody knows they're here. Not Ally, not Louisa, not Malcolm. Mullins? When they spoke earlier, Jayden isn't sure he heard him over the wind.

The broken call with Gus is a thin sort of hope.

Deal with what's in front of you. And that's getting Elliott out of the cave.

'Elliott, you said this has happened with your back before,' he says, trying to make his voice calm. 'Is it a muscle spasm?'

'Y-y-yes.'

Elliott's shivering. Jayden squats beside him, cold water swilling to his waist. He puts a hand on Elliott's shoulder, hoping he's transmitting cool.

'Okay, so stay calm,' he says. 'If you panic, you'll tense, and it'll make the pain worse. Alright? It's okay, Elliott. It'll pass. Breathe deeply, mate. You've got this.'

'L-l-leave me. You g-go. Get out of h-here.'

'I'm not leaving you, Elliott. Soon as the pain's eased, soon as you think you can do it, we're moving together. Okay?'

Words spoken into the darkness. Does Jayden believe them? The waves are consistent now, every single one coming into the cave, running up and over the rocks. The sound is hectic: slapping, fizzing, sloshing. Water finding every crevice.

Human instinct is to run. To get the hell out. But they can't.

'I can't m-move anywhere. The p-pain.'

Even over the rushing water, Jayden can hear Elliott's teeth chattering. He gets even closer to him, trying to press his body close to transfer some warmth. But, as he crouches down, Jayden is wet through. Elliott is wet through. And the water keeps coming.

'Breathe deep, in and out. It'll ease. Trust it, okay. It's just pain.'

Elliott shouts out, somewhere between a laugh and a cry.

'J-just p-pain?'

'You can control it.'

The sea? The sea, we can't control.

'You can control the pain, Elliott,' he says again. 'Just breathe.'

If it's a back spasm. But it has to be, right? If Elliott had fallen from a height, if Jayden thought he'd sustained a spinal injury, it'd be different. But the guy yelled, then fell out of nowhere. He says he's had it before. And a back spasm will pass.

But they're on a hell of a timer.

Jayden tells himself that, for every second the water is flowing in, Elliott's pain could be easing. Just enough for Jayden to lift him. To support him; to carry him out; anything. So long as they get out of this cave.

Another wave, and this time Elliott catches it full in the face; he coughs and gasps. They can't wait anymore. It's now or never.

'We need to get you up, Elliott. The water's too high.'

'C-can't.'

'Elliott, listen, I'm going to squat down in front of you, and I want you to put your arms over my shoulders. Okay? Just hang on tight. I'll get to my feet and then we're out of here. Okay?'

Jayden manoeuvres in the water, feeling in the dark for where Elliott's arms and legs are, getting a sense of his position and where the weight will come from. If he topples, they're both screwed.

'Alright? We've got this.'

Elliott cries out in pain as he tries to move. His fingers claw at Jayden's shoulder. Jayden hears a rush of water, calls out, 'Wave!' then turns his head, clamps his mouth shut, closes his eyes. It passes.

'Okay?' he says.

'O-k-kay.'

Jayden feels the weight of Elliott against his back. He takes hold of his arms and leans forward to find his balancing point. The water is at his thighs. He grits his teeth.

Elliott moans, the sound so close to Jayden's ear that his eardrum crackles.

He takes careful steps, one in front of the other. Elliott's not that heavy, but the floor of the cave is uneven, the water pulling in all directions as it flies off the rocks, gets caught in strange currents. It wouldn't take much to get knocked over.

Jayden fixes his gaze on that strip of grey. Their way out.

He takes three steps, four, five.

Another wave, waist-height this time. The power is immense, and Jayden staggers. He can feel Elliott slipping and so he bends lower to counter it. His own muscles are protesting. He hasn't worked out in a while.

'Hold on,' he says. 'We're nearly there. Hold on.'

But the water keeps coming, the force building with every wave. Jayden feels the spray on his face as it hits at his middle. It's high and getting higher. He throws out an arm to steady himself against the rocky walls, but in the darkness it catches at nothing.

I can't do it.

'We've got to go back,' he shouts. 'It's too dangerous.'

Peter drowned in the cave. Even though the cliffs and rockpools were his kingdom, a little prince in a seaside realm, he died. Was the cave pitch black then too? It was a summer's evening; light would have filtered in.

And Peter still died.

Jayden can feel a rising panic in his chest and forces himself to reset. Okay, he hasn't been trained for this exact set of circumstances, but keeping his head in impossible situations? He's been there.

You've got this, Jay.

Kieran. His partner, his brother-in-arms. Jayden will never make his peace with the way he died – stabbed in a brawl on a city street, as the two of them tried to bring order on a hot summer night – but the way he lived? Kieran was a hero. To the job, to his friends, to his family. It's the charge that Jayden needs.

He grits his teeth, shouts, 'Elliott, where's Peter's memorial?'

'W-what?'

'His memorial, you said you built one. Where is it?'

Because Elliott said the stones only get washed away sometimes.

'It's in a t-tunnel down the end.'

Jayden turns his back to the rising tide. Another wave hits and he staggers. How did he ever think Elliott wasn't heavy? Every muscle is screaming; every bone. Jayden feels his teeth clash together. He's shivering now too.

'R-reckon you can guide us there?'

'In the dark?'

No, man, by the torch I brought that I'm holding back for emergencies.

'You know this cave. You can do it.' Jayden holds out an arm, feels the cold, wet rock. 'Do I stay to the left side?'

Elliott shivers his answer, and Jayden takes a step. Water washes back and forth, as it hurls in and out again. The pair of them could go over at any moment. There could be a pit filled with water, a rock drop, anything. He can't see a damn thing, and all that he can feel – the cold, the water, the fear – is fighting against him.

Kieran's voice: Let's do this.

'Keep to the left,' says Elliott. 'L-l-left, left. All the way.'

'Anything to avoid?' Jayden laughs manically. 'Except for this whole situation?'

He feels Elliott shift on his back. Did he laugh too? Is the pain easing? It would make such a difference if the guy could walk.

'L-let me d-down,' says Elliott. 'I c-can do this.'

Thank you, thank you.

Who is he thanking? He doesn't know, but he sends the thought up and out. They need all the help they can get.

As Elliott carefully slides from his back, Jayden feels instant relief. Suddenly, he's light as a feather. He feels for the other man in the dark, takes his arm.

'You got this, Elliott.'

'Stay l-left. C-come on.'

They make their way, painstakingly slowly, a wounded man leading in the dark. Hands on wet rock, guiding. Waves at their back. Jayden's foot plunges into a dip and he stumbles. Then Elliott bumps into a rock, cries out in pain.

'Back?' shouts Jayden.

'Knee!' answers Elliott.

And, again, the urge to laugh bubbles up. A kind of hysteria. Jayden squeezes Elliott's shoulder.

'We've got this.'

'Here,' says Elliott. 'Up h-here.'

His arm brushes Jayden's, groping upwards. There's the clatter of small stones falling, just audible over the swell and slop of seawater.

'It's c-climbable. Hold me.'

Elliott's moving, feet kicking against rock. Jayden feels his back, his thigh, his leg.

'I'm up!' he shouts.

'I'm right behind you.'

'There's a l-ledge. Just feel for the f-footholds. I've got you.'

And now it's Elliott grabbing on to Jayden's arms, and his feet are holding on the rocks, and the water's no longer at their backs, showering spray overhead.

Is the tide actually receding? Or are they just staying ahead?

Jayden clambers on to the narrow ledge. He can feel Elliott lying flat, and he sits beside him, his legs hanging down into the water. He leans his back against the cold, uneven wall. Is the rock dry here? He can't tell. He's too wet.

For a second, Jayden closes his eyes. Elliott's hand finds Jayden's arm in the dark.

'If we had a phone . . .' Elliott begins.

'Yeah.'

'J-Jayden . . . this is on me.'

'I should have made us get out sooner.'

'I'm sorry. The pain. It was unreal. I felt like I c-couldn't move.'

'How is it now?'

'Like I can move again. *Just.* But . . . we can't. You should have gone, Jayden. You should have l-left me when you could.'

'You're joking.'

'Save yourself. You still c-can. How's your swimming? B-better than mine, I'll bet.'

'Look, if the tide has peaked, we're good. It'll only recede from here.'

Jayden thinks suddenly of Peter's memorial; the stones that fell as they reached the ledge. He tries to steady his breathing. 'Did Peter die on this ledge, Elliott?'

'I don't know.'

They fall silent. The cave storms with the sound of the sea. Blood roars in Jayden's ears. Is it his only chance to ask the ultimate question?

'Elliott,' he says, 'did you kill Drew Schofield?'

64

'You go, Ally,' says Lizzy quietly. 'I've kept you long enough.'

It's cold inside Star Cottage. The fire's taking a while to catch and Ally blows hard on the embers. Woodsmoke billows back into the room.

It feels like nothing's working.

Lizzy sits in an armchair, her hands resting on her knees. She still has her coat on. The cup of tea that Ally made is untouched beside her. Reggie the old hound lies by the door, his head on his paws, his eyes doleful. And, from the walls, the mantelpiece, the bookshelf, all the versions of Peter look down at them.

The house feels so terribly empty.

'Let me at least get this fire going,' says Ally. Then, gently, 'Is there really no one I can phone?'

Lizzy shakes her head. Her silver hair is held with kirby grips, but one long strand hangs loose. When the doctor came with the news of Torren's death, Lizzy's hands went first to her head then to her heart. She looked, in that moment, as if she were made of paper and would crumple altogether. But then she thanked the doctor for all he'd done, with a poise that Ally knew she hadn't possessed with Bill.

They haven't spoken about what Lizzy told Ally afterwards. What more is there to say? Plenty, probably, but any questions would feel extraordinarily callous now. Ally feels as if Lizzy has placed a secret in her hands, passing it to her for safekeeping. Or was it less studied than that? A heart's cry, at a moment of great distress? Either way, Ally has the truth. And for all that she and Jayden wanted it, she longs to give it back now.

Ally's phone rings then and the sound startles all three of them. The dog gives a sharp, single bark and Lizzy's eyes meet Ally's: wild and afraid, as if she simply can't take one more shock.

It's only Gus.

Ally hesitates.

'It's alright,' says Lizzy, 'answer it.'

'Gus,' says Ally, walking from the room, 'could I possibly call you back later?'

And that's not what Ally wants to say at all, really. Gus's gentle tones would be just right now. A port in a storm.

She's in the kitchen, looking at Torren's cap hooked over a chairback, the newspaper left open on the table. The bruised apples in the fruit bowl. Two plates, two mugs, in the drying rack. The calendar on the wall, with a view of St Michael's Mount in golden autumn light. It's an ordinary house belonging to ordinary people, but a boy died, and then much later his father. And, in between, a man fell from a balcony.

Nothing is ever ordinary.

'Sorry, Gus,' says Ally, 'could you say that again?'

His voice sounds like it's coming from a long way away.

'I said I wanted to tell Jayden that I'd had a good writing day and that he was absolutely right to tell me to stay at my desk instead of gadding about—'

'Gus, could I just—'

'—but, Ally, is there any reason he'd be in a cave?'

'A cave?'

Ally thinks of Jayden's movements: he left the Jagos' house with Elliott; he was going to talk to the Kings. She hasn't heard from him since the message she sent from the hospital.

'I thought he said a cave, anyway,' says Gus. 'The thing is, his phone cut out, the reception was dodgy, but when I called back it said "This phone is out of service" and I thought that was odd. Ordinarily it'd go to voicemail, wouldn't it, if there were no bars? I tried it twice more and got the same message. I'm sure it's nothing, but knowing you two, I thought I'd best—'

'Gus, when was this?'

'About twenty minutes ago.'

'Did Jayden sound like he was in trouble?'

'I wouldn't have said so. I mean . . . I can't honestly say. And I didn't want to make a fuss unduly, but then it's been bothering me rather, so . . .'

Ally checks her watch. It's high tide. She goes cold, from her fingers to her toes. She tries to imagine what possible scenario might have led Jayden to the sea cave but her mind jitters, refusing to focus.

'Gus,' she says, 'we need to call the coastguard.'

And now that she's said it, she can hardly breathe. Jayden is in the cave. It's high tide. His phone cut out – and that was twenty minutes ago. But he can swim, can't he? He's a good swimmer.

So was Peter.

'Let me do it, Ally. Let me phone the coastguard. Should I have done it before? I should have done it before. *Damn.*'

'No, I'll call. I know exactly where he is. At least I think I do.' Her voice jumps with urgency. 'Gus, come to the High Tide Hotel. I'll meet you there.'

Then she's dialling 999 and asking for the coastguard. She's saying the words *Trebaron Cove* and *sea cave* and his name: *Jayden Weston*. One of the dearest names to her in all the world. Then she's hanging up and hurrying back into the sitting room with unsteady steps. It's a small cottage, Lizzy must have heard her, but the woman doesn't move. She's hunched in her chair still, in the exact same pose, as if immune to all further strife. As if all the troubles in the world could rain down and she wouldn't feel them; she's already soaked through. The fire, Ally briefly notes, has caught, and the flames jump high in the grate.

Lizzy slowly turns.

'What I told you before,' she says, her voice wavering. 'Would you forget it?'

'Lizzy, I'm so sorry but I have to go. My friend . . . He's in trouble . . .'

Ally's voice leaves her.

Lizzy's face is all heartbreak as she says, 'I'll pray for him, Ally.'

65

Inside the cave, the water is all fight. It slaps at the rocks, hissing spray, hurling itself at anything in its path. Jayden shifts on the ledge as a wave pounds directly beneath them. Back here, it's black as night. The entrance, with its thin streak of dusky light, is no longer visible. All Jayden has is sound and touch. And the cave magnifies everything: the noise roars all around them, echoing off the walls and the roof; every splash feels like it could signal the end.

Because here's the truth of it: if this tide keeps rising, they're both dead. And there is nothing, absolutely zero, that they can do about it.

Trying to swim out is impossible. Even if Elliott's back held up, in this small space the force of the water would slam them against the rocks. Broken limbs at best; one strike to the head and it would all be over. No, they're trapped. Trapped in one of the toughest situations Jayden has ever been in.

He thinks of the cliff drop two winters ago, clinging to that ledge. He thinks of the man with the knife in the dunes. He thinks of all the times in Leeds when he faced violence and unpredictability: the drug-crazed, the drunken, the nothing-left-to-lose. Kieran's blood running through his fingers: the worst, the very worst of all.

But there was always something to do. Words to be spoken; moves to be made. CPR to be administered; desperate compressions that came to nothing, but it was still action, wasn't it? It was still trying. But here, now? He can't do anything. Except wait and pray. Pray that the sea falls back. That the moon stops pulling. That someone, something, somewhere, says *enough.*

Jayden isn't a religious person, but when the chips are down, when there's nothing to lose, why not call in reinforcements? He doesn't know who he's praying to exactly, but he sends words up anyway. Up – but not out.

They're swallowed by the din of the water.

Jayden has had no answer to the question he asked Elliott five minutes ago. Or was it ten? Or two? Time follows no rules in this cave. Only that, with every moment that passes, Jayden knows their situation is either getting worse – or fractionally better. The tide still rising – or starting to fall. But in this total darkness, there's no way of knowing.

Did you kill Drew Schofield?

Is Jayden going to press it?

No. He'd rather think about his children. His wife. His parents. His sister. His friends. Ally. He'd rather try to draw strength from all these good people. Because if Jayden's going to die in this cave, he doesn't want his last thoughts to be on murder. And maybe that makes him a poor sort of detective but so be it.

'Jayden.'

Elliott's voice sounds very small and distant. But the man is pushed up against Jayden's side; the ledge is barely big enough.

'Good people die, and bad people die, and there's no logic to it,' says Elliott.

Jayden groans inwardly. It's deep as thunder.

Think of the good people.

'Except when it's murder,' Jayden says. He can't help himself. 'You can't deny the logic of someone pushing a man off a balcony. Cause and effect, Elliott.'

'He knew the tide times, you know.'

'Who?'

'Drew. That summer. Dad used to write them on a board outside the hotel. I saw Drew looking at them, the day Peter died. Drew knew this cave would fill. I never told anyone that either. And if I'm going to die, then I might as well just—'

But Jayden wants to think of Jazzy's laugh, the way it bounces like a mad ball, and how it's one of his favourite sounds in the world. He wants to think of the way Benji curls into him, his son's cheek pushed against his chest, or his shoulder, or the crook of his arm: the total trust. He wants to think of Cat's eyes, electric blue and full of love – full of suffering too, not many months ago. By God, Jayden loves these people of his. And he is lucky, so lucky, to have known such love.

But to leave them? He can't do that.

He won't.

'Elliott,' he says.

And what's he going to do? Get him to finish that sentence: *Might as well what, Elliott?* But instead he says, 'We're not going to die here.' Then he says it again, louder: 'We're not going to die here.'

Then Elliott's saying it too. Shouting it; words pitched and tossed. And in the dark their hands find each other and hold on tight. Jayden feels water against his legs. Elliott's voice turns into a moan; he must feel the water too.

Rising, then, not receding.

Then, from nowhere, the cave fills with light; light so bright that they're shielding their eyes.

And despite everything he's ever learned – cool, calm, logic – Jayden thinks, *Is this it? Death?*

66

Ally is on the beach and Gus is there beside her. His arm is around her shoulders, and she feels as if he's the only thing keeping her moored.

It's a starless evening. Usually, the sea is a consoling sight, but tonight it's all menace. Waves attack the shore as if in punishment. A gusting wind blows the spray inland; it settles on their cheeks and in their hair.

All they can do is wait.

Behind them, the High Tide Hotel glitters away obliviously. But, somewhere inside, Louisa King is afraid for her husband and Malcolm King is afraid for his son. There will be hot drinks, and a member of the coastguard in a big coat, assuring people that all is being done. But Ally wanted to be out here, eyes on the sea. And Gus is beside her.

'Any sign?'

Mullins joins them. He took Steve Bradshaw into custody – charged with criminal damage – but then rushed back the moment he heard.

'Not yet,' says Ally.

Mullins stands on the other side of her, one hand on his receiver, his cap low over his eyes. He scuffs his feet in the wet sand.

'He's made of tough stuff, is Jayden,' he says.

She nods. 'He is.'

But the sea will take anyone, weak or strong; no one is a match for it, not really. The only thing to do is respect it – and perhaps even fear it.

Is Jayden afraid?

She hates to think of it.

And she hates to think of Peter Jago. All those photos of that smiling, sunny boy who loved his home, his beach, his mum and dad. Who loved his life. Peter, whose parents loved him so much they'd do anything for him. Anything at all, in life – and death.

It's not difficult to keep the truth about Drew's death from Mullins. Fear for Jayden has slammed just about every thought from Ally's mind.

'Skinner wanted to be here too,' says Mullins.

And the way he says it makes Ally think of a funeral, the detective sergeant wanting to pay his respects. She drags in a lungful of sea air; her eyes burn, and she blinks fast.

I will not cry.

'I expect he's busy with the murder, isn't he?' says Gus.

'Dead end after dead end there,' says Mullins.

Ally slips free of Gus's arm and walks a few paces down the beach.

'Ally?' says Gus faintly.

She's screwing her eyes up against the wind. There's a faint light moving out there on the water. She can't tell if it's coming or going.

Her hands are deep in her pockets, and she crosses her fingers.

'Is that them?' she says.

'That's them,' says Mullins.

But what does it mean, if a boat's coming back? It could be a bad sign as much as good. It could be terrible.

Ally feels Gus's arm around her again.

'Please,' she whispers.

'I know,' he says.

He kisses her on the cheek; so light she could have missed it. She leans into him, with all of her hope and all of her fear. And Gus, dear Gus, holds it all.

Then her phone's ringing in her pocket and she struggles to get to it. It's Cat. Finally returning her call.

Just as Ally answers, just as she says 'Cat' – breathes the word more than speaks it, really – a light appears on the water. It beams out, casting a silver glow. The darkness parts and Ally sees an inflatable boat lifting up and over the waves. She sees a man in a bulky life vest, standing in the bow.

'Ally,' says Cat, on the other end of the phone, 'tell me he's okay.'

Her voice is a wild cry. Ally can't bear it.

'Cat, the lifeboat is on its way back in,' she says. 'I can see it.'

But how many people are in the boat?

Ally holds her hand to her mouth as the boat moves closer. Mullins jogs down the sand to meet it.

'Ally, I see him,' shouts Gus. 'I see Jayden!'

67

'You idiot,' says Mullins. 'Don't they have tides up north?'

Jayden is wrapped in a blanket and doesn't look much like a tough guy. But Mullins knows he's tough as they come. Brave as they come too. Anyone else would have left Elliott King in the cave; said they were going for help, letting the fallen man take his chances.

'Thanks for getting the lifeboat out,' says Jayden.

'That was Gus and Ally. Though Malcolm King said he had a hunch Elliott might be at that old cave. Old fella won't spill the beans on why. What's going on, Jayden?'

Mullins steps aside then, because Ally and Gus want in. He watches as Ally bends to hug Jayden. She doesn't come back up for a long time. Mullins doesn't want to eavesdrop but every so often he looks at that pair and thinks, *I wish I had that.* Not that he wants to go hugging Skinner any time soon. Shell House-style knuckle-bump, though? Yeah, maybe.

He moves away. He's going soft, that's the trouble.

'Mullins. Getting your feet wet, are you?'

Skinner, sweeping in. The lights bouncing off his hi-vis jacket like they're at a carnival. Skinner's still buzzing on them nicking Steve Bradshaw. *Again.* He thought if Bradshaw was kicking off at the High Tide, it had to be about Drew Schofield.

As it happened, it wasn't about Schofield. It was about Bradshaw's girlfriend finally having had enough of him – and Bradshaw not taking it well. Which maybe is a little bit to do with Drew Schofield. *The company we keep.*

'That was a close call,' says Mullins, jerking his head in Jayden's direction. 'Ally thought he was a goner. They're busy having a little love-in.'

Skinner tuts. 'No better than an emmet, getting caught by the tide, for God's sake.'

'I think he was mostly saving Elliott King, Sarge,' says Mullins. 'Though what Elliott King was doing in that cave is another question . . .'

'He had a friend who died there, apparently,' says Skinner. 'Malcolm King thinks Elliott got spooked when old Torren Jago had his heart attack. Started spiralling. Went to pay his respects or some such.'

'And didn't count on his back giving out,' says Mullins.

'What I don't understand is why Jayden was following him in the first place. A bloke's having a midlife crisis, leave him to it, I say. Between you and me, Mullins.'

'Regrets it now, I'd say.'

Skinner sniffs. 'Where did you get to with catching up to any Shell House nonsense?'

'If they've got any leads, you mean?' asks Mullins.

'Leads. *Investigative progress.*' He loads it with sarcasm, but even so.

'Ask him yourself, Sarge,' he says.

Jayden's on his feet, the blanket slipping from his shoulders, as Mullins and Skinner make their way to him. Gus and Ally drop back as Skinner shakes Jayden's hand.

'I'd tell you to stay out of trouble, but it won't make any difference, will it?' says the detective sergeant. Then, 'Evening, Ally.'

Ally nods. She still looks shaken, thinks Mullins.

Jayden gives a half-smile. 'All's well that ends well.'

'I wouldn't say that. I've got a case that's still wide open. What did you want with Elliott King? I hear you chased him down the beach before his father even cottoned on to the cave connection.'

'His wife said his behaviour was out of character. He was hit hard by his neighbour's heart attack. I was concerned for him.'

Skinner grunts. He sounds like a bulldog, thinks Mullins; one pulling at his lead.

'No new mad theories on Schofield, then?'

'No, afraid not. What strikes me is the efficiency,' says Jayden. 'The killer got in and out and left no trace.'

'How do you know they left no trace?'

'Because otherwise your case wouldn't still be wide open, would it? They knew what they were doing, that's all I'm saying. Clinical.'

Clinical job. *Criminal job.* That's the current thinking. That's the only thinking. That an old enemy of Schofield's, some felon, breezed in and breezed out again. Luck on their side.

'What have you been up to, then, Ally? If you weren't playing in caves?'

'I went with Lizzy Jago to the hospital. We were passing as it all happened.'

'Good Samaritan? Or . . .'

'Because I've been there,' says Ally, crisp as an apple. 'My husband died of a heart attack. Now, if you'll excuse me, it's been quite a night.'

And she walks off towards the hotel, Gus trotting behind her. Mullins raises his eyebrows. Ally doesn't usually proffer that information about Bill. It must have hit her hard, seeing another woman go through what she did. By the look on Jayden's face, it's surprised him too.

Ally's reaction shuts Skinner up in any case. He huffs and puffs a bit, then suddenly decides he's had enough chit-chat. He starts to stride off – without a by-your-leave – then stops. Turns back to Mullins and Jayden.

'We've charged Steve Bradshaw with criminal damage,' he says. 'Plenty of witnesses. Mae Cunningham and Kathy Schofield have checked in to another hotel over in St Ives. Didn't like what was in the water at the High Tide, and they'll be heading back to Oxfordshire soon enough. Meanwhile, the more I hear about Drew Schofield . . . "Old-school cop" shouldn't be a slur, but it is.'

Mullins swaps a look with Jayden.

'People who carry the badge but think they make their own law,' says Skinner, 'I've no time for them. Never have had, never will.'

Skinner holds his mitt out. He shakes Jayden's hand first, then Mullins's.

'You're alright, you two,' he says. Then he turns on his heel and goes.

Mullins nudges Jayden. 'Did we just get a couple of gold stars for not being bent coppers?'

Jayden laughs, but Mullins can tell his heart's not in it. Maybe because he's not really a copper at all anymore. Or maybe because he's still thinking about nearly dying and all that.

68

Jayden packs slowly; his bones feel like lead and a tension headache burns at his skull. Part of him wants to be out of here, down the coast road, skidding into the farmyard and straight into his wife's arms. Scooping up those children of his and holding them all close. His phone call with Cat earlier was one of the most emotional he's ever had. It was different to when he called her about Kieran, when he had to tell her that terrible news. This time, it was a call of reassurance, of relief and joy. But his words left him, and Cat's did too, and in the end they just held each other down the line; listening to each other breathe.

But the other part of him? The other part is pulled in by the case. That's safety for you: how quickly normality resumes. *Right, where were we, then?* And Jayden has a weird feeling that when he leaves the High Tide, the truth that they're tantalisingly close to will disappear like footprints in wet sand.

There's a knock at his door and he knows it'll be Ally. He's already been thanked by Louisa, by Malcolm. By Elliott too, taking his hand and holding it.

You know what you did, don't you? said Elliott.

And as much as Jayden was moved by his gratitude, he wanted to send the words back his way. *What about you, Elliott? What did you do?*

As if a mind-reader, the man leant close. *I promise I didn't kill Drew Schofield, Jayden. But I wasn't in the least bit sorry to know that he was dead.*

'Jayden,' says Ally. 'Are you ready?'

She's composed herself. Back to careful, neat Ally. As Jayden clambered out of the lifeboat, his legs ready to give way, it was Ally who held him up. Who hugged him, her face wet with tears. Who said, *We can't lose you*.

'Nearly ready,' he says.

'How are you feeling?'

'Yeah, good.' Then he corrects himself. 'Like I'm a thousand years old, and my blood's still not up to temperature.'

And he shivers as he says it. But the lifeboat crew checked him, top to bottom. Both he and Elliott escaped without lasting damage. Ironically, Elliott's back spasm – the spasm that floored him in the cave – had receded to only a dull ache by the time they got to shore. *We'll get you straight in for a massage*, said Louisa. But Jayden has a feeling it'll take more than some High Tide pampering to fix Elliott.

'Has Gus gone?' asks Jayden.

'He has. I told him we wouldn't be far behind.'

'It was his phone call that saved me, Al.'

Arguably it was also Gus's phone call that nearly killed him. If Gus hadn't rung, Jayden wouldn't have been holding the handset when Elliott fell and grabbed him. *But let's not dwell on that.*

'I know,' says Ally, her voice cracking. 'He's been such a rock.'

Jayden eyes his packed bag. 'It won't take long to drive back. We've got stuff to talk about.'

'We have,' says Ally.

'In the cave, I thought it was Elliott who killed Drew Schofield. He lied to us, Al.'

And Jayden proceeds to tell Ally everything that Elliott said about how Peter Jago died. And that it was Drew Schofield who set it up.

Ally goes very quiet and still. The shock of the revelation, the teenage Drew's manipulation, takes all the colour from her face.

'But you don't still think that Elliott killed Drew?' she says.

'No. Elliott says he didn't, and I believe him. After what we went through in that cave, I don't think he'd lie to me again.'

'No,' says Ally. Then, 'I think you're right.'

She walks over to the window. Night has fallen now, and the glass throws her reflection back at her. Jayden stands beside her. They appear like ghosts, layers of dark and light.

'On the beach just now, after I left, you didn't tell Mullins and Skinner what Elliott told you?' she says. 'About Peter, I mean. And Drew.'

'No. I wanted to discuss it with you first.'

But Jayden's conscious that he basically lied to them. Mullins and Skinner won't let him forget that in a hurry.

Jayden feels her hand on his arm. 'Thank you,' she says quietly.

Their eyes meet in the reflection. On one level, he knows it before she says it.

'Al?'

'It was Torren Jago who killed Drew Schofield.'

Jayden breathes. 'You sure about that?'

'Lizzy told me. After Torren died, it all just came out in a rush. Then she pleaded with me to keep his secret.'

'But she knows you can't do that, right?'

'She was devastated, Jayden. It was terrible.'

'I know. I know it was.' And it was no picnic with Elliott either. He says it again, 'But Lizzy's got to know you can't do that.' His mind reels. *Old Torren Jago?* 'Tell me what she said to you. How did he do it?'

And Jayden listens as Ally tells him how Torren tried to speak with Drew that afternoon on the beach and was made to feel so inconsequential. As if Peter was inconsequential. And how Drew's cruelty in that one exchange was enough to hit the switch and tip Torren into action. Jayden expects a story of an escalation; another attempt at conversation going badly wrong. Instead, Ally recounts how Torren took a knife from the block in the kitchen and walked into the High Tide burning with intent. Not caring if it was Drew's wife who answered his knock at the bedroom door, not caring if she – or anyone – saw any of it. But he lucked out with Kathy and her sleeping pills. He lucked out with a power cut striking out all the CCTV. The only thing Torren didn't luck out with was Summer on her balcony filming the storm and catching him in action.

So we were right and we were wrong, thinks Jayden. Drew's death was premeditated: Torren took a knife to the High Tide. But beyond the threat of the blade, he didn't need to use it. The balcony fall did his work for him.

'Torren's dead, Jayden. All Lizzy has left is his memory. The thought of him being branded a murderer . . .'

'But he killed Drew Schofield, Al. He set off with that intention, and he achieved it.'

'The saddest thing is he felt he had nothing left to lose.'

'So why be so careful? He left no trace, Al. On paper, he's as cold-blooded as they come.'

'But it's not just about what's on paper, is it?'

'No, and that's why we have courts. Juries, Al. Not people like us.'

'But the thought of Lizzy being put through all of that, after what she's lost. She said after Drew fell, Torren ran down and checked if he was breathing. Because he did fall, Jayden, he wasn't pushed.'

'He was being threatened with a knife. For a court, I don't think there'd be a lot in it. And as for Torren checking if Drew was breathing . . . I bet he did. You don't go to all that trouble then walk away, leaving someone alive to tell the tale.'

Ally bites her lip; drops her head.

Jayden flops into a chair.

'I know this is hard, but Lizzy lied to us, Al. On multiple occasions. And Torren faked being all vague. I bet his memory was fine, wasn't it?'

'Sharp as a tack,' says Ally sadly.

'And he wasn't half as physically frail as they made out?'

She shakes her head. 'I don't know, his heart . . .'

'They consciously manipulated us to cover their tracks and obstruct the investigation.'

'We're not police, Jayden, they weren't obstructing the—'

'Come on, you think they would have given different answers to Skinner and Mullins?'

They stare at one another. Ally knows the answer is no.

'In the beginning, all Torren wanted to do was talk to Drew Schofield,' says Ally. 'As soon as he realised who he was, that's all he wanted. But the man made him feel so . . . insignificant.'

'We all feel insignificant sometimes.'

'He made Peter's death feel insignificant.'

'And I bet that hurt like hell, but Torren should have been the bigger man. Did Lizzy know he was going to kill him, Ally?'

She hesitates. 'She said she tried to talk him out of it. She did try to stop him. But she said it was like all the grief of Peter came rushing back in and there was nothing she could do. When Torren got home, they both felt sure the police would come. Torren was ready to hand himself in. But Lizzy wouldn't let him. Lizzy said she couldn't lose him too.'

'Which makes Lizzy guilty of a crime too. And while we're on the subject of who else knew . . . we've got to talk about Elliott. Whether in fact he *is* still lying to me.'

'Torren asked Elliott to look at the guest list. He confirmed that Drew Schofield was in residence,' says Ally. 'That's all. He had no idea what Torren was going to do.'

'How did Torren get into the hotel that night? Even in a power cut you need a key card.'

'Lizzy said Torren managed to prop open a side door earlier. No one noticed it.'

'You don't think Lizzy's just trying to keep Elliott out of it? Because she thinks that'll make you more likely to stay quiet?'

'She didn't have to tell me any of it, Jayden.'

Jayden pushes his face into his hands. Instinctively, he still believes that Elliott played no part in Drew's death. But it's beginning to look a lot like he was studiously avoiding talking about the Jagos. Even in the cave, when it was all out on the table; all out on the ledge.

'Look,' he says, 'at the very least you've got to bet that, when Schofield turned up dead, Elliott had a good idea who did it. Because he knew the background when no one else did. Maybe you could argue that teenage Drew thought it was just a stupid prank, have Peter stumble around the tunnels for a bit, looking for a girl who wasn't there, be made to look a fool. But, Al, Elliott told me that he saw Drew studying a chalkboard with tide times on it. Elliott reckons Drew knew exactly what he was doing when he lied about Rebecca being trapped.'

'I believe it. Drew's family had been camping here for nearly a fortnight. He'd surely have observed how much of the beach was lost when the tide came in. Which makes Drew guilty of a terrible crime.'

'So guilty that he deserves to be killed for it, forty years later? Come on, Al.'

Jayden's on his feet now. Exasperation sparks off him.

'Drew escaped any kind of punishment,' says Ally, 'and went on to live a life where he strutted around, flashing his badge, supposedly enforcing the law for everybody else. He was a bully, Jayden. Through and through. Rebecca said it, Elliott said it, his own wife said it, in no uncertain terms.'

'And he hung his so-called mate Steve Bradshaw out to dry too. But none of that's the point, Al. We can't make these kinds of calls. Because if we do, we're guilty of wrongdoing too.'

And that's the crux of it. That's the point Jayden can't move on from.

'I took an oath, Ally. When I became a constable. "I do solemnly and sincerely declare and affirm that I will well and truly serve the Queen in the office of constable, with fairness, integrity, diligence and impartiality—"'

'Jayden . . .'

'"—upholding fundamental human rights and according equal respect to all people; and that I will, to the best of my power, cause the peace to be kept and preserved and prevent all offences against people and property; and that while I continue to hold the said office I will to the best of my skill and knowledge discharge all the duties thereof faithfully according to law." I took that oath, and I meant every word of it.'

Jayden's eyes are shining with emotion, and Ally's are too.

'But you don't hold the said office anymore,' she says quietly.

A clear fact, but a low blow.

'And Jayden,' she says, 'I never have.'

69

The coast road has never felt darker. Ally's headlights pick out a narrow path as fine rain dances in their glare. They pass a sign: *Porthpella, 3 miles.*

Through all their cases, they've almost always been in harmony. Their guiding light: do the right thing. And most of the time that 'right thing' is clear to see. The only time that Ally and Jayden disagreed over a way forward was when they were looking for Saffron's biological father – and that disconnect nearly cost them.

They have three miles to fix this problem.

Ally glances at Jayden as he sits beside her in the passenger seat.

I understand you, she thinks, *I understand you completely. But I can't agree with you.*

Cat and her family are desperately waiting for Jayden to come home. They couldn't delay their departure any longer. But it felt wrong, leaving the High Tide without any sense of resolution.

It moved Ally, hearing Jayden recite the oath. Not least because she knows Bill would have spoken those same words with equal commitment and passion. But Ally is a civilian. She and Jayden are both civilians – and they're bound by their own moral judgement. A dead man can't be punished for a crime, so why punish his grieving wife?

'Lizzy admitted the crime to me, not to you,' says Ally. 'Can't you . . . forget I told you?'

'What, take the money and run?'

Because Louisa is paying them regardless – including the bonus. *The case doesn't matter,* she said. *You saved my husband.*

'What's to be gained?' Ally says again. 'I mean, really? Lizzy has nothing left. Nothing at all. Please let me give her this.'

Jayden looks pained as he shakes his head – and Ally feels terrible. He nearly lost his life tonight, because he was doing the right thing. Standing by Elliott, when all the temptation must have been to cut and run, to charge towards the light. Has her friend simply run out of good intentions? Is it time for head and not heart?

Or is it just because he's right, Al?

And it's Bill's voice she hears. Dear Bill. She knows he would agree with Jayden now, even if his beautiful big heart would have broken for Lizzy Jago.

Emotionally, Ally is still with Lizzy in the hospital, the doctor walking towards them with his eyes lowered. She's still with Lizzy in her cottage, sadness dripping from the walls, Lizzy looking like she was fading to nothing.

I'm for the little people, that's what Bill used to say. And who is Lizzy, if not a little person? Ally suspects she would be having this same argument with Bill, if he were here and if it was his decision to make.

She squints through the fine rain. The wipers squeak back and forth. To their left, the ocean unfurls, shifting and boundless. Peter is dead. Drew is dead. Torren is dead.

She tries a different tack. One of reason.

'Elliott is the only other person who could guess at the truth,' says Ally. 'And he'd never say anything, because from everything you've told me he'll always be on the side of the Jagos.'

'But have you any idea how dangerous that is? If Elliott has a crisis of conscience, if he starts talking, then we lose all our credibility, Al. Everything we've worked for will be gone.'

Is this what it comes down to? The future of the Shell House Detectives? Ally feels a swell of emotion in her chest.

A crossroads.

They've already solved far more cases than she ever thought they would. If Ally stays true to her instincts, to protect Lizzy's secret, to do what she perceives as the right thing by her, is that such a terrible way for it all to end? But it's not just Ally; she and Jayden are partners. They never took an oath, but their bond is no less true. And it's not only her decision to make.

'I get it, Al. Don't think that I don't. Keeping quiet about this, maybe that's the compassionate choice. But that doesn't make it the right choice.'

'Compassion is always right. Isn't it?'

Jayden stays quiet.

'Lizzy didn't have to tell me about Torren,' she says. 'She didn't have to say a thing.'

'It sounds to me like she wanted to clear her conscience. Like she was saying one thing to you – "please keep this secret, Ally" – but actually meaning something else.'

'I don't agree.'

'Ask her, then. Cold light of day, go and ask her. See what answer she gives you, Al.'

He's terse with her. Of course he is. He's exhausted; shaken.

Ally feels that burst of guilt again. If Cat could hear her now, she'd shut it down, with all the force of a wife's privilege. Ally remembers her bursting into A&E at the very end of their first case, when Jayden had risked everything in the dunes. Cat – heavily pregnant with Jasmine, a tower of strength – and so angry with Ally for dragging Jayden into such drama.

'Okay,' she says quietly, 'I'll ask Lizzy.'

70

What's the point?

That's the thought that runs through Lizzy's head as she stares into the fire. The log is burning white, and it looks, she thinks, just like a festive yule log. The kind Peter used to love, with chocolate icing and sugar dusted like snow, a sprig of real holly from the lane on top.

I love Christmas, he used to say.

So do I, said Torren.

And Lizzy added her voice: *Me too.*

It was always just the three of them. The three of them, and the magic they made together, the beauty they saw: cotton napkins folded into triangles, glasses sparkling by candlelight, the tree glittering with a hundred and one decorations, most of them handmade. Painted seashells, gathered by Peter. A little wooden horse carved by Torren in the work shed; a drummer boy too. Lizzy's red ribbons.

They were going on about it on the radio earlier, how many shopping days are left. Lizzy would be making the pudding in November. Even when it was just her and Torren, they always still had a pudding. But they couldn't eat it at the table, with that missing place setting, that point of the triangle; the point of everything, really. Instead, they'd sit by the fire, bowls on laps. Like two old horses at a stable door.

Lizzy doesn't know why she's thinking about Christmas. *Oh, the log, the yule log, the fire.*

Kind Ally Bright lit the fire. Perhaps she thought it would bring some comfort, or at least warmth. She wasn't to know the impossibility of that.

There have been moments of happiness, of appreciation, down the years. Living here, how could there not be? No one loved the natural world like Peter. The golden light of dawn, the sea shifting and molten, reflecting all of heaven's rays. A perfect V-shape of geese flying south, up and over the cottage and close enough to touch; necks stretched, honking cries. The infinite blue, when you all but gasp at the colour; want to take it inside of you and hold on to it always.

But she never could.

The pallor of their days has been grey. The sun, their son, gone from the sky.

Lizzy's heard of people who bounce back. She's heard of people who go on to live fulfilled and grateful lives and she respects them. She knows resilience does not diminish feeling, or love. But that isn't her and it isn't Torren.

Wasn't Torren.

Is it terrible that she envies her husband this exit? No, not terrible. Just the way of things. Until you've lived a life like Lizzy's, don't try to tell her what's right.

Everyone I love is dead.

There's a knock at her door and she thinks about leaving it. They'll go away eventually. But then it comes again – *thump, thump* – and with the fire crackling, perhaps it's a night for strange happenings. Perhaps it's Torren at the door. Torren in his big old coat, the one he burnt in the oil drum out back, and they both stared at the ashes, as if they were tea leaves in a cup, spelling out their destiny.

Once you go down a certain road, you cannot turn back.

Thump, thump.

Lizzy creaks to a standing position and walks stiffly to the door. She clicks on the outside light and sees the shape of a man through the grimy pane. She opens up.

'Elliott.'

Rain is falling outside, and it shines off his black coat; he looks as if he's walked out of the sea. His cheeks are wet too. He blinks up at her, and she sees that rainwater has caught on his lashes.

'I'm so sorry about Torren,' he says.

And without thinking – it'll surprise her later, this gesture, because what Lizzy really feels like is curling up in her shell, not throwing herself wide – she opens her arms. Elliott steps into them. He is far taller than her. He stoops, pressing his head to her crown.

She is reminded, for a moment, of Peter. An oystercatcher of a boy, long-legged, gangly, sixteen years old and far taller than his mother. The way he hugged. So strong, so tight, Lizzy would feel her feet lift from the ground as if she was a ballerina.

But with Elliott, Lizzy has the sensation that she is the one holding him up.

'I'm so sorry,' he says again.

'Come and get warm by the fire.'

'Thank you.'

But he stays standing, water dripping from his coat on to the floorboards. Outside, rain hits the windowpane like a handful of shale. The wind moans like it's got something terrible to say.

What's he doing, leaving his big hotel, his glittering wife, on a night like this? They could have waited until morning, these respects of his.

'Lizzy . . . there's something I need to tell you.'

'You know what Torren did. Or you suspect it.'

'No. Something I never told either of you. If I had . . .'

'Don't say he wouldn't have done what he did. Because nothing could stop him, Elliott.'

'If I had . . .' He looks down at his boots. 'He'd have killed Drew twice over. And probably me too.'

71

Gus is tucked up in bed, but he can't switch his brain off. Everything with Jayden. Everything with Ally. It was dreadful, that wait for the lifeboat, but what they felt when that brave little inflatable came lifting over the waves and he saw the shape of their friend? The relief was instant; it clean took his head off.

Ally told Gus that it was his phone call that saved Jayden and Elliott's lives. Well, Gus owes Jayden, doesn't he? That fateful night two summers ago, when it was Gus's life that was at risk. And, as far as he's concerned, they'll never be square in that department.

It is emboldening, though, to think he might have played his part. And for Ally to say that? Well, that's a gift in itself. And the intensity of what they shared tonight was – if it's not the wrong thing to say – a gift too.

Gus rolls over on to his side.

Maybe I should just send her the damn book, after all.

And do it now, while he's feeling vital. Appreciative. Optimistic. And before he loses his nerve.

The book is, he thinks, the next best thing to himself. *Gosh, that makes me sound awfully big-headed.* But if Ally can't accept him, the flesh-and-blood Gus, then the fact that she nevertheless wants to read his innermost thoughts – innermost thoughts wrapped up in the guise of a workmanlike police procedural – is something.

It's not an overstatement to say that Gus's friendship with Ally is his favourite thing in his life. *And, by Jove, that's despite it being tinged with romantic disappointment!* The inconvenient truth is that when the chips were down, Ally didn't want him. Or, rather, she wanted the version of him that was bolder, less hesitant, more of an all-round go-getter. And, if Gus is really honest with himself, she also wanted the version that was less petty, less presumptuous, less blundering. And, all told, that wasn't the Gus that Ally saw standing before her when Ray Finch came to town.

Such is life.

He still has a great deal to be grateful for.

Gus clicks on his lamp, swings his legs out of bed and goes over to his desk. He opens up his laptop and it responds with an electronic fanfare. No more than the sound of it booting up, but nonetheless, he appreciates the gesture.

'Thank you, Mac,' he says.

He opens up his email and taps out a quick note to her. He doesn't overthink it, God knows that's been his eternal problem, and in this, at least, he can be clear-cut and assertive. Then he attaches the document.

He hauls in a breath. Clicks send.

Whoosh.

Gone.

A sense of peace descends, because Gus knows this: if Ally says one nice thing about the book, one small, single compliment, then that will mean more to him than anything.

Barmy but true.

The clarity of this knowledge is quite liberating. He doesn't need to tie himself in knots, worrying whether he can actually finish this novel to his agent's satisfaction or not. Whether anyone will ever publish it. Whether anyone else will even read it, let alone review it. All he wants is to please Ally Bright. That's all he's ever wanted, really. And Gus knows Ally well enough to be certain of one thing: she will be kind.

Even if she hates the damn novel.

On that thought, Gus goes back to bed and finally drops off with the ease of someone who has placed their life in another's hands – and trusts that they won't drop it.

72

It's pitch black when Jayden wakes. His hand feels for his phone to check the time, then he remembers it's lost. The feeling of being in the cave rushes back at him and he attempts to steady his breathing. Beside him, Cat sleeps peacefully. Jayden's instinct was to downplay it to her, make it sound like the lifeboat was excessive; that the tide was on its way out and if they'd just waited, safe there on the ledge, they'd have been able to walk on out. It wouldn't have felt like deceit, more just positive thinking. But he couldn't take back the phone call from the beach, and the raw emotion of that moment. And these last months, after what Cat went through after Benji's birth, they've promised to be honest with one another about what they're really feeling.

They both know it was the narrowest of escapes tonight.

It was an impossible situation, Cat said bravely. And it was. Jayden couldn't leave Elliott, but staying was a terrible choice too. *Just please, Jay, next time, put yourself first. If not for you, then for us.*

Jayden shifts slightly, the bed creaking. He lays his hand gently on Cat's thigh. He doesn't want to wake her, but suddenly he feels weirdly lonely. He needs to know she's there. Down the hall, his kids are sleeping. Jazz in her bed – *me a big girl!* – and Benji in his cot. When he first came in, after Ally dropped him off, Jayden kissed them both. For all his insistence that he'd tiptoe in and tiptoe out, his love was too big for the room; strobing like disco lights, too lit-up a presence. No wonder his daughter woke. She reached up and held his face with both hands, said in a bleary voice, *You smell like the sea.* Which didn't make sense as he'd showered at the High Tide – used every one of their fancy little bottles of potions too – but then maybe Jazz was just mid-dream, as she dropped instantly back to sleep, her lips parted like a cowrie shell. Her forest-dark lashes and halo of curls. Her beauty a punch.

He would do anything for these children of his. If the unimaginable happened, who's to say how he'd be.

Destroyed, is how I'd be.

Murderous, though?

Who's to say how I'd be.

Jazz said, *You smell like the sea.* It's the middle of the night, no better time for weird thoughts to churn, but maybe his daughter was right. Maybe the experience is still imprinted on him. Maybe the sea got inside him. That feeling of seeing the lifeboat. The RNLI-printed life vests. He thought it was death, but then it turned out to be Christmas morning.

If Jayden had got Elliott out on his own, would he be feeling all-powerful? When Ally said they should follow their judgement and protect Lizzy, would he have reacted differently – no need for the authorities to step in?

No. He took the oath. If Jayden had single-handedly held back the sea, he'd have felt the same.

I'm sorry you couldn't solve this one, Jay, said Cat last night, *but you saved Elliott. And you did right by Summer and Blake too. That's still a win.*

Jayden didn't lie to his wife, but he didn't tell her that they have in fact solved it. Sort of, anyway. Between what Jayden got from Elliott, and what Ally got from Lizzy, they basically have the full story.

The fact is, Torren didn't know for sure that Drew was indirectly responsible for his son's death. Elliott said that he never told anyone. But Torren killed Drew anyway.

In the dark, Jayden reaches for his phone again, thinking maybe Ally has messaged. The bed creaks and his hand meets nothing; reflex aborted. His phone is with the fish now.

'Try to sleep, Jay,' Cat whispers beside him, half-asleep – and half-consoling, half-berating.

Jayden rolls on to his side and finds her. Cat takes his hand, and he holds on tight. When he closes his eyes, he can hear water – the rush of an incoming tide – so he keeps them open. But at some point, he must fall asleep because the next thing he knows a delicate light is pushing into the room and Jazzy's thundering over the floorboards, and Benji's wailing, and Cat's groaning 'I guess it's morning', and it's good.

It's all good.

But then he remembers everything with Ally.

73

Summer and Blake check out of the High Tide early. At the reception desk the diffusers are emitting a thick fug of scent, and it's overlapping with Louisa's equally strong perfume. Out of the corner of her eye, Summer can see Blake struggling not to sneeze and stifles a laugh. It was never his kind of place, really.

'You're not staying for breakfast?' asks Louisa, her voice beseeching. She's practically wringing her hands. She looks tired this morning, thinks Summer. Her usually immaculate appearance is a little creased at the edges. It must be the stress of Elliott's experience in the cave yesterday. Poor, poor Jayden. She messaged him as soon as she heard – making sure to send it to Cat as well.

'We want to get on the road early,' says Summer. 'But thank you. And for the whole stay.'

'Look, this weekend, I know it wasn't . . . what you were expecting. Or what any of us hoped. Obviously, we're not anticipating any kind of a write-up. But promise you'll come back another time?'

Summer tells Louisa that she thinks the hotel is great. That just because a bad thing happened here – *okay, a number of bad things* – it isn't a reflection on the place.

'Please tell your husband goodbye as well,' says Summer. 'And I hope he recovers okay after everything in the cave.'

Louisa nods. Her mouth is tight, and Summer can see the lines in her lipstick.

'He's taken our elderly neighbour's death very hard,' Louisa says, with some stiffness. 'He was barely out of that cave, and he rushed up to their cottage to pay his respects. He's . . . quite out of sorts.'

Elliott cares, thinks Summer. Just like he cared about the waitress who spilt the wine too. Summer wonders, passingly, if he still cares about his wife.

Just as they're heading out of the main doors, Summer sees Elliott about to get into his car. He must have been terrified in the cave, but Summer reckons that if you had to have anyone with you in that moment then let it be Jayden. They go over to him.

'Sorry about your friend,' says Blake.

And Summer sees Elliott flinch, as if he's touched something hot. His eyes widen like moons.

'What?'

'Your neighbour,' says Summer gently.

Elliott runs a hand through his hair and thanks them quietly. Then he notices their suitcases. 'You're leaving?'

'Thought we'd head down to Porthpella first,' says Summer.

'I've been trying to get hold of Jayden all morning,' says Elliott, 'and then I remembered about his phone. Will you see him?'

Summer glances at Blake. She told him last night about how silly she got with that almost-kiss in the bathroom. Blake was kind, how he brushed it off. *I get it. You were freaking out.* Summer's not sure she gets it; she clearly still has some work to do on herself.

'Yes, we'll see him,' she says. 'Him and Cat. And Ally.'

'Could you pass on a message? Tell him . . . Tell him that we're going to do the right thing. Together.'

'You and him?'

Her face is obviously looking quizzical, so Elliott waves his hand.

'No, me and . . . Doesn't matter,' he says. 'He'll hear soon enough, I suppose.' He glances towards the hotel. Pulls in a breath. 'Louisa, is she . . . around? We seem to have done a very good job of missing each other this morning, and . . .'

'She checked us out just now.'

'Maybe I should . . .' He closes the car door. 'Yep. Alright. I should talk to her first.' He looks down at the ground, as if deep in thought. 'It's gone on long enough,' he says quietly.

It's as if, Summer thinks, they're not here at all. Whatever Elliott King has to say to Louisa, Summer's going to guess it won't be easy for her to hear. She's reminded of how she misread Blake's change of mood; how her own insecurities made her think it was about their relationship. How wrong she was.

Their taxi glides into the car park then, and Blake gestures to it.

'Our ride's here.'

'Good luck,' murmurs Elliott.

Summer finds herself patting his arm, as if he's an elderly man, or a very small child.

'Bye,' she says, 'and thank you.'

As they walk over to the cab, Blake whispers, 'Was he wishing us good luck, or . . . saying it to himself?'

The taxi drops them at the car park, where Summer can see the purple-and-yellow wooden boards of Hang Ten.

'They do the best brownies,' she says.

'Breakfast of champions. Let's do it.'

They walk to the balustrade, and Summer leans into Blake's side as they stand and look at the sea. The sky is a riot of light and shade. The rough weather of recent days lingers in the form of murky clouds, but the blue is doing its best. And beyond the island lighthouse there's the faint trace of a rainbow.

'Look,' says Summer, pointing to it.

Blake told her everything last night: his history with Drew Schofield; why he panicked; what he's been carrying. It wasn't an easy story to hear. But she knew it was time to honour it with her own honesty. So Summer told Blake how she'd changed schools because of bullying. That the teenage girls that she knew didn't get physical, but the mind games were just as painful. That it wasn't until she started travelling, started writing, started experiencing a different world, that she left it behind her.

No, that's a lie, she told him. *I don't think someone who's been badly bullied ever leaves it behind them.*

Would you forgive them, if you met them again now? asked Blake. *If they tried to explain themselves, and apologised?*

Summer thought hard about that one.

They ruined several years of my life, she said eventually. *And I still carry that now. Maybe I'd forgive, but I'd never forget.*

Blake kissed her forehead. *How did we not know this about each other?*

Because we're both really cool now, Summer laughed.

Now, Summer takes his hand. 'Shall we go get some breakfast?'

'Hell, yes. Hey, look. The rainbow's pumping.'

And it is. Seven bands of colour, arcing through the sky; dissolving into ocean.

'Aren't you going to film it?' says Blake.

She wrinkles her nose. *Just enjoy the moment? Or take that moment and celebrate it for other people too?* 'Actually . . . yeah. It looks amazing.'

Summer gets out her phone and hits record: a panning shot that takes in the bay, the island, the implausibly perfect rainbow. Then she swivels to the sugar-sand beach, the distant wooden houses in the dunes – where, furthest along, out of sight from here, is The Shell House, the sanctuary Ally gave her. Up on the headland, the speck of a farmhouse where Jayden and Cat live. Then she zooms in on Hang Ten, and the wooden sign with the cresting wave. She says, 'Saffron makes the best coffee and brownies in Cornwall.' Because maybe Summer will write about this place, after all.

74

Kathy sits down to breakfast at the guest house in St Ives. It's a far cry from the High Tide, but the bed is soft as a fresh-baked sponge cake and the view from the bedroom offers a thin slice of sea that's a promise of more to come. Mae is having a lie-in and that's okay; Kathy's glad of her company here, but also she's happy to be on her own; unpacking the little parcel of butter, scratching it across her toast, eyeing a bowl of fruit salad; helping herself to another coffee from the cafetière that's just for her. She's the only person in the small dining room, though three more tables are set. A lorry pulls up outside the window and the light dims temporarily. Seagulls shout at each other across the rooftops.

The landlady bustles in with a fresh jug of orange juice. 'Any plans for today, love?' she asks.

'Not really,' says Kathy.

Mae will be returning to Oxford, but Kathy? Kathy is staying on here. As the widow of a man whose murder is yet to be solved, it makes sense for her to remain locally while the investigation is ongoing. Perhaps, too, it's reasonable to imagine that she feels some magnetic pull; that she can't leave her husband here on his own, even if he's dead.

But that's not Kathy.

As she woke up this morning, in the top bedroom of this skinny little grey-stone terrace, the first thought that whisked into her brain was not one of death or dread but simply this: *I'm free.* She stretched out, a starfish in the middle of the sheets. Hummed a tune from her girlhood. She felt, for a moment, wonderfully, inappropriately silly.

Doubtless there will be difficult days ahead: unavoidable bad weather. Police business. Gossip from neighbours. Incomprehensible administrative jobs. A funeral to get through, with the looming presence of Drew's indomitable mother, Margaret. Days, too, when Kathy might even miss him a little around the house. Not *him* as such, but the familiarity of a life together; thirty-plus years of marriage, after all. Just having that sort of buttress – even though it came with its own weight. But there are so many things that she won't miss at all.

Oh goodness, so very many.

Kathy has never been the type to feel sorry for herself. She fears she's become the type, in fact, to not feel much of anything at all. But she's determined to change that. Perhaps, in some small way, she already has.

The landlady tops up her glass of orange juice. It's brighter than any she has seen, and when she takes a sip her whole mouth sings with sweetness.

'Actually,' says Kathy, 'I think I do have a plan.'

I'm going to start doing exactly as I like.

75

Ally waits at the window. Out beyond the island lighthouse there's a rainbow so crisp you could reach out and pluck it from the sky. Meanwhile, in the distance, great shoals of rain clouds are moving too; the water is tinged neon. It's desperately beautiful and she tries to breathe it all in.

To root herself.

It's too early to go and see Lizzy; she needs to at least let the clock reach nine before she gets in her car. The poor woman must be exhausted, and what Ally has to say won't be enlivening either. Ally woke up this morning with a sorrowful but crystalline feeling: she can't keep Lizzy's secret for her. Jayden's words must have settled overnight, or perhaps the old adage of sleeping on it proved to be true. But she wants to give Lizzy the opportunity to see this for herself – just as Jayden said.

And if Lizzy doesn't?

Ally will cross that bridge. And as much as she dreads the discord with a woman she has so much sympathy for, at least she'll be side by side with Jayden.

There's a knock at the door and it's her partner – as if just the thought of him brought him here.

'Hey, Al,' says Jayden.

He kicks off his sandy trainers and hangs his coat up. Bends to scruffle Fox, just like he's done a hundred times. She's about to offer him coffee – just like she's done a hundred times too – when he jumps in talking.

'Look,' he says, 'when I was in the cave, I thought there was a good chance I wasn't getting out. And I also thought there was a really good chance that Elliott killed Drew Schofield. I mean, at that point, I was kind of sure of it.' He sucks in a big breath. 'But you know what? I didn't want to push the question, because I didn't want to think about it. I just wanted to think about Cat, and Jazz and Benji. I wanted to think about my mum and dad, and my sister. My nieces. All the people I love, Al, and that includes you. It didn't matter, in that moment. Do you know what I mean?'

Ally nods, eyes burning. 'I do know. It was an extreme situation. The most extreme.'

'It was the people that mattered. The people I love.' Jayden is pacing, his feet creaking the boards. 'And Lizzy loves Torren. And Torren's dead. So, what I was saying about the oath . . . You're right. I'm not police anymore. I get to choose.'

'And I respect that choice,' says Ally, 'I do. And I wanted to tell you that—'

'So maybe I choose—'

Jayden's voice overlaps hers. Beside them, Ally's phone rings. And it's Mullins's name flashing on the screen.

She holds it up to Jayden and he raises his eyebrows.

'Should I get it?' she says. 'Or . . . do you want to finish?'

'Or . . . do you?' He shakes his head. 'No, get it. We'll talk after.'

Ally feels strangely nervous as she says, 'Tim, hello.'

'Hullo, Mrs Bright. I mean, Ally. Is Jayden with you, by any chance? His phone's out of action and I thought you might be together.'

'As it happens,' she says, 'he's just walked in the door. Did you want to speak to him?'

'Both of you, actually.'

Is that a little bit of grandstanding that she detects in his voice? Mullins sounds chuffed. And it is so far from Ally's own feeling that he might as well be an alien in a spaceship as a constable on the phone.

Jayden sends her a questioning look, and she gives a brief shake of her head. She starts to mouth something and changes her mind.

'Tim, I'll put you on speaker.'

She places the phone on the table, and sits with her hands folded, head bent. Jayden hovers at her elbow.

'We had a couple of visitors down the station this morning. Elliott King and that old-lady neighbour of his, Lizzy Jago.'

Ally turns to Jayden. It's a good thing it's not a video call, because her face betrays her.

'They had a right story to tell,' he says.

And Mullins launches into it. The summer of 1988. The Schofield family and their friends on holiday. The death of Peter Jago in the cave. Then everything that unfolded over the last three days. Ally's heart beats a quick tattoo.

They came forward. They told the police everything.

'Elliott blamed himself, see,' says Mullins. 'He was only a little kid. But it was Drew Schofield's doing, all day long. They wanted us to have the full picture. When Schofield wound up dead, Elliott suspected Torren knew more than he was saying, and he kept that to himself. Obstructing a police enquiry, that is, though Skinner's going easy on him for some reason. Probably angling for a free winter break at the High Tide.'

'What about Lizzy?' asks Jayden.

'She said that all her husband wanted to do was talk to Schofield. But there must have been a scuffle, and somehow he went off the balcony. He was scared, was Torren. A gentle bloke, by all accounts. So, he did a runner. Tried to cover his tracks by burning the coat. He was that afraid of what'd happened.'

Ally looks to Jayden. No mention of the knife that Torren carried. No mention of Lizzy knowing her husband's intentions.

'It's a sad story, all in all. But it puts the case to bed, at least. Course, there'll be no conviction, not with Torren passed away. But everybody feels better for telling the truth.'

Silence in The Shell House.

'Well, come on,' says Mullins. 'Aren't you going to say anything? Mad story, isn't it?'

'It is,' says Jayden. 'Mad story. They just walked into the police station and told you . . . that?'

'If you want my opinion, Elliott looked like a bloke who'd been lugging that weight around for the best part of forty years. He was glad to set it down.'

'What about Lizzy?' asks Ally quietly.

'She said she thought about not saying anything, but in the end, she talked about it with Elliott, and she wanted it known that Drew Schofield had a hand in her son's death all those years back. That Schofield wasn't the shining bloke that the world thinks he is. Skinner tried to tell her that no one had been handing out the commendations in Schofield's direction, but that was how she saw it. That Schofield was a bully as a boy and a bully as a man and she wanted it known that Torren tried to face him – and even if Torren did wrong in not reporting it, her husband was a good man. That's how she put it.'

'And what did Skinner make of it?' asks Jayden.

'Skinner doesn't like anyone playing silly beggars, does he? Wasting police time and all that. But you can't charge a dead bloke. And maybe he's got a heart in there somewhere because Skinner went gentle on Lizzy Jago too, as it goes. He might have lost his suspect – not that Torren ever was, mind – but she just lost her husband, didn't she?'

Ally slowly exhales. Jayden drops into a chair.

'Anyway,' says Mullins, 'that's the headlines. And it's hot off the press. The pair of them are giving formal statements now. Thought you'd like the heads-up. Seeing as, you know, you've been on the case too.'

'Cheers, Mullins,' says Jayden.

'Skinner said to me, "They're losing their touch, that Shell House pair." Wanted me to pass that along too.'

'Yeah, cheers,' says Jayden again, this time looking at Ally.

'But me? See, I'm not so sure. Jayden, you were all that time in the cave with Elliott King. And Ally, you were with Lizzy Jago at the hospital. She said what a help you were, by the way, what a very big help. And Elliott seems to think you're some kind of a superhero, Jayden, when we all know it was the RNLI that did the heavy lifting. But what I'm thinking is that the Ally and Jayden I know, well, people just seem to tell you two things, don't they? They open themselves right up. Hand it to you on a plate, half the time.'

Ally and Jayden stay quiet.

'But this time, you had nothing. You're up close and personal with two people at their wits' end, all vulnerable, the pair of them sitting on the truth, and yet you're none the wiser. Or so you say, anyway.'

'Mullins . . .' begins Jayden. But his interjection ends there.

'They did the right thing coming forward,' says Mullins. 'Elliott and Lizzy.'

'They did,' says Jayden.

'I agree,' says Ally softly.

'Good, then,' says Mullins. 'We're all agreed.'

Ally almost feels like they're in the headmaster's office. And, against all odds, Mullins is the one in charge.

Underestimate him at your peril.

'For what it's worth, they had a decent bond going on, Elliott and Lizzy Jago. I reckon Elliott will look out for the old lady,' he adds.

'I hope so,' says Ally.

She wonders how this unified statement came to pass. Did Lizzy have second thoughts and go to Elliott? Did Elliott need to get his own story off his chest? Did they decide, together, that the truth – *a version of the truth* – needed to be told, and that they'd both feel freer for it?

'By the way, next time you're down at the beach, if you see some hot new surfer ripping it up, it'll be me. Saffron wants to give me lessons.'

In the background they can hear another voice, and before they know it Mullins is hanging up with an 'Over and out, Shell House.'

Jayden sits back in his chair and slowly exhales. Ally does the same. For a moment neither says anything.

'Surf lessons?' says Jayden, breaking the silence. 'Mullins?'

'My thoughts exactly.'

'I don't know about you, Al, but I could use a cup of coffee.'

And he says it at the exact moment that Ally says, 'Coffee?'

Later on, when the rain clouds have blown away and the sun has taken over the sky, Ally whistles for Fox and they step out into the day. She knots her scarf tighter as a quick-fingered breeze pulls at it. Together, they make for the sand. The tide is all the way out, and the beach is a mirror, holding every inch of the blue.

Summer and Blake dropped in earlier and managed to just catch Jayden before he left too. They wanted to say thank you. Jayden told them how Drew died: Mullins's version, not theirs. At the story of Peter, Blake was visibly moved. He said, *So Drew basically killed him.*

Did Drew Schofield kill Peter Jago? Did he study the tide times, banking on Peter's commitment to finding Rebecca taking him deeper and deeper into the cave? Ignoring the peril in a bid to save the girl he loved? Elliott felt sure of it. And so did Torren, without even knowing the full truth of Drew's manipulation; an instinct that was cemented when he saw Drew revisiting the sea cave.

Could it still have been a cruel prank gone terribly wrong? An act intended to make a fool of Peter, perhaps even scare him a little – but no more than that?

They cannot possibly know. Not now.

Ally thinks of grey areas. How right and wrong isn't always black and white.

The decision was taken away from us, said Jayden, earlier. *But we should still have the conversation, Al.*

So Ally told Jayden that she thinks she'd come round to his view.

And Jayden told Ally that he thinks he'd come round to hers.

So we're at another impasse? she smiled.

Though a better one, right? he said.

Perhaps it's alright, not to know. Not to have all the answers. One thing she's certain of is that they would have puzzled it out in the end, one way or another.

Together.

Ally looks out to the water. The sets roll in in perfect lines, like ripples in blue cloth. The surfers are out, dotting the water like seals. Gus isn't likely to be among them, not out in the deep, but she thinks of him anyway. Learning to surf is a plucky move. But then so is writing a novel. Both require a great deal of faith – with no certainty of outcome.

When she said to Jayden that Gus was a rock to her last night, Ally meant it. He was far braver than her, as they stood on the beach together, looking for the lights of the lifeboat; looking for some sign that it would be alright.

Life and death. They've been here before, Ally and Gus.

And that lightest of kisses, like a star in a dark sky.

Perhaps, amidst all that fear, that reminder of the fragility of life, Gus realised that sharing his novel really isn't a thing to be afraid of – because he finally emailed her his manuscript. It landed in the middle of the night, another star lighting up the sky, and Ally beamed to see it. The accompanying note said, *Your friend Summer seems to think we're a bit cool, you and I, so I suppose I should live up to it and throw caution to the wind and ping you the book.*

Part of her is nervous to read it, and she doesn't know why. It's a crime novel, for goodness' sake, not a love story. But this much she knows: if there's any trace of Gus the man in this book of his, then she knows she'll like it very much.

She hears the trilling of her phone and takes it from her pocket.

Ray.

Ally knows she owes him a call, and she feels bad about it. But with everything else the last few days, he dropped clean from her head. Is that a terrible thing?

'Ally,' he says.

And he puts so much in it, the way he says that one word. The way he says her name. Ally feels warmth flow through the phone, as if he's reached out over these three hundred miles or more, coast to coast, and is holding her hand.

'Ray,' she says.

'You sound pleased it's me.'

'Of course I'm pleased it's you.'

'I take nothing for granted.'

'It's just these last few days, it's been . . . a lot.'

'A case? Tell me.'

She sits down on the soft, cool sand. The wind buffets her, a slipstream of sand grains flying past her. She has the sensation that she's stopping time. That she's the only still thing on this beach.

It surprises her, how easily the connection is remade. But after those forty-seven years, perhaps three days is nothing.

'It's a long story,' she says.

'I've got nothing but time, Ally.'

'It's a sad story too.' And as she says it, her voice catches.

She can hear him hesitate on the end of the line. *Ray the good-time boy.* That's how he was when she first met him, all those years ago. He avoided the difficult conversations.

'How about I get in the car?' he says. 'Sad stories are always best told face-to-face, aren't they?'

Well, I didn't expect that.

She feels herself smiling. 'It's far too far. You'd be driving in the dark.'

'I'm a big boy. Leave now, and I'd be with you by midnight.'

'Ray, you can't. Plus, we just saw one another.'

Though for a moment she imagines stoking the fire. Warming a bottle of red. Preparing the spare room. Or . . . not. Ray has never stayed at The Shell House before.

Stupid that this thought also then lands: *But how will I read Gus's novel?*

'You're right,' he says. 'Sorry. Ridiculous idea.'

Ally scoops a handful of sand, lets the grains run through her fingers.

'But soon,' she says.

'I'll hold you to that, Ally Bright.'

Out over the water, the last of the sun turns the surface silver. It's magnificent. And life is short, so unbearably short. Even if you're lucky.

'I hope you do,' she says.

Epilogue

Torren stands at the top of the lane, directly between the High Tide and home. With the power cut, the darkness is almost absolute; the silver moon shows its face only intermittently, as gales drag cloudbanks across the black sky.

He lays a hand on his chest; tries to steady his breathing. The night swirls around him. Torren is a still point, buffeted and battered but holding fast.

Somehow.

As soon as he realised who Drew Schofield was, all Torren wanted was to talk to him. To have some acknowledgement. Not necessarily an admission of guilt but at least a recognition of the tragedy.

Tragedy. Not enough of a word, that, not by half, as if Peter's death fit some dictionary definition when it didn't, it doesn't, it can't.

So when Torren saw Drew heading off down the beach, he followed him. It was low tide, and he tracked him all the way to the mouth of the cave. Drew stood with his hand on the rock, as reverent as a man at the altar. What did it mean? Torren's eyes burnt with tears to see it. But when Torren started to speak, the look on that man's face . . . *By God.* Drew Schofield was somebody who considered himself invincible. And he batted Torren away as if he was nothing. A laugh and a jeer. Not just a dismissal, but an act of cruelty.

And that was when Torren *knew*. What he's always known, really. The tide was the weapon, but it was Drew's hand that held it, pointed it, fired it.

How can such a thing leave no trace on a man's humanity?

For Torren, it was an easy choice tonight. Perhaps that says something about his own humanity, but Torren *is* marked. How could he not be?

To lose our boy.

His big coat flaps furiously at his legs. The hedgerows sound as if they're being pulled from their roots as above him the tree canopies shake and snap. The sea is all but invisible, bar the occasional moonlight, flickering like an old film reel. He can hear it, though. The ocean is angry tonight.

And Torren?

Torren is not angry.

It was fury that drove him to the High Tide, but it is gentleness that takes him home.

Enough, he thinks.

A life for a life; the deed is done. Would he hold with that, if this were somebody else's story? He was always a mellow man before, never one for fire and brimstone. And the equation is unequal: Peter was worth a hundred Drew Schofields, a thousand, infinite. But in the end, this was all he could do.

And it felt like it was supposed to be. Mumbo-jumbo, of course, but how else can he explain the wrong turn in the driveway? What about how easily he propped that side door ajar? The power cut, giving him the cover of darkness. Then the fact that, when it came to it, the man capitulated with astonishing ease. Drunken, pathetic, he lumbered and stumbled and toppled and fell.

Torren was prepared to use every inch of that knife he held to Drew Schofield's throat. He took it from Lizzy's block in the kitchen and sharpened the blade until his eyes watered just looking at it. But, in the event, he didn't have to nick even a thread of him.

And the wife? The wife that Torren was ready to ignore the screams of, knowing full well what a hypocrite that makes him? A quick swipe of his torch beam showed she was sound asleep. At least she was spared the witnessing.

Nothing in Torren's life has ever worked like tonight. It was like swimming with the current, like running with the wind at his back. An inevitable, preordained trajectory.

This, I believe.

Lizzy, dear Lizzy, will be waiting for him at home, sunk in fear and dread. He clasped her hands before he left, and then he kissed them – just like he did on their wedding day. Just like he did the day that their boy was born. *Trust me*, he said.

He knows this won't stop here. How can it? His ears are already pricked for sirens. But he will try to cover his tracks for Lizzy's sake. He will try. But he is tired, and in truth, he senses an ending. He feels it in his very bones. And there will be no fight when it comes; not from him.

Torren takes one more look back towards the darkness of the High Tide and then he carries on up the hill. No point in hurrying; he couldn't if he tried. Whatever energy he had has ebbed and he feels every one of his eighty-two years. His feeble torch beam plays across his boots, but his eyes are on the sky now. It's black, thick with cloud, but he's looking for his star. His brightest shining star.

His sun, his son, his boy Peter.

When Torren finally sees a glimmer, it's hanging strangely low in the sky. He trudges on towards it, his heart beating a noisy tattoo in his chest. The closer he gets, the more it bobs and weaves, and he realises it isn't his star at all. It's a lamplight. A love light.

It can't be, can it? She shouldn't be out in this.

'Lizzy,' he breathes.

'Is it done?'

She holds the lamp high, and her silver hair is like magic. Her dear cheeks gleam with tears.

'It's done, my love.'

He steps into her arms, and they hold one another. His wife is stronger than anyone, and although she won't hear such talk, Torren knows that – if it comes to it – she will be alright without him.

For now, though?

Hand in hand, they walk each other home. And while the storm rages on around them, it can't hurt them. Not tonight. For once, the Jagos are untouchable.

ACKNOWLEDGEMENTS

Thank you to all of the people who've helped bring this book into the world – and made it better along the way.

Thank you to my brilliant agent, Rowan Lawton at The Soho Agency, for such wisdom and care. Thank you also to Eleanor Lawlor, and to Helen Mumby on the TV side.

I do love being part of the Thomas & Mercer family. Thank you to my amazing editor, Vic Haslam – your verve and commitment are second to none. Together with the wonderful Laura Gerrard, the editorial process is always smooth, smart, and joyfully interrogative. Thanks also to the wider team at Thomas & Mercer, including Victoria Pepe, Gemma Wain, Silvia Crompton and Rebecca Hills. Every Shell House cover is a beauty, and I'm grateful to Marianna Tomaselli for continuing to bring the series to life with such flair.

Thank you to all of my cherished friends who offer inspiration, camaraderie and kindness at every turn – you make it all so fun. A special shout-out to Lucy Clarke, who, along with my husband Robin Etherington, always reads my first drafts with such energy and positivity, no matter what.

Every crime writer needs at least one expert in their corner, and I'm lucky to have my CSI friend Zoe and my police constable friend Oli to tell me how it's done in the real world. Any inaccuracies are, as ever, down to me. I'm also grateful to the excellent crime fiction advisor Graham Bartlett for offering advice and ideas on dodgy coppers and more . . . Again, any liberties I've taken are all in the name of the story.

While I have the extraordinary pleasure of living in my fictional Porthpella all year round, trips to the heartland always fuel my writing process – and fill up my cup like nothing else.

I did much of the planning for this novel in Gwithian, on a wet, but nevertheless luminous, camping holiday last summer. A winter retreat to Marazion made sure my first draft happened on time and gave me plenty more besides.

Much love and gratitude to my family – the Halls, the Green-Halls, and the Etheringtons – for your unending love, and support. I was brought up to believe that a life lived imaginatively is the richest kind there is, and for that I thank my dear parents with all my heart.

Big, big thanks to my husband, Robin Etherington, and my son, Calvin, for your ceaseless cheering, patience, humour and love. I'm very lucky to have you both.

This sixth Shell House Detectives mystery is dedicated to my readers. I'm so grateful to you for taking a chance on the books in the first place and then coming back for more! When I started out with *The Shell House Detectives*, I had no idea what a special pleasure it is, and a huge privilege, to write a series. Thank you for being with me on this grand adventure.

ABOUT THE AUTHOR

Photo © 2022 Victoria Walker

Emylia Hall lives in Bristol with her husband and son, where she writes from a hut in the garden and dreams of the sea. She is the author of the Shell House Detective Mysteries, a series inspired by her love of Cornwall's wild landscape. The first, *The Shell House Detectives*, was a Kindle Top 10 Bestseller, with the rights being optioned for TV. *The High Tide Murder* is her sixth crime novel. Emylia has published four previous novels, including Richard and Judy Book Club pick *The Book of Summers* and *The Thousand Lights Hotel*. Her work has been translated into ten languages, and broadcast on BBC Radio 6 Music. She is the founder of Mothership Writers and is a writing coach at The Novelry.

Instagram: @emyliahall_author

X: @emyliahall

Follow the Author on Amazon

If you enjoyed this book, follow Emylia Hall on Amazon to be notified when the author releases a new book!
To do this, please follow these instructions:

Desktop:

1) Search for the author's name on Amazon or in the Amazon App.
2) Click on the author's name to arrive on their Amazon page.
3) Click the 'Follow' button.

Mobile and Tablet:

1) Search for the author's name on Amazon or in the Amazon App.
2) Click on one of the author's books.
3) Click on the author's name to arrive on their Amazon page.
4) Click the 'Follow' button.

Kindle eReader and Kindle App:

If you enjoyed this book on a Kindle eReader or in the Kindle App, you will find the author 'Follow' button after the last page.